M000206371

POWER

THE BETTY CHRONICLES

Volume II

BY A. J. MAHLER

For information about special discounts for bulk purchases please contact sales@whitebradford.com.

For additional information — http://www.whitebradford.com

Betty Thursten has a Facebook page — friend her at https://www.facebook.com/betty.thursten

Cover photo © Serov/Shutterstock

FOR MY TEACHERS

Power is dedicated to my teachers, who set the bar damn high.

To Jean Baldikowske. You knew I could do better and you opened my eyes.

To R. Warner Brown. Your love of the English language cured my incorrigible nature. A rose is a rose is a rose.

> Autumn of your life
> Old lessons rooted anew
> Fire passed—reborn

ONE

LOST

July 14, 2009 — The crack of dawn

THE RISING SUN GLINTED off the peaks as Betty bobbed in the open sea off the Venezuelan coast. Three hours treading in the seventy-seven-degree water without a floatation device and with a gunshot wound in the meat of her left calf meant she did not have much longer to live. Betty began evaluating her options. *If a shark doesn't get me, hypothermia will.* Icy-cold tendrils bore deeper into her body, their pull winning out over her desire to live. *Everything I've fought for is lost. Why am I hanging on, anyway? Gil is either dead or dying back at Ernesto's . . . Howell is a lost cause . . . my parents and brothers are vulnerable . . . even Jil has turned on me! Why not let the ocean take me to the bottom?* Betty began to slip under the waves, but she was not ready to give up just yet. The thought of her dog in a crate or adopted by some unloving slacker pulled her back up. Spitting out the ocean and gasping for air, she mumbled at the waves, "Who will take care of Surry?"

†

July 14, 2009 — Four hours earlier atop Monte Ávila

Nine-millimeter rounds fired by the guards punctured the wing fabric, making it look like black Swiss cheese, as she took off from the mountain trail on the tandem glider, one bullet ripping through her boot and lodging in the meat of her calf. Gil's final act of driving the truck off the trail jerked the glider past the cool night air surrounding the mountain. The force generated enough speed to glide away and reach the warmer air of a fading updraft, which might give her the necessary altitude for the trip over the Ávila mountain range. Betty released the clove hitch knot of her umbilical cord to Gil as the truck plunged off the precipice; she banked right enough to see the truck lights cart wheeling into the dense vegetation of the *Parque Nacional El Ávila* before the ubiquitous clouds surrounding the higher range of the rain forest obscured her view of the wreck. The flashlights of the pursuing guards pierced the night air while their Spanish commands wafted up to her prying ears. Not knowing if Gil made it out of the tangle of metal and underbrush added to her burden, swelling her heart with pain to match the rawness of the wound in her calf.

The updraft from the mountain fought against the fabric, gripping then slipping around the garish pattern of holes. The rising warm air embraced Betty, grabbing her glider, dragging the battered craft higher. Blood dripped from her left boot. Her tears faded out of sight, evaporating before hitting the Venezuelan ground below. The tears were for Gil, for her past, for what could have been but never would be. The ache in her heart pounded long after the adrenaline of the fight had worn off.

She did not make it to the rendezvous coordinates—four miles out into the Atlantic, where Bud's water-taxi service was waiting for her and Gil. Her landing was off by at least two miles and thirty seconds of thrashing terror as she unbuckled, dove deep, and surfaced beyond the grasp of the glider. *It carried me to the safety of the ocean; it's willing to carry me to the bottom if I let it have its way.* She jabbed her SOG knife blade into the fabric, cutting a strip two and a half feet long by four inches wide, which she then clenched in her teeth. *Before you get away*, Betty thought, *I need one more thing from you.* The lack of oxygen pressed against her chest, but she resisted the urge to surface by letting out a tiny bit of air. Betty slid herself along the aluminum superstructure of the glider until her hand hit the object of her desire. She cut the last full bottle of compressed gas from its perch and surfaced. She had used the other seven to generate enough lift to make it over the Ávila pass. Waving goodbye, the tip of the right wing was the last to go under; the ripstop fabric had done its job despite the pockmark holes riddling its surface. She stored the bottle in the front of her spy suit. *I'll need this if a shark picks up the scent of my blood.* Betty went under the water long enough to put away the knife and tie a compression bandage on her calf. *Have to slow down the bleeding.* She clawed her way back toward the air, shredding the surface with her hands; her lungs aching from the mounting physical drain and the coldest water in the Caribbean Sea. The fatigue from the loss of blood clung to her, a spider's silk wound as tight as a cocoon.

The mission was a failure and a trap—Ernesto Montoya had been expecting them and Betty was captured while questioning him. *Gil! You saved me again, but you can't save yourself.* Betty wanted to hold on to the hope that Gil had escaped, but it was slipping away like the glider. *Holding on to you isn't going to save me, Gil. Please prove me wrong.*

Two hours before her takeoff, Gil had located Betty, and in a daring shootout they escaped through the snare he had set up earlier to entrap Ernesto's henchmen. The C-4 explosives ripped the guards to shreds as they advanced; bullets finished what survived the explosive charges. Gil took a grazing shot to his right shoulder in the shootout, but they both escaped relatively unscathed. Ernesto fled in his Bell 206B3 four-passenger helicopter while his remaining men hunted the hunters.

Thinking back on the escape of her quarry, Betty composed a rhyme: *Rattus Rattus fleas and all / escaped before the fall / run, Ernesto, run / I kill you with my gun.* She was poetically delirious.

The waves called to her; their invitation to accept her fate grew louder. The purpose of revenge and worrying over Gil's fate gave her pause. If she would just let go, her family would be safe. If she let go, the pain in her calf would subside. The ocean was her morphine. It would make the pain go away, and it was calling to her, telling her she should not care anymore.

The waves lapped her face as she slipped slowly under again. The cold, salty water entered her mouth. She could hear a voice faintly calling to her. *Is that Gil?*

"Betty, get your shit together!" The voice both mocked and ordered her. "Since when did you give in this easy?"

Betty jerked her arms down, forcing herself to keep treading water, spitting the salty ocean back at itself. *It's not time yet.* One of the guard's bullets had smashed her beacon light during takeoff. *If the beacon flashes but no one sees it, does it still flash?* Hypothermia's firm grip was beginning to sap her critical thinking skills, but she tried to analyze the situation just the same. Betty knew the glider had landed downwind and at least two miles short of the designated landing point; her shattered radio, ruined in the poolside fight, prevented her from contacting the rescue team waiting off the Venezuelan coast. Scanning the horizon from the crest of a wave proved once again that there was nothing out here but water. *Just a vast rippling. Wait.*

She had marked her landing site with the same fluorescent green dye used by downed pilots, but it had dissipated in the rough waters. As a wave drove her higher, she could see something against the contrast of the next wave. *No!* What was left of the fluorescent green dye was being disturbed by something. A vertical fin surfaced and sliced the ocean into a wake of dye. *A great white shark's fin. Shit!*

†

Devon Miller, a new contract agent and veteran of the Navy SEALs, was waiting for Betty's signal for naught. He continuously scanned the horizon from the crow's nest with his night vision goggles, searching for the smear of fluorescent dye that should be spreading from the landing site. The rendezvous time had come and gone with no contact.

Captain Hargreave, the owner of this barely seaworthy fishing boat, kept barking at Miller that it was time to go. He clicked his mic and shrilled, "We agreed!" It was more of a shriek of terror setting in than a bark. The window of time he had agreed to had passed. Too bad for the people he was to pick up, but Hargreave was not going to risk waiting off the coast of Venezuela for the sun to rise. He turned the wheel sharply and gunned the twin engines to half speed on a northeastern heading. His excursionist and troublemaker would ignore him no longer.

Miller did not particularly care for the ship's captain or his tub, both of which were at Miller's disposal and would go where he directed no matter what the captain's opinion. Bud, Miller's contact at Control, had arranged the transportation to pick up the agents in the water. Why they were in the ocean to be picked up was not his concern. His mission was to pick up two people in the water four miles off the coast of Venezuela and deliver them to a safe house in Barranquilla, Colombia. He placed the red dot projected by the laser sight of his pistol on the map in front of the captain. When he had Hargreave's attention, he raised the dot to the man's forehead.

The old salt cut the engines back to quarter power and returned to the search pattern. With Miller's back to him, Hargreave shook his fist while uttering curses. With renewed focus on the mission and his lips clenching a freshly lit cigarette, the oaths turned to grave mutterings.

Miller would have preferred a speedboat, but the day before when he arrived at the slip reserved for this mission, Captain Hargreave was aboard the Colombian-flagged Bueno Pesquero and giving the correct sign and countersign. *Bud, you bastard, I hope you have a damn good reason for changing us to this tin cup.* They had been making a half-mile-radius circle around the coordinates for the better part of an hour. This isn't working, time to widen our scope. Miller made a wide circling motion with his arm while commanding Hargreave via the intercom, "Wider! Damn you, wider!"

The throaty hum of the trawler's engine drowned out the profane response of the captain as Miller peered into the inky distance of the night. The GPS signal was not active. No flares had been seen. The green fluorescent dye remained invisible. He began to play what-if. *What if it was me? What if I didn't make a clean escape and damage to my glider kept me from making the distance?* He made a decision. "Hargreave, you bastard child of a squid, head southeast and stay three miles off the coast."

Hargreave screamed back, "Closer? Are you out of your bloody mind?"

"You're damn right," Yes, I am out of my fucking mind for being out here with you as my partner in your rust trap of an excuse for a boat. "And you'll do as I say or by God you won't see your reward or the sun rise!"

Hargreave made an abrupt turn hard to starboard in the hopes of launching his nemesis from the crow's nest, but to no avail. His continuous muttering about the changing conditions of his employment went unheard over the now-roaring engine. A few more hours of abuse and he would get what he had negotiated for, a new boat with modern electronics—assuming the Venezuelan Navy was sleeping. The hard bargain he had driven with his contact, Bud, did not seem so rich in the poor light of the predawn sea.

The shark fin came closer and Betty felt the passing mass disturb the water. As she rechecked her bandage with hands numb from hypothermia, she rolled forward, and the cool water hitting her mouth triggered the mammalian reflex, making her gasp as she came up. The feeling in her foot seemed gone. Was it the ripstop fabric cinched too tight, or the chill in her bones brought on by her exertion and the extended exposure? Since she could not really feel her other leg, it was hard to say. She would have to loosen the bandage eventually or risk losing her leg. *Four hours. That's how long I have before I need to loosen it. But if I loosen it, the shark will find me for sure.* She thought about her options, of which there were not any. *They're too far out to spot me.* Prior to landing, Betty had strapped the emergency flare gun to her good leg. *My only hope is for the boat to circle out a little wider. A little closer than they should to the coast.* There had been a second flare gun on the side Gil would have occupied, along with four more cartridges. *I have one flare to shoot. I might need it to fend off that shark. If I wait until I see the boat, it might be too late. If I shoot it now, there might not be anyone to see it and I'm shark bait. Fuck me!*

Gauging how much longer she could hold on, Betty made her choice. Just before the night vanished, its murky cape scraping the waves as the rising sun cast it farther west, Betty launched her one and only flare. It was her last hope of rescue, but it would also tell the Venezuelans where to look. *Fucking Howell! Why didn't you plan for this?* It was a race to see who would get her first: the shark, Ernesto, or her rescue party.

Two

Lounging Around

July 14, 2009 — 1 a.m. at Ernesto's

THE BULLET RICOCHETED off the pool deck after creasing the skin of his shoulder. "Gil, are you hit?" asked Betty. Darkness hid the extent of the damage.

The acrid smell of gun smoke permeated the air. The gun battle was two minutes old and counting. Gil grunted that he was all right. "Get your sorry little ass to the truck," growled Gil.

"What about your sorry little ass? You think I'm going to leave you here?" Betty reached over and brushed Gil's hair with her left hand. Gil leaned his back against the overturned bar as he probed his shoulder for the extent of the damage. Satisfied that it was merely a scratch, he declared, "McFluffy needs to improve his damn suits!" Betty, kneeling beside her partner, gave Gil a peck on the cheek before she shot an advancing guard with the MAC-10 in her right hand over Gil's chest. The sound of the bolt action was all you could hear, thanks to the silencer.

"Who do you think is gonna get the glider in the air? I'll get out the usual way, you take the glider and make the rendezvous," commanded Gil.

Betty did not like the idea. The glider was a tandem, designed to handle the weight of both operatives, or Betty and Ernesto if they took him alive. With the crappy weather and cool night air, the liftoff was questionable. "Gil, I'm not going to leave you—"

Gil interrupted Betty before she could finish. "You bet your sweet ass you're leaving!"

"You just saved my ass—just returning the favor." Betty ducked as Gil aimed over her shoulder and fired.

Gil was visibly bleeding, but the bandage he was about to apply would cure that. "Who do you think the medic is here? There isn't enough lift to get both of us off the ground, and I'm shark bait if we're in the water for more than a couple of minutes." Gil shot a guard sneaking around a low wall to Betty's right.

Betty put her arm back into her left sleeve, stopping halfway before zipping up to shoot the next guard stupid enough to come out of the main house with his flashlight on. *Time to reload and find my night vision goggles.* It seemed a little awkward to be in a shootout with her breasts hanging out of her usually tight-fitting bulletproof spy suit. Gil and Betty crouched behind an overturned teak daybed from the poolside cabana; the adjoining cantina looked like the result of a serious bar fight, with broken glass and pools of dark liqueur covering the deck. Fifteen minutes before, all had been quiet. Gil had rescued Betty from Ernesto's trap and killed the pursuing guards by blowing the explosive charges reserved for just such an emergency.

This rescue reminded Betty of the other times Gil had secured her safety: arriving after her gun battle in the apartment above the bar in downtown Caracas and the ensuing car chase; dropping into Gil's arms on the rubber boat from the container ship full of munitions; and the guard on their first mission together. *The pig. Why does he always have to piss me off?* Then there was the train ride in Panama where she kissed Gil in front of Dr. Salizar and the passengers to divert their attention from her being late. She did not mean to, but she *did* enjoy that kiss.

†

July 14, 2009 — 12:30 a.m. at Ernesto's

Gil and Betty felt safe in the darkness of Ernesto's abandoned compound after his helicopter faded into the night. This stage of their mission concluded with the knowledge that even if their bonus objective fled, they had succeeded in their primary targets. What started as a thank-you hug turned into a passionate kiss. Betty grabbed the back of Gil's neck and pulled him close as she ravaged the lips she so desired. Gil grabbed her neck and supported her back with his other hand as he pressed in. Betty slowly moved her free hand from Gil's shoulder, feeling his rib muscles and the small of his back. The MAC-10s and backpacks dropped to the ground.

A. J. Mahler

A chaise lounge was close by, so Betty pulled Gil to it as she lay down on her back. Gil opened the front of her blouse with deft fingers before unzipping her spy suit to reveal her subtle curves framed with firm muscle. Gil moved his lips and tongue down her neck, kissing and cupping her breasts as Betty reached down to his trousers, feeling his longing underneath. Perhaps it was the result of the adrenaline rush or pent-up emotion from past missions; Betty did not care as she removed Gil's pants, unzipped his spy suit, and eagerly slid her hands down Gil's firmly muscled rib cage, stopping at his hips for only a moment before grasping his cock and balls firmly in her hands.

Gil sighed "Ahhh" before unzipping Betty. He allowed her to linger before he began tenderly kissing her body as he pulled her suit down. Her exposure left her feeling vulnerable to both Gil and an intruder should an interruption occur. Both felt vulnerable in a way that neither had expected. Betty had given up hope of ever planning out her life again, like she had done with Tom and José. Gil wanted more than the ephemeral moment; he wanted to keep Betty safe now and beyond this mission. A feeling he once had with Sally.

"Things are going to get complicated." Gil slid his hand between Betty's thighs.

Grasping his ass, she pulled him forward, Betty was ready. She wanted him and he wanted her.

The foreplay of action had prepared both of them. Betty's moans echoed Gil's rising thrusts. The rush of blood, the shivering of Betty's muscles, the release Gil felt as their pheromones merged into one for just that moment.

†

"I suppose we shouldn't linger, though it would be worth it." Betty smiled demurely without letting go.

"Yeah, get your ass up out of that lounge, we have places to go!" Gil goaded. She finally let him pull out. He lingered for a moment before dressing to admire the beauty before him. His reverie was shattered when he felt the sting in his shoulder and watched the pool deck explode from the impact of the bullet sent to kill him.

"Fuck me!" Gil cried, reaching up to feel the wet warmth of his own blood as he dropped to the ground and rolled away. He grabbed his MAC-10 to kill the asshole that had just interrupted his thoughts, but Betty fired first.

She rolled to the right, pulling her clothes mostly back on as she scrambled for a fresh magazine in her backpack. There was only one more guard, but Gil took him out with a double tap. More were likely to appear in a moment or two. Chagrined, Betty thought, *I just can't catch a damn break!*

THREE

TAKE TWO AND CALL ME IN THE MORNING

BETTY GRIMACED AS SHE inspected the superficial wound just below Gil's right shoulder. Gil handed her a bandage and she applied the large adhesive square. *It's my fault he's shot. Gil did his job—the electricity was shut off, the backup generator disabled, and the guards distracted. I'm the one who didn't get my job done.*

A month before, Betty and Gil had slipped into Ernesto's compound on a reconnaissance mission after taking the guards out, one with a laxative and the other with jumper cables to the family jewels. By all accounts, the mission went well despite the weather; they successfully breached the perimeter without notice, except for the incapacitated guard. That mission's results gave Bud Stux's Intelligence Team back at Control the necessary information to put together tonight's mission.

"We can make the generator explode by reversing the power cables. They'll burn up and the evidence will be destroyed in the resulting arc." Bud proudly pointed at the animated depiction of the generator's demise.

"What prep work do we need to do?" Gil looked skeptically at the diagrams before him.

"Not much."

"You guys always say that!" erupted Betty as she pushed her mission papers toward the middle of the conference table.

"Come on, guys, we're a team—let's act like one." Howell attempted to bring order to the charged environment. "Only people we absolutely trust are in this room. There is no mole here."

"Easy for you to say," harrumphed Gil.

"Right, you're not the one in the field getting shot at or barbecued by electricity," Betty interjected.

Bud Stux raised his hand to get everyone's attention. When that did not work, he placed his fingers in his mouth and blew. The earsplitting whistle stopped the bickering and focused the team's attention on Bud. "Listen! It's a natural gas generator with a liquefied petroleum tank backup."

"Right—so?" asked Gil.

Bud's normally nasally voice went up half an octave in his excitement. "If the natural gas line ruptures and ignites from a lightning strike—"

"Lightning strike? How the hell are we going to arrange a lightning strike?" Betty interrupted with disbelief.

"Easy! You shoot a spool of very thin copper wire into the clouds with the other end wound around your strike point. Piece of cake!" Bud looked very pleased with himself.

"And you've done this before, right?" Gil was looking for reassurance. "This isn't going to be an alpha test for some new piece of untried equipment?"

"Tell me this is proven technology?" Betty pleaded.

Bud tried to reassure them, patting at the air with his palms as if he were calming an animal. "No problems! Definitely not like the rocket-launched moped."

"Thank God! I still have bruises."

"I never said you could jump off a one-story building onto a moving flatbed truck!" Bud protested, slapping his palms on the table.

Pouting, Betty folded her arms, slouched in her chair, and glared at Bud.

With an exasperated swing of his arm, Bud declared, "I helped design this for a military application before I came here. Definitely production quality." He gave a reassuring nod. "Definitely." Bud sounded like he was trying to convince himself and the others at the same time.

"Right," Howell said decisively, dimming the lights slightly and using his laser pointer to circle the presentation screen. "We knock out the power, blow the backup generator with the"—Howell looked at Bud, who indicated a rocket shooting into the sky with his index finger— "lightning rocket, which blows the backup propane tank filled with LP fuel. The explosion is the distraction, and the ongoing fire from the natural gas line keeps the guards busy while you"—Howell pointed to Betty—"sneak into Ernesto's bedroom to interrogate."

"While I disable the remote shutoff valve and secure the perimeter until she's done," Gil concluded, nodding.

Howell gave Gil a stern look to remind him not to interrupt. "So, we go next week."

Gil nodded again. "Right."

"Modify the power grid and transformer in full view of the guards"—Betty was ticking off the list on her fingers—"come back that evening during the resulting power outage."

"Remotely triggered," inserted Bud.

"Better be on time!" Gil said.

Betty glared at both team members for interrupting her. "Subdue the guards, enter the compound undetected during the explosion of the backup generator."

"The cameras will be off." Bud felt the heat of Betty's glare. "What? How hard can it be with no—"

"Shut up, Bud!" Tom and Gil simultaneously yelled at Bud before he could do any more damage or incite Betty further.

Ignoring Bud now, Betty turned to Howell. "I go to Ernesto's suite, subdue, bind, and interrogate him using the truth serum, STP-17."

Gil picked up the litany with his mission points. "I prepare for our exit, clear the path to the truck, and we exit via the glider off Monte Ávila—"

"Waraira Repano," pronounced Bud.

"What?" Gil waved his hand at Bud while squinting to stay focused on his thought process.

"Waraira Repano. It's the indigenous name for the area," Bud explained with a pontific air. "Shouldn't you know the local terms if you're going to pass yourselves off as locals?"

Betty looked wearily at Howell. "Can I kill him now?" She turned to glare at Bud again; his chair squeaked as he started to back away from the table.

Howell shook his head no before looking back at Gil and indicating he should continue.

Gil gave Betty a glance. "I'm concerned about the glider not making it over the pass." He did not want to alarm her, but now was the time to work these things out instead of in the field. "If we end up launching before dawn, there won't be enough thermal lift to make it over."

"I've added power boost to the glider," mumbled Bud.

"A power what?" asked Gil.

Betty jumped in. "The glare from your rockets will be a signature we can't hide."

"No-n-no!" Bud stammered. "It's all air pressure. No flare."

"And this has been tested, right?" Betty glared at Bud.

"Well, not exactly." Bud continued hurriedly to keep Betty from interrupting him. "You just pull the wire for each canister and the CO2 tank will push you higher. It's just plain physics. Think Harrier Jet."

Howell rubbed his forehead and sighed.

"I guess . . . there wouldn't be any reason for us to leave before dawn anyway, right?" Betty sought reassurance.

Gil decided to change the subject. "As I was saying, I've set the charges to protect our flank and rear."

"And guard the suite while I work. Don't forget that part!" Betty said.

"Yes, I'll wind back after setting the charges to guard your ass."

"You better not forget!"

"I'll save your ass as always." Gil grinned as he said it.

"Now, kids—focus." Howell paused and then cleared his throat. Looking at Betty, he slowly said, "I'd rather you ended the interrogation early if there's a problem."

"Terminate him?" asked Betty with a hint of pleasure.

"No. Only if your life depends on it."

"Why not? If I get everything we need, why not?" Betty said like a petulant child.

"We don't know for sure if Ernesto ordered José's death. You only need to wait a little longer for your revenge." Howell tried to sound reassuring, but it came off as chiding.

"I have a problem with this." Betty looked annoyed. "When you recruited me, you promised we would get the bastard who killed José!"

"We will." Howell turned to Bud. "Has any new information come in to confirm or deny Ernesto Montoya's involvement in José's murder?"

Bud looked at his boss with a mixture of horror and disapproval. Betty almost grinned as she thought, *I think the little shit just peed in his pants!* She covered her mouth to prevent anyone from seeing her smile.

Bud stammered, "I have nothing to add at this time—pro or con."

He pulled out a handkerchief and wiped his clammy brow.

"You're working on this, right, *Bud*?" Betty emphasized his name to make sure he knew she was holding him responsible, then turned her gaze on Howell to glare at him.

Howell met her eyes. "Primary missions first. Secondary objectives come second. Are we clear?" The staring contest might have gone on for some time if the lights had not flickered to get Howell's attention. He looked up at the ceiling. "I'll be back in a moment. Bud, go over the instructions on the rocket-lightning thingy, will you, please?" Howell did not wait for Bud's acknowledgment.

Bud reviewed the steps for Gil and Betty: how to attach the cable and spool, how to launch the rocket, clearance requirements for safety, and what to expect. Before he could finish Howell returned.

"Right, Betty, if you get all of the questions answered on the list and you think Ernesto did it, you have a go. If there is any doubt, you spare him . . . for now. We need to bring him in for a more thorough interrogation and, if we are lucky, turn him."

Betty reluctantly accepted the modification with pursed lips and a barely perceivable nod.

†

July 14, 2009 — Midnight at Ernesto's

Each guard cast a dancing elongated shadow as they debated the proper protocol for dousing the fire. The shutoff valve was stuck. One man had witnessed Red Adair blowing out oil wells with explosives in the deserts of Kuwait during the first Gulf War. Another had seen a massive Soviet water tank do the job. Because the buildings were not in imminent danger, they had time to debate their options. Calling in the local fire department was low on the list. Inside the empty hallways of the main living quarters, the remaining sentry posted outside of Ernesto's bedroom door was now propped up against the wall, sitting cross-legged, his head bowed down, and a sedative dart sticking out of his neck.

Ernesto was asleep when Betty entered his suite, thanks to the influence of a sleep aid. He did not like storms. With the assurance of knowing he was guarded, he felt he could afford to knock himself out as needed.

Betty rolled Ernesto Montoya onto his back. "This will hurt a little." Using the same white plastic flex cuffs commonly used by the ATF for drug dealers, Betty secured Ernesto to his bed before he was fully alert. He did not look surprised to see her and he did not cry out for help, but then again, the STP-17 she had stabbed into his neck probably helped.

With Ernesto's wrists bound and the addition of her little cocktail in his system, there was not much on his agenda for the evening besides whatever she had in mind. The questioning started with the simple and expanded to the complex.

"Where do you keep the Cabal's money?" Betty asked.

"Money?" Ernesto replied.

Betty could not decide if he was covering or just not understanding the question. Her Portuguese was perfect, thanks to José, so it could not be a translation error. "We know you handle vast sums of money."

Ernesto pouted. "Just bookkeeper."

Because of the truth serum, Ernesto was cooperating somewhat, but his answers were clipped and imprecise. He's so out of it . . . I wonder if he took something before bed . . . maybe it's reacting with the serum, thought Betty.

"How do you move the money?" Betty asked. Bud had explained to her that the Cabal used the darknets, websites that no one could see if they did not know where to look—let alone have the correct encrypted software and passwords.

Ernesto smiled vacantly at no one in particular. Betty ratcheted up the process. *Press on!*

She pulled out a slip of paper Bud had given her with an IP address, port number, and a security code. These were just guesses, so she was supposed to let Ernesto only have a quick look. She flashed it in front of his eyes. "We know how you connect your servers. Why don't you just tell me what I already know?"

Ernesto's face scrunched for a moment as he tried to reach for the paper and was reminded that his hands were bound to the bed. He shrugged his shoulders slightly and sighed. "I have never seen that before."

Ernesto's answers felt true, but his responses were frustrating Betty—she needed to link him to José's death, and this would not cut it.

Gil should be busy preparing our exit. Ten more minutes to interrogate Ernesto before all hell breaks loose. Daylight is only a few hours away. She climbed on top of Ernesto and placed her hands on his shoulders. His nose inches from her face.

"Who do you work for?" asked Betty.

"I work for many people, beautiful lady," stated Ernesto.

"Names. I want names of your investors, account holders, and directors," Betty persisted.

"Paul, Timothy, Carlos, Samuel . . ." Ernesto listed many more first names.

Evidently, last names don't exist in his world . . . this isn't working. "Who gives you your orders?"

"Father."

"Father has a name?"

"Father Tom tells me what to do."

Ernesto is an orphan—he must mean a priest. "Anyone else?"

"No one else. Just Father." A tear crept into Ernesto's eye and trailed down his check.

The Jesuits! How could they possibly be controlling an international banker? Betty checked her watch—five minutes left, tops. She pounded away at the banker, question after question. Control had created a list of subjects for Betty to focus on, yet everything was a dead end. None of the remaining interrogatories on her list seemed to elicit any useful information. *First names have value . . . if you can tie them to other information.*

"When you have a problem you cannot fix, who do you call?" Betty was getting desperate and began to ask random questions.

"What kind of problem?" asked the compliant Ernesto.

"Say you needed some muscle, a hit man." Betty asked, searching for who had killed José.

"Oh, depends, but I suppose Max or Michel . . . sometimes Yuri," replied Ernesto.

Betty felt like her world was crashing. *Was Yuri the assassin?* Yuri was dead, buried in a nondescript grave in rural Virginia. A plot of land set aside for bodies Control needed to get rid of—bodies no one would miss. The lab had photographed him, tested for every known chemical, and saved samples of his body tissue for future testing needs. He was finally given a simple burial, with only the gravedigger and two agents present to ensure the body made its way to a final resting place.

The possibility that Yuri Vasilyev, Dr. Salizar's assassin on the train in Panama, might have been José's murderer did not comfort Betty much. Yuri had been a tool for someone like Montoya; killing Montoya would bring satisfaction and closure to Betty, but only if she knew he was the one responsible. *Damn it!* Betty considered the irony of wishing Yuri had lived. *He died trying to escape; his foot barely caught the steel beam of the bridge or his jump to the river might have succeeded. If he had lived, I could've found him again!* During their encounter, Yuri only divulged some cryptic information about Dr. Salizar killing his family.

Control's search into Yuri's background exhumed mostly medical information: Dr. Salizar's hospital network had treated Yuri's wife and child. His wife had died during childbirth thirty years before, and her body parts had been harvested for ten different transplant operations that day. Control's front company, a medical device manufacturer, had gotten access to the information in the course of performing a contract for modernizing the hospital's record system. Per the contract, the programmers had all the records electronically stored and copies saved. During the briefing session on Yuri's postmortem, Howell solemnly looked at the information before divulging, "His boy survived childbirth but was switched with a stillborn." Flipping through the file, Howell said there was more, but it was not pertinent to her mission, thus she did not need to know. This was before Betty had learned of the possible connection between Yuri, Ernesto, and José.

Betty's fingers encircled Ernesto's neck. *Damn it, Howell!* Her fingers began to tighten, and Ernesto's breathing became labored. A surprised and scared look came over the previously calm and submissive banker. Betty was not sure if she was choking Ernesto because he might have ordered the hit or because she was still pissed off at Howell. As quickly as she started, she stopped.

Betty grabbed a syringe from her kit and quickly stabbed the large needle into Ernesto's left nostril. Ernesto yelped as Betty injected the electronic tracking device into the sinus cavity of his skull. McFluffy's tracking device could be followed on the ground from up to a kilometer away, or via satellites 240 kilometers above the earth using triangulation. Ernesto's skull shielded the barb-encrusted capsule from detection or modification. Its shadow profile matched the surrounding bone in the unlikely event his head would need an x-ray. Fortunately, the memory loss caused by the STP-17 would keep him from recalling that anything had been inserted into his sinus cavity.

Betty would have preferred shoving the needle a couple of inches farther into Ernesto's skull to kill him, but without being one hundred percent confident he ordered José's assassination, she would have had undying guilt and nightmares. He would have to wait for his comeuppance. Right now, Betty needed to end the interrogation before the guards regrouped and checked on their master.

FOUR

THE PRICE OF KNOWLEDGE

May 5, 2009 — Observatory Circle, Washington, D.C.

"WE'VE BEEN DANCING AROUND this for too long. When are you going to tell me the truth?" exclaimed Tom Howell Jr.

"Now, Tom, be fair." Tom Howell Sr. attempted to pacify his son. "I have tried to guide you in your career."

"Guide me? More like command me!"

"You have fought me the whole way . . . we could have had this conversation years ago," said Tom Sr.

"Enough lecturing. I chose my path, but it turns out you've manipulated me at every turn through cat's-paws and subterfuge."

"I was only trying to guide you."

"No wonder I'm good at the spy game!" replied Tom Jr.

Tom was with his father for lunch. Instead of their usual, the Capital Grille, this meeting needed to take place in a secure location swept for listening devices and devoid of personnel, even those cleared for top-secret conversations. This meeting was taking place at the home of Tom Howell Sr., a handsome Georgian colonial in the Observatory Circle area of Washington, D.C., close to the second- and third-tier embassies—an area with naturally high security. Lunch consisted of tomato bisque soup and Reuben sandwiches. The cook had left the house after serving the food. Barnes, the butler, was out on errands, and the groundskeeper who doubled as a security guard was working in the garage.

"Tom, your mother and I have always been honest with you."

"Honest? You call keeping my family's history from me honest?"

"We have also withheld information from you in order to always tell you the truth."

"So you are going to finally . . ."

"I'm an old man now. Next month I will be eighty-nine. I don't have time to beat around the bush." Tom Sr. took a deep breath, as if to ready himself for the next part.

Tom Jr. interjected, "Tell the truth? You've been lying to me since I was born! Like you always said, the best lie is the truth with details left out."

"As I was saying, we have always told you the truth by leaving out certain details you did not need to know, nor could you understand." Pausing to sigh, Tom Sr. continued. "You have been working in Control since graduating from college. Your work has been exemplary." Tom Jr. tried to hide the warmth of satisfaction at the rare compliment from his father, but Tom Sr. noted the relaxing affect it had. "It is time for you to learn some of my darkest secrets."

Tom Jr. looked skeptically at shallow wells of his father's eyes. "I'm not your confessor, nor do I wish to be."

A rumbling cough and dark spittle erupted from the old man into his waiting handkerchief. "If I were to die before telling you, they would be lost forever. You are the only other to know. A secret is no longer a secret if more than one person knows."

A crack appeared in the junior Howell's stony face. "I'm not sure you can die."

"I assure you, I will die. However, out of respect for the dead, I assume you will only use a mirror to check for my breath rather than sticking a pin in my face." He paused again to sigh and drink some water before returning to his story.

Tom relaxed in his chair ever so slightly and prepared himself for a whopper of a tale.

The gruff voice began with a false strength borrowed from the past. "I was entrusted by Allen Dulles, the station chief of Switzerland in 1945, with a small fortune and the mandate to create Control after the conclusion of World War Two because of the damage caused by Soviet and Chinese agents compromising the Dogwood chain of informants. Dulles knew the Office of Strategic Services was about to be disbanded or reworked into a new organization. His job was to remove as many double agents and moles as possible before that conversion. Mine was to create an entirely new entity outside the rules and regulations of the U.S. government with ten million dollars of Nazi gold and ten million dollars of forged British banknotes. In today's market, that would be . . . hmmm . . . about two hundred and fifty million. While loading the British banknotes from the warehouse, I also located the printing press and plates the Bernhard Operation had created for forging U.S. one-hundred-dollar bills. For a time, I literally was printing money to keep Control hidden and moving forward."

"So you're a counterfeiter and Black Ops specialist with a pedigree." Tom Jr. said wryly.

Senior cleared his throat and glared at his son. "As you know, Allen Dulles eventually became the first civilian head of the CIA, the successor organization to the OSS, seven years later. Allen knew he could count on me to take care of any operation too sensitive for the CIA. Our motto then—and should be now—'Abort if report,' meaning we should abort any mission with the possibility of linkage to us or the U.S. government. We do not exist, and no one should find out about our missions.

"I hand-selected the staff and agents for complete secrecy and loyalty; any sign of disloyalty resulted in liquidation. We erred on the side of caution more than once." Tom Jr. watched wide eyed and tense as his father paused again to take a drink and sigh. Tom Sr. soldiered on. "It was my order that resulted in the protection of our secrecy. I . . . hmmm . . . Tom, you never knew your uncle Jack. Jack was a brilliant civil engineer who created the bunker of Control. He surveyed the land, ran the construction crew, and ordered the materials. Everything in that building came about because of Jack. I ordered Jack's lobotomy." Tom Sr. put his head in his hands for only a moment and then straightened himself.

"You told me he died in Korea! You did lie!" Tom declared.

"No, I told you we lost Jack during the Korean War, not because of the Korean War. I allowed you and many others to assume he was a war hero, which he truly was in the clandestine sense. Jack understood the total need for secrecy. He also had a problem with alcohol and a loose mouth when drunk. He knew the price he would have to pay; however, I could not order his death. What I did to him was worse than death: he survived for only a few years before his mind broke completely after the procedure. Jack was institutionalized . . . well . . . along with a few others."

"You bastard!"

"More people died building Hoover Dam then we lost building Control!" roared the old, proud lion. "I assure you more lives have been saved or improved by Control's existence than by that damn dam!"

Tom Jr.'s lunch turned unappetizing, and what he had eaten felt like it was coming back up. The illusion that Control was only for the good of the country was now slipping away. The price paid for complete secrecy—ordering the lobotomy of a sibling—seemed too high. Tom's younger brother died shortly after birth, leaving him an only child. This was followed by a miscarriage, and eventually, his parents had stopped trying. Fate left the future of Control at his feet and that load seemed too heavy to lift; yet he was drawn to the challenge with a perverse sense of duty to country and family.

Sensing the cloud in his son's mind, the steamroller of a patriarch eased up for a moment. "Tom, it is not all darkness when it comes to Control. You would not know, but your mother was blind when I met her. Her father, Dr. Fritz Lieber, was in Germany before World War Two and therefore was coerced into joining the Nazi Party's SS medical unit. His research into the transplantation of tissue interested the higher-ups, leading to tremendous latitude to investigate his theories. Just as you may have heard, the jet engine was first successfully used by the Nazis, and likewise medical breakthroughs also came from people like your grandfather, Dr. Lieber."

The torrent of secrets bewildered Tom. He was drowning in information; he wanted to ask questions, to complain about details, or just scream. But he dared not interject lest his father stop the flow. His mind raced to store the data without analysis before the next flood of information.

"Your mother was blind, her retinas scarred beyond use from measles contracted at age five; Grandfather Fritz vowed to find a cure. The only avenue appeared to be a complete eyeball replacement, but that was impossible at the time. He devoted himself to grueling hours of research and experimentation, starting with transplanting corneas using Dr. Vladimir Filatov's technique and the advances of the Spaniard, Dr. Castroviejo. These methods could not solve your mother's blindness, but they were a start on the right path.

"Fritz had many patients from which to choose, such as soldiers wounded in battle—anxious to regain their sight and willing to be guinea pigs. Fritz's bosses were pleased with the successes and unconcerned with the failures. Complete eye transplantation seemed within reach with the new drugs developed to prevent tissue rejection. The ending of the war meant the end of his lab, and the tribunals would have meant his possible imprisonment. We rounded up scientists such as your grandfather at the end of the war to move them to the U.S. to further our own scientific endeavors. We gave the doctors new identities, washing away their sins. Fritz refused to come to America. He insisted on moving to Argentina, where many fellow Germans and Nazis settled out of sight." Tom Sr. gulped his water to quench his now-dry throat. He was no longer used to speaking for such great lengths, and the strain was beginning to show in his voice.

"I set Fritz up in Argentina and stayed for three years to see if there were any other potential scientists for our research labs. I found Josef Mengele during this time . . . mad as a hatter. His science was an abomination of cruel intentions. I told Dulles where he was and suggested the newly formed Israeli State might be interested in him. At the time, they were too busy protecting their borders. Years later, they just missed that 'Angel of Death' by a mere two weeks."

Tom Jr. pushed his food around on his plate, needing to do something besides just sitting there.

"Fritz took on an early disciple of Dr. Castroviejo's, a young and inventive Dr. Salizar. Together they embarked on an amazing journey, discovering new drugs. Some prevented rejection of transplant tissue, and some promoted nerve growth. I, of course, provided the necessary money for their research. This is the one time in the past sixty years I abused my oath of secrecy. I had fallen in love with your mother. She was fifteen when I met her. We married when she was twenty and I was thirty-three.

"I traveled back and forth for five years while Jack finished the construction of Control. It took ten years to build the structure and bring it online. Electricity came from an underground steam geyser. Water collected from the condensing tower provided all the potable water we needed. We were a self-sufficient city: hydroponic food, livestock, electricity, and running water. We brought in everything else undetected— but, I digress." Tom Sr. paused to clear his throat, his thoughts returning to his wife, Julia.

"When your mother died, I did not tell you she committed suicide. By now, you may have guessed that your mother was one of the first successful recipients of full eyeball transplant surgery. What you did not know is that your mother suffered bouts of depression. Just before the final episode, I replaced a nosy housekeeper; your mother refused to take the anti-rejection medicine, and the new woman did not understand the vital nature of the pill. Tissue rejection ensued, and your mother lost her sight once more. It tore her apart, and she took her own life." For the second time, Tom Sr. put his head in his hands, and this time Tom saw his father shake with emotion, but only for a moment.

Upon regaining his composure, Tom Sr. continued. "This, as you know, happened after her sixty-seventh birthday, just after you were allowed to come home. Perhaps that is the one consolation I have, her convincing me to relent and reconcile with you."

That was all the old man could take. He waved Tom off. They would continue again at lunch the following day.

Tom Jr. did not know what to do. He felt an urge to put his hand on his father's shoulder, to console him as he had seen his mother do a hundred times. However, the knowledge Tom had gained also revolted him, making him want to get as much distance from his father as possible. *What have I gotten myself into? Am I as corrupt as my father? Can I keep these secrets?* Tom slowed as he walked to his car; the burden of knowledge seemed to settle in his calves and leaden his feet. *Tomorrow?* He was just hoping to get through the rest of the day.

FIVE

THREE-RING CIRCUS

July 28, 2009 — Washington, D.C.

THE TRAPEZE ACT BETTY PERFORMED lacked a net. Her law offices were the anchor of her reality, the platform from which she would launch herself into the void of Control operations. Her real world—the one she felt most alive in—was out in the wilds of South America. The predictability of her office was a nice backdrop to her spy work. Reality was dull and boring. Spying was exciting and invigorating. The adrenaline rush of a job well done under pressure kept pulling her back. The surreal world of Control had a tangible form that Betty held on to every chance she got. She was looking for answers that a pad of paper and a blue pen could not give her. She enjoyed her work helping immigrants enter the United States but she loved destroying the plans of terrorists and the World Order Cabal. Time at her desk afforded the opportunity to savor the taste of her missions: sitting back after a good meal of adrenaline, sipping a strong Colombian coffee, and evaluating how she had performed. Occasionally, Howell would show her a medal she could not keep; her preferred reward was that full feeling at her desk.

Lately, everything seemed to lead back to Caracas, Venezuela. Something big was happening there. Unfortunately, the leads were now cold. Ernesto Montoya was no longer visible, despite the transponder Betty had implanted in his skull. His low-key entourage had moved to another compound before he could be located on the ground or via satellite scan. Gil disappeared into the arms of the Cabal: either dead, missing, or imprisoned somewhere. The loss of her partner was devastating, and it was crippling her operational effectiveness. Howell had insisted she take some time to get her head together and catch up on her legal career before deciding if she was still in the game.

"Betty, I trust you; you're a great asset to Control. I know you can do your job, but I'm worried that *you* don't know it."

"Howell, what the hell are you talking about? Gil is probably dead because of me. He wouldn't leave with me on the glider. He bailed me out of the trap Ernesto set for us . . . I owe him my life . . . What do you think I'm feeling?" Betty did not say what she was thinking, *Gil might not be dead if I hadn't had sex with him. We would have gotten out on the glider before the replacement guards arrived or even left by a different way . . . together.* Betty lingered on the thought just a bit longer. Was it the passion and the sex, or did she love Gil? *Tom doesn't need to know about the sex on the poolside chaise lounge—that I do know.*

Howell had mistaken the flush of red on her cheeks as guilt. "Betty, take the next two weeks off. I don't want you to do anything but your legal work and yoga for a while. Center yourself and decide where you want this to go. I'm not in a hurry. I'll stop by your office next time I'm in D.C."

Betty hated Howell for saying it and for being right. She needed time away to get her thoughts straight. It was getting harder to concentrate on work, let alone keep track of the minutia of her life. She frequently found herself doodling houses, dogs, and babies. *Do I need to bail out of Control? Is it time to move on to a permanent reality?*

Betty had an uneasy feeling that would not go away even when she immersed herself into her legal work. The stranger symptom was her frequent desire to vomit. An urgent need to find the nearest waste basket grabbed her whenever a strong aroma drifted by. Smells and thoughts specific to her memory of Gil did not trigger the nausea; instead, those evoked a warm yet sad feeling, a longing for what could have been—and if she allowed herself, a hope of what could be.

Margaret cornered Betty after the last client meeting of the day.

"Ms. Thursten . . . Betty . . . may I ask you a question?" asked her legal assistant.

Betty rolled her eyes. She was not in the mood for twenty questions. "What is it, Margaret?" Betty suddenly had the urge to run to the toilet to vomit.

"Betty . . . you know I don't pry . . . but have you been feeling OK?"

Betty knew she was not depressed. She was sad and angry over what had happened to Gil, but not depressed. "Margaret, I am not depressed, if that's what you're thinking. Yes, I have been a little down. You know that project I was working on to find the person who killed José? Well, I've hit a dead end . . . and, a close friend was hurt because of my search." Betty could not tell Margaret the whole truth, so she gave what breadcrumbs she could.

"I don't think you're depressed," said Margaret as she gave a snorting-halting laugh. "Betty, do you use birth control . . . pills I mean?"

Betty was not ready for this question. Margaret's rather personal interrogatory was a two by four to her tortured stomach. She had been using Depo-Provera to protect against pregnancy for the past five years. She was forgetful when it came to taking a daily pill; the three-month protection provided by the shots in her thigh or abdomen seemed to be the better way to go. When or if she ever got married, she could stop the shots and start having kids nine or ten months later. Betty had missed her last appointment before the mission to question Ernesto Montoya. "Margaret, I don't know why this is any of your business, but I started using Depo Provera with José."

"Betty, Depo-Provera has a three-percent failure rate." Margaret said as she turned and walked away.

Betty's open mouth felt dry. *It doesn't mean anything. She pries into everyone's life to make up for her lackluster home life.* Betty remembered meeting Margaret's husband at the firm's last Christmas party. *Burt is such a pig!*

Margaret tended to know what was going on and with whom. She frequently cornered a coworker to tell them their astrological reading for the day. Betty did not believe in astrology or fortune telling, but she did believe that some people were more in tune with their surroundings than others. Betty placed her hands on her belly and closed her eyes, attempting to feel her inner self and hear what her body might be saying. With shock and self-awareness, she grabbed her black leather attaché case and bolted out of the office. A pregnancy test from the drugstore was most definitely in her future.

Six

THE MARCH OF TIME WITH MR. MISTY

July 28, 2009 — Washington, D.C.

BETTY'S CALENDAR SHOWED a missed July 6 appointment for her quarterly Depo-Provera shot. Upon returning from Venezuela, the answering machine message brought a cold sweat to Betty's brow before she reminded herself that it usually took almost a year for fertility to return. "Ms. Thursten, this is Sarah from Dr. Callahan's office. You missed your appointment. Please call our office to reschedule as soon as possible." Betty had been at Control planning the missions. Her calendar was not in her quarters to remind her. Did her body make her forget? Was the clock ticking? Betty's thirty-fifth birthday had come and gone. She only had five more years before the risks of childbirth started to climb and no permanent relationship in sight. Tom and Betty had planned on two children before his assignment to Iraq. She had spent many hours imagining what it would be like to be a mother: holding a baby in her arms, nursing, raising toddlers, and even their first days in school. The end of her relationship with Tom gave her pause until she became serious with José. In time, Betty became comfortable with visualizing her future children once more, until José's murder. Death seemed to follow her even before she became a spy, and now, being a mother seemed a luxury she could not afford.

Betty read the instructions over again, just to be sure: "Within two minutes, the round shaped window will reveal a + (pregnant) or − (not pregnant) result." The second hand of Betty's watch swept around at its usual pace, giving off the seesaw sound of the movement. Her frenetic mind swung back and forth between the possible outcomes. One path led to a child she envisioned cherishing while simultaneously feeling the anchoring weight of a family to care for, on her own. The other path continued her trajectory before the passion of the moment with Gil, but now not so bright with promise. The absence of that very child that would root her to a community forced her to linger on her mortality. Passing on what little she understood of the world to her baby seemed more purposeful than killing bad guys, where every time one went down, another took his place. The revenge business did not seem nearly as satisfying as raising your own little villains.

The excruciating wait was nearly over, yet Betty refused to look at the results even when the watch declared time was up. Which did she want? Both were scary. A child would end her spy career and hamper her legal one. The absence of a child dulled the meaning of her life. This seesaw of emotion tilted back and forth as she gathered the strength to decide which path was right. After another half minute had elapsed, Betty peered at the indicator, knowing neither would fully complete her.

"Crap!" She got what she wanted, but did not need.

On the plus side, Betty now understood why she felt sick to her stomach, ready to vomit in the morning and again at the whiff of any old odd smell. Then again, she wished the test showed negative. She wished that the cause of her ill feelings was only her anguish over Gil. She longed for him each night in bed—longed for the man, the lover, the comrade, and the friend. Howell's warnings for Betty to take care and not to fall for Gil were no match for pheromones. Betty had avoided temptation, only to walk into the trap at her most vulnerable moment. Had she made love to Gil because she was ovulating for the first time in four years or because he had saved her life? She hoped it was because they had found a deeper connection.

Betty dialed the number for Dr. Callahan's office but hung up as the line was answered.

If this was Tom's baby, how would I feel? If I had gotten pregnant before he left and I knew he wasn't coming back . . . would I keep the baby? But I thought he was coming back. Just like I want to believe Gil is coming back. Betty drifted deeper into thoughts she had packed away, thoughts she had not intended to return to; she let herself linger in the depths of her love and desire to be with Tom. The man she once thought she knew before Iraq, not the man she now knew as her boss. To a much happier time in Georgetown when they lived in the loft apartment overlooking the Potomac River.

Seven years earlier — Georgetown

"Tom?" prodded Betty.

Tom was deep in thought, staring just over Betty's left shoulder at the front window of Café Bonaparte. "Huh . . . what? Oh, I wasn't listening, was I?" It was a lazy Sunday afternoon, and the light dancing in the window was mesmerizing him.

"No, Tom, you weren't. Do you know what we were talking about?"

"I could fake it, but you would know better, wouldn't you?"

"I was telling you about Jil's sister Ruth. How she was starting to date my brother Rob?" Betty said, hinting at the past five minutes of a one-sided conversation. "What exactly are you presenting tomorrow that has your undivided attention? I want to work that into my story so you'll hear me."

"I could tell you, but—"

"—then you'd have to kill me. I know . . . hardy, har, har! You wish you were a secret agent."

"I really do wish you had a security clearance, it would be a lot easier."

"I suppose I could change careers, get a job with the Pentagon just so I can keep an eye on you." Betty winked.

"You'd never find me. That is such a huge building." His thoughts rolled back to 9/11 and his brush with fate. "I didn't even know anyone who was on the side the plane hit. Oh, sure, I know people who know people, that kind of thing."

"Do you want to talk about it?" Betty cocked her head inquisitively.

"Oh, I don't think so . . . there isn't really anything to talk about." Tom was lying; he had been in the targeted section of the Pentagon only hours before the terrorist strike. Had he allowed a coworker to keep him for coffee, he might be dead. The work he was now involved with would save many lives, but too late for his old friend, a comrade he would never talk to again.

Tom's distance today had little to do with an impending presentation. His mind kept returning to thoughts of the delicate thread keeping everyone alive, fate and circumstances. The metronome of his responsibilities drew him away from Betty.

"Tom! You're doing it again," said Betty.

"Let's get out of here—I think I've had enough of coffeehouses for a while. Let's go for a walk with Surry, down by the river. Maybe have a picnic dinner? Lie on a blanket and gaze at the sky. It's a beautiful day." Tom's mind drifted away again.

"Sure, it would be nice to have a picnic. What do you want to eat?"

He refocused squarely on Betty. "I don't know, maybe get something from the deli?"

Betty liked the idea of lying on a blanket. She started picturing her head on Tom's chest while he napped and she worked on her brief. She had quite a bit of reading to do before Monday. Surry could play with her friends or play catch with Tom. She loved to chase after the ball, like it was a squirrel. Sometimes the ball would take a big hop four or five feet off the ground and Surry would leap up, laying herself out in midair, stretching to catch the ball in midflight. It was awesome to watch her get up to speed on a long throw. Surry was their surrogate child. Someday they would have children; two would be enough, perhaps a boy and a girl. There was no hurry yet. Betty liked the idea of Surry still being around when the children were old enough to throw a ball for her.

"Betty?" said Tom.

"What? Oh, I guess it was my turn to go to never-never land!" Betty blushed. She grabbed Tom's left hand and headed out the door with her bag on her left shoulder.

"It is a beautiful day, isn't it?" marveled Betty.

†

Time had passed quickly since that day in the misty past. It was the first of many derailments for her life's master plan: Tom's departure, José's death, joining Control, and now Gil. Time for children was running short. Betty wrestled with her conscience for hours before she knew what to do. Ultimately, the thought of either trusting another man like she had Tom, so totally and completely—or binding her soul and future to something so fragile as another's life, like she had with José—brought the seesaw to the ground.

"Dr. Callahan's office, this is Sarah. How may I help you?" said the sweet voice.

"This is Betty Thursten. I need to schedule . . . an abortion."

SEVEN

GIDEON'S BOOKING

May 6, 2009 — Observatory Circle, Washington, D.C.

"GIDEON, DELIGHTED TO SEE you." Barnes took the man's hat and escorted him to the sunroom where Tom Howell Sr. sat in his chair looking out over his back yard, seemingly lost in thought, just an old man waiting to die.

"Barnes, tell the gardener that the boxwood hedge on the periphery is not level nor is it straight. If he thinks my vision is failing or my attention dimming, he can look for new employment."

"Yes, sir. This is Mr. Crenshaw as you requested." Barnes waved his hand at the seat the thirtysomething trim black man was supposed to take, but Gideon stayed standing, waiting with his right hand on the high-back chair.

"Sit," insisted Tom Sr.

Gideon moved forward just perceptibly, then drifted back to the balls of his feet. "I'm not sure I want to."

"Your hesitation speaks higher of your intellect than your résumé. Please, Gideon, take a seat and make yourself comfortable. Shall I call Barnes back to get you a drink?"

Gideon shook his head no. He hesitated for another moment, looking over his shoulder at the path back to the door before sliding resolutely onto the soft cushion of the exquisite fabric. The chairs were at a ninety-degree angle to each other, intended for viewing the garden rather than face-to-face conversation.

"*Now* would you like a drink? Coffee, tea, or . . . perhaps something a little stronger?"

"Espresso, if Barnes hasn't lost any of his barista skills." Gideon looked out in the general direction of the boxwoods but could not see any flaw in the gardener's work.

"You are here because Barnes says you can take care of a job for me."

"I'm here because my last job paid poorly and I am running out of money." Gideon looked back at the crumpled heap of a man.

"True. We are all motivated differently. I will make it simple for you. You will be paid the equivalent value of two ounces of gold every week that this man stays alive." Howell Sr. glanced at a portfolio sitting on the low table in front of Gideon. "That is all you have to do. Your expenses will be paid: travel, equipment, walking money; your payments will accrue in whatever bank account you wish, and it will cost you nothing to go about your normal day."

"Twenty-four-seven surveillance and protection is at least a three-man job."

"He spends most of his time"—the old man wheezed in and out while resisting the urge to clutch his chest—"in a secure location that you don't have to worry about. Your job starts when he arrives and ends when he returns to that location."

Gideon glanced up at a smiling Barnes, who had entered with the coffee tray. "You knew I would want your old brackish sludge, didn't you?"

"You used to hate this 'brackish sludge,' if memory serves." Barnes looked over at his master. "He preferred Americano in the beginning, but he's a bright young man who grew to understand the finer luxuries of life—after a little instruction and inducement."

"Hmmm. Don't we all with the correct teacher." Howell Sr. reached for his coffee and turned his head slightly so Barnes could adjust the oxygen tube constricting his thick neck.

Gideon gave a smile and a nod of appreciation to Barnes for the excellent espresso before turning his attention back to the dossier of the man he was to protect. "Is he to know I'm watching him? He might object."

"Oh, he won't like it one bit, but you aren't being paid to make him happy."

"I'm not being paid anything yet. I haven't taken the job."

"Gideon, you took the job when you agreed to Barnes's request to come here."

Gideon made a motion to leave but settled back into the chair as Howell Sr. waved his hand for him to stay seated. Neither man spoke for a moment. Instead, they both stared out the window at Mandala tending the garden.

"Mandala does the most exquisite work. You see, he hates imperfection more than he hates gardening."

"I don't follow you."

"You hate being broke more than you hate being on retainer. You will never have to find another job the rest of your life if you manage this properly. Your contact will signal you when your subject leaves the protection of his castle. Well over fifty percent of your time will be yours to do as you wish, and you will have plenty of money to spend tending your 'garden,' whatever you choose that to be."

"What happens if I decide to quit?"

"This is a lifetime appointment. You will be the ripple following his wave from here to the horizon."

Gideon sipped his drink and stared at the garden below. The land dropped off to a slight ravine behind the house, giving the viewer a high point to observe the grounds. "That's what I thought."

"I don't like turnover. Identification and training are too time consuming to pick the wrong candidate."

"How long has Mandala been with you?"

"Longer than Barnes. Hmm. Forty or more years, I suppose."

Gideon saw Mandala look to the house for a moment as Barnes relayed the message to the gardener. Then Mandala aggressively grabbed his shears, shaking his fist at the window while uttering a sobriquet for the old man before marching over to the boxwood hedge to amend his errant trimming.

"He knew it wasn't perfect, didn't he?" asked Gideon.

"I don't ask anything of my people they don't truly want to do. Otherwise, I picked the wrong man or woman for the job."

"I want half of the money to go into a separate account. For my mother."

"That isn't necessary, Gideon. I already have set up an account for your mother. As long as she lives and you do your job, she will always be taken care of."

Barnes appeared to escort Gideon out.

Gideon rose to leave, turned to look directly at his new master, and stated, "Golden handcuffs."

"Yes. Yes, they are."

EIGHT

THE TRUTH HURTS

July 15, 2009 — 2 a.m. at Ernesto Montoya's compound

"UHGH . . ." GIL'S LUNGS compressed from the force of a ham-hock fist. The thug in front of him was not pulling any punches.

"Who do you work for?" asked a man in black. Between swollen eyelids and the harsh light, Gil could not make out the leader's features. Everything beyond the range of the lamp was a shadow. As the thug's face pierced the veil of the hundred-watt light bulb again, Gil noted a knit cap and thick eyebrows, giving the sinister appearance of a vulture.

The shadow motioned to the thug.

"Uhgh . . ." Gil repeated.

"Why were you sent to kill Mr. Montoya?" said the man in black.

"I was not sent to kill him." Gil coughed as he spit out the words. Lying was not going to help. He was not supposed to answer any questions. The bitch of it was, he would rather die than give any valuable information. The truth could not hurt in this situation, though he was not going to admit that Betty was involved. *Maybe give the bastards a bone. Something for them to chew on instead of me,* thought Gil.

"Lies!" screamed the man in black. He nodded to the thug, who dragged a body into the ring of light. "This is your partner. We found him trying to finish what you started."

Gil grimaced at the sight of Sanchez. Sanchez's forehead was missing a large section of skull and flesh above his eyebrows where a bullet had exited. Without seeing it, Gil knew there was a small entry wound at the base of the skull. Someone had caught him by surprise and did not bother with the niceties of an introduction. "Shit . . . never seen'm before."

The thug hit Gil with his knuckles square on the jaw. *That's going to leave a mark.* The taste of blood, the hot iron of hemoglobin, the wet feeling of a trickle down his chin, and Gil unable to wipe his mouth with his hands cuffed behind the chair all increased his rage and resistance.

"Once more. Who sent you? What were you doing with Mr. Montoya? Who else are you working with?" grilled the man in black. Again, Gil spit blood and saliva toward the darkness and the last known position of the voice. If he was going to die, he was going to do it with dignity and spirit. He was not going to let these assholes have their way.

Gil had gone through survival training for Special Ops. Solitary confinement in complete darkness for what seemed like a week started his training; the beating by a team of sadistic trainers while an officer and a doctor stood by completed it. Gil had signed several forms giving his permission to gain this exclusive training. The interrogators giving the beatings knew how to hurt Gil without causing permanent damage. The doctor was present to make sure Gil survived. The government's investment up to that point had cost too much to let a trainer get too enthusiastic in the simulations, but the beatings had to be realistic—Gil had to know what he was going to be up against if he ever did get caught.

This time he had no illusions about his fate. He had no worth to Ernesto's goons beyond the perceived value of the information he could divulge. There would be no hostage negotiations or trading of prisoners. Once they were convinced he had no further use—he was fish bait.

Something electrical was beginning to hum. The radiating element began burning the remainder of the last victim's flesh still attached to the device. Now glowing in the shadows, the smoke curled into the bright curtain of the light. The smell of scorched flesh reached Gil's nostrils.

"Well, Mr. Spy. Perhaps you like barbecue. We have a local delicacy you may prefer—Caracas chicken." The thug used a large knife to cut Gil's sleeve and then tore the material off. "Spread the oil on first, Manolo, it brings out the flavor!" laughed the man in black.

Manolo used a brush to paint olive oil onto Gil's shoulder and bicep. Gil's shoulder joints ached from the tight binding behind his back. He could barely move; pulling on the handcuffs just caused the metal to bite deeper into his skin. Resistance was an act of disobedience and not good for his health.

The vulture of a man standing before Gil grabbed the electric branding iron, the metal glowing in the darkness; Gil could make out the distinct shape of a capital "W" surrounded by a circle. *This is not going to feel good*, thought Gil.

"Are you sure you do not have something to tell me, Mr. Spy? Give me something, anything, and we do not have to do this. Manolo likes to play with his iron, but he must do what I tell him. Give me something so I can tell Manolo no más," said the man in black.

Manolo snarled and laughed maniacally as he came closer with the scalding iron. *This is one tattoo I'm not looking forward to.* Gil cleared his throat, buying a few seconds while his mind raced. *What can I tell the bastard that doesn't matter?* At war with himself, Gil fought the desire to avoid the iron. He knew instinctively that any information he gave would only delay things. Once he caved on the iron, it would become their favorite tool to elicit new information from Gil. The point of the torture was to find his weakness, what he was afraid of; which device would evoke such terror that Gil would have no option but to talk.

"I've always wanted a brand, but can you turn it upside down? I was kind of hoping for an 'M.' Hell, make it an 'M' for Manolo, 'cause when I come back for you, I'm gonna shove that iron up your ass so far you'll taste burnt shit in your throat."

"As you wish. Manolo, let's see if Mr. Spy truly likes the brand."

"Wilhelm, may I have a word with you?" a voice said from farther out in the darkness.

"Michel, this is none of your business . . . yet. You can have the scum when I am done getting information out of him," said the man in black.

The voice moved closer. "I do not think you understand, Wilhelm. I cannot afford for an infection to—" The flash of two muzzle blasts from the darkness dropped Wilhelm and the thug.

"Gil, my son, it is a pleasure to finally meet you. You have your mother's eyes."

Gil felt a prick at his neck and his eyelids began to get heavy. As much as he fought the urge to go to sleep, it was no use. Darkness came, sound faded away, strong hands propped Gil up, and the handcuffs were unlocked. The last thing Gil heard was a cart being rolled up to his body and a wheel squeaking, complaining of the impending load it was about to bear. Then darkness overcame Gil; complete and utter darkness.

NINE

DATE WITH THE DEVIL

May 12, 2009 — Observatory Circle, Washington, D.C.

"**I** REALLY MUST TELL THE COOK to make smaller portions, but with so little time left . . . why should I care?" asked Tom Howell Sr.

"How do you live with yourself?" Tom eyed his father with disgust.

"Well, no mincing words today, are we? It isn't all gruesome. We've stopped terrorists from blowing up innocent people; toppled evil regimes hell-bent on repeating the reign of the Third Reich; even developed amazing medical technologies that have benefited mankind," said Tom Sr.

Tom Jr. stared alternatively at his silverware, napkin, and plate. A seemingly unpalatable filet mignon, fresh green beans with slivered almonds, and new potatoes in quarters with a light glaze stared back at the scion of Control.

"Yes, I not only ordered the assassination of evil men, I ordered the lobotomy of my own brother. Is that what you're thinking?" accused Tom Sr.

Tom Jr. nodded, his face solemn and determined, and then he returned to staring contemptuously at his father. He was determined to make it through this lunch without killing him. Tom could do it with his bare hands, but today he had brought a 9mm SIG Sauer pistol. Barnes, the butler, did not greet him at the door or do the customary search and removal of his pistol. This had puzzled Tom and somehow made him feel less empowered to do the deed. His father knew he would come armed and yet warmly welcomed his own assassin to his hearth.

Tom Jr. had not been able to sleep after the last meeting; instead he fitfully turned or stared at the ceiling as he searched his soul to determine what kind of man he himself had become. *Could I order the lobotomy of my brother? Is that actually an option, let alone an alternative to assassinating—no, murdering your own sibling?* He had tried to back his thinking up and consider why Uncle Jack had taken the job knowing the ultimate price he could pay for the opportunity. *"Death by police,"* they call it. *Did Uncle Jack grow too weary to continue on, expecting a quick bullet to the back of the head?*

"How could you order the lobotomy of your own brother?" Tom Jr. now demanded as he felt for his pistol in the shoulder harness.

"Your Uncle Jack was a gifted engineer and a brilliant man. He was also an alcoholic who . . ."

Tom slammed his shooting hand on the table and violent spit out the words, "You knew he was a loose-tongued alcoholic, yet you dangled the choicest of jobs in front of him, with the sole condition of sobriety for the rest of his life." His words burst from his mouth so harshly that his spittle landed on his father's jacket.

A guilty and cowed Tom Sr. quietly uttered, "I needed someone I could trust, someone who could design Control and keep the design a secret."

"Pathetic! Excuses! There were probably a hundred men capable of the job, and you obviously would have had no compunction killing someone who wasn't your brother." Tom Jr. found it difficult to look at his father. He was not sure if it was because of his outburst or his disdain for the wizened old heap. Tom could imagine his father's weakened state was caused by the long, slow draining of his soul rather than time and neglect.

Tom Sr. weakly continued on without taking up his son's points. "There are no complete plans. Only incomplete sets, kept in separate locations with different protocols for retrieval. Jack had the only complete drawings in his head."

Tom looked coolly back at his father. "So because your brother decided to end his life by taking that one drink he swore to give up, you fucked him by giving him a lobotomy. Nice." He waved his hand dismissively and casually brushed it against the pistol hidden under his jacket.

The old lion gathered himself and tried to strengthen his argument. "The *one* condition of his involvement was that he would never drink again. Not even mouthwash."

"Didn't you hear me, old man? Your brother committed suicide when he drank that celebratory Scotch!"

"The penalty for drinking even one shot of alcohol, intentionally or by accident, was death." Tom Sr. paused to wipe his forehead.

"But you didn't kill him, did you? You made him suffer . . . to pay for that one drink."

"I couldn't bring myself to kill my brother. In a way, Jack suffered for my weakness. He even asked me to kill him once when I saw him after the lobotomy. I couldn't do it. I've suffered for that lack of will, and so did Jack. Thankfully, he died two years later. He saved his daily medication and overdosed."

Tom Jr. sat silently for a long time, gathering his thoughts and making up his mind. His outburst was long overdue, and the good feeling of chastising his aged father seemed too little, too late. Self-righteous indignation would have value only if he walked away from Control at once. He now believed his father would let him walk away. No lobotomy, no assassin's bullet in the middle of the night, no accident on a dark highway. He could walk away and be rid of the burden, leaving it here on the table. The pistol. If he placed the gun on the table and walked away, he would not have to speak another word to his father.

Yet, he had Control in the palm of his hand. He could use it for any purpose he saw fit. He could do it the right way. Or would he make the same choices as those before him?

His father gave him all the time he needed to process his thoughts.

At last, Tom Jr.'s shoulders fell in sign of resignation. A decision had been made and a path determined. "Thank you, I understand." Tom Jr. looked up and scowled slightly at the man he saw in a new light. He straightened his napkin and adjusted his silverware so as to look away from—what? He saw a creature craven enough to torture his own brother, not out of anger or rage, but for fear of exposure. "I don't agree with the method or result, but I understand now," he said quietly. He finally understood what kind of man had raised him. Without knowing why, he had fought for so long to distance himself from this man. It was something he could sense but not name until now—a man without mercy.

A pitiless, ruthless, driven man who would stop at nothing to maintain his power and control; remorseful, perhaps, but only because he still had a soul and could see down the road as he headed for eternal damnation.

Tom Sr. began to cough uncontrollably into his napkin. Tom Jr. started to rise from his chair, but Tom Sr. waived him off. The fit subsided in a moment. "I am not long for this world. Tom . . . I've stopped the treatment of my lung cancer." Tom Sr. paused to take a sip of his water and then took a longer sip of his 1931 Quinta do Noval Nacional port.

Tom Jr. now realized why he entered his father's home without Barnes requesting the usual surrendering of his pistol. The old man wanted to die, but he did not have the guts to take his own life, just like his Uncle Jack. Yet Jack found the will after the lobotomy.

Tom relaxed. With knowledge came power. Suddenly, the smell of the fine meal and the taste of a rare vintage port seemed palatable.

TEN

TO CATCH A FALLING STAR

July 14, 2009 — The Caribbean Sea

DEVON MILLER GRABBED the collar of the floating body that had just gone under the water. He kicked his legs hard to counteract the drag of the deadweight of the special operative he hoped he was saving. Miller's wetsuit and the buoyancy of his gear was not enough to keep him afloat, but it helped some. He could now tell it was a woman by the feel of her body and the length of her raven hair. From thirty yards out, Miller had seen her head go under the water. There was two, maybe three minutes to get her back up and breathing again. No telling how many times she had gone under and pulled herself back up. Maybe it was the sound of the approaching boat, the recognition that she was about to be saved, that allowed her to let go . . . knowing that someone was near to catch her fall.

Hargreave circled the Bueno Pesquero as Miller pulled the agent to surface and checked her breathing. Betty, roused by the arm around her neck and shoulder, began to fight off what her reflexes said was an attacker. Miller had his answer. "Relax. It's OK. We're here to pick you up. Shhhh. It's OK. You're going to be fine. The boat will be here in a moment. Just relax."

Betty began to believe she was going to be OK and stopped fighting. She could hear the motor of the Pesquero as it came around.

Miller grabbed the dragline and pulled them both closer to the boat. Hargreave reversed the propeller to stop the trawler before he reached over the rail and helped Betty up the ladder. She sprawled akimbo on the deck of the boat, and before she could say a word, Miller began checking her wound while Hargreave gunned the motor to head back to Colombia.

Miller was a former Navy SEAL medic who had been to hell and back during training; he knew what it took to survive in these waters.

He also knew that this woman should be dead. Between the gunshot wound to her calf, the loss of blood, and the ten-foot waves throwing her about, she should have given up long ago. Something had given her strength beyond normal comprehension. A strength he could respect and understand.

"Hold up, Hargreave!" Miller was not going to leave a possible second agent in the water. "There are supposed to be two of you. Where's your partner?" he asked. No time to wait and see if the Venezuelan Navy noticed their foray into territorial waters.

Miller tried to cut through the spy suit to inspect Betty's wound and gave up. Instead, he pushed the fabric up to her knee to reveal the extent of the damage.

Betty looked down at her bleeding leg and muttered, "He didn't make it out."

Miller looked wounded, as if it was his fault.

"He was alive when I left in the glider," insisted Betty. "I don't know where he is now. He'll have to make it out on foot or by car. He was hit, but in OK shape . . . he's a medic, so . . ."

Miller signaled to Hargreave: no one else to pull from the water, time to head back and warm up. He wrapped Betty in a black thermal Mylar blanket before sending an encrypted message back to Control via secure satellite phone that simply read "1." Miller silently relished his success as Betty settled herself into one of the worn cushioned seats of the cabin. Part of Betty felt sorrow for the loss of Gil, while another part of her silently cheered him on, knowing that if anyone could get out alive, it would be Gil.

The captain's quarters had been cleared for her privacy. Miller started an IV drip for Betty after rewrapping her wound, checking her vital signs, and asking if she needed anything. Betty shook her head no as she swallowed the offered ibuprofen and prepared to get some rest. As he left to check on Hargreave, he was certain he could hear the sound of crying—sobs, really.

Betty lay still in the bunk, reliving the past few days. Her feelings for Gil and her operational failures preyed heavily on her mind. Gil had compensated for her lack of field experience, but that moment of passion was probably their undoing. Burdened by the knowledge of her responsibility, Betty finally drifted off, but she slept poorly.

ELEVEN

MARGIN OF ERROR

THE GENTLE SWAY AND HUM of the *Bueno Pesquero* combined with the warmth of the wool blanket wrapped snugly around her should have given Betty a warm fuzzy feeling, but it did not. She pensively waited for her water taxi to dock so she could get her jet ride back to Washington, D.C., and the "reality" of her day job. Her mind raced with self-judgments and thoughts of a life half over. The smell of the greasy food Miller brought her a few hours into the cruise tripped one memory in particular.

†

Summer 2006 — Three years before the crack of dawn

Betty quickened her step as she turned left at the corner. The car had been following her for half a mile. It was a Chevy Impala made to look like an undercover car. The dead giveaway was the swivel light on the driver's side. The black paint job, black rims, no chrome, and souped-up suspension said I am serious business, even if a badge was not there to back it all up.

The car was driving extra slow to stay one hundred feet behind Betty. It inched up to match her pace until something blocked its forward progression. Then it would swerve around the obstacle and get back in place one hundred feet behind.

As Betty ducked into an alley, she could hear the motor roar to life. *Who is this asshole and what does he want?* Betty hid behind the dumpster on the left side of the alley before the stalker could turn the corner. The Impala inched into the alley, and the driver's side window rolled down to reveal a middle-age man with a receding hairline. It was tough to tell what color his hair had been before he dyed it to hide the gray, but auburn was a good guess. The cheap blue windbreaker was obviously an attempt to look like any generic enforcement officer. The cheap gold watch nearly sealed the deal.

Betty leapt from the cover of the dumpster and used her heightened adrenaline level to drag the man out of the window before he realized what was happening. In the time it took the oaf to start saying, "What the—" Betty had him on the ground with her knee on his throat and her fist poised to punctuate her fury. The Impala limped down the alley, slowly gaining speed until a pothole caused it to veer to the right and hang up on a full grease-trap dumpster. The hood crumpled slightly and took on an oily sheen from the grease that sloshed over the lip of the container.

"I'm going to ask you several questions. You have one second to start answering each question. If I don't like your answer, I will dump your body in that grease trap over there," warned Betty. "Where is your ID?" Betty leaned harder when her stalker reached into his jacket. "I didn't ask you to get it, I asked you where it is. Remember, the grease trap," Betty said as she jerked her head toward the Impala now covered in grease.

"In my shirt pocket," said the man, choking from the pressure of Betty's knee. Betty reached into the shirt pocket and pulled out a cheap plastic ID case. The card inside indicated he was a private investigator with a Virginia license to practice.

"Well, Paul Margin," said Betty as she glanced back and forth from the ID to the man under her kneecap, "you have some explaining to do. Do you carry a weapon?" Paul shook his head no. Betty patted him down anyway. There was no weapon. "Tell me, Paul—may I call you Paul?" The private dick nodded yes slowly, trying carefully not to damage his larynx under Betty's kneecap. "Well, Paul, I don't like being followed. Who are you working for and why are you following me?"

"A friend of mine was worried about you, said you lost your fiancé recently. I was supposed to just keep an eye on you . . . follow you around . . . make sure no one made a move on you," he squeaked.

Betty was about to pursue who his friend was when she noticed out of the corner of her eye a small girl, about seven years old, holding on to the hand of her mother. They were wearing matching outfits and had the same sandy yellow hair. Both the girl and the woman stood in awe with their mouths wide open. Betty felt the rush of adrenaline wane. Looking down at Paul, she gave a low growl and said, "Leave me alone! If I ever see you following me, I will put you in the nearest dumpster and lock the lid!"

Betty released the private eye as if she were throwing his shirt to the ground. Her glare kept Paul supine as she backed away; he lay there, his hands showing palms up. Betty walked past her audience and told the little girl, "Never take grief from any man."

Betty rounded the corner and headed east to get back on track. A sudden moment of panic hit her. *I must be getting paranoid! Now I think that cab is following me. I swear he is the same cabbie that has picked me up the last couple of times.* Just as quickly, she let the thought pass as a fare jumped in the back of the Scat Cab and took off.

She had an appointment with Dr. Callahan to keep, just her annual exam. She wanted to stop taking the Depo-Provera. José was gone and she was not planning to be sexually active. The risk of osteoporosis convinced Betty to only take the contraceptive when she was in a relationship.

✝

"You can call me Doc." Miller carefully removed the bandage from Betty's leg to check her wound. "I could remove the bullet, but it can wait until you're in a hospital with a blood transfusion."

The gentle swaying of the boat and "Doc" Miller rechecking her wounds tickled her memory about Dr. Callahan. Something she could not remember at the moment. Was it time for her annual exam? Did she need to start having mammograms? She felt like she was forgetting something. *It doesn't matter. Nothing matters. I failed Gil. I let my partner stay behind. Even if he was always giving me shit, I want him here, now . . . with me.*

"Do you want to talk?" Miller inquired.

Betty shook her head no and looked away. She had only spoken a couple of words to her rescuer and had not even thanked him. She looked back and blurted, "Wait. Thank you." She turned away again and tried to get comfortable in the bunk, despite the latest dose of medication not quite keeping up with her pain.

Miller looked at her for a minute or two before heading back to check on Hargreave again. As he left the cabin he could hear her take a deep breath and a long exhale, then a muttered "Fuck" before she began crying herself to sleep.

"Man, she's dealing with some shit," Miller murmured loud enough to be heard.

"You'll be dealing with some shit if we don't get out of Venezuelan waters before that patrol boat catches up to us." Captain Hargreave handed Miller his binoculars.

Miller took a long look at the Venezuelan Coast Guard boat as it tried to ply a line to intercept them. "Point-class cutter. Maybe the Pelicano or the Petrel. Could be the Alcatraz. Best they could do when they were U.S. Coast Guard boats was maybe sixteen or seventeen knots, but those tubs are ancient now." Miller paused to ponder just how ancient their pursuer's craft would be. "Probably fifty years old." he continued, then turned and looked at the captain and asked derisively, "What can this tin can do?"

Hargreave grinned in the direction of the pursuers. "This is probably her last run." He looked directly at his antagonist and playfully offered, "What do you say we see what the old girl has left in her?" He pushed the double-throttle levers to full forward, and the rhythmic humming of the past day became a deafening roar as the trawler lurched and began chewing up the ocean surface. "We only have a few miles to go before we enter Colombian water. No problem."

Miller reflected that this was the first time since he met the captain that the man actually had a smile on his face. "You would make a wonderful privateer, even if you're a pain in the ass most of the time."

Twelve

Round About

July 29, 2009 — Somewhere in Europe

HOWELL'S WORDS SPOKEN in Gil's apartment so many years before taunted him as he lay in his cell.

"What do you mean I have your mother's eyes?" Gil had asked the intruder in his kitchen.

"I was shocked the first time I saw you." Tom Howell Jr. squinted slightly as he stared at Gil. "Your eyes have the same green and hazel aura as my mother's—very distinct in coloration and texture. I got my father's eyes, though not exactly," he said, shrugging.

The dingy room turned cell was wearing on Gil. The only window was painted, barred, and nailed shut. The only furniture consisted of an army cot and an aluminum chair designed to look like an antique wooden office chair. Michel would come to his room and sit in that chair for hours trying to get to know Gil. It was not an interrogation. It was an absent father getting to know his son after being in the shadows, unknown and hidden. Michel would elicit stories from Gil by offering information about his birth mother and family. The walls were nearly soundproof. The combination of metal lathe and thick plaster muffled any sounds from the next room.

Michel had cautioned him to rest and get well. The doctor had come into his room several times a day at first, checking Gil's wounds, writing down his temperature, administering antibiotics, and changing his dressings. The level of care was equal to what he would have received at a military base. However, the vigilance and prophylactic nature of the antibiotics bothered Gil. Michel was not questioning him about the mission or operational details; he just wanted to talk about Gil's childhood. Gil would not cooperate until Michel produced grainy photographs of Gil from his youth: photographs he had never seen before, taken from a distance using a telephoto lens, proving Michel had spied on him since early childhood.

"Your mother was an angel I could not resist," said Michel. "I was the devil, seducing her while my brother was away. Yuri was always on some secret mission for the Belarus KGB while I stayed home in the capital, Minsk, as part of the Presidential Guard. I was to look after Elena while my brother was away. It was a crazy time. Minsk was growing rapidly, rebuilding after the destruction of World War Two. Nearly all of our city was destroyed and eighty percent of the population was killed. We—Yuri and I . . . how do you say it? We were enforcers; we took care of the enemies of the state." Michel paused long enough for Gil to absorb what he was hearing.

"What does this have to do with me?" asked Gil.

"While Yuri was away, I seduced your mother and you were conceived. Yuri had no reason to suspect, but Elena and I knew the truth. When it was time for you to be born, again Yuri was away, so naturally I was there for Elena—she did not survive childbirth," said Michel as he cast his eyes downward.

"Yuri claimed Dr. Salizar killed his wife, my . . . mother. Which story is true?" queried Gil.

Michel cast his gaze at his folded hands. "I told you that I am a devil. I will not deny my role in this."

"What do you mean, your role in this?" asked Gil.

"Elena was dying. She was hemorrhaging blood internally. Her uterus had ruptured along the scar from her previous C-section. Dr. Salizar had recommended a C-section for your birth. Elena wanted to do a VBAC, or vaginal delivery. I allowed her to go through with it despite the warning signs," said Michel.

"What were the warning signs?" asked Gil.

"Elena had complained on the way to the hospital that something felt like it had ripped. She couldn't breathe quite right. There was not any sign of bleeding until labor was far along. A transfusion started to bring her blood pressure back up . . . but it was too late. Dr. Salizar did an emergency C-section to save you. Elena died on the table while Salizar performed a hysterectomy." Michel sighed heavily.

"So my mother died. But why was I given up for adoption?" asked Gil.

"Your mother had one other child, your half brother Michel, named after me. He is five years older than you. Times were different then in Belarus. Minsk was a crazy place with so much going on. There was not anyone to take care of a baby for Yuri. I knew he would have to give up his work as a KGB officer to look after you. Dr. Salizar made a suggestion—no, an offer. Another couple, your parents, lost a child that same day in childbirth. Dr. Salizar offered to have you adopted by this American couple. He was a marine at the embassy. His wife unconscious . . . you were substituted. Only Dr. Salizar, I, and your adopted father, Edward, knew of the switch. Yuri thought his son—my son—died in childbirth with Elena. We buried the Richardson infant three days later with your mother," said Michel.

Gil, sitting on the edge of his military-issue bed, soaked up every word of Michel's story. He had a half brother. His parents never told him of the adoption. He looked enough like his mother that no one questioned his parentage, least of all Gil.

"There is more to the story, but it will have to wait. I am quite tired. My kidneys are failing, Gil. I am not long for this world. I will rest and be back to visit later." Michel said as he got up to go.

"Why are you holding me? You aren't interrogating me." Gil looked quizzically at his biological father. "I don't understand."

"Tomorrow, you will understand. I promise," said Michel with a slight smile beneath tired eyes. The guards opened the door when Michel called out to them. One had pepper spray while the other had a stun gun at the ready. They were not showing deadly force, but there was no question that Gil would not be leaving this room.

The single forty-watt lightbulb in the ceiling fixture lay bare and dangling above his bed. He did not have control over the light; it stayed on during what Gil thought of as day and was turned off at what he presumed was bedtime, probably around nine p.m. It would come back on around six a.m. With his light off, he could tell the building still had power because of the hall light that would come through the crack at the bottom of his door. Gil could press his face down to see a limited view of the outside world. With his ear to the crack, he could hear the guards' banter, but not knowing Belarusian left him with meager scraps of intelligence.

Gil's daily routine would begin with the sudden lighting of his bare lightbulb. A power drop caused by the daily surge in electrical use from nearby heavy equipment would correspond with the changing of his guard, presumably at seven a.m. He could smell coal burning, hear the din of metal on metal, and feel the vibrations of what he assumed was massive machinery. He imagined factories revving up for the day's work. If only he had such purpose to his day.

A knock at the door, just one rap, was the only courtesy given to Gil when a visitor was about to enter. It gave him all of a second to gather himself for the doctor or Michel. The two guards were always present at these moments. Always the same two heavyset thugs wearing black turtlenecks and sometimes black leather jackets, indicating by the smell of tobacco that they had just returned from taking a break.

"Michel, what a surprise," said Gil. "I didn't expect to see you so early this morning. Where's the good doctor?"

Gil's bandages were off. He was still healing, but no infection had set in, thanks to the antibiotics. Michel offered him a glass of water and his daily antibiotic dosage. As Gil swallowed the pill and drank the water, a guard handed Michel a food tray.

"Eggs and toast. Your cook is not very creative, Michel," Gil judged as he took the tray from Michel after placing his drink on it. Gil usually placed the tray on the aluminum chair while he ate, but now he kept it on his lap so Michel could sit down.

"No, please, use the chair, Gil. I will sit on the edge of the bed with you, if you do not mind," said Michel.

"OK." Gil dragged the chair to the foot of the bed.

"I have already eaten, you see; the good doctor allows me only liquid diet. I know not what is in those, eh, damn things, but they are not too bad," Michel said with a slight laugh.

"Makes my eggs and toast seem a little more appetizing," remarked Gil. "So, yesterday you were telling me about Elena, my . . . mother. You said there was more."

"I do not want to upset your breakfast. Eat first and then I will tell you," said Michel.

"I cannot imagine what you could tell me to put me off my breakfast. I was a Special Forces operator," said Gil.

"Yes, Gil, I know. My pride burst when you made the cut," said Michel. "I kept an eye on you throughout your career. My boss would occasionally give me hell about using assets to track you, but he believed I would eventually make you a double agent." Michel pulled a small stack of three-by-five pictures from his breast pocket. He shuffled the photos for a moment and produced a shot of Gil at one of his military graduations. A similar photo had been on his parent's mantle, but from a different angle.

"I don't know what to say," said Gil, pausing midbite while egg yolk dripped off his raised toast onto the plate.

"Gil, Elena died giving birth to you. Dr. Salizar was not just an ordinary doctor. He was a pioneer in transplant operations. Yuri was one of his early attempts at full eye-transplant surgery," said Michel.

"What does this have to do with Elena?" asked Gil.

"I'm getting to that." Michel feigned a hurt look. "Please allow an old man to tell his stories."

Gil moved the tray and offered the chair to Michel, thinking it would be more comfortable for the old man. "Please sit down," said Gil.

Michel moved to the chair. Gil took his place on the bed, leaning against the wall with his back propped up by his pillow. He now felt like Michel was telling him a bedtime story.

"Yuri was KGB. Before you were born, before your half brother Michel was born, Yuri lost his eye in a scuffle with a traitor to the state. The man fought like a devil to escape as Yuri cornered him in a bar in East Berlin. The traitor gouged Yuri's eye as Yuri choked him from behind. The eye popped out of its socket and was dangling by the optic nerve. Yuri hung on tight and broke the traitor's neck. A local doctor put the eye back in, but the eye couldn't be saved. He was referred to Dr. Salizar, who offered to help, in exchange for."—Michel looked like he was searching for the right words—"our professional services."

"Services?"

"Yes, you know . . . espionage, protection, enforcement . . . eh, uhm, the usual duties of a KGB officer, but in a private capacity."

"Go on."

"He had just perfected the transplant surgery and special drugs to help with anti-rejection and nerve regeneration. A suitable donor was found—a criminal who was about to be executed. The surgery was mostly a success. Yuri could see with the new eye after several months of recovery. It was not perfect vision, but it was better than no vision. Yuri was to take the anti-rejection medicine the rest of his life . . . but a mission for Dr. Salizar to repay the debt went poorly. Yuri couldn't take his medicine while in captivity and lost the eye. A rather awful infection set in, which led to the scar on Yuri's face," said Michel as he unconsciously rubbed his eyes.

"OK, but what does that have to do with my mother?" asked Gil.

"Dr. Salizar was ready to perform another eye surgery. He had new drugs ready and a candidate for the surgery, his sister-in-law. We already knew our Elena was dying; Yuri and I both owed a debt to Dr. Salizar. I approved the harvesting of Elena's eyes and other body parts. I signed her death sentence. Dr. Salizar said she had a slight chance of living but offered to wipe the slate clean. I let her go." Michel said this as he buried his face in his hands.

"Who . . . who was Dr. Salizar's sister-in-law?" asked Gil.

"Her name was Julia, Julia Howell," recounted Michel.

Gil was stunned. Tom Howell's mother? That would explain why Tom had said Gil's eyes reminded him of his mother's. "You said you owed a debt to Dr. Salizar, a debt beyond Yuri's eye surgery, you mentioned a debt you both owed," prodded Gil.

"My kidneys were failing. I was starting dialysis when Dr. Salizar offered to transplant one of Yuri's kidneys to me. It was a perfect match; we are . . . were twins," said Michel.

"Is that why you have me here? Why you've made sure I didn't die at the hands of Montoya's thugs? Why the extreme care in my healing to make sure I don't have any infections?" asked Gil.

"Gil, I want you to do this for me because you want to . . . but I can take your kidney anyway if you do not agree. I am a patient man, but I am dying. I will be dead in a few weeks or months without a new kidney. Yuri's other kidney was to be mine, until your partner Betty caused Yuri's death. Your probing into Dr. Salizar's life required Yuri to kill Salizar. Yuri couldn't allow Salizar to live, and I couldn't allow Yuri to die.

"Dr. Salizar's son, Eric, has taken over the hospital network. He will be performing our surgery. You are very healthy and do not need two kidneys to live. I need only one kidney to live," said Michel as he got up to go. "I am too tired to talk. I will come tomorrow. Think about what I have told you and what you need to know to help me." Michel picked up Gil's empty breakfast tray.

"Go to hell!" said Gil.

"I am. It is only a question of when," said Michel as the guards let him out.

THIRTEEN

DOING THAT THING SHE DOES

May 28, 2009 — Somewhere in Washington, D.C.

T HE TRAY SEEMED HEAVY to Jil, but the breakfast was
perfect: an omelet with fresh sautéed vegetables, toast with
blackberry jam, two strips of bacon; hot Brazilian coffee in
a ceramic mug, extra large, with hazelnut flavoring, and a dollop of
whipped cream. A single yellow tiger lily in a tall thin vase adorned
the tray next to the three daily newspapers: the Wall Street Journal, the
Washington Post, and the New York Times.

Jil carefully made her way to the bedroom, balancing the food
and the coffee with precision. The carpet felt good on her bare feet. Her
floral print silk robe was open, the ties dangling down and her cleavage
exposed. Evident to a casual observer, the air conditioning was causing
her nipples to press against her garments, especially the silk teddy in a
light shade of peach with lace around the bodice.

The casual observer today was Dr. Eric Salizar. The younger Dr.
Salizar laid in Jil's king-size bed watching CNN and keeping an eye on
Fox News in the picture-within-a-picture. He wanted to make sure the
news did not have any superfluous information about his now deceased
father. All that he heard was the preapproved headline: a brilliant
transplant surgeon and researcher, Dr. Gualtiero Salizar, died of sudden
cardiac arrest while traveling by train in Panama. The news drones did not
mention the commotion of the attack, the hysterical passengers fleeing
the scene, or anything referring to Yuri Vasilyev's fall and broken neck.

Eric was just a young boy when his father placed him on a step
stool so he could assist with Yuri's eye surgery. As a thirteen-year-old, he
performed his first solo transplant surgery on a dog to repair the damage

caused in a fight. His father was an impatient man. Eric was to be in medical school by eighteen and in the hospital under the good doctor's tutelage before he reached his twenty-third birthday. Greatness required many accomplishments at a young age, and he did not disappoint his father. There were other doctors learning from the great man, but only Eric learned the family secrets. By his sixteenth birthday, he personally mixed the anti-rejection and nerve-growth drugs from the raw rain forest ingredients, extracting the essential oils and blending them per his father's instructions. An elite list of clients depended on Dr. Salizar's techniques and his unique drugs for guaranteed results. Some of the medicines worked equally well for tissue regeneration or wrinkle removal—a rather nice side affect the ultra-wealthy appreciated and could afford.

Crucial to the success of the surgeries was the matching of the genetic material used to reduce the rejection and enhance the regrowth of connective tissue. Dr. Salizar subjected elite clients to genetic screening for matching potential donors who either gave freely or surrendered their treasure after an untimely death. Generous remuneration to the donor or their families kept things quiet. Poor relations of elite clients became willing or not-so-willing donors. The members of the World Order Cabal could afford to pay any price for what they needed.

"Oh, Jil, thank you." Eric was pleasantly distracted from the newscast. "That smells delicious."

She placed the tray on the side table next to Eric with a slight smile. As she bent over, her cleavage was in his face. "Hmmm . . . you look delicious," Eric said as he ogled her.

She sat down on the bed near his waist. He picked up the napkin and silverware. "Jil, you seem distant—maybe you're tired and need to come back to bed?"

Jil smiled a small, tired smile. She placed her right hand on Eric's bare chest. A small tuft of black hair covered his finely sculpted muscles. One thing that Eric took care of was his body. She bent over at the waist and gently kissed Eric's nipples, flicking her tongue while she slid her hand down under the waistband of his silk boxers. Eric leaned back into the supportive pillows piled high at the head of the bed. He tossed the remote with his left hand and placed the silverware and napkin back on the tray with his right. Grabbing Jil's head with both hands, he caressed her temples as she kissed lower and lower down his well-defined abdominal muscles accentuated by his deep tan and dark olive skin. *He definitely has his father's skin color,* thought Jil as she pulled down the boxers while Eric lifted his body up. His interest in the food and TV waned markedly.

Jil looked up at Eric and said, "You will take care of it, then? You will do the surgery for my mother?"

Eric seemed bored by this comment, yet at the same time he was anxious for Jil to continue what she was doing. Better to go along than spoil the fun. "Of course, we must find the right donor, ahhh . . . first . . . hmmmm . . . yes . . . we must find the right . . . ahhh . . ."

Jil completed her task at hand; it only took a few moments between Eric's desire and Jil's skill. She covered Eric with the sheet and left to get dressed for her day. She had a meeting with Senator Bolden in two hours and she needed to confirm her mother's flight to Europe for the operation.

She dialed her cellphone from the privacy of the kitchen. "Daddy? It's all taken care of."

Larry Harper blurted, "But what about the—"

"No, everything is taken care of, you won't have to worry or do anything except get Mother ready. Ruth will meet us and stay during her recovery."

"I don't know how you convinced him, but thank you, Jil. Your mother's breathing has become quite difficult, and the oxygen doesn't seem to work like it use to. She'll be ready," said Larry.

"I know, Daddy. Her lungs are shot. It's time. The surgery will be hell, but the new drugs are supposed to work wonders for her recovery. We're doing the right thing."

Larry was not to know all the details—especially about his daughter Ruth donating her lobes—until after the operation was complete. Jil's smoking afforded her the excuse of being a bad candidate. Ruth was to be the only and best option. During the recovery, Jil planned on emphasizing that Ruth's healthy lungs and genetic match to her mother were a godsend.

"I am so proud of you," Larry cleared his throat, "You are being so strong."

"We all need to be strong, Daddy." Jil flicked her cigarette at the closest ashtray. *Especially Ruth!*

"You're right, of course. Have you spoken to Ruth? Does she know the sacrifice you're making?"

"I don't want her to know just yet. Let me tell her, OK?"

"Of course, I wouldn't dream of getting between the two of you!"

"Good. I'll call you when the date is set and your tickets are ready. Everything will be taken care of. You and mother have nothing to worry about." She hung up without saying goodbye before Larry could ask any more questions.

I'm the one in charge for a change. Jil pulled a long drag from her cigarette and blew a smoke ring at the ceiling. *God, it feels good to have real power for once.*

FOURTEEN

ROGUE MAIL

July 29, 2009 — Old Town Alexandria

O N THE TOP SHELF of the hall closet was the last box from the Georgetown loft apartment left to unpack. Betty and Tom had spent many beautiful moments together in the cavernous space they had renovated. Betty especially cherished the evenings spent on the couch overlooking the Potomac and the cityscape. This particular box had haunted her for years, tucked away high enough that she would not notice it, yet ever present when she wanted to think about the memories. This treasure trove contained the letters, cards, and notes to and from the couple as they courted one another. Some lover's poems. Thank-you cards for a special kindness. An assortment of birthday, anniversary, and holiday cards, even a few shopping and honey-do lists mixed in. Betty had saved them all, whereas Tom abandoned everything when he did not come back to her after his tour in Iraq.

Perhaps it was the pain of the rejection or the sorrow she cradled from her abandoned hopes and plans. When she was with José, the cards stayed in the box unless José angered her or did not give her the level of attention she needed. These moments gave her the excuse to revisit her past and the feeling of love she felt from being with Tom—a love that seemed unconditional, complete, and everlasting. Until he took it all away. She pretended that he was only away temporarily and would be back to collect the letters, and her heart. That this time apart was just a temporary inconvenience tempering the fire, containing the heat of their passion, and preserving the possibilities that only time would reveal.

When she felt unloved, all the cards dumped onto her bedspread gave her a pool of feelings and emotions to bathe her soul; a cleansing of her raw inner self that felt the denial of love from her parents, siblings, and extended family. The depth of the hurt in her soul scared her during the infrequent visits she made to her psyche: the distorted belief that she was unlovable, the raw pain of not fitting in, and the excruciating temptation to place all the world's problems on her shoulders. If she could just be a better person, get better grades, a better job, or be prettier, all the doors in the world would open, including the one to a loved one's heart. Only Surry seemed to understand, but her dog's unconditional love only slightly filled the void that lingered deep within her. The child she planned to abort made her even more vulnerable to these thoughts. Her one chance at unconditional love from a child—her child—was scheduled for termination.

†

Three years earlier — Old Town Alexandria

On a particularly dreary Saturday, with low clouds and oppressive humidity lingering like a layer of clothes you cannot take off, Betty took the step stool from the kitchen to the closet and pulled down her box of memories, intent on dwelling on the one time in her life she believed, even if only for a short while, that she was truly lovable. The brown cardboard box—marked with permanent pen by some stock clerk at a department store with the cryptic message "Defective, hold for review"— felt heavier than usual and nearly slipped from her grasp. During the move, she had grabbed the closest box to dump the pile of memories into from the drawer of her dresser, with the plan of getting a secretary's desk or a rolltop to sort and store the paperwork into individual cubbies. Hot spots of memories she could focus on, dipping her toe as needed instead of drowning in her past. The perfect desk had not materialized and the letters stayed in the plain yet poignant box.

José's discovery of the box and perusal of her private correspondence nearly caused the end of their relationship. He had been indignant that she would want to keep any memories of past relationships once they were engaged.

"Betty, look what I found," bellowed her lover.

"What are you doing?" Betty growled as she grabbed the box from José. "You have no right!"

"No right?"

"These are mine."

"Aren't we to be man and wife?"

"What?"

"Why do you keep these secrets from me? Why would you want to keep these, anyway?"

"I wouldn't expect you to understand." Betty closed the top of the box by intertwining the flaps.

"Am I not enough man for you? Isn't my love enough?"

"This isn't about you. It's about me." Betty put the box back into her closet.

"If you are seeing others, it is about me!" José became indignant.

"I'm not seeing others," Betty said tersely.

"Then why keep them if they are old lovers. It is like having them in bed with us." José swept his hand over the duvet and pillows piled high on Betty's bed.

"You're one to talk! Have I ever asked you about your old lovers?"

"That's different," countered José.

"How the hell is it different?"

"I don't keep mementos or trophies. I don't relive the memories."

"Oh, because I like to reread old letters, I'm somehow less committed to you. Is that what you mean?" Betty looked at her engagement ring and then at her fiancé. "Fuck you, José!"

Tenderly, realizing he had gone too far and despite his belief that he had done nothing wrong, José backpedaled his position and attempted to soothe her. "Sweetheart, darling, I am just a jealous man. I only want you to love me."

"Right now I don't know if I can love you." José's love seemed conditional to Betty. She lived in fear of him withholding his love when his temper flared, while she dared to believe its fullness when he caressed her in bed.

"This is nonsense." José waved his hand dismissively.

"Maybe for you—for me, this is real. These letters matter. If you love me, you'll forget I have them and leave me to my memories." Betty wanted to pout and show how much José was hurting her, but instead she just looked pissed.

"I love you." José said in a pleading voice.

A. J. Mahler

Betty scowled at her fiancé. "No, you don't." Betty took her engagement ring off her finger and flung it at his feet.

José knelt down on one knee, scooped up the ring, and asked, "I ask you again for your heart, your soul, your love. Be my partner and my wife." He held the ring out with his left hand and placed his right hand on his heart.

"Promise me you'll forget the letters."

"What letters? See, I have no recollection."

Betty took the ring and put it back on her finger. She believed for just a moment that she could be loved. Yet, her mind drifted to the letters. She fought the desire to take them to a room by herself to check the record, to tally the love others had professed and then abandon them for good. "Love me, José," she whispered softly into his ear.

José heard, "Make love to me, José," instead, and he did.

†

Betty put the cards and letters back into the box, pausing on a card. It was her mother's Thanksgiving invitation for Tom to join the family for dinner and the holiday weekend—separate bedrooms, of course.

FIFTEEN

THE DECISION

November 27, 2002 — Rochester, N.Y.

"BETTY IS READY. I think you need to bring her in." Bob Thursten slapped Tom's knee to emphasis his point.

Sitting next to Bob on the twin bed, Tom kept his voice low. "My father also thinks Betty is ready to join Control. I just don't know if it's the right decision."

"What's holding you back?"

"She doesn't know the truth about . . . about her parents. She doesn't have the military background." Tom shifted uncomfortably as he danced around his true feelings.

"Of course, she'll need training to be field ready, but she's been training for years without knowing it: camping, orienteering, and scrapping for attention with her brothers." Bob confidently gave his litany, his job well done, but before Tom could interject, Bob raised his hand and tilted his head to acknowledge an exception, her one serious weakness. "Maybe she doesn't have enough martial arts training yet, but you got her to take that rape defense class, and she's enjoying the jujitsu classes. It won't take her long."

"It's not the training so much . . ."

Again, Bob interrupted Tom, but this time his voice took on a mentor's tone. "You have fought your father for the last ten years. You'd be in charge by now if you had listened to him. Instead, you went off on your boyish adventure to become a military officer. I think you've become too regimented in your thinking."

"What do you mean?" Tom drew away defensively; his relationship with his father was a sore point.

"Some of the best agents come from nontraditional sources. We need agents who can insert into the social strata that an officer never could."

"I'm not following you."

"Betty can walk into any room and be the center of attention or be a wallflower. She has charisma that she can turn on and off at will."

"True."

"Between hanging with Jil and her legal training, she can now read a room in an instant." Bob smiled knowingly, like the Cheshire cat.

"Well, I guess I just don't know if she's cut out to be a field operative," Tom scratched the back of his hand nervously.

"What do you think a field op is? All hand-to-hand combat? It's about finding the weaknesses of the person in front of you so you can use them to your advantage. Sometimes that means strategic arms, and sometimes it means charming the pants off a target." Bob paused to look squarely at Tom. "Are you too emotionally involved with Betty?"

"No . . . no, it isn't that," Tom lied.

"Your sexual chemistry is obvious." Bob nudged Tom with his elbow. "Her mother would prefer you two didn't have sex, but I understand—human nature."

"But . . ."

"You know Betty will need to seduce targets, right?" Bob looked intently at Tom, trying to discern the depth of his weakness.

"Oh, well, I suppose I'm detached enough to accept that . . . I don't know. I guess I'm a little confused." Tom began rubbing his temples, fighting the urge to leave the room and end the conversation. *If my father were asking these questions, we would be in a fighting match by now.*

"Search your soul, Tom. Is this about you, Betty, or Control? Where is your allegiance?"

"I know you've been working with my father for a long time . . . I know you've risked your life as a double agent, but how much longer can you really pull this off? What happens next?" asked Tom.

"I promised your father that I would commit my life to Control. If I die tomorrow because of a mistake or just plain bad luck, either way, I prepared for that eventuality. I understand it's not if I die so much as how and by whose hand. Your father had the right to take my life fifteen years ago after I created my part of Control. I made that bargain. Your father found another use for my talents and for that"—Bob paused while he looked around his son's bedroom for a moment—"I am thankful. I would not have seen Betty grow up and become the successful lawyer she is if I hadn't been willing to become a double agent."

"I don't understand how you could have been willing to die so young—so full of potential."

"You should understand, I'm just a soldier, like you. If my commanding officer says attack that machine gun nest and, by the way, you have almost no chance of surviving, it's still my duty to attack that enemy position."

Tom looked distraught and confused. *Is it my duty to watch Betty die?*

"It isn't about fair. It's about duty. I'm not saying I'm prepared to die. I'm saying that I am prepared to take on any mission and give it my best shot. I expect to succeed, and so far I have." Bob smiled with pride.

There was a sound outside the door. Tom and Bob looked at each other and stopped talking. The door began to open slowly, and suddenly there was Betty, looking sheepish and surprised.

"Daddy?" said Betty.

"Well, Bets. What a surprise, we were just talking about you. Sit down right here next to your dear old dad."

"What's going on here Daddy? What are you and Tom up to?" Betty went on the offensive to cover up her true intent—having sex with Tom.

"We were just trying to figure out what you are doing with your life, just trying to see where you are going. What do you think?" deflected Bob.

"I think I'm going back to my room. I just came in because I heard voices and was wondering what was going on." Betty tried to look put out.

"OK, darling, head to bed. Tom and I were just wrapping up anyway."

Tom looked uncomfortable. Betty thought it was because she almost got them caught. Bob knew it was because Tom was in love with Betty.

Sixteen

Angling for Answers

July 31, 2009 — Somewhere in Europe

"YOU'RE GOING TO GIVE ME a kidney, whether you want to or not. If I have to sedate you and remove it without your consent, my surgeon is willing to do the job." Michel had entered the makeshift cell as before, bearing food and charm. This time the charm slipped away quickly as the raw truth of the situation abraded any remaining civility.

Gil looked pissed, but Michel was too busy pontificating to notice or care.

"I've certainly paid the price for him to do the work!" Michel said haughtily. "I won't try to convince you that you should do it for love. I have no illusions about our relationship." He slowly shook his head no and pushed out his lower lip to hold in a pose before continuing his sermon. "I am merely the genetic father. Edward is your real father. He has loved you and raised you as his own. I am just the surrogate who donated the sperm in a moment of weakness." Michel concluded with his hand raised with one finger pointing to the sky. "My brother and sister-in-law deserved better. I am what they got."

Gil looked away, unwilling to acknowledge the legitimacy of Michel's claims.

Michel controlled the future of Gil's life. If Gil did not cooperate with Michel, then Michel would just take both of Gil's kidneys and be finished with his bastard child. If Gil worked with Michel, he could keep a kidney and continue his life as it was, but there were no guarantees that Michel would not be back later for more body parts. Michel was not looking for family holidays together or any kind of bonding. Just one kidney and Gil could go about with his life. Assuming Dr. Salizar's research into organ regeneration from stem cells was viable before Michel needed the other one.

"How do I know you aren't just going to take both kidneys anyway?" wondered Gil.

"You do not . . . but understand . . . I want you to be in the best frame of mind going into surgery. It is best that we go into this with a positive mindset. We will both heal better if we understand and agree with what is happening," said Michel.

"What if I kill myself—what would you do then?" asked Gil.

"Harvest both kidneys and start surgery immediately. The surgeon and operating room are ready. We will part you out before your body gets cold. To preserve the kidneys, I have life-support equipment to keep your blood circulating," Michel explained coolly.

"I'm sure I could find a way to damage my kidneys . . . to . . . to make them unusable to you," said Gil.

"Well, I suppose if you truly prefer dying to cooperating and living . . . I might as well call the doctor now. He wants to wait a little longer to make sure we are both ready, but he will do as I ask."

"So Christ-like: dying I destroy you, living I restore your life. Will you drink my blood too?"

Michel considered his fingertips and the cleanliness of his nails. "I should just take both kidneys and dump your body," he replied casually, as if he were describing a used facial tissue.

"What's the recovery time? When will you release me?" asked Gil.

"Small incisions are made in the abdomen to insert laparoscopic instruments." Michel made a hole with his left hand and stuck his right index finger through the gap. "The laparoscope contains a miniature camera that guides the surgical team. A three-to-four-inch incision allows the removal of the kidney. You will be closed with self-absorbing stitches and able to walk around immediately after, but you should not lift more than twenty pounds for four weeks. We will release you twenty-four hours after the surgery. Where would you like to be taken?" asked Michel.

"Where would I like to be taken?" asked Gil incredulously. "You're kidding, right?"

"No, I am quite serious. You deserve to convalesce somewhere nice that suits you, no?" Michel held his hands out as if he were holding a present. "The Riviera, Black Sea, Tuscany . . . whatever you desire, as long as travel is safe for you. The islands off your America will have to wait a few days—at least, until we can arrange your travel papers," clarified Michel.

"Maybe I don't need to kill myself." Gil looked sharply at his father. "What if I just kill you?"

"Gil, you will be dead within five minutes of my body hitting the floor. The guards outside have been through the same training as your Special Forces. They are watching you with a live feed. They could probably save me before you could do permanent damage, but they have been instructed to kill you in that scenario or if you try to take me prisoner to effect an escape—avoiding the gut, of course. I am expendable—no, expiring? Without your kidney I will be dead soon anyway," stated Michel.

Gil sighed. He was in a corner.

"Please, give me a moment. I need to use your toilet." Michel stood up and walked to the three-by-five space across from the bed, a converted closet. "One of the symptoms of my disease is frequent urination."

Gil's food and necessities arrived three times a day. Clean clothes exchanged for dirty. It was all very clinical and thorough. At the insistence of the guards, he changed his own bedding to avoid any possibility of a hostage situation. He had lived in considerably less civilized conditions for far longer with less sleep or food. But even while on assignment and covertly watching his quarry from the same position for hours, at least it was his choice and he was in control. Captivity was killing Gil. He had nothing to fight and no exit without capitulation. The food was decent; the bed was reasonable. The doctor was efficient and kind. The only thing lacking was Gil's freedom.

Donating was the key to his release. The risks were low, though he would have to be careful about hand-to-hand combat in the future. He could not afford to have his remaining kidney damaged in a something so banal as a bar fight.

Why am I resisting? My choice is donate or die. Gil thought about his situation. *I feel sorry for Michel, but is this Stockholm syndrome?*

How can I not be falling into that psychological trap? Here is a man giving me information I've never had access to before. Hidden stories about how I came to exist and why I've ended up in this room thirty years later. Hell, Michel says my own mother doesn't know about the switch. Dad's distance—was it just his way of dealing with military life or because I was adopted? Growing up, Gil never knew when his dad was about to ship out. Now, with so much time to reflect on his life, he realized, *It was me who was distant.*

"OK. I will agree to the surgery, but you have to tell me everything about Yuri, Elena, and yourself before we start." Gil averted his eyes until Michel exited the exposed space. Now, looking his biological father in the eyes, he continued, "I want to know who the doctor is performing the surgery and where I am now." He creased the corner of his eyes in a squint and pointed his index finger like a gun at Michel's chest. "When I am satisfied that I know everything, I will submit willingly." Gil dropped his hands to his lap in resignation and sighed. "That is what you want, right? My willing submission to the surgery?"

"Very well. We will begin tomorrow. I am too tired now to continue. I will give you two days to ask all your questions. Then we must commence the operation. I will inform the doctor to prepare his team," said Michel as he knocked on the door to leave.

Then Michel gave a slight knowing smile. "You will know things I should not tell you . . . but I suppose the price is worth it." Once again, the guards were there with pepper spray and a stun gun in case Gil tried anything. With intense resignation to the inevitable, he did not.

Seventeen

Through the Tree Narrow

August 5, 2009 — Old Town Alexandria

WALKING PAST THE FIREHOOK BAKERY on South Union Street, one block from her apartment in Old Town Alexandria, brought back memories of the pies Betty's mother Beth used to make. The fresh aroma of apple, pecan, pumpkin, and strawberry rhubarb pulled at her. Betty remained ensnared by the aroma while a young mother and her infant child blocked what remained of the sidewalk, which was mostly encroached by a bramble of tree roots making a break for the street. Waiting for the woman to finish dusting off the baby's binky and move on gave Betty time to savor the smells and contemplate the unwanted bun in her oven. *What is it about being a mother?* thought Betty.

†

November 28, 2002 — Rochester, N.Y.

It was the morning after the clandestine operation into Bill's room to have sex with Tom. "Hmmm. That pie smells delicious, Mom!" Betty commented as she entered the kitchen.

"Yes, now, don't let that boy of yours sneak a taste. These pies are for Thanksgiving dinner."

Betty rolled her eyes and smiled.

"Did you sleep well?"

"Yes, Mom, I did," said Betty as she began trying to work the knots out of her muscles without looking like she was stretching too much. Sharing a twin bed with Tom was intimate and fun, but the day was going to be ripe with sore muscles if she did not pull out her yoga mat soon.

"Well, I'm sure old twin beds aren't as comfortable as your bed at home." Beth beamed with pride as she observed how much Betty had matured. "Your father and I are glad you came to spend Thanksgiving with us. Your brothers will be here later. Rob says Ruth will be coming with today. Won't that be nice?"

"I thought Rob and Ruth had broken up," countered Betty.

"Oh, those two, they love each other, but something always seems to get in the way. They always end up back together, though." Suddenly Beth seemed distracted as she peeked around the corner of the kitchen door at the sound of voices in the living room. "Aha! There they are. Tom and your father are talking business again. You know your father, always meeting someone about who knows what and he says it's just guy talk."

"They were talking in Bill's room last night. I . . . I heard voices and checked in on them. Daddy said they were talking about me, but I don't believe him," said Betty

"Bets, if people were actually talking about me ten percent of the time I think they are, well, they are way too interested in my tame little life," stated Beth.

"Mom, are you glad you had kids? I mean, you've always shown your love for us unconditionally. You've given me so much. But . . . I . . . I don't know . . . were we worth the trouble?" asked Betty.

"Well, there have been times when you kids were damn inconvenient to have around, especially when your father and I were trying to have some hanky-panky or talk dirty to each other," Beth winked. "But, we found ways."

Betty blushed slightly, "Yes . . . yes, you did." She could think of several times her parents were not as discrete as they may have thought they were.

It was Beth's turn to blush a little, so she changed the subject. "Bill's run-in with the law over that Greenpeace incident gave me gray hair. Rob's friends in junior high brought no end of worries, and his grades . . . well, I wasn't sure he'd make it through high school," said Beth.

"I guess we all had our rough patches," Betty said, wanting to defend her brothers.

Beth tilted her head slightly and pertly smiled before summing up her thoughts. "But on the whole, you kids have brought such joy to your father and me. So, yes, despite the diapers and the accidents and the grief, you were more than worth it."

"Thanks, Mom."

Betty hugged her mother.

"Tom and I have talked about kids . . . not that we are getting married or anything . . . just talked about what we want in life."

"It's important to do that—talk."

"I've thought about how you raised us, going back to work teaching when we were in school."

"Raising you was more important, but it was nice to go back to work."

"That dovetailed so nicely into our lives," Betty finished Beth's thought for her. "I think I can do it with some help. We'll have to get a nanny or a regular sitter, but after five or six years, I should be able to bring my career back up to speed."

"Your career is important, but at the end of your life, will you remember the briefs you wrote or the times you spent with your children?"

"Well, that's what I meant. I would wait until they are in school before going back to work."

"You were mostly baked by the time you were twelve."

"Baked?"

"By sixteen there wasn't much I could do to change you."

"Well, you did teach us to be independent thinkers."

"Just remember, the first ten to twelve years is the most important time you can spend with your child."

"I guess I see what you mean."

"That and when they become real adults and you don't have to worry about them . . . as much," concluded Beth.

"Well, I'm not in a hurry."

"Good. No reason to start until you're really settled."

†

Betty shook her head to clear away the thoughts of the past. The child was sucking on its binky, satisfied that all was right with the world. Betty was able to pass the tree and felt like she had just crossed a threshold of sorts. *I'm going to keep the baby,* thought Betty. *I don't know how I'll make it all work. I doubt Tom will support me in this, but what's he going to do about it?*

"Hi, Betty," said Grace Arthur, the agent who managed Betty's new apartment. Grace was just leaving Firehook Bakery and had a parchment bag in her right hand and a coffee in her left.

"Grace!" said a startled Betty. "Sorry, I was deep in thought."

"Anything nice?" asked Grace.

"Yes, I suppose so." I didn't realize how much I miss Mom. "Grace, I have to talk to someone. Can I join you for coffee sometime?" said Betty.

"Just grab a cup inside . . . the Brazilian is quite sharp and the Venezuelan is nutty . . . the coffee, that is," finished Grace, winking. "We can go down by the river and sit on a bench. I was just headed over there to enjoy the day."

She waited outside while Betty bought a cup of coffee. Grace's comments about the different blends intrigued her. It was almost as if Grace was commenting about Betty's past—the Brazilian being José and the Venezuelan being the crazy mission that led to Gil's capture and Betty's pregnancy. *I'm just imagining that . . . Grace would have no way of knowing anything about my past or recent history. We've chatted a lot, but never about business or any personal issues. I must be reading into things too deeply,* she thought.

Betty chose the Venezuelan. The coffee was hot and smelled delicious. The two women chatted about nothing in particular while they walked to the bench. The day was beautiful. Maybe Grace was just what Betty needed.

EIGHTEEN

A ROSE AND ITS THORN

July 29, 2009 — Control

"**D**AVID, I NEED TO TAKE a couple of days' personal time." Howell threw himself down into the overstuffed brown leather chair across from David's desk. His abrupt entry and tense shoulders belied his casual flopping into the worn, high-backed office chair. "We don't have any active issues, so I expect you to handle anything that comes up. Code Vinegar if you need my attention. Otherwise . . . leave me alone until next Monday." Just as abruptly, he got up and left before David could finish typing and turn his wheelchair around to greet his boss. *David the protégé. He can handle it,* thought Howell. *If anything big comes up, I'll lift my head up, but damn it, I need a break. Dealing with my father is killing me. That SOB has been pulling my strings since I came out of the womb.* Walking down the corridor, his neck and shoulder muscles tightened visibly as he passed a portrait with a vague likeness of his old man. *No more! I'm taking control of this situation. I'm the one with the power now.*

David was an enigma—an Oxford-trained mathematician with an emphasis on mathematics of optimal control. He left Oxford under dubious circumstances that included charges and countercharges involving the May-December marriage of Vice Chancellor Delaune, who claimed David seduced, raped, and killed the vivacious Lady Delaune. However, David maintained he was the third leg of the latest Delaune ménage à trois, experimenting with extreme bondage involving intricate knots, pulleys, and two of the lovers acting as counterweights. The elderly and impotent vice chancellor fainted in the midst of the act, which caused the strangulation of his young wife, and David, while preoccupied, did not cut the rope in time to save her. It was agreed that David would join the British Army to become a paratrooper while Lord Delaune resigned to his manor to write his memoirs.

So, being a hard-charging, in-your-face kind of guy, David applied to join the SAS Special Forces unit. His selection and successful completion of the training led to a mission in the Mideast where he caught a friendly-fire bullet in his back resulting in paralysis from the waist down. Post-recovery, David's recruitment by Control provided Howell a sharp intellect and intimate knowledge of Special Forces operations. He was a natural.

Howell's secure phone rang directly to the cloistered residence of Tom Howell Sr. "Barnes, I don't care if he likes it or not. I will be there in three days, not tomorrow." *Until then, I plan on thinking about anything besides Control.* He dropped the connection while Barnes was still sputtering. *For five years, I've played my part, giving all of my time and soul to running my part of Control.* His share of the day-to-day operations of Control had ramped up markedly in the prior two years. At the current pace of change, he would be in charge of the whole operation before Christmas, only four short months from now. *I'm due for a little R&R. I have to take care of myself or cracks will develop.*

Normally, just to make the point that he could, Howell would have gone to dinner at the Capital Grille and stolen a bottle of wine from his father's locker. Being in the late stages of lung cancer, the old lion slept his day away and rarely, if ever, ventured to his old hunting grounds. Yet the wine locker stayed stocked despite Howell's pilfering. *I see it now; the wine was just one more string he could pull. I need to shake things up. Something fresh,* thought Howell. *It is time to cut the strings of the puppeteer.*

After the usual harrowing flight from Control to D.C., Howell eschewed the available limo and hailed a waiting cab, calling out "Eighteenth Street Lounge" as he settled into the back. Betty and Tom had once gone to this haven of DJ music. He was not looking to relive his time with Betty, but he certainly would not have minded.

The cabbie, a smartly dressed black man wearing a vintage Cavanagh felt fedora, looked back at Howell in the rearview mirror periodically as the duo traversed from Ronald Reagan Airport onto Arland D. Williams Jr. Memorial Bridge. "The Bridge of Sighs," muttered the cabbie.

"What?"

"This bridge is the one Flight 90 crashed into. The Bridge of Sighs."

"I'm not following you." A perplexed Howell looked up from his briefing papers he had somehow managed to take on his vacation.

"Back in '82, a 737 crashed here on the Fourteenth Street Bridge, broke apart, and landed in the water. Six survived the crash but only five were rescued."

"OK, I remember."

"The only survivor who wasn't rescued was Arland D. Williams. They named this span for him."

"OK. Right," Howell replied quizzically.

"He gave his life rescuing the others from the frozen Potomac. My uncle was in the traffic jam and saw the whole thing."

"Must have been pretty crazy." Unsure if he wanted the conversation to continue, Howell tried to sound slightly bored.

"Man, it was insane. He couldn't do anything to help them. Just watch and help the crazy cat who dove into the water to encourage the victims."

"Sure, it must have been tough on everyone. Not much you could do."

"Heroes, man. They were all heroes, brother. Without heroes where are we?"

The drive was uneventful for the next ten minutes, but as they turned left onto Massachusetts at a streetlight, the cabbie said, "If you don't mind me saying, you don't look like the type."

"What type?" Howell squinted slightly, trying to get a clearer view of the driver.

"The sort who goes to the Eighteenth Street Lounge." The cabbie hurried to soften his statement, "I suppose."

"I do mind you saying it, but what type do you think I am?" said Howell.

"More of the Capital Grille set, if you don't mind me saying," said the cabbie.

"Stop the cab!" Howell screamed as he reached for his bag and the door.

The door locks went down.

He tried the door but it might as well have been welded shut. *Fuck! No strings attached and I'm still screwed.*

The cab sped up and took a sudden left off Dupont Circle onto Connecticut Avenue. The cab accelerated and began to weave in traffic throwing Howell about in the back of the cab. This was the correct direction, but the driver's maneuvering and the locked doors indicated things were not right. There were no seat belts and Howell had nothing to hold on to. He jammed his left foot under the seat and pressed his right against the passenger side of the car. *What the fuck? Who does this asshole work for? Gotta get the hell out of here!* raged Howell in his mind. He tried to hold onto the shopworn, slippery vinyl, seat with his left hand as he pulled out his SIG Sauer P226 and pointed it at the back of the cabbie's head. "Pull over or I splatter your brains all over your fucking fedora!" screamed Howell.

The cabbie ducked as he slowed down. "OK, man, I get your point. Can't a guy have a little fun?" The cab slowed down to a stop just a half block from Howell's destination. The doors unlocked and Howell jumped out. Before he could get around to the driver's door or even close the passenger door, the cab sped off. Howell memorized the cab's license plate and ID number. *World Cab Co. # 304 J125435, black man with a vintage felt fedora, his ID said Samuel . . . what was his last name? Doesn't matter, probably all fake anyway.* Howell repeated the information to himself until he had it down. *Even if it leads nowhere, I still need to check this out.* A hipster on a skateboard came to a screeching blunt-stop before reversing his direction; Howell quickly realized he still had his pistol out. *Not the time to attract attention.* "Crap!" blurted Tom as he tried to regain his sense of balance and control of the situation. *I'm close to the mansion, but they know I'm going there.* Tom spied the Fly Lounge and ducked in.

The night was young and the crowd sparse except at the bar. It was quite a departure from his previous destination. The Eighteenth Street Lounge was located in Teddy Roosevelt's mansion. The velvet and dark wood accents evoked a more gracious living style juxtaposed against the modern DJ music. The Fly Lounge, on the other hand, was in a basement across the street and the décor was early aluminum airplane. At least Howell could keep an eye on everyone in this smaller space. *I have to get off the street for a minute and decide what the hell I'm doing,* thought Howell.

He found a spot with a good view of the door on one of the long red benches behind a small, round aluminum table. The Plexiglas top was inset with a champagne bucket of ice. An attendant leaned into Howell, her chest showing, her red lace bra slipping out of the faux flight attendant uniform, and said, "We have a bottle service special tonight, one-hundred-fifty-dollar Skyy vodka. What's your pleasure?" Her whole demeanor implied that for the right tip, she was ready to provide anything he desired.

Howell was not sure what all she was offering beyond the vodka; spotting her name tag just to the right of her push-up bra under heavy strain, he tried to gain his composure. "Sure, Skyy vodka . . . Vanessa." Howell started to pull out several hundred-dollar bills from his wallet before Vanessa could stop him.

"Oh, you're fine, I've started your tab already," said Vanessa as she leaned a little closer, her right hand on Howell's left thigh as she put two shot glasses on the table. Kneeling down, Vanessa placed the already chilled vodka bottle she had been carrying on her tray into the ice bucket. "Is there anything else I can get you? Do you need some company? There are some very nice girls at the bar who would love to join you."

"No, I'm fine for now. Thank you, Vanessa," answered Howell standoffishly.

Vanessa slowly pulled her hand along Howell's leg until her hand came to his knee. She pushed gently on his leg to bring herself back up to standing, dragging her fingernails slightly as she let go.

"How do you like your vodka?" asked Vanessa.

"Chilled is fine," said Howell as he reached for the bottle.

Vanessa reached out, placed her hand on top of Howell's, and gave him a most agreeable smile. "Oh . . . that's my job." She looked directly at his crotch and then back at his eyes. "I'm keeping my eye on you . . . in case you need anything else." She licked her lips as she fondled the bottle of vodka while pouring his drink. Holding the bottle with one hand, she jammed it back into the ice bucket and slowly let go before sauntering seductively back to the bar to talk to one of the waiting girls.

Howell sat back as he sipped on his chilled shot.

A tall, leggy brunette walked over to Howell's table. The sequined dress shimmered like the desert heat, but the curves were real. Howell felt a shiver of recognition, especially when she bent over exposing her ample cleavage, and said, "Do you mind if I join you? The boys at the bar are a little childish for me."

Why not, thought Howell. "Sure. Would you like a drink?" And before he could reach for the bottle, Vanessa was pouring for Howell's new guest. Howell said into Vanessa's ear over the din of the DJ, "Is this one of the girls you were talking about?"

"No, but I've seen her here before," said Vanessa.

The now-seated brunette leaned into Howell and offered her hand as she pressed her ample breasts into his shoulder and huskily whispered into his ear, "Susan."

"Tom," said Howell as he delicately took Susan's hand and gave it a slight squeeze.

"It is a pleasure to meet you, Tom," Susan said as she snuggled next to him and sipped her chilled vodka.

"You look familiar, but I cannot imagine where I've met you before," said Tom.

"Oh, what makes you think we've met before?" asked Susan.

"When you were walking over here you reminded me of someone. Oh, you obviously aren't her, but you reminded me of a coworker I knew back in, ah . . . I guess it was eight years ago," said Howell.

"What was her name?" asked Susan defensively.

"Babs . . . ah . . . Barbara McGillicutty, but she was a blonde. Her face was not as pretty as yours," said Howell.

"Never knew her," smirked Susan.

NINETEEN

SHARK ATTACK!

May 15, 2009 — Observatory Circle, Washington, D.C.

"'**Y**OU OUGHT NOT TO PRACTICE** childish ways, since you are no longer that age.'" quoted Tom Sr. "Homer, the Odyssey."

Tom Jr. pivoted his 9mm SIG Sauer pistol from his father's heart to a head shot. "I'd shoot, but I know it's what you want. I know you're dying a slow, painful death."

Tom Sr. swallowed and quietly cleared his throat.

Tom Jr. sneered at his father. "I understand you don't have Mother's strength of will to kill yourself."

Tom Sr. started to object but decided that provoking his son on this point would not get the result he yearned for.

"Did you ever consider that Jack was committing suicide the day he got drunk? Suicide by cop, they call it." Tom Jr. waited for his father to defend himself.

The old man squirmed slightly in his seat but stayed mute.

Tom Jr. continued, "He knew what he had created. He knew there was never going to be another project like it for him. What else was there to live for? To be your lackey? Your boot licker?"

Fat fingers fumbled with the oxygen tube, attempting to improve the fit into his nostrils.

Tom Jr. glared at his father. "Is that what you think of me? Your errand boy? Does your action item list conclude with 'Get Junior to pull the trigger'? If I did, the secrets would stop. What if I did kill you and walked away? Would Control die a natural death, or do I need to put a bullet in your dog for you too?"

Tom Sr. winced but did not answer.

"Barnes would dispose of your body and I'd dispose of your cur."

With all his might and faltering lungs with every word, Tom Sr. finally snarled, "You don't have the courage or the balls!" The last word rumbled out of the man with spittle for emphasis.

Tom Jr. narrowed his eyes. "Oh, yes, Father, I could kill you right now. I have the balls and the cause, but your button-pushing isn't working, is it?"

"I have given you everything you need. What more can I do"—he wheezed in and out—"to induce you to give me relief?"

Tom pondered his father's question for only a moment. "What if I said the price of a quicker and painless death for you was the end of Control?"

"Control will survive my passing. Others will do what you cannot or are unwilling to do. There are contingency plans." A great racking of sound and sharp motion grabbed hold of Tom Sr. and shook him violently.

"I'm going to keep coming here every week to see this through. Then I'll decide what to do." Tom Jr. moved the pistol slightly to his right and pulled the trigger. Plaster exploded behind Tom Sr.'s head; he did not flinch, but he did blink his eyes to clear them. Plaster dust settled on his thin comb-over as he licked his lips and began to rub his hands, thick with bulbous fat. Tom Jr. tilted his head slightly, listening for running feet. "Now I know." He slowly put the pistol away in the holster hidden under his jacket. "No one is listening in on our conversations." Tom looked directly at his father with a knowing glare. "Someone would have come to dance on your body. Or to kill me. You now know that I can pull the trigger, and will. 'Oh for shame, how the mortals put the blame upon us gods, for they say evils come from us, but it is they, rather, who by their own recklessness win sorrow beyond what is given,'" he quoted. "Zeus, Homer, the Odyssey." He smiled slightly. "As you were saying, Father?"

The ancient spymaster gently shook the plaster from his hair, wiped his face with his napkin, and made an effort to straighten his red satin smoking jacket. He sipped his water and cleared his throat before starting. "The ruin of the original Control began shortly after I 'retired' in 1978. That whole mess Carter created in the desert could've been averted had I stayed on. The back channel to the CIA ended with the death of Dulles in 1969. All the old lions were dead. I was the last of that pride. In the sixties, Congress was looking for blood after Kennedy's assassination, along with the mess of the Vietnam death squads. The CIA didn't know where it stood and was pulling back. The direct link died with Dulles and we did not arrange for a replacement. There was no one either of us trusted with the secret of Control.

"We were truly on our own. We counted on being invisible. Canceling any mission that even had a hint of transparency. I could have gotten the hostages out in forty-eight hours with a few phone calls to start civil unrest and generate distrust between factions. In the mayhem of that environment, five specialists could walk in and drive the hostages out in trucks with signs six feet high proclaiming 'Hostage Rescue Mission' in Persian! No helicopters to strand in the desert, and all the hostages rescued. Minimum force for maximum results. Hell, the operation would've cost less than the price of the equipment Carter lost in the desert," explained Tom Sr.

"You had contacts in Iran during the hostage crisis?" Tom Jr. screwed his face up in disbelief.

"We still do. We could take out the Iranian nuclear program in one day . . . if we were willing to expose our network. For now, we are waiting to see what comes of their progress. Need to keep an eye on the Koreans and Chinese, no reason to hurry." He waved off his son, as if he should already be seeing these connections. "The Chinese were sponsoring the North Koreans and they were providing the technical support to the Iranians."

"You say 'we' and that you 'still do.' My understanding was you're only providing an advisory role to Control. You make it sound like you're part of the day-to-day operations," said Tom Jr.

"Well, I wouldn't be much of a spy, now would I, if I didn't have my sources and resources. Of course, I am still the final arbitrator of Control. I know where all the bodies are buried," said Tom Sr.

"Literally!" said Tom Jr.

Tom Sr. frowned at his son for his lack of deference. "Tom, why do you keep coming here week after week if you don't intend to do something with the knowledge I'm giving you?"

"I suppose I'm trying to understand you and what you've been up to these past sixty-five years. I want to know what really happened to our family. I'd like to know more than just the first names of my relatives. For instance, I don't even know Uncle Guali's last name or where he lives. I've only seen him maybe twice in my life. Aunt Helen has been to see Mother many times over the years, but I know almost nothing of my only living uncle . . . I'm assuming he is still alive," said Tom Jr.

"Your uncle—Guali, as you know him—is alive and a successful man in his own right. Dr. Gualtiero Salizar."

"Why didn't you tell me? Why haven't I seen him since I was a boy?"

"He has been busy taking care of his business. That and he's still upset about your mother's suicide."

"But why? Why would he hold that against you?"

"His skill restored your mother's sight. It was my job to make sure she stayed on her medicines."

"What does he offer Control?"

"He has a chain of hospitals around the globe. I will admit that we use his facilities from time to time to our advantage. Some agents have received life-saving operations without any trace of medical records. Guali doesn't know about Control directly, only that I send him work."

Tom Jr. interrupted his father again for clarification. "What kind of work?"

Tom Sr. strangled the urge to rebuke his son for the interruption and for his lack of insight. "When an agent is damaged beyond routine medical care or in a way that would raise questions in our society's regular medical system, Guali patches them up. Sometimes as good as new and others as best he can. Some he's to record for future reference and others he's to disavow."

Tom Jr. wanted to interrupt again, but a slight frown from his father as he started to mouth the question on his mind stopped him.

Senior cleared his throat and wiped his brow before continuing. "Unlike your Uncle Jack, Guali has never uttered a word that would divulge any indication of Control's existence, but I want to make sure none of the patients I've sent him talked under anesthetic or that he has become too curious about the cause of these unique injuries. So far he assumes we are just run-of-the-mill mercenaries. Or so I used to believe."

"OK. We check out Guali's level of curiosity, but why compare him to Uncle Jack?"

"Jack couldn't stand the thought that his greatest work would remain a secret long after he died. His pride is what did him in—that, and the alcohol. Guali tried to treat his disease. He was able to diminish Jack's desire and strengthen him, but eventually, well, you know what happened," said Tom Sr. as he looked away to stare out of the bulletproof glass of the old Georgian town house.

"Tom." Tom Sr. had a grim look on his face as he looked his son directly in the eye. "It is time to reevaluate Dr. Salizar's commitment to secrecy. I want you to send your best agents, Betty and Gil, down to Panama. Salizar will be there in July. He is planning on riding the Panama Canal train and then going on a cruise from Colón through the Panama Canal back to Ciudad de Panamá. Your agents are to quiz him. Feel him out for what he is willing to talk about, ask him about terrorism. I believe a group funding terrorists is compromising him. I need to know if this is true. I need to know if it's time for action."

This news and the orders that followed were shocking to Tom Jr. He tried to keep his face from showing any emotion. Now was not the time to play into any of his father's Machiavellian tendencies. *Is he trying to shock me, spur me to action, or just test my will?* "Very well. I have Gil scheduled for another job, but I have a new agent General Getner brought on that will suffice on short notice." Tom Jr. was not about to admit he still had feelings for Betty or that he was concerned that Betty was falling for Gil. Tom Jr. had his *own* secrets.

TWENTY

FROM HERE, I CAN SEE ETERNITY

June 28, 2009 — Control

"**B**ETTY, I NEED TO KNOW exactly what happened in Panama and on your mission with Slim in Venezuela."

"I've told you everything over and over again. In the cab, the debriefing here, and again you ask." Betty did not want to be here, in the bowels of Control, preparing for the next mission to Caracas. It was her birthday, and Howell had not even acknowledged the importance of the day for her. *I have better things to do today than go through this bullshit!*

"Do not leave out any detail, no matter how minute you think it is . . . I need to put this puzzle together," Howell paced back and forth in front of the whiteboard in the planning room.

"Tom, you aren't telling me everything! What are you hiding from me?" asked Betty as she sat forward in her chair, poised to do bodily harm to her former lover.

Howell instinctively moved back a few inches and then recovered his composure. "I sometimes forget that you don't completely trust me."

"That isn't all you've forgotten!" Betty said indignantly.

If Howell understood her true meaning, he was concealing it well. "If I tell you what I know now, it might influence your memories. I need you to start from the beginning. After you've told me everything you remember, I'll fill in the blanks for you . . . I promise." Howell regretted saying he promised the moment it crossed his lips, but Betty did not take the bait.

She gave up, for the moment, the idea that Howell might acknowledge her humanity, and drifted into spy mode. "Slim kept a close eye on me from the start of the mission," started Betty. "I thought he was just interested in me sexually. I told you about that incident in McFluffy's lair, the fitting for our new spy suits. I assumed you wanted us to become comfortable being in the presence of each other naked." With her hazel eyes slit, Betty glared at Howell. "The situation reeked of a deal between McFluffy and Slim, but I have to admit, it was kind of fun to see Slim squirm like he did." She smiled briefly as Howell nodded for her to go on.

Betty took a deep breath before continuing, "On the flight in the chopper to the drop zone near the dam, Slim seemed a little uncomfortable; he was acting like he didn't trust me completely." Betty paused as she visualized the moment. "He was checking my work while we set the explosives. I was pissed at the time and told him to get moving."

Howell nodded thoughtfully and rubbed his chin.

"He kept falling behind." Betty added for emphasis, "He was chomping that damn cigar the whole time. Slim was supposed to be covering me as I made my way to the warehouse to pick up the nuclear material."

"Was he?"

"I told him to put the cigar out, that smoking it would get him killed. I could tell where he was by the ember."

Howell signaled for her to continue. "You didn't say if Slim was in position."

"He was moving toward the Qaida camp. He wasn't supposed to move there until after the explosion. The charges were set to go off in fifteen minutes or by manual detonation by the handheld detonator in Slim's big mitt. I don't know why, but the charges went off early, by about five minutes—"

"Did you have enough time to do your job?"

Betty glared disapprovingly. "I was just getting in position at the back door and had located the capsule about thirty feet inside the building. The explosion caused the terrorists to drop their projects and run for the front door. I had about two minutes to get in, grab the capsule, and get back to the boat before the wall of water hit the building."

"I see."

"Our rendezvous point was only two kilometers by road, but I wasn't going to be clear of the water in time to go that way. I stuffed the capsule in my backpack and prepared to take the brunt of the wave with the skiff like a boogie boarder—"

"Always adapting. Excellent."

Betty paused to take a drink of her water; she ran her finger over the ring left by the glass on the hardwood table as she relived the adrenaline-laced moment of the raging water. "I grabbed a tree limb to get off the river when I was approximately even with the plantation." Betty looked Howell in the eye. "I had to navigate the gully washes without any light, so I was slowed down a little." She decided to skip the part where she nearly gashed her face open on the rocks when she tripped. "I arrived at the plantation with enough time to locate Miguel and interrogate him before catching the copter."

"How do you know he didn't handle the terrorist camp per his mission objectives?" Howell tapped his pen on his pad of paper for emphasis.

"When I surveyed the housing area before moving in, I spotted Slim behind a shed. The yard light clearly showed his outline. Hard to miss a seven-foot giant with a glowing ember."

"He could have driven down and beaten—" Howell did not finish his sentence.

Betty looked Howell in the eye and said, "I knew he was up to no good."

"How did you know?"

"Everything was wrong. He wasn't following protocol."

"And?"

"A feeling in my gut." She placed a hand on her stomach to emphasize the point.

"Those feelings are usually right. He didn't"—Howell looked like he had a bad taste in his mouth—"take care of the camp. We verified." He frowned and reluctantly waved his hand twice for her to keep going.

"I moved into position and nearly made it to his hiding spot. I stepped on a cistern cover just feet from him . . . he turned and engaged me immediately."

"Had you made any signal to him or did you identify yourself with the call sign?"

Betty's hot gaze made him sit back from the table. "He clearly knew who I was and had every intention of killing me. I managed to get him in a submission hold and thought I had him when he went slack sooner than he should have. As soon as I turned him over I realized he'd taken a cyanide capsule."

"How?"

"His mouth was foaming."

Neither said anything for a moment. Howell was thinking about how much he loved Betty. She was thinking about how she had wished it were Howell laying dead on the ground.

Unintentionally smiling from the thought that it was Betty's birthday, Howell sat forward and wiped his mouth. "What next?"

Thinking Howell could read her thoughts, Betty hung her head slightly and refocused. "I stripped his body of any and all identifiable material and dragged him under a fuel tank. I used his damn cigar to ignite the fuel to burn any evidence." Betty looked up at Howell and earnestly said, "I told Slim smoking kills!" Betty sat silent for a moment. Burning Slim's body had taken a toll on her psyche.

"When I picked you up outside the Froggy Bottom Pub two days later . . . you were tying one on."

"I was trying to forget."

"Did you tell anyone . . . anything?"

"No. No, I didn't." She had not told anyone what she had done, but being with the other adrenaline junkies, Bobby and John, had allowed her to forget for a moment what Slim had brought on himself.

Howell let her reminisce in silence for a moment. He was not in a hurry, and prompting her to continue would not help. After a minute of reflection, Betty said, "I found the dogs he had killed. I guess I didn't care so much about burning his body after I found the dogs. He didn't have to kill them! He had stunners. Slim got what he deserved." Howell nodded his head in agreement, but did not say anything. Betty paused to mourn the loss of innocent life before she continued, "I grabbed a truck the workers abandoned to investigate the fire. There wasn't any time to check on Miguel. I just made the chopper in time."

"OK, I guess that covers Venezuela. What about Panama?" Howell was ready to move on, even if Betty was not.

Betty revisited the water ring on the table. "I was held up at Lorenzo's factory. A worker lost a finger and the floor went crazy. I skedaddled when Lorenzo said I should go without him to the train . . .

that he would meet up with me the next day in Colón. Then a funeral hung up my cab. Gil kept the train in the station by bribing the conductor. It was such a scene when I got there, all those people wanting to know what the delay was. I started a fight with Gil . . . it seemed like the thing any couple would do in that situation. The crowd was satisfied that everything was in order and went about their business."

"And Salizar?"

"He took note of our lover's spat and the subsequent make-up-and-make-out session."

Howell seemed to take keen interest in this part. Betty thought it was because of Gil. Howell was trying to decide what interested him more: news of his dead uncle or the make-out session.

Betty continued, "He kept a voyeur's eye on us the rest of the time. We followed him into the club car and bought him a scotch. He told us how his wife disapproved of his drinking and quizzed him about what alcohol he bought on his trips. He let others pick up the tabs and honestly told his wife he didn't buy."

Howell smirked slightly at the thought of his uncle outwitting his aunt.

"We were just getting acquainted and priming him for the cruise back when Yuri came up and injected him. What did you find out about the solution?"

Howell snapped out of his familiar revile. "Yuri used a compound we haven't seen before, but it was made up in part of synthesized venom from scorpion, cobra, and a local favorite—aranhas armadeiras or banana spider. Salizar's heart and breathing stopped, his muscles paralyzed. He was in immense pain for the few moments he was conscious. Once injected, it would have been impossible for him to give you any information. A few drops injected under the skin and you stop breathing; your muscles are frozen. If you don't receive the antidote within five minutes, you suffocate. Salizar's dosage was massive and injected directly into his carotid artery. The local authorities determined the cause of death as a banana spider bite combined with Dr. Salizar's advanced age and fragile health," recounted Howell.

"But what about Yuri?" asked Betty.

"Oh, I have more on him in the next room." Howell smiled a little too nicely for the situation and waved his arm toward the door.

"Whatever," she harrumphed, but she moved to the next room as ordered.

As she walked through the door, she was shocked to see an eight-inch round single-layer cake with vanilla frosting, two plates and forks, and a knife to cut the slices.

"Happy birthday, Betty!" Howell looked like the cat who ate the canary. "I wish everyone could be here to celebrate, but you know I'm the only one who knows your birth date here."

Betty began to cry and rushed from the room and back to her quarters.

"Jesus! I can't ever seem to get it right with her." Howell grabbed a fork and took several bites of the abandoned cake before tossing it in the trash and heading up himself. "Not bad, not bad at all."

Twenty-One

Operator!

May 12, 2009 — Washington, D.C.

"**E**RIC, IT'S HANDLED. Just make sure my mother gets the treatment and your problem will be solved," said Jil.

"How can I trust you that it will be handled after the surgery?" Dr. Eric Salizar drilled Jil.

"You can't, but you will have my mother in the recovery room. The job should be completed to your satisfaction before she leaves the hospital." Suddenly concerned about the background noise, Jil asked, "Eric, are you calling on the secure phone I gave you?"

"No, I am calling between surgeries at the hospital. Why?" asked Eric.

"Damn it, Eric! Your father would never make this kind of mistake. Do not let it happen again!" said Jil as she slammed the phone down. She took a deep breath and counted to ten. It was time to release the hound. Jil had developed contacts throughout the world during her time working with Senator Bolden. One in particular, a girl named Sally, had specialized in compromising military personnel and Secret Service agents who could potentially be turned or used as unwitting double agents. Sally had shown great promise until she tried to work too many guys at the same time. Her transfer to Eastern Europe on special assignment would give her reputation time to cool down before reinsertion into Washington, D.C.

Jil picked up the secure line and dialed a foreign number.

"U.S. Embassy, Minsk, Belarus. How may I direct your call?"

"It is time for the Wooden Dragon to speak."

"I'm afraid you have the wrong number," said the operator as she hung up.

Sally wrote down the note "Wooden Dragon to speak," folded the paper, and placed it in an envelope. She addressed the envelope:

Yuri Vasilyev
KGB
17 Avenue Nezalezhnastsi
220050, Minsk
Belarus

The envelope could not go into the day's outgoing mail, so she placed it in her purse for later. Sally smiled, pleased with herself, but paused for a moment as she contemplated what she was doing. A worried look overtook her countenance as she realized the danger she was putting herself in by transmitting a coded message to a foreign national for the murder of another. She performed the sign of the cross and mumbled an Our Father and several Hail Marys as she gathered her things. With one last pause to twist the ring Gil had given her—before he had discovered her in bed with a target—she screwed her courage to the sticking place. She kissed the ring as if it were Gil's cheek and set forth, determined to do what it took to return home and recapture her man.

✝

That damn Yuri better get this right, thought Jil. *That man has been patiently waiting for his turn to get revenge. Thank God, the leash has been pulled tight until now. Casper needs updating. I'll do it on my way home tonight. No . . . wait! I have the lobbyist dinner at six uptown. It'll have to wait until the morning.*

Jil picked up her phone and dialed a local extension.

"Parker," a male voice stated.

"The dinner tonight? Did you bring your clothes or will you be going home first?"

"Miss Harper, you know I am always ready, but I do have to pick up the suit from the cleaners. It should be ready in an hour."

"OK, that gives you two hours to get ready. Do not be late." The handset dangled in her hand for a moment over the base. "Parker?"

"Yes, I'm still here," answered Parker. He had learned patience and not to hang up too soon when Ms. Harper called.

"Pick up some roses for Senator Bolden. I am sure he has forgotten his wedding anniversary today. She likes roses, lots of them; at least two dozen, *yellow*, not red. Be sure the stems are de-leafed; have the card read, 'To my ever-loving Doris on our 34th anniversary. You are my rock.' Have Bolden sign it and then send it on via the limo to their house. Have the limo driver remove the crap flowers Bolden's office probably sent over and replace them with the yellow roses in a crystal vase. The address is—"

"I have the address, Ms. Harper. Two dozen yellow roses delivered with Senator Bolden's personal message the card. Will do, anything else?" Parker tapped his pen impatiently on his pad of paper, anticipating the list growing longer.

"Yes, add a one-point-five-liter bottle of Dom Pérignon 1988, and wipe that smug grin off your face," rasped Jil. The cigarettes and booze were starting to take their toll on her larynx.

Parker knew his boss well. Harper & Associates prided itself on inside information including which man or woman in power might need help remembering the little details. Bolden's staff would have reminded the senator of his anniversary and lined up a box of drugstore chocolates paired with a medium-price wine, and a bouquet of pollen-laden flowers, which would surely cause her allergies to be aggravated. She would enjoy the chocolates, but she would regret it later. She was competing against much younger and slimmer women, as Jil could attest, having been the senator's mistress in the past. The official election cycle was over for the next five years, and the good senator might just think he could trade Mrs. Bolden in for a trophy wife. Jil Harper was not taking any chances. "Stability is always the key," Jil was fond of saying.

Twenty-Two

Denmark by Any Other Name

May 13, 2009 — Washington, D.C.

"**M**S. HARPER, ARE WE CLEAR on the particulars?" said the voice with a Danish accent.

"Yes, Casper." Jil shuddered at the sound of his voice. "You will allow Ruth to travel to Århus for the operation as long as I place the agents for the trap."

"Good, but what about the senator?" said the distinct male voice.

"Senator Bolden is willing to change his stance on the finance bill if minor changes are made to the language. Even if it's unenforceable, he needs to be able to say he caused the modification. I've taken the liberty of crafting language that appears to tighten the capital requirements but in practice has no real effect on your operations. The trick is graduated increases tied to taxable events. Since your operations are primarily tax free, the graduated increases are effectively moot. That and the Federal Reserve is loaning you money at negative rates for any bad assets you might want to dump."

"Hmmm. That might work. I want the legal staff to review your language, to make sure we aren't setting any precedents." Casper's voice seemed to brighten as he recognized her ingenuity.

"I'll send the language over now via encrypted e-mail." Jil felt a bubble of pride at solving a problem before presenting it to her "boss."

"The Yuri issue?" Casper's voice took on his more usual dark tones.

"Yuri has been set in motion. He is to leave the operatives alone for now unless he is provoked. The trap is being set for them in Caracas." Jil hesitated to ask for anything of her master, but she asked anyway. "Is it necessary for the woman to be killed after interrogation?"

"You do want your sister to be available for your mother's surgery, do you not?" Casper's voice sounded like honey and vinegar.

"I . . . I just was hoping there would be another way. Very well, as you wish. The two agents are to be trapped and interrogated at Ernesto's in Caracas," confirmed Jil.

The call was over. *That damn voice! He never compromises. I'd rather face God down than ever cross Casper!* Jil's hand was shaking uncontrollably. She knew what she needed to do, but it was going to take a stiff drink to make the next call. The wet bar in her office was stocked for any visitor or occasion. Jil's taste seemed to change with the circumstances or the person in front of her. *Scotch, yes, a double of scotch and I can keep going. Only another hour before the lobbyist meeting. I can't get sloshed, but I certainly need the edge taken off!*

Two fingers of Johnnie Walker Blue Label over ice in the Waterford crystal glass seemed about right. *A thirty-dollar drink. My clients get the best . . . sometimes I deserve it . . . right now I need it.* Jil drank the fifty-year-old rare blend and poured another. This one she carried to her desk to sit down in her brown leather swivel chair. Her office was plush with thick carpet and soft velvets. The mahogany was thick and dark. It looked more like a man's office and projected the power money could buy. *Money is power . . . power is money,* thought Jil. *This next call sucks.*

Jil put a smile on her face to make her voice match. Dialing the long code for Europe with her pencil gave her enough time to straighten her spine. "Ruth? We have to talk. Have you heard about Mother?"

"Jil, you know I'm cooped up in this mansion."

"Yes, you poor thing." Jil was reminded of George Burns's old saw "Sincerity—if you can fake that, you've got it made." She stripped the sarcasm from her voice for the follow-up question. "How are they treating you?"

"I guess if I'm going to be a prisoner it beats London Tower, but they haven't even heard of cable here and they will not let me on the Internet."

"How do you get along?"

"My Danish is getting better."

"Ruth . . ." Jil paused long enough to take a pull of the Scotch. It was starting to warm her and take over her words. *Thank God for the Scotch . . . I don't think I could go through with this without its warmth and its courage,* thought Jil.

"Yes, Jil, I'm here," Ruth was not quite sure if Jil was still on the line after the extra-long pause.

"Ruth . . . Mother needs an operation."

"Operation?"

"Her lungs are about to give out."

"What do you mean?"

"She's on oxygen and about to die." Jil rushed the words to keep Ruth from interrupting and to keep herself from faltering. "There's only one way for her to survive—she has to have a partial lung transplant."

"But—"

"Yes, if Mother dies, Father dies with her. You know he won't perform as expected if Mother dies."

"That isn't—"

"He'll be too despondent and will not want to live, let alone make sure we do." She did not mean to, but by pausing to take another sip, it gave Ruth enough time to ask a question.

"Of course Mother should have the operation. Did you find a suitable donor?" asked Ruth.

"Yes. You." *What else is there to say?*

"Wh- . . . wh- . . . what did you say? Jil, I thought you just said I'm to be the donor."

"Yes, Ruth, you are the donor. You will not be giving up all of your lungs, just a part of each lung. You've never been an athlete. You could shop all day and not notice a difference after your recovery. And with the drugs developed by the Salizars, your lungs should actually grow back." Jil tried to be reassuring but did not believe her own words; Eric assured her it was on the horizon, even if it was not going to happen for Ruth right away. *Better to hold out a branch of hope,* thought Jil.

"Why don't they use the drugs to fix Mother's lungs? Why do I have to donate? What about you, Jil?" Ruth sounded rattled as she peppered Jil with questions.

"I'm a smoker, Ruth. Yes, I know I need to stop, but my lungs aren't suitable for transplant. You've never smoked and are in good health. You're also an excellent genetic match to Mother. I'm closer to Dad genetically. Ruth, you know the bastards holding you are out for blood. We haven't paid the money back Daddy lost, so if Daddy doesn't do what they want they'll kill us all. Daddy can't live without Mother.

If Mother dies, Dad dies. If Dad dies, you and I die. That's the deal. By saving Mother, we save ourselves," said Jil.

"You mean you save yourself!"

"That isn't fair!"

"I'm as good as dead stuck in this place, and you know it!" exclaimed Ruth.

Jil took a deep breath and an even deeper drink of her Scotch. *I can't afford another drink right now . . . but damn it, I am!* "Ruth, I'm not a viable candidate. You're the only one who can donate tissue to Mother. If you don't do it, Mother dies. If Mother dies, Dad dies. If Dad dies, you and I both die. What part of that equation don't you understand?"

"Jil, I'm scared. I've never been so scared in my life. The only decisions I make each day are what clothes to wear. I had a life before all this."

"Well, what do you want me to do?"

"I don't want Dad's money!"

"This isn't about money anymore!"

"Damn it! This isn't fair and you know it!"

"You know I'd give both my lungs if it mattered!" protested Jil.

"I want Mother to li—"

Jil stared at the bottle just out of reach and with frustration she yelled, "Then donate!"

"—to live because she's my mother."

"Fuck you, Ruth." Jil punched the speakerphone button and placed the receiver on her desk to retrieve her medicinal alcohol.

Ruth's voice cracked over the speaker as she returned Jil's volley. "To hell with you and Dad! You are both selfish, worthless people. Fuck you! I'll do it, but for Mother, not you!"

"Good."

"I better have time with Mother before and after the operation, or so help me God, I will come after you and rip out your lungs!" The line went dead.

As Jil was pouring one more Scotch before her dinner with the senators, the phone rang an unusual tone. *Thank God! He's finally learning to use the secure line.*

"Have you and your sister made up your minds which one is donating?" asked Eric.

"Well, we had a big fight, but we agreed that Ruth would do it. She pulled rank on me, being the older sister and all," lied Jil.

"But you're the better genetic match—even with your history of smoking, you're the better candidate!" said Eric.

"She is my older sister. She has the right. Please don't bring it up again—she'll think I put you up to it. She feels she owes it to our mother and will not listen to reason," said Jil.

With a heavy sigh and a pause to think through this new wrinkle in his work, Eric said, "As you wish. Just remember, if we use Ruth's lung tissue, the odds of success are not as good."

"I . . ." Jil paused to remind herself to fake sincerity and that she represented her entire family in this decision. "We understand. We trust you and know you'll do the best job possible. She'll make it." She has to!

After hanging up the secure line, Jil downed the top-dollar sipping scotch in two gulps, wiped her lips with the back of her sleeve, and yelled "Fuck!" as she hurled the heavy, cut crystal glass against the brickwork of the fake fireplace across from her desk. Then she picked up her clutch and touched up her makeup, straightened her posture, and grabbed her wrap.

On her way out, Jil stared into the mirror next to her door and through a forced smile said, "I never did mind the little things." As she passed through the threshold, Jil was not quite sure who had stared back, but it was not the girl she once knew from her days in the beauty pageants.

Twenty-Three

Laundry Time

July 31, 2009 — Washington, D.C.

JUST ONE WORD, "Vinegar," was all the text message from David read, and it made the hairs on the back of Howell's neck stand up. *Crap, what the hell is going on? First, the cabbie tries to kidnap me, now David is signaling that something is coming up on the radar at Control*, he thought.

He reviewed the previous evening in his mind. He had spoken to David before leaving. *No problem there.* Howell had taken a random cab to his apartment after waving the Control limo off at the Ronald Reagan International Airport. *They couldn't have known I was coming unless . . . my apartment is no longer secure and I'm a target. Time to move an agent to my apartment—no, a contractor who knows nothing. This will confuse the enemy when they probe the change and we might spot their operator—figure out the who and the why.* Howell would make all the arrangements himself so no one else would be exposed. *Devon Miller is showing promise.* The resource file on the former Navy SEAL was in his attaché. *This would be a good opportunity to see his operational skills . . . test his mettle . . . with Gil gone, someone is going to have to step up and be Betty's partner. She needs a strong man she can bounce off and fight alongside of, like her brothers.*

Looking through the file, he came upon a memo signed by his father authorizing the use of a contractor to discredit Miller as an actively gay man to force his discharge. *Son of a bitch! That slimy bastard! How does he sleep at night?*

Reading through the dossier revealed the twisted logic and heartlessness of the senior Howell. Using the military's "Don't ask, don't tell" policy as a wedge, a contractor falsely implicated that Miller was a gay man, providing Control with a veteran SEAL and excellent candidate for an agent. The contractor became Miller's roommate before establishing his sexual orientation to their friends. When Miller discovered the malicious lies, he beat up the roommate who purposefully lost the fight and claimed domestic abuse. This forced Miller's retirement at the peak of his abilities, without burnout. He would be resentful and hungry for revenge. *Perfect storm for recruitment: cruel, brilliant, and morally void—just the type of work I would expect from my father.* Howell thought of his dead Uncle Jack and imagined his ghost lined up with all the other fallen heroes sacrificed for the sake of Control by his father. As if he was asking Uncle Jack's ghost for approval, Howell blurted out loud, "If I don't give Miller a chance to redeem himself, who am I really helping?"

Howell dialed the direct line to David after contemplating the finer points of his ever-expanding responsibilities.

"David? I'm on a secure line now," stated Howell.

"There are reports that the Panama mission may be compromised."

"Why? What have you got?"

"We're seeing activity related to the assets left behind by Slim."

"Any direct threat?"

"We don't think our people are in danger directly, but things aren't adding up."

"I can come in now if you need me."

"No need for you to rush back, but I felt you should be aware that things are speeding up."

"Do you need my input?"

"Not now, but soon."

"I doubt this is related, but there was an attempt to kidnap me last night."

"Harvey said you took a cab."

"I don't think the cabbie expected me to be armed or he would have gone about the kidnapping a different way."

"Could it just have been an attempted robbery? Just random bad luck?"

"It wasn't a coincidence. Clearly tactical."

"What do you want me to do?"

"I want you to arrange a contractor for my apartment."

The sound of David typing could be heard over the connection, "Do you have someone in mind?"

"Locate Miller for me."

"Righto," David acknowledged.

"After this, I want to bring him in and prep him for replacing Gil." Howell rustled through his paperwork as he thought out the next twelve hours.

David cleared his throat. "Uh, sir, we don't know that Gil is dead yet."

"Don't mistake my planning for the future for a lack of compassion or hope," Howell sternly reminded his second in command. *Jesus, I'm starting to sound like my father. God help me!*

"I understand." David started typing again, preparing the orders for execution.

"Right. OK. It is"—Howell looked at his watch—"eight a.m. Make contact with Miller and arrange a meeting for me. I want him to be in place within four hours."

"Anything else?"

"We need to get a handle on what's going on before we initiate the Panamanian train and Caracas glider missions."

"Yes, sir." More typing sounds from David's end punctuated the connection. "There is one more thing on the agenda this morning."

"OK." Howell acknowledged he was ready.

"José de Jesus Silva wishes to meet."

Howell absently looked at his watch again as if time was preciously ticking away. "I suppose I'm the only one he wants to see."

"He will be at Our Lady Queen of the Americas taking confession after the eight a.m. mass."

"The usual meeting place?"

"Yes, use the last confessional. He will enter after you."

"David, José is not a real priest. In fact, he is about as far from a man of faith as you can find in our line of work," said Howell.

"Sir, José is compromised. You are the only asset available for this meeting," said David.

One of Tom's early jobs for Control had been as José's contact as a field officer. Any competent agent could have accomplished today's meeting, but Howell's familiarity would allow him to get close enough to terminate José discretely after debriefing him. David did not have to paint the details for Howell to understand the situation.

"Oh . . . I see . . . David, you chose correctly to interrupt my R&R," Howell said as he disconnected the secure line.

Twenty minutes later, a simple text indicating an address and time came to Howell's phone—"2153 P St NW 1130"—which caused him to smile. *David is getting very efficient.* Howell would have plenty of time to meet José at Our Lady Queen of the Americas near the Colombian embassy, which was only a half mile from a Metro station. This Catholic church specialized in serving the Spanish-speaking population of Washington, D.C. All masses were said in Spanish.

No more cab rides for now. Better to be in the open surrounded by people. He would be harder to follow, but his prosthetic leg would give him hell by the end of the day. *Be invisible.* Every move he made now, he needed to remember the Control credo that being undetected was more important than accomplishing any single mission. *No sloppy work.* Howell felt his jacket for the SIG Sauer P226 in its holster under his arm. It was too hot to be wearing a jacket, but he did not have a choice today.

Howell arrived at the church at 8:55 a.m., after five transfers between metro stations and buses. There was a small line at the back of the church for believers waiting to confess their sins. They attempted to look indifferent when Howell walked up to an unused confessional and entered while they stood in line. The light above the door immediately showed "Occupied," and a figure in black came out of a vestibule to enter the priest's side of the confessional.

"Forgive me, Father, for I have sinned. It has been a while since we last spoke," said Howell.

"Señor, you know I am not a priest."

"Father José—"

"Please, no blasphemy. It is bad enough that we meet here under false pretenses. You may not be the believer you once were, but I still must confess my sins, even if I must disguise the details. God knows what you and I are doing, but the confessor only needs to be a conduit," said José de Jesus Silva.

"José, you are most wise to cleanse your conscience in a manner bereft of details. The mission, it was carried out to our satisfaction?" asked Howell.

"Yes, the two were cleanly assassinated."

"And the hit?"

"It appeared to be the work of a rival cartel. Our man has ascended to the leadership role and is now in charge."

"Good." Howell checked his watch. *Time to wrap this up.*

"Gracias." José's tone turned cold as he continued, "However, there is one consideration you may have overlooked."

"Yes?" Howell paused as he removed his pistol and silencer.

"The second man was to be wounded, not eliminated." José sounded unusually perturbed over the death of a traitor.

Howell screwed the silencer onto the pistol, covering the noise with his own voice. "I'm afraid that is my fault. You know we do not allow visible traces. You know it has to look perfect. The information was found in his home, was it not?"

"Yes, he was pinned as the inside man from the rival cartel and eliminated as a double agent." José gritted his teeth as he placed his right hand on the grip of a M1911 pistol hidden under his priest frock. "Señor Howell, he was my cousin."

"José, if he had lived you, would have died."

"It is a family matter now, and some are not so easily consoled," remarked José in a slightly less hostile tone.

"We chose to take his life instead of yours. I would think you would be somewhat grateful, but I can understand the family difficulties."

"We all make mistakes." José's grip loosened on the pistol, but he hesitated to let go.

Time's up! Howell prepared to raise his pistol. "Please accept my condolences and pardon my presumptuousness." He could hear sirens in the distance coming closer.

"I suppose I can see it your way, now that you have clarified your position. I will pass on your anonymous condolences." José removed his hand from the pistol hidden under his frock and settled himself into his seat, getting comfortable now that the tension had eased. "Now, on to today's business"

What? Howell hesitated.

"A man with a Wooden Dragon tattoo named Yuri Vasilyev will be on the train in Panama. His mission is to . . . what's going on?" José shifted forward as if he was about to leave. He began moving for his pistol, realizing he had been foolish to relax. It was too late now.

The sound of the paramedics outside the church and the confusion of the parishioners intrigued by the commotion reached the confessional.

José shifted back and looked directly at Howell through the screen. "You bast—" José's words abruptly ended as blood began to drain from a small hole in his forehead. The combination of a subsonic round, the silencer on the end of Howell's P226, and the commotion of the EMT crew was sufficient to mask the end of José de Jesus Silva.

Howell unscrewed the silencer and put the firearm away in its holster. The ambulance siren was quiet outside the church. *Crap. He was going to tell me something I needed to know. Two more minutes! I needed two more minutes. I should have kept him on task instead of letting him rehash the past . . . It's done. José was the only person who knew I was in D.C. this weekend, besides my father.* He wiped for fingerprints and left with his handkerchief in his hand, dabbing at crocodile tears at the corners of his eyes to hide his face. Another loose end was tidied. He was invisible again. It was regrettable that he had to leave such litter in the church. The confessional would be cleaned in seconds and without a coroner's report; the news would be bereft of any notice.

Howell gave a slight nod to the EMTs, Grace and Harold, as they made for the confessional. The parishioners were startled and focused on the uniforms. A man with his hat in hand took one step toward the confessional door Howell had just exited, but stopped as the medics pushed past him. Before the true priest in the next booth could finish, José's body rolled out of the church on a stretcher with his face covered. Two minutes after dying, José was on his way to his new home: a burial spot in rural Virginia. The gravedigger and two agents would attend the brief funeral sans eulogy. *If you can't say anything nice, don't say anything at all about a turncoat.*

One task off the to-do list. Now to meet up with Miller, thought Howell as he briskly walked to the Metro one-half mile away. A call to David would have to wait. Texting Yuri Vasilyev's name even on a secure cellphone was not a good idea. It would just have to wait until he could ensure a secure conversation. *Who is Yuri Vasilyev working for? What is the importance of a Wooden Dragon tattoo? Do I spread this intelligence or keep it to myself? Father would wait. The mole would warn his Cabal masters and further damage our mission. Two Josés dead now: Betty's and now another. Obviously a dangerous name.*

TWENTY-FOUR

TO TELL THE TAIL, OR THE TAIL OF TWO CITIES

THE SAIGON BISTRO WAS LESS than a mile from Our Lady Queen of the Americas by foot. The logical path was to head south on Phelps Place and take the dogleg left to the stub of 22nd Street. This route was short and obvious. It would only take ten minutes at a brisk walk, if Howell went directly. Considering Howell walked on a prosthetic leg, had just assassinated a Colombian native, and was being followed by an unknown organization—plus the Russian embassy was only two doors down from the church on the east side of Phelps—the best route was anything but short. It was only 9:05 a.m. He did not need to be at the bistro until eleven thirty, and he was only two miles from his father's house.

Time to pay a visit to the old neighborhood. That way I'll see if anyone is following. If they know who I am, they know who my father is. I won't actually arrive at Father's; I'll just go in that direction, thought Howell. Taking a left out of the church, he headed west on California Street toward Massachusetts Avenue. His parents had moved to the area when he was a small boy; because of his mother's agoraphobia and his father's lack of attention, he had spent many hours exploring the streets in and around the embassies on his own.

After a couple of blocks, it dawned on Howell that he would be passing the Venezuelan embassy. With so many Control missions focused on this hostile nation of late, he was curious if his presence would set off any alarms. He slowed down just before crossing 24th Street. As he neared the turn of the century brick house, he paused in front of the Venezuelan flagpole planted in the postage-stamp-size front yard.

"Just enough grass for a dog to piss on," said Howell out loud, then thought, *I better be moving on.* Looking over his shoulder, he spotted a well-dressed man in a fedora about one hundred yards back. The man seemed to take a sudden interest in the shine of his shoes. "This is what I was waiting for," said Howell under his breath.

He began walking briskly down California toward Massachusetts. The Turkish, Japanese, Indian, and lesser embassies were just around the corner. He was only a long block from the main arterial street of the area, but his stump was already beginning to hurt from the constant strain of the fast gait combined with the frequent twisting to check over his shoulder. The man in the fedora picked up his pace and gave up any pretense that he was not following Howell. *There is usually more than one on a serious tail. There is probably a car nearby talking to the walker. I need to lose this guy and the car,* thought Howell, grimacing as he quickened his stride further.

He was going to be a sweaty mess before long with his jacket on, but the SIG Sauer in its holster made Howell feel better about the situation. He reached into the inner pocket and retrieved the silencer. Taking his gun out to put on the silencer was not an option. If he hurried, he could thread the silencer onto the gun before he turned the corner. He slowed his pace down to stop the throbbing from his amputated leg. *I don't want to attract any more attention. Something doesn't feel right.* The barrel of his pistol extended through the bottom of the holster, allowing attachment of the silencer while the gun was stowed. This made the pistol very long, difficult to pull, and more likely to be visible as a bulge under his jacket. But with the fourteen subsonic rounds still in his magazine, he could handle almost any adversary in near silence. The only noise would be the slide action of the P226 and the sound of the bullet's impact. Neither would be noticeable in the rumble of D.C.

The tail ducked into the gap between the Slovenian embassy and the neighboring house. *He must be trying to cut off the southern route on Massachusetts Ave. He'll come out of the Marshall Islands and be on the run to intercept me at the corner,* thought Howell. His options were limited. The Japanese and Indian embassies were reasonably safe havens; if he did not have a pistol with a silencer, he could slip into either and lose his tail. *I don't think they want to grab me. They want to know whom I am meeting with.* He quick-dialed "9" on his phone for a remote answering machine that Control screened for active-agent caller IDs.

"Massachusetts Avenue and Rock Creek, ten minutes," said

Howell after the electronic beep.

The church meeting was quick—they couldn't have seen anything, thought Howell. *Wait, the man who tried to go to the confessional when I left . . . he stopped when Grace and Harold showed up. He had a fedora in his hand. How did I miss that?* He could not wait to make his move on Massachusetts. *That street is too busy.* He needed time to position himself and the tail in a more secluded spot. This turnabout was dangerous if the intentions of the tail were lethal. Fedora was going to draw attention to himself by skirting the embassies. *The police will poke their heads up from their newspapers if things get any more visible.* That would prevent Howell from interviewing his tail. Instead of ducking through yards like Fedora, he decided to keep on toward Massachusetts Avenue. *Hopefully, he won't have reinforcements.*

Checking both directions on Massachusetts, Howell felt assured that he was not in imminent danger despite his tail. He headed northwest toward the Naval Observatory, less than a mile away. He was not going to reach it before making his move, but he wanted the tail to think that was his destination. Past the Lesotho, Turkish, and Belize embassies lay the Islamic Center next to the Oman embassy. *If I want to lose Fedora, I just have to go through here and make some noise. They won't catch me, but the guards will slow him down,* he thought That was an attractive option, but Howell really wanted to know who was following him and why. Just past the Islamic Center was Waterside Drive, which led to Rock Creek Trail. Any chase car would be lost on the trail and in a dilemma as to how to proceed.

Sure enough, Fedora was following on Massachusetts and a chase car was visible when Howell stopped to admire the Turkish embassy. Looking over his shoulder to his right, he spotted a late-model black Audi A8 four-door sedan rolling along Massachusetts at a leisurely rate. The distinctive large vertical grill of the Audi A8 made it especially easy to spot. Howell continued on to Waterside and headed down to the path while the car and the tail talked briefly. Fedora followed Howell into the wooded area as the Audi stayed behind on Rock Creek and Potomac Parkway. He was closing in. *Fifty yards.* Howell slowed to allow the tail to come closer. He began to limp noticeably and headed for the Omni. Fedora talked into his cuff and the Audi gunned it toward Shoreham Road and the hotel.

The situation was now perfect. Howell and the tail were now out of site of the road and any eyes in the sky. He spun on his good leg and drew his P226 on the tail who was now only twenty-five feet behind him. Fedora was startled to have become the quarry and was ill prepared for Howell's quick turning of the tables. With careful aim, Howell fired twice in succession, placing a slug in each shoulder of his tail. Fedora, with a bewildered look on his face and hat flying to the ground, grabbed each bloodied shoulder as if he were assuming the X of Eucharistic adoration. Howell placed one more round into the tail's right thigh, dropping the man to one knee. Howell approached, then planted his leg and used his artificial leg to knock the spy onto his back. Before the man could recover and radio his situation, Howell kneeled with his good leg on Fedora's chest with his P226 pointed at the man's head.

"Do you speak English?" asked Howell.

"Da . . . yes." Fedora looked a little scared.

"Why are you following me?" asked Howell.

"Go to hell!"

Howell moved the barrel to the side the man's left ear and fired into the ground, causing a blast of earth and grass to spray on the man's head.

"I will ask again. Why are you following me?"

"We only observe coming and going. Not intercept you," answered the tail.

"Much better." Howell smiled to acknowledge Fedora's improvement. "What name shall I call you?"

"Boris. You call me Boris."

"Where is Natasha?"

Boris's grimace turned to a strained quizzical look. Natasha was his lover at the embassy. There was no reason to believe his captor could possibly know about this connection. "Natasha? Who Natasha?" he proclaimed with his heavy Belarusian accent before wincing from trying to shrug his shoulders to sell the lie.

Howell inwardly laughed. He of course was making a joke, referring to the famous antagonistic couple from The Rocky and Bullwinkle Show, Boris and Natasha. *Unbelievable! He's lying. There is a Natasha . . . probably his mistress.*

"OK, Boris, sure. Natasha isn't in the chase car." *I don't have a lot of time, but what the hell!* "She's back at the embassy, isn't she?" Howell winked at Boris.

Boris swore under his breath in Belarusian. "OK OK. Natasha is in embassy. What you want?"

"I'm going to search you. I know it's going to hurt, but put your arms behind your head or I will make the pain go away . . . for good," assured Howell.

Boris grimaced, and despite the obvious pain, put his hands behind his head. Howell patted the man down and removed a Makarov pistol from its holster. He ejected both the magazine and the chambered round before tossing the pistol into the woods. Reaching back into the jacket, he pulled out Boris's identification. The man's name actually was Boris—Boris Izhevsk. He was a Belarusian national with diplomatic immunity and an embassy guard out of his jurisdiction.

"Boris, I do not like to be followed. There isn't a *good* reason to kill you right now. Your people already know where I am, so you are my message. Next time I *will kill* anyone who follows me—without asking any questions. I could've taken your knee, but I only wanted to slow you down. You don't want to die, and I doubt you want to have your leg fused."

Nodding slowly and continuing to grimace, Boris asked, "I put my arms down?"

"It hurts, doesn't it? Imagine that pain in your knee all the time. That would really slow you down, wouldn't it?" said Howell as he pulled his pant leg up to reveal his artificial leg.

"Yes. I not die and keep leg. Thanks to you, I be going home. I lose mistress and privileges. I kill you later, we meet again!"

Howell flipped the gun in his hand; holding the silencer, he struck Boris in the temple hard enough to knock the man out. "Good luck with that, Boris."

Keeping the man's identification would give Control valuable information, even if it was faked or forged. Just to make sure the man was really out, Howell gave him a vicious kick to the ribs, nearly losing his balance on his artificial leg. "Yeah, you're gonna feel that in the morning, Boris," remarked Howell.

He was about to leave when he noticed a tattoo extending past the cuff of the man's right sleeve, which had rode up Boris's forearm during the struggle. He knelt down and pulled the man's sleeve back to reveal a Wooden Dragon tattoo on his right forearm. *Damn! Just like Yuri's.* There had to be a connection—both were from Belarus. *Some sort of a combat unit insignia, I suppose.*

Howell traced his way back to a side path, the grass ground down to the dirt by many feet, which led to his family's neighborhood. He did not want to lead anyone to the house, so he walked Rock Creek Drive briskly to Massachusetts Avenue. The Scat Cab was waiting for him—a cab he was glad to see for once.

"Travis, it is a pleasure," said Howell. *I can always count on Travis. He did such a nice job watching over Betty. So much better than that rent-a-cop, Margin.* Shortly after José's murder, Howell had hired a man named Paul Margin to keep an eye on Betty, partly to assuage his guilt over not being able to protect her from his world and partly to keep her from looking into the murder on her own. Margin's job was to shadow her until Howell could arrange something more permanent with his father. They had wanted to recruit her, but too soon after her fiancé's murder would push her further away rather than draw her in. After the incident in the alley when Betty discovered Margin was tailing her, Travis was tasked with keeping a more respectful distance and watchful eye on Control's future agent.

"Where to, mister?" said Travis.

"22nd and P Street, please. No hurry," Howell emphasized as he rubbed his aching leg and reseated the prosthetic leg. *Boris will be a little slow getting around for a while. Suppose I should call Grace, just in case he didn't find his pistol,* thought Howell as he dialed the number for the D.C. cleaners. "I may have left a small mess behind during brunch in the Rock Creek Woods about five minutes ago. There was some action; I may have left behind a piece or two."

"We've already been to one of your parties today—are there going to be any more? Do we need to call in extra help?" inquired the voice, caramel and sticky.

Howell's answer was curt. "No, I only planned the one party; brunch was a last-minute invitation. Is this a problem?"

"Oh, no problem. Just trying to plan my day. We appreciate your business and look forward to serving you again soon," said the saccharin voice.

With that unpleasantry completed, Howell looked through the usual papers in the possession of a foreign security agent like Boris. *Wait . . . The inside of the back cover of the passport had a slight bulge.* Howell took out a penknife and delicately sliced the inside edge, exposing a thin sheet of paper just slightly smaller than the cover. The top-right corner was a black-and-white image of a dragon, just like Boris's tattoo on his arm. Next to the image was a series of letters and numbers, each with the name of a city below them.

5xx723bq	20c9ed9d	ois094jf
Frederikshavn	Buenos Aires	Århus
887gr9i2	mv0d9d33	13kj3d9s
Caracas	Tongyeong	Göteborg
u2d93kd5	938dd80u	2kd9w0ad
St. Petersburg	Washington DC	Shanghai

This means nothing to me, thought Howell. *I'll have to run this by McFluffy and Bud.*

The remainder of Boris's papers were normal—no other hidden compartments or obvious secret meanings. Just the same, these would end up with Bud as well. *It isn't even ten a.m. What will I do for the next hour and a half?* thought Howell. He pulled a card out of his pocket. 'Susan Miranda, Property Management, 1425 P St NW, Washington, D.C.' *What the hell, why not,* he thought. He dialed the phone number.

"Hello?" said a seductive feminine voice.

"Susan? Tom Howell. We met last night at Fly."

"Oh, yes, Tom. How are you? Are you still in D.C.?" asked Susan.

"Yes, for the day. Turns out I have an appointment not far from you for lunch. Do you have time for coffee?" suggested Howell.

"Oh, I suppose I could sneak out . . . why not? Timing?"

"I could be at your office in ten minutes. Will that work for you?"

"Yes"—the clipped sound of shuffled paperwork and computer typing resonated in the background—"enough time to clear off my desk."

Tom Howell hung up on his new lady friend. After five years of deprivation, Susan was an object of great interest, even if it was just to talk.

"Travis, please take me to the 1300 block of P Street. I'll walk the last little bit," said Howell as he rubbed the end of his leg where his knee should have been.

TWENTY-FIVE

Is OCD Cleaner?

August 5, 2009 — Old Town Alexandria

"**S**URRY!" BETTY YELLED. *It's going to be one of those mornings,* she fretted. Surry was chewing the long-handled plastic measuring spoon Betty had washed earlier and placed on the counter next to a new can of coffee grounds. Grace would arrive for coffee in about fifteen minutes and Betty needed to recenter herself; yet, her focus had become a moving target as the pregnancy evolved. *A teaspoon will do, but it seems tedious compared to the scoop,* thought Betty.

Coffee on the bench at the Potomac had been an impromptu plan after Betty had run into Grace at the Firehook Bakery. Her penthouse overlooked the park where they settled in for their second serious talk since Betty had moved into the building. Just as they were getting comfortable, Grace had received an urgent phone call.

"Yes." Grace listened to the caller for almost a minute before speaking, "I see. That will not do. If we don't clean it immediately, a stain will set in." She paused to listen again. "Two paramedics?" A puzzled look on her face turned to a knowing smirk. "Precisely. I will take care of it personally."

Grace hung up her cellphone, paused for a moment to collect her thoughts, and turned to face Betty. "I am so sorry, Betty, when can we get together again for coffee?"

"Is something wrong?"

"Oh, dear, it's just a mess one of the tenants caused. Blood is so difficult to clean if you don't deal with it right away. Not to worry, it will only take a couple of hours to clean up. Would one o'clock this afternoon be OK?" asked Grace.

"Oh, that would be fine. Come up to my . . . my place," stammered Betty as she mentally stumbled, remembering her penthouse apartment had once been Grace's. "I'll have some coffee brewed."

✝

Betty picked up the water pitcher with the filter on top to fill the coffeemaker. As she turned to pour the contents, Surry came charging into the kitchen with a tennis ball in her mouth. The recently mopped floor was still slippery, and Surry slid into Betty's legs. The water pitcher dumped most of its contents past the coffeemaker and down the gap between the refrigerator and the counter. "Oh, damn it, Surry! I just mopped the floor!" howled Betty before it dawned on her that Grace could be outside her penthouse door any moment and she needed to be careful with her language. "Rats, what a mess." Betty dropped a couple of kitchen towels in front of the small gap between the cabinet and the refrigerator to sop up the water that had mostly flowed off the counter and onto the floor. She refilled the coffeemaker reservoir and hit the brew button.

A knock at the door started Surry barking and looping back and forth between the kitchen and the front door. Betty mentally bit her lip to keep from cursing again and calmly called her canine back to the kitchen. "Lay down," she firmly told Surry. "Stay!" With the kitchen and Surry in as good a state as she could manage, she crossed the open floor plan to the door.

"Grace, you're early! Did everything work out?" asked Betty as she welcomed her guest into the foyer.

"Oh, Betty, it's lovely—the decorating you've done."

"I was about to show you around, but you already know the place, don't you?" said Betty, giggling.

Surry poked her head from the kitchen into the living room, carefully observing the dynamics of her master and the tone of conversation. Surry did not like Grace.

"Very tasteful. The couch looks like you bought it just for this space!"

"Thank you, but it came from my previous place."

"Oh, but it's perfect. Large, but not dominating," assured Grace.

"It was a fabulous loft apartment. The ceilings were twelve feet high. It was a huge space, sixty by twenty feet," Betty recalled.

"Sounds wonderful!" said Grace.

"Oh, it was a mess at first . . . we put in a lot of elbow grease."

"Tell me about it."

"Plaster falling down, trash all over the place, and the floors were a disaster. It took two weeks of nonstop work. But in the end, we had an awesome place when we were done and they didn't even raise the rent!" Betty prattled.

"I bet you and Tom were happy there," said Grace as she smiled.

"Ah, yes, we were." Betty furrowed her brow and thought to herself, *I don't remember ever telling Grace about Tom.*

Surry began a low, slow growl from the kitchen and placed one paw onto the wood floor of the living room.

Grace glanced over at Surry and back at Betty. She had accidentally divulged the extent of her knowledge of Betty's past and tried to change the subject. "You seem to have settled in nicely. You're managing just fine without a roommate."

"Grace, I never told you who I had been living with," insisted Betty.

Grace deflected the query with a wave of her hand. "Betty, you listed him on your application as a reference. Of course I checked your references and he mentioned your living together."

"Oh, yes, of course, how silly of me!" said Betty. "It's the attorney in me, always looking for the buried truths, I suppose. Please forgive me, Grace."

Grace patted Betty's elbow and gave her a reassuring smile.

Seeing the physical contact set Surry off. Being half Weimaraner, she had a protective streak that forced her to action. Baring her teeth and barking loudly, Surry quickly approached the two and placed herself between her master and the intruder.

"Betty!" Grace cried out for protection as she leaned back and defensively raised her hands as a barrier.

"Surry! Off!" Betty grabbed her dog's collar and dragged her into the master bedroom, closing the door. She turned and began apologizing to her landlord. "I'm so sorry, really! I don't know what got into her." Betty bit her lip and tried to console Grace as she smoothed her clothes and calmed herself.

"No worries, my fault surely." Grace tried to sound convincing.

After a few more moments of trading apologies, Betty remembered the pretense of their meeting. "Oh, the coffee! Sit where ever you like and I'll bring you a cup."

Grace moved to the kitchen table and sat down. She fidgeted with the place mats and napkins before accepting the cup of coffee from Betty. She took a deep smell of the aroma. "Thank you."

Betty pulled the sopping wet towels from beside the refrigerator and placed them in the sink. "I really have to apologize. Surry bumped me while I was filling the coffeemaker—clumsy me, I spilled the water. I think all the commotion before you arrived had Surry all stirred up.

Grace waved the incident off. "Don't think about it again, it's forgotten," she declared.

Betty felt it was time to broach why she had asked Grace up for coffee. "I don't know why I want to talk to you about this"—Betty took the seat opposite with a mug of her own—"but I suppose it's because you remind me of my mother's younger sister, or maybe the older sister I never had."

"Well, that's a fine compliment!" Grace smiled wickedly, as if she had a private joke she would not share.

"Tell me about your family . . . you said you had a son, that you lost him?"

"Oh, Timmy. He was a momma's boy."

"Aren't they all?"

"He'd do anything for me."

"What did he do?"

"We worked together, you know . . . managing things . . . the apartments and such. He was a hard worker."

"I imagine, just like you?"

"I would have liked for you to meet him." Grace looked down at her coffee cup wistfully.

"Yes, I would have liked that too, I'm sure," assured Betty.

"Timmy was a good boy, always watching out for me. His father wouldn't have anything to do with him, though he did take care of our bills," confided Grace.

"It must have been hard raising a boy alone."

"Oh, we had our ups and downs." A smile of satisfaction crossed Grace's face. "It wasn't easy doing it by myself, but it was rewarding."

"So it was worth it . . . having Timmy? Did you consider having an abortion?" Betty asked shyly.

"Oh, sure, I thought about it, but Roe versus Wade was still new. It was a different time." Grace shrugged. "On the whole, I would not change anything . . . anything except losing Timmy."

"How did you lose him?" It was Betty's turn to comfort; she placed her hand on Grace's.

"It was an accident. He was in the wrong place at the wrong time."

"I'm so sorry. What happened?"

"He was shot by a man being hunted by the police just because he got in the way."

"That's horrible!" exclaimed Betty.

"The police say Timmy actually was trying to help the man before he understood the danger and the nature of the man he was dealing with. Timmy was like that, kind hearted," demurred Grace. "Oh, look at the time. I've been doing nothing but talking about me. What was it you wanted to talk about, Betty?"

"Hmmm . . . I think you've actually answered what I wanted to know. I'm so glad you came for coffee."

"I enjoyed talking with you too. But I couldn't have been the confidante you were looking for. I mean—suddenly leaving you yesterday and doing all the talking today."

It was Betty's turn to give a knowing smile. "Sometimes hearing someone else's story is as good as telling your own worries." Betty moved her chair back to signal it was time to go.

"Well, I certainly would be glad to visit again." Grace gathered up her cup and napkin to take to the sink.

"We'll have to do it more often," Betty said as the two women rose from the table and said their goodbyes at the door. With a warm feeling, Betty thought to herself, *I think I know what I'm going to do.*

"Yes, we will. Next week?" Grace asked as she walked out into the hallway and down the stairs.

"Maybe Thursday?" Betty wondered if Grace was going to her apartment just one flight down or to her office down the street. *Why am I thinking like a spy?*

After she let Surry out of the bedroom, Betty went to the kitchen to clean up, including the mess she had created when Surry bumped her. The refrigerator was on rollers, so Betty unplugged it and wheeled it into the middle of the kitchen to mop up the remaining water. Just as she finished, she glimpsed a scrap of paper was stuck to the bottom support bracket of the refrigerator. "What's that?" Betty asked Surry.

Surry tilted her head to better hear and understand her master.

It was a small, damp, pink piece of paper—a Post-it note. In smeared ink it read:

Tom—José—messy. Intercept police forensics, clean. ASAP!

Betty's hand began to shake. *What could this mean? Grace's phone call earlier . . . about blood and paramedics! Grace is a cleaner. She cleaned José's murder! Tom knew too much . . . things only known if he'd been there. How could I have been so fucking blind!*

A paralyzing, intense rage mixed with despair gripped Betty. The solid framework of her past life became unstable again. The brightness of this new reality glared like an interrogation light on a prisoner—her heart. The blows of Howell's abuse hurt as the knife of knowledge twisted in her soul.

Twenty-Six

Say 10ish?

"**D**R. CALLAHAN'S OFFICE, this is Sarah. How may I help you?" said the sweet voice.

"This is Betty Thursten." She sounded harsher than she meant to, so she took a deep breath before continuing. "I need to cancel my appointment for tomorrow." *I need to cancel with Grace too!*

"Did you wish to reschedule, Ms. Thursten?" asked Sarah in a kind and understanding voice.

"No, I've decided to keep the baby," stated Betty. *Then again, maybe I need to interrogate Grace.*

"Well, let's get started on your prenatal appointments, then. You're still early in the pregnancy. You should be around three weeks, right?" asked Sarah.

"Yes, it's been almost a month since . . . yes, three weeks." Betty tried not to think of Gil. *He isn't available to help make this decision.* Even if she knew where he was, Betty did not feel a need to consult Gil on having an abortion. However, now that she was keeping the baby, Betty thought, *Is it fair to have his child without his knowledge? What am I thinking? I don't even know if he's alive!*

"OK, Ms. Thursten, I have you down for two weeks from today, Thursday, at ten a.m. Will that work for you?" asked Sarah.

"Yes, OK." Betty gritted her teeth. *If I cancel coffee with Grace . . . no! Coffee with a sedative and some STP-17 instead of cream and sugar!*

"Will the father be coming?" Sarah asked in a nonjudgmental tone.

Betty sighed and tried to reign in her racing thoughts. "No, he isn't available." Betty tried to imagine how she could get a hold of Gil.

Why isn't he here to help me? Just like him to be held hostage when I need him. He should be here for the appointment and to help interrogate Grace! Time to track him down. Time to have a few words with Howell about José too.

"Ms. Thursten?" asked Sarah hesitantly. "Are you still there?"

"Yes, oh sorry, Sarah." Betty shook her head to clear her mind. "I was deep in thought."

"So, Thursday at ten. We'll see you then." The sound of the phone ringing in the background cut out as Sarah hung up on Betty.

Betty put the cellphone down on her kitchen table. *I need to make a plan. I don't want to show my hand to Howell or I won't have the assets of Control I need to save Gil . . . then again, Howell is keeping information from me. That had to be Grace's handwriting on that note, which makes it obvious that . . . that bastard Howell killed my José! Time to find out more on Grace. Then I'll go cut Howell's balls off and shove them down his throat. I told him I would kill him if he ever lied to me. Only, I never said it would be quick. This might take awhile.*

Betty let the sharp edge of that thought dig into her psyche before taking a deep yoga breath to center herself. She had to be calm for the next call. Betty switched on secure communications and dialed Howell's direct line.

"I'm glad you called. I have new information on Gil. When can you come in?" asked Howell.

I wasn't expecting this! "Why can't you tell me over the secure line?" Betty thought she was being a little too curt, but it was hard to check her emotions on this call. *I really don't want to see that prick eye to eye; no telling what I might do,* she thought.

"You know why. This may be a secure line, but we still have the mole issue. How soon can you get to the shuttle? I'll have the flight deck cleared and ready on your say-so."

Something's up, thought Betty. *He's too eager for me to come in.* "I have to take care of something here tomorrow morning. I can be there by two." Betty did not like the idea of going to Control. She needed to be the one calling the shots, and that meant staying away from Howell. As she disconnected the line she thought, *Damn it! I'd rather be going back to Ernesto Montoya's hideout, guns blazing, than go to Control right now!*

This next call should be secure, thought Betty. Grace's home number was unlisted, but Betty had it anyway. She could see through the cover now. Bosley Rental Agency. *That would be Howell's sense of humor.* John Bosley was the chief private detective for the Townsend Agency in the TV series Charlie's Angels. *There might even be other agents in this building, but I doubt it.* Setting Grace up as a rental agent gave her complete flexibility in time management and plenty of places to hide evidence, people, and even bodies. *I need to learn some of her hiding places before I kill her. She won't see this coming and I'll be able to subdue her quickly.* Betty calmed herself with her breathing exercises. *OK, I'm ready.* She dialed Grace's number without the encryption of a secure call. *Don't want her to know I know!*

Grace always knew who was calling from the caller ID, except she tried to sound as if she was unaware that it was Betty on her phone. "Hello?"

"Grace, this is Betty. I need to ask you something, I didn't get the nerve up to ask you over coffee."

"OK."

"May I come over tomorrow?"

"Sure, what time?"

"Say around ten a.m. I'm staying home tomorrow from work to take care of a few loose ends." *I have a few loose ends, all right . . . and Grace, you're one of them!*

Grace suddenly sounded more like her usual chipper self. "I'll have some coffee ready."

"Oh, that would be lovely." said Betty.

"But can you make it nine thirty? I'm meeting a prospective tenant at ten thirty—that will give us enough time and I can still be ready for my meeting," suggested Grace.

She's hedging, trying to gain control, thought Betty. "OK, that'll work. I have a conference call then, but I can move it if I make the arrangements now." *Two can play this game!*

After hanging up, Betty began to prepare her kit for the next day: sedative, truth serum, plastic flex cuffs, surveillance gear, stunners, weapons, and a mix of audio and video recording devices. *Time to start keeping an eye on Grace Arthur. I need to establish a baseline before I assault her at home tomorrow.* Betty already knew the building. Finding a spot to do surveillance from was more the issue. She had only a few hours to gather as much intelligence as she could. Their building was the tallest for a couple of blocks, but the Strand Theater to the east might give enough of a view from the roof. *Looks like I'll be doing some night ops*, she thought.

TWENTY-SEVEN

DO NOT TAKE THIS PERSONALLY

August 1, 2009 — Control

HOWELL VIOLENTLY STABBED the stop button on the audio playback. "David, this seals it. The mole is Getner."

A nervousness pervaded David's tone. "What now?"

"I am taking control."

David looked at him with a smirk.

"Little 'c' control," elaborated Howell.

"I knew what you meant." David tried to cover his mouth, but the corners of his eyes belied his change of mood. "I just imagined you taking your ball and bat to go home."

"I guess a little levity can help . . . ha!" Howell then wiped the smile from his face. "I need you to step up and run the Black Ops group for me. I can't do it all."

Howell closed the briefing packet compiled by Bud Stux, Control's information technology specialist. The evidence was conclusive that Getner had divulged information known only to him and Howell: José de Jesus Silva's cousin was an expendable double agent who provided low-level intelligence through José, who then reported to Howell. Getner's mistress acquired the identity of the cousin, which led to his status being exposed to the terrorist cell in Colombia. The death of José de Jesus Silva in the confessional was an unfortunate bit of collateral damage. "I wish this had been an isolated incident. In hindsight, it's clear that the leak sprung over a year ago."

"Well, it's obvious he was the source of the leak. How did you figure out so quickly who his mistress was and the connection?"

"It is a small world, my friend . . . a very small world."

†

July 31, 2009 — Washington, D.C.

"Thanks for meeting me on such short notice." Tom paid for the two coffees with a crisp hundred-dollar bill. The barista examined the bill closely, holding it above his head in the spotlight over the cash register and running a special marker across the face to check for authenticity. "I wish I had been able to stay longer last night—we were having a good time."

"Yes, well, I just went home. There didn't seem any point to staying after you left," Susan batted her long lashes.

"I see."

In a sex-kitten voice, she asked, "Do you take anything in your coffee? I like cream in mine." She turned and flipped her hair as she began a sultry walk to the condiment counter.

Distracted, Tom replied to her retreating figure, "Hmmm. Just black."

Susan proceeded to adulterate her coffee with the half-and-half as Howell picked up his change. When he turned around, he noticed her purposefully bumping into another patron and spilling the dairy product on her dress front. "Oh, look what you've done!" she exclaimed in the direction of the hapless man oblivious to his part in her manipulations.

"Susan, are you OK?" Howell looked perplexed by what he had just seen.

"Just look at my dress!" Susan grabbed napkins to wipe her ample bosom but only managed to spread the liquid around, causing her cotton dress to cling even more to her curves. Her lack of a bra became exceedingly evident.

"We should probably go get you cleaned up, I suppose."

"Luckily, my apartment is only a couple blocks away. Come on, it will only take a moment to change. We can sit on my couch and talk while we drink our coffee."

Howell was wary of the offer but intrigued by the possibilities. Last night at the Sky Lounge, just as he had started to warm up to Susan, David had sent an update on the Betty situation that required him to call in for additional consultation. In order to make a secure call, Howell had to cut the evening short and return to his apartment early, alone. Now, with her attempt to manipulate him by dousing her dress, he had the chance to pick up where they had left off.

"Sure, that sounds like a good idea." Howell faked a smile.

Once at Susan's apartment, she tossed her personal items onto the side table near the door. She left her phone with her purse and began taking off her dress in view of Howell on her way to the bathroom to clean up. "I won't be a minute," she called out.

"Take your time." Before he could walk to the couch in her living room, a text came to her phone, which automatically showed the first part of incoming messages and the sender despite having a screen lock. "Tonight?" was the message and the sender was Getner. "Holy shit!"

"Is something wrong?" called Susan from her bathroom.

"No, I . . . I just remembered an appointment." Howell covered as best he could. He tried the usual pin numbers most commonly used: 0000, 1234, 1111, 2580 . . . He heard her go to the adjoining bedroom and rifle through her closet. Nothing was working until he thought to use the first four digits of the value of pi: 3141. *It worked! Strange, Susan doesn't strike me as the math type.* His time was running short. He did not want to be caught snooping. As he quickly scrolled through her messages and emails, he heard the sound of high heels clicking on the wood floor—Susan was shuffling in front of her mirror, checking herself out before making her appearance. He put her phone back after marking the messages he had opened as unread.

"What do you think?" Just as Howell sat down, Susan came into the living room wearing only a sheer robe over a red bustier, thong underwear, and garters holding red stockings. Her four-inch stilettos made her look leggy and tall.

"I think my appointment can wait."

†

August 1, 2009 — Control

"What do you want me to do first?" David's excitement translated into fidgeting with the wheels of his chair.

"Arrange my departure for D.C."

"You just got back."

"I need to clean up the loose ends," replied Howell as he turned to leave the room.

"One question."

"Yes, whatever you need to know," said Howell, looking back over his shoulder, then turning to look him in the eye. David was sitting in his wheelchair ten feet from the new director of Control.

"What is our authority—what is the chain of command?" asked David.

"Well, that's an excellent question. What I can tell you is that Control is the offspring of Dulles and the OSS. President Merryweather renewed our 'charter' by putting General Getner in charge of the assets that remained of the old Control. It lay in disarray from neglect and paranoia," Howell paused for a moment reflecting on his reluctant rise to the top. "The chain of command is my father, me, and now you, along with the other department managers."

"Is it true your father started Control?" asked David.

"Yes. He was the first director of Control and ran operations until 1978. There were several successors of various degrees. The last long-term successful operational status was ten years ago. The Black Ops group just came out of mothballs when Merryweather renewed our purpose. The rest of the organization churned on, selling medical equipment and services while continuously collecting intelligence. There was no reason to shutter that side. My father was casually overseeing the situation until the president asked for his help."

"I understand, but how does Getner fit in?"

"He is a distant cousin to Merryweather. Merryweather needed someone who he believed he could trust with his life."

"But Merryweather—"

"—is dead. We are now on our own."

"So, we continue the arc. We're still commissioned to end the Cabal." confirmed David.

"We are the last defense. Every other resource has been compromised—the U.S. government, the Department of Defense, Homeland Security, CIA, NSA, state governments, and local governments of the major metropolitan areas, including their police and fire departments. Whatever group you want to check out, you will find the Cabal has infiltrated or has influence at will. They have unlimited money at their disposal and an unlimited supply of people who want a piece of the power that money represents."

"That's a little daunting when you put it that way, almost overwhelming." David cast his eyes toward his feet.

"Well, if we were going after every corrupt person, yes, we would be fools on a fool's errand."

David puffed out his chest a little. "I suppose I've overcome greater odds, personally."

"We're just going after the command and control. Our focus is on disabling the leadership, but as you know, we have to do it without anyone recognizing our hand in cutting off the head of the dragon."

"How do you propose to do that?"

Howell felt as though he was lecturing, but he needed to get David squared away on their mission. "They must turn against each other or die of natural enough causes. If we are too obvious, we will be visible and our own end will come quickly." Howell looked down at his own feet. David's paralysis from the waist down gave him cause to appreciate what he had. *I'm lucky, I suppose—at least I can still walk around, even if I have to strap this damn leg on every morning,* thought Howell as he reached down to touch where the side of his leg transitioned from artificial to real.

"Yes, focused and invisible. I understand. Thank you, sir," said David as he idly rolled his wheelchair back and forth an inch as if to say the conversation could end, if Howell was ready to move on.

"One more thing, David, Betty is on leave as of now, but she must be watched."

"You're kidding, right?"

"I wish I was. Bud has prepared—" Howell slid a folder marked with a large red slash across the top over to David.

David eyed the folder suspiciously. "Why is Bud putting together a watch file on Betty? She's doing great work, even with the trap at Ernesto's."

"She's pregnant and wants to keep the baby," explained Howell.

"Well, that would put her out of commission for a time. Wait, we can always use a pregnant woman in the field—there are situations." David let the sentence hang, testing the waters of his new position as Black Ops director.

"The point is, her priorities are changing. I believe she is salvageable; I don't want this to spin out of control like Getner," said Howell.

"How could we have salvaged Getner?"

"If we had known about his mistress earlier . . . we could have corrected."

"Corrected?"

Tom hated sounding like his father, but the conversation required a direct message. "My father was Getner's boss. If we had uncovered the situation sooner, before any damage occurred, he may have given the general a chance to deal with the problem himself . . . or maybe not."

"I understand." David regretted asking for clarification.

"Never let yourself be sucked into that situation. Women will present themselves to you from time to time. You will never know who is an active agent for the Cabal or if there is just some innocent interest. You cannot trust anyone outside of Control. This is war and we are the frontline." Howell hated himself for being preachy. *God, I sound like my father, a man who had many mistresses. What a hypocrite—both of us.*

"The pointy end of the spear; I understand." David sat up a little straighter.

"You can stay here to make my arrangements. I only have one call to make before leaving and can do it from another phone. Be careful, David." Howell turned and left the secure meeting room, which was deep in the heart of the building. There were no listening devices, cellphones, cameras, or personal items allowed on this level of Control. There was an absence of people as well. This area was for deep planning: for conversations that could not be on the record, even within the confines of Control. Access was limited to the highest levels of management. The secure level was partitioned to provide individual offices of varying sizes to accommodate the needs of the staff. Normal protocol would have dictated that David leave and Howell remain to do his business, but with David's disability, it was easier for Howell to move and be sure no one— not even David—could hear his next phone call. Today, Howell trusted no one, not even his closest advisers.

"Barnes?" The butler invariably answered the secure telephone line.

"Yes, Master Howell."

"Is he awake and alert?" asked Howell.

"I will fetch him for you. Give me just one moment." Barnes had been with Tom Howell Sr. for over twenty years. He was a model of perfection. He could have been a Black Op and possibly was at one point. Under the slightly concealing butler uniform, Barnes did not appear to be as strong as Tom Jr. was but he was stout enough to help the old man in and out of bed, let alone all the other situations a geriatric aid performed.

"What the hell do you want?" asked a grumpy voice on the other end.

It could be the encryption, but I think he is gruffer than usual, thought Howell. "Venus caught the fly."

"So it was him."

"You were right about the mistress being the key to his betrayal."

"Do you think he intentionally compromised the organization?" queried the dying spymaster.

"No, based on the communications David and I just reviewed, it is obvious he was being manipulated into giving more information than he intended. It was all innocent talk, but a knowledgeable person would be able to put two and two together."

"So, it is up to you to deal with this. Clean it up."

"Not up to killing your own dog?"

"Son, if this body would allow me, I would be there in a few minutes to not only kick your ass, but to put my own dog down, as you so astutely put it." The old man felt a flicker of the old fire in his belly.

Howell gritted his teeth. "I'll wait." *I am his only remaining option. I can afford to prod this wounded lion.*

Senior harrumphed and paused for a moment before continuing. "You are in charge now. Getner is now a liability we can ill afford. You must tie up the loose ends. I want it done by tonight. No point in delaying the inevitable."

"Do not take this personally, Father, but you are a cold-hearted bastard."

Tom Sr. chuckled. "Son, you have no idea. Come over for lunch tomorrow. I want a full report and I have some things for you."

"I'm dying to find out what that could be," said Tom Jr. with a smirk that carried through the secure encrypted connection.

Tom Sr. was irritated by his son's snarky tone. "No, I'm the one dying. Do not . . . forget who holds all the cards. Trust no one and only you . . . handle this." Off to the side, Tom Sr. spoke to Barnes, ". . . get . . . my . . . oxygen . . ." A coughing fit blasted through the phone connection.

"Father, are you all right?" asked Tom Jr.

"Never . . . better . . . damn it . . . Barnes." Tom Sr. disconnected the call.

†

Howell fidgeted with the short stack of top-security file folders on his desk as he replayed the conversation in his head. His deep thinking was interrupted by the sound of "dah-di-di-dah-di" being tapped out on his door. Howell tapped "di-dit" on his desk to finish the rhyme "Shave and a Haircut." "Come in, Bud." Howell warmly greeted his director of information technology.

Bud fidgeted with his baseball cap, embroidered with PWND and the cartoon image of a chess pawn standing over a fallen king. Pulling the cap down over his forehead with the bill just barely over his eyes, Bud said, "I have a problem."

"You never come to me with just a problem—and no solution."

Bud spun his hat around backward and leaned in toward Howell's desk. "You know I'm not a people person."

"How can I help you?" Howell wanted to agree with him, but gave a knowing smile instead.

"I don't like where you seem to be headed with Betty."

The smile left his face. "I'm not sure what you mean."

Bud ticked off his list aggressively using his left index finger, starting with his right pinky. "First Gil, then Getner, now Betty. You seem to be losing staff rather quickly." He held his middle finger a little longer than necessary and was becoming more visibly agitated than when he came into the office.

Howell felt like he was dealing with a petulant child used to getting his way. "We haven't lost Betty. You're doing a great job keeping me in the loop of things I need to know, like her call to the clinic."

"I don't like it," Bud harrumphed.

"You already said that. Why don't you like it?"

"You seem to be headed toward"—Bud placed his right index

finger at his temple with his thumb cocked—"terminating her." He pulled the imaginary trigger and grimaced.

Howell looked like he was revolted by the thought, but with a hint of knowing that was what Tom Sr. had recommended. "Farthest thing from what I'm trying to do, Bud."

Bud ticked off a new list of items. "I know the history, I know how you were tasked with bringing her into Control, and I know the irregularities in her family history."

"Bud, you are supposed to be gathering intel, not analyzing it. That's why we have the 'A' room."

"Those nerds . . ."

"Said the pot calling the kettle black." Howell derisively wagged his finger and tilted his head at the man he considered his top nerd.

"Those analysts aren't privy to everything. They aren't going to know about you and Betty."

"What about Betty and me?"

"You're in love with her. You're her boss. She just got pregnant by someone else. Do I need to draw a picture?"

"Bud." Howell paused for effect and to make sure what he said next was crystal clear. *How much does he need to know? What doesn't he already know?* "You are correct. I love Betty. Recruiting her was damn difficult for me. If we weren't part of Control, we'd have a family and children right now, but I made the right choice."

Bud smoothed his hair before resetting his PWND baseball cap, his personal statement on his computer prowess. Prowess he gained by eschewing all social engagements beyond the computer screen. He had friends online, but most of them were his tools or resources. None of them knew his real work or that he loved to make quiche for breakfast.

Howell attempted to look serious yet encouraging. "Control is our life. A choice I irrevocably made, just like you."

"Get to the point, please. I have a program running that I need to go check." Bud was lying. He could check the status of his running programs with his smartphone. He just hated to waste time chitchatting with other humans.

"Betty made a choice also. We need her. I think you love her too." He softly tailed off the last few syllables as he mustered a mixture of empathy, sympathy, and sincerity.

Bud looked away from Howell. His mind raced as he calculated what he could do to help Betty without Howell's knowledge—and stay out of trouble.

"Make sure I know what I need to know so we can keep her alive and in Control. OK?"

"OK." Bud got up and left as abruptly as he had come in, resetting his cap once more as he left Howell's office.

Bud smiled as he walked back to his office. A smile born of the knowledge that he now had an unrestricted license to protect his queen, which empowered him to remove any obstacle from her path—even if that meant hiding information from Howell, if necessary.

Twenty-Eight

Business, Not Pleasure

August 1, 2009 — Washington, D.C.

"TOM, WHAT THE HELL do you think you're doing? Put that gun away!" scolded General Getner.

"General, the leak has been traced back to you. I do not relish this job. I did not ask for the assignment—you sought me out. You must have known I would find the mole eventually. Did you really think I would fall for the red herring of Miguel or McFluffy?" Howell chambered a round into his SIG Sauer P226.

"What the hell are you talking about? Mole . . . I'm no more the mole than you are," said Getner as he fostered a haughty attitude.

"I arranged a mission that only you were briefed on. There was no operative; just a man I labeled as one, who deserved to die. His own people killed him, after he was tortured for several hours. We traced the communications from Washington, D.C., to Caracas and Århus. Would you like to know who made the communications?" asked a confident Howell.

"I'm not following you. I made no such communications. This smells fishy!" said Getner.

"The call did not originate from you," Howell informed him.

"What are you trying to pull here, Tom? President Merryweather's death left only two of us. Now that Control is a rogue organization, it's just you and me. How could you believe I would turn on my own people?" asked Getner.

"You're wrong, Getner. One more knows about Control: the one who arranged your assignment with Merryweather. The one who started the whole mess fifty-five years ago," retorted Howell.

"Your father," said Getner matter-of-factly.

"Yes, my father. How could you betray the trust of my father and expect to live out your life? He would be here himself to kill his own dog, if he weren't housebound and dying," said Howell.

"I didn't realize he had reached that stage." Getner stared at the floor for a moment. "I haven't spoken to him in months." Looking directly at Tom while keeping his voice calm and respectful, he said, "I'm sorry. I truly am. It's no way for a man to die. He has accomplished such great things, you know."

"The greatness of my father's accomplishments will have to be judged by historians many years from now. A hill can look quite tall standing at the base, but from a distance it is merely a bump," said Howell.

"How dare you disparage your own father! His mission was set in motion in a different time. The world was in complete turmoil. I may have not served in the Great War, but I was forged in the heat of that fire." Getner's pride and fury made him forget for a moment that he was a doomed man.

"Be that as it may, our issue at hand is the leaking of information detrimental to the very organization you are praising," said Howell.

"I . . . I haven't done anything to hurt Control!" stammered Getner.

"You broke a core rule," said Howell.

"Who the hell do you think you're talking to?" Suddenly incensed, Getner tried to redirect the conversation. "Maybe you had a hand in Merryweather's killing!"

"You're grasping," Howell replied while checking his watch. "You know he was assassinated by the Cabal for not following their directives."

"You know he died taking our secret to his grave." Spittle flew from Getner's lips. It was dawning on him that the devil had come to collect his soul.

"I wish I could say the same for you."

"He was an honorable man, just like me," said Getner. "I thought you were one too, but now I have distinct doubts about your status." A plan was forming in his mind. He needed to distract Howell and retrieve the pistol tucked between the couch cushion to his right. He had never actually killed a man, despite all of his years in the military. Could he actually pull the trigger?

"My status is not the one in doubt." Howell said firmly as he checked his watch again. I need to wrap this up.

"Put the gun down. Let's put our heads together and figure this out," pleaded Getner. His shaking hands belied his even-keeled voice.

His anxiety and seething rage is dangerous, thought Howell.

Getner slowly moved his right hand down the couch cushion as his left hand grabbed his handkerchief from his right breast pocket to mop his sweating brow and distract Howell. The M1911 was loaded, with a round chambered. The safety was off. He only needed to move his hand a few inches more.

"Put your hands back in your lap, if you don't mind, General." Howell derisively enunciated the last word.

Getner pulled his right hand back to his lap as he put his handkerchief away, feigning indifference. "I don't know what you're talking about, Tom. Will you put that damn thing away! You're making me nervous—you might accidentally fire that pistol," said Getner.

"As you should be well aware, I was trained by the best. I don't make mistakes. Don't you want to know how the Cabal manipulated you?" asked Howell.

"Manipulated? I still don't see how you think I'm the mole," said Getner.

"It came from your mistress, Susan Miranda, a.k.a. Babs McGillicutty. You told her secrets that you thought were harmless—only, they weren't," said Howell.

"Susan? What? Babs? I vetted Susan myself. She had security clearance while working for the DOD. What makes you think she passed any information?" As soon as the words escaped his lips, a light went off for Getner.

"Susan, aka Babs, milked you for information," said a disgusted Howell.

Getner could only protest. "I have no idea what you're talking about. She came over every once in a while. We had sex. She wasn't nosy. I didn't tell her anything. What the hell? A man has to satisfy his needs!"

"Thankfully you haven't revealed the location of Control, but you have compromised me and others. We are known agents now. I was tracked in D.C. My apartment is being watched. A cabbie attempted to kidnap me," said Howell.

"What the hell? How could I have compromised you, let alone anyone else?" asked Getner.

"I can only surmise, but information was passed by Susan that only you and I knew." For a brief moment, Tom let the truth set in. "Do you have anything to tell me? I really don't see any point in delaying the inevitable."

"Inevitable? Who do you think you are? I am your commander. Put that pistol down and come to your Goddamn senses!" cried Getner as he began to shake with anger. "Fuck you, Howell."

"You know the penalty for what you've done. It is business, not pleasure, I assure you," said Howell as he pulled the trigger.

His call to Grace was answered on the first ring. "It's time. One bag, extra large," instructed Howell. "Military honors, please. He deserves at least that."

"I understand. Be out in fifteen minutes or it will be two bags," Grace jabbed.

Howell knew Grace was mostly kidding. She took her job seriously and did not make mistakes. *But she'd probably do it if I gave her half an excuse*, he thought.

Rifling through the drawers of Getner's desk revealed no secret documents or any indication of his involvement in Control. *The safe.* It was behind the reproduction of George Washington crossing the Delaware. Swinging the picture to the left, Howell dialed the combination that only he and Getner knew, or so he hoped. If Susan had gotten into the safe, then the game was over. It would only be a matter of time before the whole organization unraveled if she had access to the documents inside. Thankfully, the seals were still in place, indicating that no one had tampered with them since Getner and Howell had last reviewed them.

There were no plans or names, just coded documents giving access to bank accounts, deeds to properties, and lists of compromised government officials who were vulnerable to blackmail, or who were targeted for elimination. *Enough to end Control if the codes are ever broken.* The deeds included the burial ground where General Getner was headed and the ten-thousand-acre parcel where Control was hidden. Being real government documents, their encryption involved shell corporations with P.O. box addresses and empty offices.

Twenty-Nine

Power Equals Money

August 2, 2009 — Observatory Circle, Washington, D.C.

"TOM, YOU ARE LETTING THINGS slip out of control. What is your plan to bring things back to where they belong?" asked Tom Sr.

Barnes had let Tom Jr. in and promptly exited the house. Lunch was New York strip steaks with baked potato, green beans with almonds, and a Cypher Winery Phoenix Syrah. Tom Sr. had been impatiently waiting for Tom Jr. to arrive.

"It is a pleasure to see you as well, Father. Are we so short of time that there is no room for the usual pleasantries?"

"Matter of fact, yes," grunted Tom Sr.

"Well, in that case and since you asked, I plan on bringing Betty back around."

"She's pregnant," said the old lion judgmentally.

Tom Jr. sighed. "Yes, the pregnancy and the Gil situation are intertwined."

"Abortion?" The old man aggressively attacked his steak as if it was his last meal.

"She had planned on aborting the pregnancy, but now she has convinced herself to keep the baby."

"Put Grace on it," suggested the old pro.

"Grace attempted to talk sense into her, but Betty is difficult to persuade when she has her mind made up," Tom Jr. pointed out.

"You need to get that asset under control. If you cannot manage her, you need to eliminate her."

"I understand." *I'd sooner kill you than Betty.* Tom Jr. seethed under his calm exterior.

"About Gil, what is your plan? He would have talked by now. Have you located him? Are any assets in route to deal with the situation?"

"We think Gil is in an industrial location not far from downtown Minsk. It is our understanding that within twenty-four hours an opportunity to breach their security will occur."

"Why so long?"

"The ring around Gil is quite tight. There is little leakage of information, but we have seen some asset movement by associates of Yuri."

"Yuri, eh? These beans are marvelous. You haven't touched your steak yet."

"Even in his death he seems to have a reach far beyond our initial reckoning." Tom cut a small piece of the rare and bloody meat, primarily to appease his father.

"Son, you will find out one of these days just what it means to control someone from beyond the grave."

"Father, if you are intending to exert control from the grave, you can disabuse yourself of that notion right now. I'd sooner walk away then let you run my affairs from the afterlife." Tom was for once enjoying the meal before him.

The old man erupted in a violent coughing fit, his chest heaving with effort. Tom stayed in his seat, waiting to see what would happen next.

"Damn it, I think I just tore some cartilage!" said Tom Sr., holding his left side as he leaned slightly forward. "Don't think I'll live long enough to die from the cancer."

"Can I get you anything? Some medication, a doctor? Do you need to go lie down?" asked Tom Jr. as he made a motion to stand up.

"Sit, I've been through worse. Damn lungs are shot. All the money and power in the world and I can't buy another day on this earth if I wanted to." Tom Sr. turned up the oxygen ratio on the portable unit by his side.

"Why don't you get a lung transplant? You know you could get to the front of the line by making a call."

"I waited too damn long. The cancer has spread all over. I'd probably die on the table. I'm eighty-nine years old, overweight, and ready to die." He drew in a painful breath, but what choice did he have?

"You'd be doing me a favor to pull out your pistol and shoot me now." Another drag on his oxygen tube gave him a sharp pain as his rib cage expanded with his lungs. "I'd rather die a day or two early than try to sleep with this torn cartilage tonight." He tried to lean back and grimaced as he grabbed his side. He pushed his plate away, hardly touched. "Oh, hell."

"That's just it. You're headed to hell and there is nothing you can do."

"Son, I don't have enough time left and I'm done with pleasantries, as you stated," he growled. "Either shoot me now or hear me out."

"Well, I won't shoot you, so state your piece."

"No rush to have the place to yourself, eh? When I die, Barnes will give you everything you need. You will own this place and a couple of others: the Maine hunting lodge, the Colorado cabin."

"I do miss the cabin." Tom Jr. began thinking of the skiing trips of his youth, until the reality of his missing leg jerked him back to the present.

"Your name will be added to all of my bank accounts."

"Why?"

"No probate or public trace of the asset transfer." Tom Sr. used his cane to push the paper closer to Tom Jr. "Sign that piece of paper in front of you and it will all be taken care of before I kick the bucket." There was a pen sitting on top of the paper. "Better hurry or Barnes will have to reanimate my corpse to complete the transfers."

Barnes really does take care of everything. "I suppose you would just fake my signature if I didn't acquiesce." Tom Jr. reluctantly signed the paper at the bottom below the legal language granting him a small fortune and started to place the pen back down on the table.

"Keep the pen. It's my Montblanc. I won't need it anymore."

Tom Jr. put the pen into his suit coat pocket.

"Signed a few death sentences with that one," added Tom Sr.

Tom Jr. pushed his plate away. His appetite replaced by the weight of the accursed pen in his breast pocket. "There are some things I didn't need to know."

"Who are you training to replace yourself now that Getner is out? The management of your team, that is?" Tom Sr. pointed his cane at his son for emphasis.

"David. He's ready, and with his disability, he won't stray far. He was a competent field man, and he has the desire and the knowledge. That, plus I trust him."

"Trust no one! Hasn't Getner taught you anything?" The cane slammed down on the table for emphasis. "Read what you just signed. You need to be more careful!"

"What point are you trying to make here, Father?" asked Tom Jr. as he picked up the sheet.

"You did sign an asset transfer, but I could have made it anything. You hardly looked at the damn thing. You keep saying how you don't trust me, then you trust me with your signature. You are going to have to watch your ass a lot closer than that, if you want to survive this job!"

Tom Jr. baited his father. "You trust Barnes and your staff."

"I trust them because their lives are dependent on my life." Tom Sr. grimaced as he took a breath. "If I die before transferring power, like the pharaoh's staff, they die with me. It is their job to make sure there is stability. They are worthless if there is no stability. You will have to keep them on their toes and under a death sentence to trust them until the end!"

"I think I want to live my life with the ability to sleep at night," replied Tom Jr.

"To each his own." The decrepit old man took another slow, painful breath. "Best wishes to you kid." And another, slower, but deeper, purposeful breath. "Now, get the hell out of my house. I think I'm going to go lie down and die." He leaned back and closed his eyes.

The old man cannot get up without Barnes's help, thought Tom Jr. *Moments after I leave, Barnes will have him tucked in bed.* Tom did not believe that Barnes was so loyal because of a death threat. *Someday I'll know the truth . . . perhaps sooner rather than later.*

THIRTY

SPLITTING THE DIFFERENCE

August 5, 2009 — Old Town Alexandria

THE SCOPE PIERCED THE LIVING room window with Grace in the crosshairs. Normally, Betty would have it mounted on a M110 sniper rifle, but that seemed a little excessive for this situation. Grace was not on Betty's termination list—yet. A monopod perched on the edge of the roof of the Strand Building gave her the stability she needed and the ability to move quickly out of view. The purpose tonight was to observe Grace and determine her habits, to prepare for a clandestine entry into her apartment to find some facts. The sun had already set to the west of Betty, so her matte-black tactical gear and clothing made her a shadow of no concern on the roof.

How could I have fallen for her story? She seemed to know me too well. Her excuse about the rental application doesn't fit . . . whoa! This woman has a serious case of OCD! Betty's running internal diatribe and dialogue cataloged everything she witnessed as Grace cleaned what appeared to be an already spotless apartment. *Pretty thorough . . . kind of early for a spring cleaning . . . oh . . . she's wiping for prints! Is she practicing, or making the room sterile? Gloves, net cap, and ultraviolet light to check for biomaterial!* Betty lost Grace as she left the field of vision provided by the window. Scanning the other five windows of the apartment, Betty spotted Grace in the kitchen.

A kettle was boiling on the stove, but Grace ignored it, which seemed odd since the steam would clearly be causing a whistle. *Is she completely nuts? What the hell is she doing with that kettle?* Grace removed a large object secured in butcher paper from the refrigerator. After carefully unwrapping the item and placing it in a large Pyrex dish in the sink, she covered the mass with hot water from the tap and placed a meat thermometer in the water. Grace finally reached for the kettle. She slowly added the boiling water while watching the thermometer until the needle read 140 degrees. Betty's scope gave her a better view than if she stood over Grace's shoulder.

The frost on the ice cleared. Grace pulled away and revealed the true nature of her work, causing Betty to exclaim, "It can't be! Oh, my God! A hand?"

Betty did not see Grace leave the kitchen because of her focus on the hand. *What is she up to?* She swept the scope over the apartment until she spotted Grace in the living room as she sat down in an overstuffed chair with her back to the window.

Let's see what she's looking at, maybe get a feel for the setup. Of all the visible rooms, the living room revealed the most to Betty. Two large windows exposed most of the area and Betty's slightly higher position afforded a good angle. The usual furniture of a single middle-aged woman: floral prints, not too feminine, but definitely not a man's home. The chair across the way seemed out of place: *its well-worn leather, a table next to it, and a reading lamp that did not match the rest of the furniture. There's a dog-eared book on the table with a bookmark . . . Robert Ludlum . . . Bourne Identity . . . not likely Grace's taste. It looks more like a shrine. The dust!* A film of dust covered the table, interrupted by two small semicircles on opposite sides. *She doesn't dust the table? That is so out of character. Her son was dead before she moved from my apartment to this one. Did she just move everything from there to here, just as it was?*

Panning the room, Betty spotted a table with photographs. What she saw made her heart skip a beat. It was not the picture of Grace with her son, or even the fact that that the son could pass for one of Betty's brothers or Howell. What caused Betty's heart to skip a beat was a photograph of a younger Grace standing next to Betty's mother on a dock in front of a sailboat. Another picture hung to the left: an intimate picture of Grace, her teenage son, and a younger Tom Howell Sr. *The roof is spinning,* thought Betty as she put the scope down to use both hands to steady herself. Dropping into a cross-legged position, Betty rubbed her eyes as if to remove the image she had just seen. *Grace knows Tom's dad? Grace's son is Tom Sr.'s? Grace is my aunt? That would make her son my cousin! My head is spinning . . . this is too much!*

After ten minutes, Grace returned to the kitchen to check on her progress. After putting on latex gloves, she examined her trophy and checked for flexibility of the fingertip flesh. A gold ring and a watch became visible. The severed wrist, three inches above the carpel bones, gave enough room for the watch to stay put. Refocusing the scope on the watch, Betty could now tell it was a Rolex. *A class ring of some kind.* Betty shifted to her left to get a better view of the kitchen as Grace drained the water from the Pyrex. She dried the hand with a cloth towel before spraying a light coat of something shiny on the fingertips of the hand. She then opened a box, which contained a SIG Sauer pistol.

I doubt that needs to be cleaned, thought Betty, but sure enough, Grace wiped the pistol down before using the severed hand to apply incriminating fingerprints. *Whose hand is that—and is he still alive?* Betty had discerned by the size of the hand, the coarse black hair, the condition of the nails, and the direction of the thumb that this was a man's right hand. *He wore a watch on his right hand. The ring . . . a class ring from Annapolis . . . turn the damn hand just a little to the left, please, if you don't mind, Grace, I want to see what kind of watch this navy officer wore. Is he naval intelligence, average officer, or—what?* Betty knew that while a watch could just be a watch, certain specialty watches were preferred in the intelligence community. An expensive watch could indicate wealth or connections. In any case, it would at least give her a handle on who the former owner might be. Especially—even if unlikely—he was still alive. *An Oyster!*

Grace carefully placed the pistol back in its box. *She's wearing gloves, and she's already wiped the apartment down. No traces to find their way onto the gun from her or the environment.* Grace placed the hand into a ziplock bag and into a smaller Pyrex dish, filling it with water from a gallon jug of distilled water prechilled in the freezer. Grace placed the dish back into the freezer portion of the Sub-Zero stainless-steel refrigerator.

Betty packed her equipment and returned the scope case to her backpack. It was time to leave, take some acetaminophen, and place a cool cloth over her forehead. *What do I do with this information?* thought Betty as she climbed down the stairs into a stark new reality.

THIRTY-ONE

CAN YOU GIVE ME A HAND?

BETTY THREW HER BACKPACK at the couch and reached for a family photo album. *What the hell? I don't remember any photos of Grace or her kid growing up. I only had Rob and Bill. There weren't any close cousins, aunts, or uncles! Jil is the closest to a sister or a cousin I had. It didn't seem strange then . . . but now . . .*

The album contained pictures of her family doing the usual holiday events: camping trips, fishing trips, parties, and graduations. It had always been something to explain when other kids talked about their grandparents. Betty's had all died young, before she was old enough to know them. There were pictures, of course, but no real memories of the people in the photographs. Jil's grandfather had died at sixty-two of a heart attack. Jil's grandmother had died of breast cancer at the age of fifty-three. Because Jil had similar circumstances, it did not seem that strange to Betty to grow up without grandparents.

Betty dialed her parents' home phone, hoping to catch her mother.

"Hello, Thursten residence," trilled Beth.

"Mom, I need to talk to you about our family. There are some things you haven't told me," accused Betty through gritted teeth.

"Betty, the phone is not the way to talk about this. I will catch a shuttle flight down. We can meet for dinner tomorrow," said a suddenly serious Beth Thursten.

"Mom, I . . . I'm sure it's just a misunderstanding," stammered Betty.

"No, it's time we talked. I will meet you for dinner at your place, say six p.m.?"

"Timmy Arthur," was all Betty said.

There was a long pause on the line before Beth replied, "Betty, there are things you obviously need to know now that you did not need to know before. Please don't say anything more on the phone. I will be there tomorrow night."

The line went dead.

I must be on to something . . . Mom would not be coming if there wasn't something there. Her meeting with Grace at nine thirty in the morning crossed her mind. *Grace knows, but will she tell the truth?* Betty put the picture album away. *What the hell have they been hiding from me?* As she was about to pull her hand away, another thought flitted by. *Wait a minute, there aren't any pictures of me before I was one! There are pictures of Rob and Bill in the hospital with Mom after their birth. There aren't any of me!* Betty pulled the first album out, the one with the oldest pictures. Beth had made duplicates from the negatives to give to each of the three kids—personalized albums focused on each child with an appendix of the other kids. Betty flipped to the back of her album. Sure enough, there were pictures of Rob or Bill having their diaper changed, but none like that of Betty. No pictures of her nursing with Beth; no stroller pictures until Bill was with her in the double stroller; no first step shot. Even her earliest photos were with a post-infant Bill. Betty did not exist in any photos until her younger brother was at least six months old: making Betty about one and a half years old. *This doesn't make sense . . . unless . . .*

Betty dialed her father's number. She rarely called him on his cellphone, but this was important and he always answered her call even when he was in meetings. The phone rang into Bob Thursten's voice mail. *Mom must have called him already, warned him not to talk to me!*

Betty began writing down a new family tree. *If I write it down, maybe I'll see what is going on.* Beth and Grace were sisters. Timmy Arthur was her cousin. Grace had a different last name from her mother's maiden name of Calvin. The only family-type picture with an adult male indicated that Tom Howell Sr. was Timmy's father, and Timmy looked enough like Tom Howell Jr. to be his brother, so Betty drew a connection to the Howells.

She stared at an early picture of the three siblings: Betty and Bill together in the stroller with Rob standing while holding onto the handle. Her skin color was more olive and her hair darker than the boys'—much darker than her fair-skinned parents. The family line had been that an earlier unknown relative must have been dark complected, causing Betty's coloring to come out recessively. Betty did not imagine her mom having an affair, and Beth had always said she looked more like her dad. *I really don't look like either of them, though, do I?* Her gaze bore into the past presented by the pictures. *That perfect past of two doting parents who encouraged me to try anything and run with the boys.* Her relationship with Jil now seemed like a correction set in motion by Beth to compensate for a feminine deficiency of Betty's, almost as a tutor on the finer social graces. *Why have I been so blind to this for so long?* She tried to calm herself. *I have to let this go. I can't solve it tonight.* Only a few hours from now, Betty was going to be meeting Grace as "Aunt Grace" for the first time. Until then, her top priority needed to be rest.

†

The climb down the stairs in the morning seemed harder than Betty imagined. *I cannot go in with guns blazing; I have to get Grace to tell me about my family. I will start by commenting on how much the picture looks like my mother, then connect to Tom Howell Sr. in the other photo.* A sinking feeling in Betty's stomach reminded her that the situation could turn ugly. Grace was a professional. She cleaned bad situations for the likes of Tom Howell Sr. and had hidden much over many years. What could Betty hope to uncover in a few minutes over coffee? She would have to find a way to slip some STP-17 into Grace's drink. Control had stolen the secret formula for the truth serum from the Russian KGB and added a little twist to make it work orally.

Betty pressed the doorbell. She could hear Grace coming to the door and checking the peephole to be sure it was Betty at the door.

"Well, hello, Betty! I'm so glad you were able to drop in," said Grace with a crocodile smile.

"Hi, Grace." Betty forced her own smile as she walked into the apartment. The layout was similar in shape but smaller than Betty's penthouse.

Grace moved to the dining room table and placed her hand on the coffee urn. "May I get you a cup of coffee, Betty?"

"To be honest, I could really use a vodka tonic about now. I've had one hell of a morning," said Betty, shaking her head side to side slightly.

"All right. It's a little early, but what the hell, I'll join you." Betty watched Grace move over to the kitchen and fill two cut crystal glasses with ice from the same freezer as the hand. Betty had a clear view of the kitchen and the refrigerator.

She grimaced at the sight of the pan that held the severed hand sitting next to the ice maker. The thought of a drink filled with that particular ice ran a chill up Betty's spine.

Grace poured the tonic from a bottle in the refrigerator and pulled a half-empty bottle of Absolut vodka from the kitchen cabinet. While Grace was preparing the drinks, Betty turned away to shake the thought of the gruesome artifact of the freezer and poked around looking at the photographs. *The pictures—what the hell? Rearranged? Where are the pictures of Mom and Tom Howell Sr? They're—gone! She "cleaned" her own house before I came here?* Timmy's table had been cleaned and the latest edition of Elle magazine graced the surface. The well-worn leather chair now had a feminine, red rectangular cushion. Betty sighed and thought, *This is going to be more difficult than I thought.*

"Here you go. Cheers!" said Grace as she *handed* Betty the drink and raised her glass in a toast.

Betty took a sip of the vodka tonic that thankfully lacked any discernible taste of flesh as she steeled herself for what was to happen next. "So, Grace, there is something I need to ask you about. Was your maiden name Calvin, by any chance?"

Thirty-Two

It's Back Again

July 13, 2009 — Caracas, Venezuela

GIL BURST INTO THE GARAGE Control had set up for the Caracas mission. Their equipment was spread out on folding tables, and Betty was going over each piece for the third time. Gil immediately began helping Betty prepare for the evening's adventure. "The vendor is in place. The food has been prepped with the laxative."

"What's going on with the weather?"

"Just some clouds. Perfect for a 'lightning storm'!"

"Those clouds just don't look right. Ops said there was going to be a moonless night, but I don't think they meant a rainstorm."

"The weather will be fine. Help me check the glider . . . time to head up the hill for the test flight."

Three hours later, Betty stared out over the horizon from the heights of the mountaintop overlooking Caracas, Venezuela. The test flight to check the air currents above the city of four million souls went as planned. After tying the tandem glider down on the Toyota Hilux roof, Betty lost her grip and slipped off the tire; Gil caught her gently with his rough hands.

"Your eyes have the most amazing hazel color," said Gil as he slowly placed Betty on the ground.

"You have the most unusual green eyes I have ever seen," she replied as her hands gripped Gil's firm biceps. "You were really solid up there on the glider. I felt like we were in sync." Betty stared at Gil's left eye, then his right, checking for variations in the starburst green. Gil's eyes radiated from a center of yellow green to a vibrant outer ring of green blue.

"I—" Gil started to say something when Betty leaned in and kissed him firmly on the lips. Tongues chased each other and darted in and out as hands grasped one another, Betty and Gil firmly locked together. Gil's right hand supported Betty's neck and head as his left drifted down her back, caressing her lower spine.

Betty gripped Gil's neck with one hand as she reached down and pulled Gil's ass closer to her. "Mmmm," she moaned slightly.

Gil slid his left hand lower to Betty's ass, gripping her firmly, sliding his right hand down her back to the other cheek. As Gil pulled her up, Betty jumped lightly onto Gil's hips, straddling her partner.

"We . . . I can't do this now . . ." Gil whispered into Betty's ear. "I mean, I want to, but I can't . . . not until after the mission. I don't want to blow this." Reluctantly, slowly, Gil lowered her to the ground. *I've screwed up every relationship I've had.* He tried to put her down, but she would not let go. *Maybe I can get this one right.*

"Do you mean the mission?"

"No, us." Gil pointed to the sky. While satellites tracked their moves via GPS-enabled phones, Control had a drone flying high above them with the ability to spot an object one square foot in size.

"I understand." She disentangled herself from the man she had been thinking about since he caught her in the dinghy. "We have plenty of time," she said, smiling as she tore her eyes from the green heaven and slowly turned her head away.

"Betty, are you ready for this?" Gil brushed a strand of her raven hair from her face so he could see her eyes. *I think I love you.*

"Who do you think you're talking to? This is not my first mission, Gil!" said Betty as she took a defensive stance.

"I remember when you got that scar . . . our first mission together." Gil stood with his hands on his hips and a snarky look on his face. During their first mission together, also in Venezuela, Betty had stopped watching the guard when she lost sight of Gil. The guard, an Islamist terrorist posing as a fundamentalist, slapped her; his ring cut deeply into her forehead, causing an injury that required stitches. She had recovered her composure and took the guard out. Gil now wagged his finger at her. "Don't get distracted like that time."

Betty swung her toe at Gil's shin but missed by an inch. Gil was not sure she missed because he reacted in time or because she pulled back a little bit.

"Whoa, now, wild thing! We're on the same side. I'm just trying to say I care. Don't do anything stupid—I don't want to have to rescue your ass again." But I'll die trying, Gil thought.

"You love playing hero, don't you?"

"It's a cute ass and worth saving, but . . ." Gil turned and walked toward the Hilux. "Mount up. Let's get this show on the road!"

†

July 31, 2009 — Somewhere in Europe

"Michel, I cannot explain it." Dr. Eric Salazar dropped Gil's arm after checking his pulse. Gil was sedated and resting. "The food is the same as the guard's."

"The antibiotics?" inquired Michel.

"No . . . no . . . there must be something else." The doctor looked puzzled as he racked his brain for a cause.

"You are the doctor, how is this possible?"

"He has no cuts or abrasions to explain the illness. It is most certainly some form of induced dysentery."

"When will we be able to do the operation?" Michel's face looked tense.

"Not until this dysentery is past. He is losing too much fluid. The IV will keep him under control, but his kidneys are working overtime," said Dr. Salizar as he adjusted the drip.

"How long has he been delusional?" asked Michel as he pried Gil's left eyelid back to check the pupil.

"He became feverish about thirty minutes after you started dialysis." He rechecked his watch for accuracy. "This is the third time he has had dysentery. Search his quarters again. There has to be something he is using to cause this."

Both men searched the small space several times more, looking where the other had repeatedly. Frustrated, Dr. Salizar began crawling on his hands and knees to see under every visible surface.

"Michel, under here!" Dr. Salizar lifted up a soiled rubber balloon that had been wedged behind the toilet.

"What is it, Eric?" asked Michel.

"This is no doubt what he has been ingesting to cause the dysentery. I thought your people searched him thoroughly." said Salizar.

"He would have had a small amount of time to hide it during transit before I got him to the plane. I don't know how he could have . . ." Michel's mind began to drift off as he imagined the only obvious hiding place for criminals and POWs. "No, I suppose we were not completely thorough—no cavity search." Michel rubbed his forehead aggressively as he tried to refocus his thoughts.

"It will be another week before he will be ready. You will have to continue on the dialysis until then," stated Dr. Salizar. "You aren't in renal failure yet. You still have time. Do not worry, my friend, it will all work out."

"I am counting on you. You know I have already paid the debt to your father." Michel looked to the heavens and silently asked for forgiveness, though he was not a believer. Insurance, perhaps, for the afterlife, if it did exist for him.

"Yes, I know you have."

"I have also given you everything you have asked for." Michel felt the need to emphasize that the younger Dr. Salizar was in his debt.

"And then some." Eric nodded solemnly.

"Don't fail me." Michel's upper lip quivered ever so slightly as fear crept into his mind. The fear that hell awaited him in the afterlife, and that every day gained on this earth kept his eternal debt at bay a little longer.

"Have we ever?"

"This is my son. I want him to live a long life; at least until you are able to generate organs like you claim," said Michel.

"Not to worry, Michel. That is only a decade away. The stem cell research is progressing nicely." Dr. Salizar lifted his left eyebrow and wryly commented, "I could try it out on you now if you like."

"I am a patient man, Eric; I will take his kidney and wait until the guinea pigs have proved your methods before I take that risk." Michel rubbed his lower back gently.

THIRTY-THREE

REMOTELY PAYING ATTENTION

July 13, 2009 — Control

"**D**AVID, ARE YOU ON TOP of this mission's next phase?" asked Howell as he came up from behind and placed his hand on David's shoulder.

"Yes, sir. I have the drone and satellite phone feeds linked. The GPS information is coming in," replied David.

"Where are they now?" asked Howell as he peered over David's shoulder at the screens.

"They are just leaving El Ávila. The glider test went well . . . but I am concerned." David tapped a screen to his left to show the drone footage of the flight while he fine-tuned the view on his right from a satellite phone feed.

"Exactly what is your concern, David?" Howell asked as David began the replay of the recent drone optical feed. "Hmmm, I see your point. Amazing."

"McFluffy has outdone himself again. If I understand it correctly, he stitched a thousand cellphone cameras into an array."

"Aye! There were a thousand and twenty-four, laddie." The meatball of a man, McFluffy himself, bounced into the room with an encrypted thumb drive for David. "Shove this into your system, Davie, and you'll really be spot'n some good stuff!"

"Enhanced?"

"Aye! You might say that." The thistle-bearded scientist winked, causing his caterpillar of an eyebrow to wiggle. "You can spot a budgie on a bramble."

After David loaded the latest software from McFluffy, the image on the screen became even sharper. "The resolution on these cameras—

good God!" David cleared his throat. "We're the only ones with this capability, right?"

McFluffy was already halfway out the door. "Aye, we are the only ones." His face became serious for a moment. "That boy wonder of ours, Bud. I couldn't have done it without him." His Scottish brogue had become easier for the staff to understand, or maybe McFluffy had simply trimmed his beard. "No one else has figured it out—yet." With a wink and what might have been a puff of smoke, the old master tinkerer disappeared around the corner.

David zoomed in on the clear imagery. The drone was flying seven miles above the operators, yet the smallest detail could be seen of their activities. "Sir, should we abort the mission?" asked David as he tried to turn his upper body around to look at his boss.

"I don't see why. This happens more than you would believe. Haven't you seen a 007 movie or two?" asked Howell with one eyebrow cocked. "Missions are dangerous and highly charged emotional affairs. These two have been working closely together for months. I had hoped they could keep it totally professional, but I'm also a realist. There is a chemical response to the adrenaline, testosterone, and estrogen floating around out there. They would have to be complete robots not to react. I'm not surprised." Howell wanted to add, but kept to himself, *That should be me down there with Betty straddling my waist! Damn leg.*

David stopped trying to turn around and instead used the mirror strategically placed on his desk to talk to his boss. He had to keep an eye on the screens while he talked or he would have turned his wheelchair around.

"Move Sanchez in close . . . just in case," said Howell. Sanchez was their Venezuelan equivalent to Grace. "If the team screws up, he will have to clean up any mess in a hurry." *Damn it, Betty, get your shit together, girl!*

"Yes, sir." replied David as he entered a code into the computer. The code initiated a text message to the secure phone in Sanchez's possession. The prearranged code was indecipherable to anyone monitoring the cellphone traffic. It was simply "2a," meaning move to the second position and await further orders.

†

Betty looked out the window of the Hilux as they made their way down the mountain. *Things are getting complicated. If I didn't know better, I'd say I was ovulating,* thought Betty as she felt her abdomen. *I'm not getting any younger. Only five more good years to have a baby, if I want one.* Betty shook her head to clear her thoughts. She could not think of children at a time like this. She could not think of children at all until her mission of extracting vengeance for José's death was completed. Howell had promised that this high-risk mission to collect intelligence would pay off personally for Betty—she would have the chance to find out who had killed José while unveiling the larger Cabal organization. Ernesto was the key: he knew the players and managed their money, and he alone could unlock the door to the vengeance Betty sought. *And if Howell gets what he wants out of the deal, all the better.*

"Are you even remotely paying attention to what I am saying?" asked Gil as he gave Betty a slug to her left shoulder to get her attention.

"Of course I am—you're just going over the details of the mission for the fortieth time and boring me to death!" retorted Betty as she slugged Gil back.

"Careful now, I might drive us off the cliff." Gil feigned jerking the wheel hard to the right as if Betty's hitting him could have doomed them to their deaths. "I was just saying, that if for some reason we're unable to meet at the rendezvous point, I'll be placing C-4 throughout the place. I will have the main detonator, but if you need to arm them, just slap the charge with your palm and you will have five seconds to get the hell out of dodge. The timer isn't going to wait; you can't leisurely walk away. Five seconds, you got it?" asked Gil.

"Are those the new timers from McFluffy?" asked Betty.

"Yes, these are Wi-Fi and GSM-enabled charges. I can detonate them, time them, or create a wave effect . . . anything we need. Can you believe there's an app for that?" asked Gil as he showed off his new iPhone, specially modified by McFluffy.

†

"Anything good on TV?" asked Howell as he pointed to a screen on David's right.

"They are just getting back into range for the edge feed," answered David. McFluffy invented the edge feed system using satellites and regional antennas. He had recently upgraded the communications grid to include drones, which Bud had helped program. For this mission, he had put small cameras in the dash for a 360-degree view. The camera system was connected via cellular towers with a satellite backup to ensure extended coverage. In the back country, a drone could be flown to retransmit the signal to the normal channels. While on the satellite feed, only snapshots came back to Control, whereas on the edge feed of the cellular connection, full-motion video was available. "Here it comes," said David as he turned up the volume.

The sound was tinny but slowly improved; the video feed was a bit choppy, but with so little action going on, it did not matter.

"Those clouds are coming in pretty quick. I don't like what I'm seeing," Betty was saying as she pulled out the binoculars to scan the horizon. "David, I know you're listening. What the hell is going on with the weather? It's supposed to be dry tonight, right? I mean, this isn't going to be like last time, right?" She still was pissed about the squall the night she had to drive a crappy, broken-down car with lousy wipers to breach Montoya's security, even if she did get to send a jolt into the guard using the jumper cables.

David reached for the mic button. "Uh, yeah, I'm here. The weather report is updating as we speak. Can't vouch for the earlier forecast. Hold on." He clicked his mouse several times to find the correct feed out of the six regional forecasts he was following. "We have a squall moving in off the coast. It will be mild with intermittent downpours. Shouldn't be a problem for a couple of pros like you two." David sounded more confidently than he felt.

Howell clapped his hands twice. "Listen up, you two, I need you to be focused and ready to improvise. No plan survives first—"

"—contact with the enemy." Betty interrupted Howell before he could finish, sounding perturbed. "We know! David, why didn't you tell us our fearless leader was with you?"

"Well, I suppose it's time for radio silence, then. Good luck. Bona fortuna," said Howell as he signaled David to cut the microphone.

"God, I hate it when he gets all sanctimonious on us!" Betty lashed out, knowing Howell would still be listening.

THIRTY-FOUR

MS. CALVIN, I PRESUME

August 6, 2009 — Old Town Alexandria

"**I**T WILL TAKE JUST A MINUTE for the drinks." Grace placed a large block of ice into a plastic tub and began stabbing it violently with a pick.

"You sure are going to a lot of trouble . . ." Betty began looking around the living room. *The pictures . . . they're missing! The chair and the table . . . everything has been cleaned; anything of Grace's past that connects her to me or Howell—gone.*

"I like to make my ice from distilled water," Grace grunted as she chipped away.

"Is there a difference?" *These pictures aren't the ones I saw earlier, but the frames are the same. Bizarre!*

"Oh, yes! The ice is clear and much better tasting than the city water." She was putting the chipped ice into the cut glass tumblers.

"Doesn't chipped ice melt faster?" *I didn't imagine those pictures. I know I'm not hallucinating!*

"It does," Grace agreed. Her thoughts seemed to wander until she finished with, "You're right."

Grace is hiding her connection to me. The connection is so strong that she had to switch the pictures out. "Couldn't you use a regular ice tray with the distilled water?" *Even the picture of Timmy is different.*

"But I like the look of the chipped ice, don't you? Here you go. Cheers!" said Grace as she handed Betty her drink and raised her glass in a toast.

Oh, my God! The ice came from the freezer with the hand in it! If I didn't need this drink right now . . . Betty took a sip of the vodka tonic.

No discernible taste of human flesh, so she knocked back a big swig and steeled herself for what was to happen next. "So, Grace, there is something I need to ask you about."

"Sure, anything." Grace gave a large smile as if she had swallowed the canary.

"Was your maiden name Calvin, by any chance?"

The smile left her face for a moment. "Calvin? No, my maiden name is Smith. My mother was Juli Smith. Why do you ask?" Grace asked as she tilted her head slightly.

"Oh, you just look so much like my mother."

"Thank you . . . I think."

"I'm probably misremembering, but I vaguely remember a picture of you and my mother on a dock . . . in front of a boat of some kind," ventured Betty.

There was a flash of something in Grace's eyes . . . a fire of recognition, like a caged animal trying to find the best way out of the trap. *Gnaw a paw off, pull hard, or cry for help . . . none of the options look good for you, Grace,* thought Betty.

"Bless your heart—you're too kind to think of me that way, to want me to be your aunt. Why, I would be delighted if it were true," replied Grace.

She won't take the bait, thought Betty. But I'm sure she knows I know the truth. Why does she keep denying it?

The two powerful women were performing a dance of words, weaving back and forth without a direct confrontation.

Betty pondered her next move. *I don't want to push this too hard . . . she is a force to be reckoned with,* she thought. "I'm sorry, I don't mean to pry or invent a connection. I suppose I have so few living relatives." She sighed for effect. "Actually, just my parents and brothers."

"You don't have any grandparents left?" Grace picked up Betty's drained glass. "Do you want another?" Grace asked with one eyebrow raised.

"You must think I'm an alcoholic!" Betty responded, now on defense. "No, thank you. Now I think that coffee would be the better choice." Betty noted that Grace's glass was just as empty as her own. "No, my grandparents are all dead, I'm afraid: breast cancer, heart attacks, the usual litany."

"No cousins, aunts, or uncles?" asked Grace, bustling to the kitchen.

I need to turn the tables here; I'm the one who is supposed to be asking the questions, thought Betty. "I have some distant cousins, but I haven't seen them in ages. What about you, Grace, what's your extended family like?"

"Well, I knew my grandparents, naturally, but they have passed on long ago. My mother and father died around ten years ago. I was the only child my parents had," said Grace as she handed Betty her coffee. "No cousins to speak of, at least that I know of. My mother kept to herself and my father was an only child. I suppose I leaned on my friends' families when I was younger."

"Me too!" jumped in Betty. "Oh, Grace, do you have any honey? I'm on this weird diet . . . trying to stay away from processed sugar." *I have to get Grace out of the room long enough to put the serum in her coffee*, she thought.

"Well, yes, I believe I do. Give me just a moment," said Grace as she started to get up with her coffee. "Can you have biscotti?"

"Yes, that would be lovely," said Betty, thinking fast. *She'll need both hands to get the biscotti. She can't take her coffee and bring back the honey and a nosh!*

Grace left the room with her coffee still steaming on the side table between them; the coffee, adulterated with cream, would easily hide any flavor of the truth serum. Betty slipped the vial from her waistband where it had been hiding; the vial cap pried off silently with her thumb, and the contents slid into the caffeinated elixir. She hid the vial safely back in her waistband before Grace could turn back to the living room with the honey and biscotti on a tray. After adding a dollop of honey, Betty blew gently on her sweetened coffee, and her voice turned silky smooth. "Thank you, Grace. It's very kind of you to find some honey for me."

"Oh, no trouble at all."

"I don't usually put anything in my coffee, but I've been craving sweets on this diet."

Betty forced herself to focus on something besides Grace's coffee. *She'll know I've done something if I focus too much or too little on the coffee*, she thought. *I have to wait five minutes for it to take effect.* "What is it like to manage the apartments?" she asked, wanting to start off with something that Grace would be comfortable talking about truthfully. *Not like the truth is her strong suit.*

"Well, it's like having an extended family, I suppose. I'm here to help when there are problems, when the tenants have their triumphs and failures." Grace stopped long enough to take a long taste of her coffee. The cream had cooled the brew enough to make it easy to drink.

Betty carefully observed Grace's physiology, watching for clues such as increased pulse, sweat beads, nervous ticks, or absentminded touching of her arm. These and other clues like blink rate, head tilt, lip wetting, and such were all indicators she learned during her training at Control. "Do you think it has made up for your lack of extended family?" probed Betty.

"I suppose it has, but I get to pick my tenants." Grace winked at Betty.

"I do like the idea of that, being able to pick and choose your family. Does it take much time to handle the apartments?" continued Betty as she blew on her coffee before taking a small sip. The vodka was starting to loosen the tension in her brain. Not so much that she lost focus on Grace, just a little more comfortable with talking to someone who happened to keep a severed hand in her freezer.

THIRTY-FIVE

PATADA EN EL CULO

June 23, 2009 — Caracas, Venezuela

B ETTY WAS BEGINNING TO PANIC a little. "There isn't
enough time."

"There's never enough time." Gil flung cabling, large
tools, splicing kits, and the like into the back of their new utility truck.
He smeared tar here and there, scraped the paint with his knife, and
knocked dings into the panels.

"Everything is last minute out here in the field," Betty swept a
heat gun over fresh paint.

"Not a bad job! You may have missed your calling."

"Gee, thanks." Betty aimed her tool at Gil's crotch as a tit-for-tat;
Gil jumped back several feet to avoid the searing heat.

Wet paint depicting the octagonal logo of La Electricidad de
Caracas, the local electric company, emblazoned the doors of the truck.
Applying heat would dry the paint quicker, allowing time for several thin
coats of paint to prevent runs. Vinyl lettering would have been easier and
preferable, but Betty was improvising; the technician who had created
the vinyl lettering introduced a couple of glaring typos into the Control
version of the logo: "Le" instead of "La" and "da" instead of "de." In a
few weeks, she and Gil were to break into Ernesto Montoya's compound
to question him. The cameras and security in general were a problem;
the utility truck and their uniforms would allow them to get close and
interact with the guards, discover procedures, and identify weak points.
Their cover included a story that the local substation was malfunctioning
and would need repair work immediately. Subsequently, Gil and Betty
would return to the bunker for additional briefings and planning based on
the information brought back.

For now, their new ride was ready to roll. Thirty minutes later, they were pulling up to the compound.

The guards were attracted to Betty's cleavage spilling out of her uniform. Her red-laced underwire bra pushed her breasts to the point of escape just for this purpose. Gil's fluency was not nearly as good as Betty's, so she kept herself between the guards and her partner— not a particularly difficult proposition, given her slutty disposition for this mission.

Just visible below the short-sleeve shirts of the guards were black dragon tattoos; the tails of the serpents arced low toward the elbows of their left arms, and the bodies of the ancient beasts graced their bulging biceps. The tattoos would look intimidating to most intruders—or perhaps it was the AK-47s the guards were holding. Neither in particular attracted Betty's attention. She had a mission to perform, and guns were no match for her abilities. Her charms and good looks were distracting enough to get close without showing a weapon or flexing her own muscles.

It was always more desirable to disarm and disable than to destroy. Destruction brought too much attention. Ideally, a security breach relied on detecting human weaknesses, and Betty was an expert at that, especially the male kind. She and Jil had spent many days shopping at the mall and drawing the attention from boys of all ages. Her exotic good looks gave beauty queen Jil a run for her money, even though Betty always felt inferior.

Betty put her charms to work as she approached the guards after getting their attention by slamming the truck door. While they were looking at her, Betty bent down to pick up a stray bit of copper wire on the sidewalk, her breasts straining to fall out of her uniform. In Spanish, Betty called out to the men, "You two need to be careful—thieves are stealing all the copper wire around here."

"Ahhh, we don't worry about basureros! Those garbage collectors don't come near our compound," scoffed the first guard.

"They know better than to come near here," added the heavier guard. "Now, beautiful chica like you? That is what we worry about!" The guard leered at Betty as he tried to suck his gut in a little tighter.

Gil came slowly out of the cab of the truck as if he did not give a damn about doing any work. The contacts he wore changed his eye color from vibrant green to muddy brown. The temporary black hair dye helped him blend in. "Let's go—lunch time," declared Gil in his rehearsed Spanish.

"¡Te voy a dar una patada en el culo!" Betty pantomimed her words by making a kicking motion in Gil's direction. Turning back to the chuckling guards in front of her, Betty continued, "We need to change out the transformers on this block. We are going to be turning the power off for at least six hours."

"No problem, we have generators. Do whatever you want," scoffed the skinny guard.

"Well, make sure you have enough diesel. I don't want you crying because the tank ran dry while we are eating our lunch," retorted Betty.

"Yeah, no problem, we have a dual fuel generator with an eight-thousand-liter tank, we can go for days. Just take your time and do the job right," said the guard with the slight paunch. "Just watch out for the basureros! They will steal your truck and your copper wire." said the guard, laughing.

Betty laughed with the guards and Gil chuckled slightly before saying, "Come on! Let's go eat."

Betty glared at Gil. "Go get in the truck, you lazy, good-for-nothing . . ." Turning back to the guards, she continued. "We will be here for a couple of days getting things in place. Any decent food around here?"

"Roberto comes around every day at noon; he should be here any minute now. He always has some of his wife's good cooking. Armando here cannot get enough of it!" The skinny guard pointed at his partner's expanding midriff.

"Te voy a dar una patada en el culo, Julio," said the heavier guard as he turned toward his partner. Apparently, Julio had struck a nerve.

"Armando, you are just pissed because your chica doesn't like your belly and won't do you no more!" teased Julio

Betty saw her opening and said, "I think it's kind of cute," she said, turning and walking away, swiveling her hips as she headed for the truck.

The guards stopped arguing to give this chica bonita their undivided attention as she climbed into the truck. If Gil had taken this opportunity to slip through the gate, he doubted anyone would have noticed.

As they drove away from the daydreaming guards, Betty summarized her thoughts. "Gil, I bet McFluffy could blow out their electrical system and the generators with a tricked-out transformer. Send a message to him with the pictures you took. Maybe we can get a crew in here in time."

"I could have walked in waving my arms the way they were screwed tight to you. Hell, you could walk up to them, flash a little tit, and I bet we both get in," declared Gil.

"I will pretend you didn't say that. If we need to use that as the backup plan, OK, but me flashing my breasts is not going to knock the cameras or the security measures out. They aren't that big!" Betty gave Gil a sneering scowl capable of causing spontaneous combustion in a lesser man.

THIRTY-SIX

FALLING GRACE FOLEY

August 6, 2009 — Old Town Alexandria

*J*UST A FEW MORE MINUTES *and she will be under the complete influence of the STP-17,* thought Betty. *Then I can start to ask the hard questions. But first, I need to ask questions I know she'll answer truthfully without hesitation.* "So you are your mother's only child. What was it like to be an only child?" asked Betty.

"Oh, I never said *I* was an only child. I have an older sister from before my mother married my father."

Grace's sudden reversal on the breadth of her family tree startled Betty. "You—you said your mother only had one child." *The pictures! Damn it! Why did she change the pictures?*

"I am the only child my mother had with my father. He died in the Korean War after I was born but before I could meet him," said Grace as she looked past Betty at her pictures.

Feeling a bit shaky, Betty hesitated, wanting to turn around to follow Grace's lost-in-the-past gaze, but it only lasted for a moment, so Betty pushed on. "What is your sister's name?"

"Bethany," said Grace with no hint of emotion in her voice.

The serum is working! She can't lie any more. "What is your sister's last name?" asked Betty with anticipation.

"Thursten."

"And her maiden name?"

"Calvin, after her father's last name," said Grace.

Betty felt both the thrill of being right and the utter agony of uncovering hidden folds in the fabric of her family. *All my life I've wanted a broader family tree and now I want to prune it!* "What is your father's last name?" Betty was not sure she wanted the answer, but she could not stop now; nor could she show any signs of wavering as she interrogated Grace.

"Foley, Jack Foley."

"What happened to him?" *Why is her maiden name different?*

"He was a marine first lieutenant. He died in the Chosin Reservoir," said Grace matter-of-factly.

"I thought you said your maiden name was Smith," said a confused Betty.

"Oh, it is. My mother and father did not have time to marry before he shipped out. Mother didn't know she was pregnant until after Jack left. I was his farewell gift, so to speak." Grace still looked into the distance, but she no longer seemed to be focusing on the pictures—or on anything, for that matter.

The serum has her now! "How was my mom's . . . Bethany's last name Calvin? I thought her mother's last name was Smith?" asked Betty, stunned.

"Oh, same reason. Bethany . . . Beth came about because mother married John Calvin the day he went off to join the marines during World War Two. He died during the D-day invasion." Grace's words began dragging with obvious pauses between thoughts.

"How old was your mother when she had Beth?"

"Mom was young, only sixteen when she got pregnant, but it was the war. John was leaving to die for his country. How could she not give herself?" asked Grace.

"Yes, how could she deny John that?" *Grandma played Russian roulette and lost that spin. Then again, I wouldn't be here if it weren't for John Calvin,* thought Betty. "Tell me about my mother."

"Oh, I never knew your mother." Grace looked back at Betty, focusing for a moment on her interrogator as if she was trying to remember something.

"Beth, my mother Bethany," prompted Betty.

"Beth isn't your mother. You were . . . adopted."

"Adopted?"

"Beth is Rob and Bill's mother," explained Grace with a furrow in her brow. "Don't you know this?"

"No, I didn't," said Betty as she stared at the knot in the pine floor at her feet. Her stomach churned with emotions. *Jesus, I was looking for information, but this is not what I expected.* Betty looked away, bit her lip, and began rubbing the web between her left thumb and index finger. Beth would scold her if she wrung her hands in public. By using her finger inside the envelope of her hands, her "mother" would not notice. "What happened to my parents?"

"Oh, your parents died . . . in a car accident. They were Bob Sr.'s handlers . . . for the KGB."

"The KGB?" asked Betty.

"A Spanish couple . . . if I remember correctly."

"The Russian KGB? What was my dad doing with the Russian KGB?"

"Not the KGB of Russia . . . the KGB of Bulgaria."

"Oh. I see," said Betty. *What the hell did the KGB have to do with my dad?* "Why did my father . . . why did Bob have a KGB handler?" asked Betty.

"He was passing . . . computer designs to the . . . commies," Grace started to seem a little spacey.

"Bob was a communist spy?" asked a stunned Betty, shaking her head to clear what could not be possible.

"Oh . . . well . . . not exactly. He was a"—Grace searched diligently for the correct words—"double agent, actually." Grace drained the last of her coffee to wash down the tail end of the biscotti. "Can I get you some . . . more coffee, Betty?"

"No, thank you." Betty's reality continued to shift quicker than she could keep up. *Adopted? My father is a spy? A double agent? What else could I possibly not know?* Betty's thoughts raced. *I need to pull it together here. If I don't settle myself down . . . I need to process this later!* "Who does my father work for? The CIA, NSA, the military?"

"Well . . . no. He works for us, dear."

Betty's look said deer in the headlights. Her mouth formed the word "What" but nothing came out of her mouth.

"Haven't you been briefed? Oh . . . I suppose not. Compartmentalization. No reason for you to know Bob works for Control if you didn't figure it out on your own," said Grace. Somewhere in the back of her mind, Grace knew she was saying things she should not, but she could not stop herself. It was a liberating feeling, but completely out of character. She had risen and gone to the kitchen to fetch the coffeepot. Returning, she stated nonchalantly, "I don't know why I'm telling you all of this . . . I usually keep these thoughts to myself!" She laughed as she shrugged her shoulders. "More coffee?" Somehow, Grace seemed in control of this interrogation despite the truth serum.

Passively Betty held her cup for Grace to top it off. Her mind reeled from the onslaught of new information, her former reality shattered, the past now open for reinterpretation. Which of her memories were real, and what was imagined or planted? *Who am I and how did I get to this point? Did I make these choices or was I set up?* Everything about being a secret agent seemed so easy to Betty: training, firearms, fighting, flirting, even changing tactics at the drop of a dime. Was it her destiny to be a spy? *I thought I just had a gift for this work. My fucking parents! Had they trained me from birth?*

The truth serum would start to wear off soon; another dose was not an option, plus Beth would be arriving in town at any moment. *Do I still call her Mom? Can't worry about what to call her just yet.* Betty needed to wrap things up and get out before Grace recovered her wits, since her aunt would never knowingly tolerate an interrogation. Best to be gone and allow the hollow memories of a casual morning drinking coffee to take hold. Betty took her coffee cup to the kitchen, rinsed it out, dried it, and placed it on the rack with the other dishes. There really was no other evidence that Betty had been here. Grace would remember that Betty had stopped by, but the conversation would be a blur, or so Betty had been led to believe.

"Grace, thank you so much for the coffee. You are such a good listener. I feel much better now. And thanks for being such a good friend!" *A nice warm and fuzzy exit. Give the feeling like I did all the talking. She won't even remember.*

"Anytime, dear . . . anytime." Grace closed the door behind Betty and threw the bolt.

"Holy shit!" said Betty under her breath. *Mom . . . or Beth will be arriving in a few hours. Not much time to figure this all out.* Betty gritted her teeth and scolded herself, *Always move forward.*

Thirty-Seven

Out from the Cold

"**B**ETTY, I CAN'T GIVE YOU this stuff. You don't have the clearance." Bud stammered his weak denial as he stared at the visage of Betty on his screen. For Bud, rules were made to be broken. He had a crush on Betty and had tried, unsuccessfully, 321 different ways to get a date with her. Evidence clearly indicated that either she had not noticed or what he had to offer needed to be changed. Bud was uncomfortable trading company secrets for his holy grail of a date; but he had come to realize that without such currency, he had no chance—thus all the more reason to give it a shot.

Control policy forbade office romance, but management often turned a blind eye to this particular human weakness. Anyway, in Bud's case, there was no romance, only desire. "What the hell! You're gonna say no anyway," Bud said as his pen wavered over his personal log book. A ledger of numbers encoded to denote the failures and lack of successes without context would mean nothing to anyone except Bud. This journal was for his eyes only and not something to keep on a computer, which could be hacked.

"Bud . . ." Betty started to counter, not quite sure what he was talking about. Perhaps it was the encrypted connection causing the loss of intangible information, the nuance of a word. *I swear he's about to ask me out on a date!*

"One date, guaranteed kiss at the door . . ." Bud asked nervously, not believing the sudden courage he felt, and before it could pass, he blurted out, "And I get to put my hand on your ass while we kiss." Bud was stunned he said the last part out loud.

"You think Line X is worth that much?" teased Betty, not sure if the kid even had the cajones to try putting his hand on her ass.

"Betty, if you're asking about Line X, then you know the public stuff French President Mitterrand released." Bud was visualizing the dossier in his mind. He had looked it over intently because of the geek factor.

"Sure, I know the details. We sent over faulty chip designs and rigged software to blow up the Trans-Siberian Pipeline. We also gave them the rejected shuttle design, but those aren't the details I'm after." Betty was trying to make it sound like the dossier was an afterthought.

"The U.S. didn't just send over faulty designs to blow stuff up or delay projects. Fully functional chips and designs went over as well. On purpose. Go ahead, you can guess why we did it and what our involvement was and kiss my ass. Or you can meet me and find out the real details." Bud was beginning to gain confidence in his newly discovered position of power.

What the fuck? thought Betty. *Did he just grow a pair?* "Bud, I don't really care about the details of the 'what.' I want to know the 'who.' What I really want to know is if Bob Thursten was part of the project."

"You're trying to get information out of me!" Bud exclaimed.

"Bud, Bob is my father. There are things out there bigger than me, you, or even Control. There are things I need to know." Betty did not like begging. It was not in her nature.

"We are all expendable here—you know that." Bud was getting nervous. Betty needed to set the hook or lose Bud forever as a source.

"Bud, you know the rules against fraternizing. If I ever hear you mentioned this to anyone, I will cut your balls off," Betty stated coldly.

"Wait—d-does that mean you . . . you agree to . . . to the terms?" stuttered Bud.

"When do I get the dossier on Line X?" Betty asked sharply.

"After I take my hand off your—your ass—I mean af—after the kiss. I will meet you at Five Guys, 107 North Fayette Street. Near your place, Thursday." Bud started to feel full of himself. He could get used to this.

"Bud, how do you know where I live?" Betty started to feel the burn of anger. *Who does this little shit think he is?*

"I . . . I'm the dispatcher for SCAT Cab Company. Didn't . . . didn't you know?" stammered Bud.

"You and I have a business date, Bud. There are some things you are going to tell me before you get that kiss. Do you understand?" Betty growled. *The things I have to do to get what I need!*

Betty had decided to search the Control database for information on Line X after her last conversation with Grace. She wanted to know as much as possible before asking Bud. There was the usual public information. Classified information for an agent of Betty's clearance showed the interconnections of the various spy agencies of France, Germany, and the U.S. involved in resolving the Line X espionage ring of the Soviet Union. The Soviets were far behind in generating the technology necessary to keep up with their enemies. Rather than develop their own designs, they sent hundreds of spies searching for specific technologies patented by the multinational corporations of the world. Colonel Vladimir Vetrov, an engineer by training, gathered this information from the spies in the field.

His mission was to evaluate and distribute the collected information to the appropriate people in Mother Russia. Earlier in Vetrov's career while working in France, a French businessman bailed him out of some trouble over another man's wife. Ten years later, after becoming disillusioned with the Communist regime of the Soviet Empire, Vetrov defected to the West through his French contact and divulged the compromised names and technologies. Rather than shut down the spy network, the U.S. began using it to send faulty designs back to the Soviets. One victory that was visible from space was the explosion of the Trans-Siberian Pipeline. The demise of the evil Soviet Empire was sped up by the loss of eight billion dollars of oil and gas revenue from Europe.

Between Grace's admissions that Bob Thursten had been sending information and designs to the Communists and the background of the Line X file, Betty was starting to see her father's role as something much larger. *I'm supposed to be at Control in two hours . . . no matter,* Betty thought. *I know which buttons to push. Howell won't mind me meeting with my mother; hell, he probably already knows.* Shaking her head to clear the noise of conflicting information, Betty exclaimed, "Madness, this is all madness!"

Thirty-Eight

Once upon a Dime

"WHAT THE HELL am I going to do?" Betty was nervous. She was pretending to be waiting patiently by flipping through old scrapbooks from her childhood. Fifteen years ago, Beth had compiled the books for the children. Pictures, cards, letters, mementos—little bits of the children's history that would have been lost to time if not preserved, items that meant little to anyone else. They seemed less important this morning, now that Betty knew her true heritage. The baby pictures looked contrived. The smiles and hugs— fake. Every situation now looked more staged than the snapshot of Betty and her "brothers" beneath the artificial Christmas tree. Her childhood indoctrination led her to believe she looked like them; comments about similarities now stood out. Focusing on these supposed similarities burst the bubble of perception. Betty was ready to throw away the evidence of the lie that had been her life, but these mementos had been the foundation of her family history. She would hold on to them until she could create a new, more accurate picture of her life.

On a page two-thirds of the way through the book, Betty spied a Mercury dime taped securely to the page with packing tape. Regular transparent tape would have sufficed to keep it secure, like many of the other objects in the book. Beth had used glue elsewhere, yet the paper lacked any signs of glue. Why would she have taken the extra precaution of using packing tape on the dime? *There is more to this than meets the eye, kind of like everything else in my life.* Betty pondered the dime. As she examined the page, she noticed the news articles radiating out from where the dime had been secured. A dim memory surfaced to explain the coin in her scrapbook.

Her father had given it to her when she was only five years old.

At the end of the day, they would go through his pocket change looking for silver coins. The U.S. stopped minting with pure silver after 1964 and stopped using forty percent silver for larger coins in 1967. Silver prices were at an all-time high when the Hunt brothers tried to corner the market in 1979. Silver had gone from six dollars an ounce to nearly fifty dollars an ounce by January 1980. At that time, the Hunt brothers' profits on paper totaled approximately $4 billion. The company Tiffany had placed a full-page ad condemning them:

> We think it is unconscionable for anyone to hoard several billion—yes, billion—dollars' worth of silver and thus drive the price up so high that others must pay artificially high prices for articles made of silver.

The commodities exchange, Comex, finally reacted to the outrage and danger of a cornered market by requiring the Hunts to put up an additional $100 million of collateral to back their bets. Their inability to meet the demand raised the possibility of default and caused a steep decline in the price of silver despite the eventual billion-dollar line of credit established to backstop the brothers. On March 27, 1980, the Hunt brothers' finances collapsed with the commodity price of silver.

Articles detailing the cornering of the silver market by the Hunts flanked the winged liberty head of Betty's 1945 silver wafer—articles that explained the minutia of financial exchanges. A typed note on the reverse side went into detail about the hidden forces laying in wait for the Hunt brothers. Shadowy figures who told the commodity exchange what to do and when. What punches to throw and when to pull them. Betty rubbed her finger across the typed page, feeling the bump of the dime under the paper. *Wait. . . there's an extra bump, a tiny round bump!* Betty turned the page over and fingered the packing tape, trying to decide how to remove the dime. In a sudden burst of purpose, she rushed to the kitchen junk drawer to get a box cutter. *I'm tired of not knowing! They've used me all my life, used me for their purposes. It's time I took control!*

The sharp razor cut the tape cleanly. She used the point of the blade to lift the tape away while holding the dime down. A moment later, the coin was free from its former prison and Betty carefully flipped it over exposing the fasces, a Roman symbol of authority made of rods surrounding an ax; on the U.S. dime, it symbolized America's willingness and strength for war. However, in ancient times it represented a judge's power to give the death sentence. Next to the fasces, on the right above the Latin phrase, *E pluribus unum* ("Out of many, one") was a small circle about a millimeter in diameter.

Betty put the scrapbook down to retrieve her magnifying glass, which was an heirloom from her grandfather, or so she was lead to believe. *I don't know what to believe anymore!* She passed the glass over the foreign object. *A microdot? I need a microscope. Damn it! Why don't I have a microscope?* Betty looked at her watch, the Rolex GMT-Master her Uncle Buck had given her when she graduated from Georgetown Law. He claimed to have worn it as an aviator during the Korean War. *Who was he really? Are any of my family, friends, or relations even real? Who can I trust?* More to the point, her mother would be arriving from the airport at any moment. There was not enough time to find a microscope and inspect the information on the microdot. It would have to wait. Betty carefully placed it into a small manila envelope that formerly held a safety deposit box key. Scotch tape secured the dime but made the discovery of the treasure obvious. *Did Mom put this here on purpose? How could it be anyone but her?*

"Time to put things away and get dinner ready," sighed Betty as she put the scrapbook back on the living room shelf, her finger sliding off the binding, tracing the spine as her mind wandered. Thoughts of her childhood raced through her mind. *Who was who? Secret agent or civilian? What clues from my past can help me now? So many possibilities . . . I have to get a grip here!* The shelf now had a path in the thin dust indicating the book's recent removal. Betty pulled her shirtsleeve down and used it to wipe the dust from the shelf. *Damn it! I just need to clean more often.* Betty patted the soiled sleeve on her jeans to knock off the dust. *Where are Dr. Seuss's Thing 1 and Thing 2 when I need them!*

A half hour later, as Betty pulled the tuna fish casserole from the oven, her doorbell rang. *Shit, Mom . . . Beth got here quick from the airport!* Betty began to hurry. As she turned to put the casserole dish on the table set for two, her hand slipped slightly from the hot pad, causing the 350-degree glass dish to sear her thumb. Startled, she yelled "Fuck!" as she dropped the dish; the hot tuna fish casserole splashed across the tile floor.

She was angry that her thumb throbbed with pain from the burn; angry her "parents" had lied to her all these years; angry that the woman at the door was not her mother, but the usurper who may have even killed Betty's actual mother.

Surry had been watching the food intently as Betty took it out of the oven and was quickly in position to help clean up the mess. "Surry! Back!" Turning toward the door, Betty shouted, "Hold on, I'll be there in a minute!" Surry found herself suddenly pulled back from her treasure and summarily escorted to the bedroom.

"Beth . . . Mom, oh, hell. I just dropped the casserole!" said Betty, sucking her thumb as she opened the door.

"Oh, honey, let me see," Beth reached for Betty's wounded thumb.

"I don't need you to look at it," scolded Betty. She tried to regain her self-control by changing her tone. "I just need to put some aloe on it."

"That's what I was just about to suggest." Beth furrowed her brow as she gave her daughter a hug and a kiss on her cheek. "I love what you've done with the place!"

"Thanks." *Do I even call you Mom anymore?* Betty looked pensively toward the kitchen and then back at Beth. "Let's go out to eat. It wasn't that great of a dinner anyway."

"Only if it's my treat!" exclaimed Beth.

"No, my treat, don't even think of reaching for the check," stated Betty sternly.

"Well, let's clean this up. Where's Surry? I bet she'd love to help," chuckled Beth.

"I put her in the bedroom. Oh, damn it, I need to ask you things we can't talk about in public." Betty scooped the worst of the disaster up with the dustpan while Beth searched for the broken shards of glass scattered on the floor.

"We'll order takeout then. Chinese?" asked Beth as she threw away several dangerous-looking pieces of casserole dish.

"Sure, the Dragon is just around the corner. The food looks and smells better than it is and they give you too much of the things that don't matter," Betty quipped. *Just like your parenting . . . I need to reel my emotions back in. It's time to start getting some straight answers!*

Thirty-Nine

First, Do No Harm

August 3, 2009 — Observatory Circle, Washington, D.C.

"**T**OM, YOU HAVE TO CHOOSE: either incapacitate her mind or terminate her employment. She is too dangerous to the organization as a loose cannon," said Tom Sr.

"I never wanted to recruit her in the first place! It was you and Bob. Always, you and Bob. He knew this was a possibility. How could he want this for his daughter?" exclaimed Tom Jr.

"Betty was not their daughter. She was adopted. Her parents were Bob's handlers for the KGB. They were Spanish nationals who died in a car crash when Betty was one. I'm surprised you didn't know this. It's not in her file, but you should have figured it out," scolded Tom Sr.

"That's not my point." Tom Jr. was getting frustrated with his father, as usual. "They raised her as their own. She may not have been their blood relation, but they treated her like one."

"Oh, they raised her right. They raised her to be an agent. The original thinking was she would be the perfect double agent to send back to the KGB, but by the time she was a teenager, it became clear she was headed for something bigger," said Tom Sr.

"What do you mean, 'something bigger'?"

"She's the whole package. Brains, looks, and brawn . . . or rather, the focused skill of a martial artist. The Thurstens raised her as an asset. She is expendable," stated Tom Sr.

"I think she can be brought back in. There is still time. She has not talked to anyone but Grace and Betty figured out Grace was one of us. No harm . . . yet."

"What part of this equation don't you get, son? She's a broken asset. She cannot be reeled back in. She's gone rogue, so put her down before she takes you down with her. If you cannot see to your own self-preservation, I can't help you." Tom Sr. shook his head and raised his hands up to show his frustration with his son.

"My self-preservation? Fuck you! Just because Betty's not playing by the rules—your rules—you want me to clean her?" Tom Jr., enraged, was stabbing into the table with his index finger, causing the dishes to rattle.

"I warned you *not* to get emotionally involved. You were just supposed to give her a mental checkup . . . see if she was ready to become an agent. You were not supposed to move in with her, let alone become engaged!" Tom Sr. stabbed his own finger into the table.

"We weren't engaged. I promised her I'd come back from Iraq . . . oh, what's the point." Tom was getting frustrated with the direction of the conversation.

"Tom, bedding her down was one thing—I could understand that—but to move in with her and woo her? You only needed to know if she was emotionally stable enough for missions, Tom, I warned you!"

"Yes, I was supposed to be as big of a bastard as you. I was supposed to follow her, make contact, and get to know her. I used the dog to do it, remember? I did what you wanted, I determined she wasn't ready, and when I reported that, you concurred. What was wrong with me keeping the relationship?"

"Because someday she was going to be all in, and you were going to be the one to manage her. Maybe not directly, but certainly indirectly. I think you have seen for yourself the problems that crop up when you're involved with an employee." Tom Sr. paused the lecture and stared at his now-chastised child.

Tom Jr. looked down at his plate. *The bastard is right, but I can't give him the satisfaction.*

Tom Sr. continued. "You've held her back. She could've been a better agent if you had not hamstrung her with your relationship. I agreed with Getner on cutting the relationship off, but damn it, Son, you never should've been in that situation. If you'd cut the relationship before going to Iraq instead of leading her on, telling her to hold out for more, she would've moved on and we could've brought her in while you were on assignment." Tom Sr. stopped to gasp for air before beginning to cough violently, spitting blood out into his napkin. Pain racked across his face as he attempted to rein in the fit before it shook his body apart. His rib cage was still tender from the cartilage he tore the previous week. This made the pain in his chest even sharper. "One of these days I'm going to break a rib doing that," rasped Tom Sr. as the coughing fit subsided, "if I don't die first."

"Father, do we need to call the doctor?" asked Tom Jr.

"No, there is nothing he can do but shoot me up with painkillers. I have what I need here—enough morphine to keep me from caring. Probably enough to end it, but you know I won't do that." Tom Sr. barely shook his head.

"Sadly, you won't, will you? You could save us all a lot of trouble."

"Call Barnes back. I think we're through for the day . . . you . . . I . . . I . . ." Tom Sr. passed out before he could finish the sentence.

Tom Jr. came around the table and checked his pulse and breathing. "The tough old bastard is not ready to die just yet," he muttered. Dialing the number for Barnes, Tom studied the yard outside the bulletproof glass of the dining room. The garden was immaculate; not a blade of grass looked out of place. Just as his father would not tolerate an agent going off the script, he would not tolerate a weed in the grass. *Survival has its price. The only ones left owe him their lives. Is this really how I want my life to end up? Using my children as tools to accomplish a mission? Everyone and everything expendable?*

Barnes did not say anything when he took the call.

Tom Jr. stated, "All done," and ended the connection immediately. Barnes would be by the old man's side in less than five minutes. *Someday, I'm going to look at Barnes's file. What could Barnes possibly owe him? Or what does dear old dad have on him?*

FORTY

BLACK NOIR

August 6, 2009 — Old Town Alexandria

MSG-LADEN COMFORT FOOD *may not have been such a good idea,* thought Betty, *or is it the job of interrogating my adopted mother making me feel queasy? Better get this over with.* "Why didn't you tell me I was adopted?" asked Betty pointedly.

Beth was suddenly defensive. "You're a smart girl, Betty. I thought you knew and didn't want to bring it up."

You're kidding, right? Betty sneered at Beth. "What kid doesn't want to know about her birth parents?"

Beth was buying time, unsure of where the inquiry was going. "Now, Betty, you're upset. I understand—"

"Don't mother me! Damn it! Just tell me the truth. Who were my parents?" Betty's terse reply caused Beth to sit farther back into the chair.

"OK, I'll tell you what you want to know." Beth adjusted herself in her seat as if she were settling in to tell a bedtime story. "Your parents were Spanish. Your father was attached to the Spanish embassy. We became friends about two years before you were born."

"How did you meet them?" Betty's tone softened. *She seems to be telling the truth.*

"The Spanish embassy was given a tour of the IBM facility that your father—Bob—worked in. He was working on advanced computer technologies that IBM was trying to sell in Europe. This was around 1972, I think." Beth looked over into the living room at the bookshelf. "You actually have a picture of your parents in the first scrapbook."

Betty stood up quickly to retrieve the volume from the shelf. Beth made no effort to move from her chair. *The scrapbook seems heavier than I remember. Heavy or not, the truth lies inside. Do I really want to know? How could I not want to know?* Betty placed the leather-bound book in front of Beth.

"Let me see . . ." said Beth as she flipped through the first ten pages. ". . . Here it is." Pointing to a black-and-white photograph, she said, "Peter and Isabella were very serious most of the time, but opened up nicely at parties." The photograph depicted a group of adults at a table in a restaurant, smoking, eating, and drinking. Young versions of Bob and Beth were sitting with Peter and Isabella, the women next to each other and the men sharing a story, cigarettes waving in the air. Flanking them, only half in the frame, was a fifth man who was standing to the side of the table. The smiles on the faces of the couples indicated they enjoyed one another's company.

Betty focused in on her birth mother, Isabella. It was difficult to tell much about the woman, seated behind a table as they were. Her hands were thin with long fingers. *Her eyebrows, were they dark and full like mine? If she's my mother then they were obviously plucked to make them narrow and precise.* Isabella's hair was coiffed in a late '60s style, similar to Audrey Hepburn's *Breakfast at Tiffany's* updo: her black hair in a French twist and a cigarette between the first two fingers of her right hand with her ring finger and pinky curled toward her palm. Isabella's right elbow was planted on the table with her left hand cupped around; a slight, knowing smile, almost a look of desire, as she listened to Beth talk. *A racy story? Perhaps a party they were going to after dinner? What is she thinking?* Her father, Peter, had slightly wavy black hair combed back and held in place with Brylcreem. He looked a little like Antonio Banderas: swarthy skin, prominent chin, and sculpted cheekbones. He also looked very happy.

"Peter doesn't sound like a Spanish name," questioned Betty.

"Oh, his parents were Marxists. They named him after Lenin," explained Beth.

"Wait—Vladimir Ilyich Lenin?"

"Yes, but he went by Peter in America. His little joke."

Betty scrunched up her face, not getting the inside joke. "What?"

"Peter the Great. He thought it was hilarious." Beth subverted a smile and laugh at Betty's fierce look.

"Where was this taken?" Betty inquired as she turned back to staring intently at the photograph, trying to peel the years back.

"We were at the Copacabana in New York." Beth looked wistfully at the photo, seemingly remembering a time of happiness.

"The Copacabana? I can't place how I know that name." Betty squinted at the photo as if she could see something that was not there if she just tried a little harder.

"You've seen *Goodfellas*, the restaurant that Henry Hill takes his date to—the one where they go through the kitchen to get to the dance floor." Beth sighed. "That was the place to be at in New York back in the day."

"How did you get in?" Betty seemed surprised that her parents could actually be hip.

"Now, Betty, Bob, and I were not always so 'square.'" Beth actually made the shape of a square in the air with her index fingers. "Peter knew Tony Lip, the maître d'. He is the other man in the photo. He was sitting down with us for a moment just before the photographer came over. He didn't want to be in the photo, so he got up to leave."

"Tony Lip? Wasn't he in The Sopranos?" asked Betty tilting her head as if it would clear her memory.

"And *Goodfellas*," added Beth in a smug voice. "It was a crazy time."

I need to get her back on track fast. "Why was Dad—Bob giving computer designs to the Russians?"

"Betty . . . you're putting me in an awkward position. You—you aren't supposed to have this kind of information," Beth stammered as she tried to regain control of the conversation.

"He was a double agent, sending faulty designs to the Soviet Empire. He was feeding the Line X agents. I know a lot, but I want more."

"I'm not sure I can tell you much more, your fa- . . . Bob is the one who knows details. I'm just on the periphery, you know?" Beth was sidestepping the issue.

"Were both my parents spies? Were they the handlers for Line X?" Betty looked at Beth rather pointedly.

"OK. I will tell you what I can and no more," said Beth with the tone of a mother who has given up protecting her young. "You know that they will kill you for digging where you don't belong, don't you? Lord knows I tried to protect you, to keep you from this life. Didn't I prepare you to be a professional? Aren't you at least grateful for all the hours I put into your education? Damn it! I raised you as my own child, my own daughter!" Beth slammed her fist on the table, scattering the unattended fortune cookies and sauce packets.

"Beth—Mom . . . I know you gave me more than I would have had in an orphanage. You gave me an amazing education—some would argue the best possible—but I fought for everything I got. I had to fight Bill and Rob every day for your attention." Betty was not going to let herself get defensive. "Don't you dare tell me that I got more than I deserved!" A tear was at the corner of Betty's eye. *Damn it! I am not going to cry!*

"Yes, you fought the whole way. Sometimes with us and some-times against us. I'm not sure how I survived some of the rounds in the ring with you." Beth stared at the overturned, half-eaten boxes of Chinese food on the table. "Can you forgive me for my mistakes?"

I am not going to let her manipulate me! "Of course I forgive you for your mistakes, just as I hold you accountable for manipulating me when you did." *I need to get her back on track.* "What were your orders regarding me?" demanded Betty.

"We were to raise you as our own; to train you to be a spy without your knowing it. You were to be a natural, trained from birth." Beth's chin rose, and a haughty tone crept into her voice to match her pose. "Your success would be dependent on a broad education and a fighting spirit. I think I succeeded in my mission. Of that, I am proud."

Betty heard the muffled sound of a metallic click under the table, the sound of Beth cocking a gun. "Oh, I have a fighting spirit alright," countered Betty, who had been pushed too far. She slammed the table into Beth's gut, tipping Beth's chair over, and spilling the woman onto the floor. A gun flew from Beth's hand as she tried to recover her balance. Betty pulled a knife from the counter and charged forward, kicking the gun out of Beth's reach. "Damn you, bitch! I should kill you right now!" screamed Betty.

FORTY-ONE

OVER THE CLIFF

August 1, 2009 — Somewhere in Europe

"GIL, YOU REALLY MUST LEARN to behave better. I cannot have you trying to hurt yourself. If you keep giving yourself dysentery, you could die. Now we cannot have that, can we?" Michel let go of Gil's hair, dropping his head into the pillow. Gil was strapped down to his cot and unable to move his arms or legs. "Is this the way you want to repay me for saving your life? Yes, you're right, they were going to kill you after they got what information they could from you."

Gil hacked and spit at Michel, landing a large loogie on his father's lapel.

"See how you treat me?" Michel pulled his hand back as if to slap Gil across the face. "You know I will not hit you, not when you are so close to being ready to help me." Michel leaned back and gave a hearty laugh that weakened quickly. His face grew pale from the exertion. "You won't be escorted. I know that is what you want. You want the chance to subdue one of us and use that to your advantage. Do not bother. We will shoot any guard who lets you get the upper hand. From now on, you will be restricted to bed and will be using a bedpan."

✝

August 6, 2009 — Old Town Alexandria

In Beth's new position, hands pulled behind her back and secured to her chair, she seemed to change her attitude. "Betty, you don't know what you're doing!"

A gag hung below Beth's chin, which Betty pulled up over her mouth. "Shut the fuck up!" Betty pushed the chair hard enough to spin Beth away from the table and against the wall. *I tried to play nice. Time to get the truth serum back out.* Betty pulled out a black clutch with a syringe and a bottle inside. She used an alcohol wipe to sterilize Beth's arm. "So, you don't want to cooperate voluntarily, so be it." Betty violently wrapped and tied a rubber hose around Beth's bicep, snapping the elastic material to make sure it was snug. *I hope that leaves a mark.* "We'll do it the hard way." After locating a vein, she jabbed the needle with quick precision. Betty plunged the truth serum into Beth's vein and pulled the needle out. Beth flinched but did not resist. "That should only take a minute. Too bad you might remember what led up to this . . . unfortunate turn of events. I'm not sure what the next step will be from here. You shouldn't have pulled a gun on me, Beth."

Beth's cellphone rang. Beth glanced at Betty. She looked like she would give her left arm to hold the cellphone in her right hand; forcing herself to regain control, as she turned away from Betty, she slowly shifted her face into a mask of calmness. *Either the serum is kicking in or Beth knows who's calling her.* Betty reached into the purse and took out the phone. The display read "ICE" and the area code 585, which would indicate the number was from Rochester, New York.

†

August 3, 2009 — Observatory Circle, Washington, D.C.

Barnes rushed in, pushing past Tom Jr. to quickly listen to Tom Sr.'s chest and feel for a pulse before turning back and glaring at the son. Barnes opened a medical kit and made several quick injections into the old man's neck. The pale skin seemed to change from a waxy white to a light pink almost immediately. Barnes tossed the needles in a clinical fashion into a biohazard container.

"Is he all right?" Tom asked, pausing before heading out the door.

"Your father is not well. He is not long for this world and the medicines have a shorter positive result each time." The butler sounded as if he were reciting a medical pamphlet, describing the drug to a layman.

"I'm sorry if I got him too excited, but he brings it on himself. I think he is looking for a confrontation with me. I think he wants to die."

Tom looked at his shoes and then back at his father's caretaker.

"It would be best if you did not come back for two weeks. Nevertheless, he will expect you next week as scheduled. It may be your last meeting. Make it worthwhile, Master Howell."

Tom's cellphone was ringing. It was David. Odd. . . David should have just texted a message. He would know that Tom was at his father's house from his phone's GPS. *Oh, hell, I'm not going to find a more secure location to take the call.* "Yes."

✝

August 3, 2009 — Somewhere in Argentina

"Michel was the one who killed the guards and stole the prisoner." The man in black military commando clothes stood at attention in front of the desk of Ernesto Montoya.

"Well, the old bastard is not ready to pass on to his good night." One by one, Ernesto was turning the pages of a report. He did not look up at his head guard. The men changed from time to time, but there was no real difference. He called them all Max, the name of the first guard. "My God, that was thirty years ago." The current security man knew better than to respond to Ernesto's verbalized thoughts. The original Max gave his life willingly thirty years before, by jumping into the path of an assailant's bullet. Ernesto was sure the new Max was equally prepared, but the act would be less noble with the latest body armor. "Best not to dwell on these things." Ernesto closed the report and asked, "Do we know their current location?"

"We have traced them to Belarus, possibly Minsk. We are searching." Max did not even look down at Ernesto; his eyes stared straight ahead, above the balding head of his boss. If this conversation were taking place in the open, Max would be scanning from side to side without ever looking directly at him. Finding and eliminating threats was his primary mission.

"Michel is not a threat, but we cannot allow him to get away with this—transgression." Ernesto tossed the report aside and looked directly at Max. "Can we?"

†

August 3, 2009 — Washington, D.C.

"Miss Harper, you have let us down. Why didn't you tell us about your relationship with Betty Thursten?" asked the voice with the Danish accent.

Jil held the phone tight against her ear; the wind was strong and making it difficult to have a conversation. Cupping the phone with her left hand, she kept the whistling sound from irritating the man on the other end of the phone. "What do you mean by 'relationship'? I've known Betty since we were children. I assumed you knew. We were roommates when you first made your presence . . . known."

"We are referring to Ms. Thursten's clandestine activities. She seems to be more than you have let on. Are you trying to help her?" questioned the silky voice from far away.

"I have no idea what you're talking about. Betty is an immigration lawyer. Sometimes I help her get a client special access. I've forwarded the information on the clients to your office. I'm not hiding anything from you!" Jil was getting nervous. These people did not care if you screwed up due to ignorance; they meted out punishment just the same.

Suddenly the voice spoke icy words intended to run shivers through Jil's spine. "Jil, be so kind as to find out what your friend is up to? Be a dear and poke around—with those delicate little hands of yours. You know how we hate surprises."

Forty-Two

Strained Relations

August 6, 2009 — Old Town Alexandria

BETTY TRIED TO IGNORE the incessant chirping of her own cellphone. By the ringtone, she knew it was Bud Stux. *Why can't the little geek just text me?* The STP-17 was about to be fully effective; there was not time for idle chat with Bud. *God, he probably thinks he's my boyfriend now!* "Crap!"

"Mmmfff." Beth's habitual attempt at correcting Betty's language fell short.

Just as the phone stopped chirping, it started again. *He is not going to stop until I answer. What the hell could be so important?* Betty grabbed the phone off the counter and stared at the display until it stopped ringing. *No messages. Bud had called five times already.* As soon as it started chirping again, Betty took the call. "This better be good!"

"What took you so long to answer?" Bud was whispering. "I have important news. I can't tell you over this connection, though."

"Then why are you calling me incessantly?" asked Betty sternly.

"If you had picked up earlier, I could tell you!" Bud was speaking very quickly, as if he needed to get off the phone before someone overheard him. "Call me in five minutes at this number."

"I'm kind of busy right now. What is this about?" Betty was annoyed and began ticking off in her mind a short list of all the issues she was dealing with. *My "mother" is ready to be interrogated; my true Spanish parents died in a mysterious car crash while working as spies for the Russians so my surrogate parents trained me as an asset that is expendable; my fiancé José was murdered; Tom is a spy who has been using me and may have killed my fiancé; my "aunt" lives downstairs with a severed hand in the freezer and works as a cleaner for the same secret spy group as me; my best friend is working under duress for the people I'm tasked with defeating; Gil is probably dead and buried in a shallow grave because I was not smart enough to get us both out and I'm pregnant with his baby; and I'm fraternizing with a computer geek to get information about my adopted father who I suddenly don't give a damn about. What on earth could be all that important?*

Bud must have turned a corner and was free to talk for just a moment without being overheard. "Gil survived." Click. The connection ended.

Her world turned upside down. Dropping hard onto a kitchen chair, Betty stared past Beth out the window at the Potomac River. There was a knock at the door, and Grace was calling for Betty to come open it. Surry was barking in the bedroom, pawing at the door. Betty's phone began to ring and this time it was Tom calling. Betty suddenly felt nauseous. Tears began running down her cheeks. She placed her hands on her womb, feeling the sudden contractions of her uterus. Something was not right. Nothing was right. Her world was collapsing around her with little to hang on to. *Gil. I'll hold on to being with you again.*

"Betty, is everything OK?" The muffled sound of Grace's voice from the other side of the door called. "I heard quite a commotion—I'm worried about you." Grace used her manager's key to unlock the deadbolt and the doorknob. The security chain kept her from getting all the way in. "Betty, are you OK? I'm really worried about you."

"I'll be all right." Betty got up from the kitchen chair and moved closer to the front door. "But I think I'm losing my baby." Betty needed to stall. "Come back in a half hour if I don't come get you, OK?" Grace could not find her sister tied up in the kitchen. That would be hard to explain.

"Betty, you should let me in—you could hemorrhage! Let me help you!" pleaded Grace.

"I'm OK, Grace. Really, the worst is over. I'm sure of it. I will call you in a bit. I promise." Betty urgently needed to get to the bathroom.

"Do you have anyone with you? You should have someone with you."

As Betty edged to the door, she thought, *Strange. Grace seems to know that Beth is here. No . . . I'm just reading into things now.* "Bye,

Grace. I'll talk to you in a little bit." Betty placed her shoulder into the door and threw the deadbolt. *Not that it would stop her, but this may slow her down.* Betty propped a wooden chair under the doorknob and hurried off to the bathroom, letting Surry out to guard the door as she passed the bedroom. Grabbing the garbage can to throw up in, Betty sat on the toilet. The contractions became intense. The taste of her lunch on the way back up was enough to put her over the edge. Betty spewed vomit into the trash can. Tears streamed down her eyes, the taste of bile, betrayal, sorrow, and loss combined with the knowledge that Gil had survived, mingled into a potent mix.

Somewhat recovered, Betty washed her mouth out, flushed the toilet, and moved on. *Time to go.* Betty went to her closet and grabbed her bag. She always had a two packed in case of an emergency: one for work and one for espionage. Betty grabbed the tiny manila envelope with the microdot, her cellphone, and Surry's leash. Surry was going to have to spend some time at the kennel. *I'm going to have to travel light and might not be back anytime soon. No, not the kennel. I can't let Grace get her.* Surry began licking Betty's hand. *But who can I leave her with?* Surry nuzzled her as if she was trying to tell Betty something. *Margaret! She'll take care of my girl until I get back!* Betty slipped Surry's leash over her neck, removed the chair, and reached for the deadbolt. Surry began to sniff loudly and growl at the door.

Grace was outside the door again. "Betty, I'm worried, are you all right?"

Jesus, did she even leave? "Grace, I'm going to the doctor's office. Can you back up? Surry's very protective right now. I don't want her to hurt you," Betty lied. She sure as hell wanted Surry to take a bite out of Grace, but could not afford the distraction right now.

"Oh, OK good, I'm glad you're going. I'll take the stairs so you can take the elevator. I'll push the button for you right now." Grace actually sounded concerned.

"Thank you, Grace!" Betty did not want Grace seeing her bags. She put the spy duffel back in the closet after removing some papers and her passports. *This is way too much stuff to explain. I can get new tactical gear anywhere.* Betty peered out the door to make sure Grace had left. Looking back over her shoulder, she could see that Beth was beginning to stir. The serum was wearing off. "Holidays are going to be awkward

. . . oh well," sighed Betty as she began her exit. *Nothing here I ever have to see again. These memories are replaceable. Nothing was real anyway!*

Betty's phone began ringing again. *Tom! Damn it!* "Yes."

"You need to come in. There have been some issues and new developments. We need to talk. Now." Tom spoke firmly, half asking, half ordering.

"I have to go to the hospital right now. I just miscarried. I will come in when I'm released," lied Betty. *This should stall them. Give me time to sort things out.* Call-waiting signaled that Bud Stux was trying to call her again. "I really have to go." Betty hung up on Tom and took Bud's call. "Bud."

"Why didn't you call me? Never mind. Gil is a captive in Denmark. I tracked him down through a shipping company in Minsk. They hid him in a shipping container that had foam sprayed over it to hide it. Pretty clever, really." Bud seemed to be pausing to take a breath.

"Slow down. You found Gil, or a trace of him. Do you know where they're holding him?" probed Betty as she rode the elevator down to the first floor.

"Of course," Bud stated as if Betty was questioning his ability. "He's in a warehouse next to the shipyard."

"I'm going off the grid. I'll have to get a new cellphone. How can I contact you?" asked Betty.

"Tweet me. It's @stuxboy. No one knows about that account. Be careful, Betty—they are on the cusp of terminating your contract. Tom is the only one keeping them from canning your ass!" He hung up before she could ask him anything else.

Betty dropped the phone into the gap between the doors and the wall of the elevator shaft before walking outside with Surry. *Unbelievable!* The usual driver was waiting for her in his SCAT Cab Company taxi. He turned his duty light on as she walked out the door. *I can't risk taking that cab even if Bud is the dispatcher!* A Mercury cab was driving by in the opposite direction. Betty whistled a shrill sound with her fingers in her mouth. The cabbie looked over and braked hard. Betty ran to the cab. The SCAT driver jumped out of his cab in pursuit, but Surry growled violently at the man, snapping at his crotch, allowing Betty to get her bag into the Mercury cab. Surry backed into the cab and the startled driver drove off.

"You got a problem with that guy?" The driver had a pensive look. He was of Middle Eastern descent with a large scar across his cheek. The name on the cabbie's license said Hamid.

French accent—Moroccan, perhaps. "No, no, he and I had a fight over a lost bag."

"You're not gonna try to skip out on my fare, are you?" asked Hamid as Surry growled slightly. The cab headed north toward the capital area.

"I called his boss and he's pissed at me. Listen, I need to get to Maryland. I have two hundred dollars here for you." Betty tore the bills in half and gave the cabbie half of the pieces. "Don't call this in. And turn off your GPS. I'll give you one of the halves when we cross the state line and the other half when we get there."

"Lady, I can't turn off the GPS, they will fire me," pleaded Hamid.

He didn't complain about the price, thought Betty. "I will give you two hundred more to cut the cable. Now."

"Fuck! Three hundred more, but I want the bills in one piece." Hamid pulled a knife out from under his seat and held it up for Betty to see.

"Fine." Betty passed the bills through the sliding Plexiglas opening and the cabbie cut the cable to the GPS unit.

"Address?" he asked.

"I'll tell you as soon as we get close. Take 95." Betty was keeping all her cards close to her chest.

FORTY-THREE

CLEANLINESS IS NEXT TO GODLINESS

August 6, 2009 — Control

"**I** THINK YOU BETTER TAKE this call." David pushed the phone toward Tom.

"In a minute, David, I'm trying to get Betty to pick up her phone. She's still home, according to the GPS signal." Tom slowly lowered his cellphone when he saw the number calling on David's phone. It was Grace.

Tom pushed a button. "Yes, Grace, Tom here, I have you on speakerphone for David."

"She's gone. Beth's tied to a kitchen chair. Did Harvey get her?"

David read a report on his screen and shook his head no. "Harvey says Betty took a different cab, a Mercury Cab number 8975. That dog of hers tried to eat Harvey's family jewels for dinner."

"Tom, do you want me to clean up here?" asked Grace with a hesitant tone.

"I think I know what you are asking, Grace. Put Beth on the line, please," said Tom

"Tom, why am I still tied up? Please ask Grace to let me loose," pleaded a spacey-sounding Beth.

"Beth, what happened?" asked Tom, perturbed.

"She—I pulled my Glock from the holster. I was going to capture her as you requested or . . . terminate her, if necessary. She kicked the table into me when she heard the gun cock. She went berserk, Tom!" Beth's voice sounded shaky.

"Beth, what did you tell her? This is important."

"She drugged me, but I don't remember her asking me any

questions. I . . . things are all muddled up—I don't know . . . I can fix this. I'll find her and . . . I'll talk some sense into her. I raised her . . . I can fix this!"

Grace's voice chimed in. "I think Betty had a miscarriage when she started the interrogation. There was a maxi-pad wrapper in the trash and vomit as well." She sounded robotic. "She took a bag with her but left her tactical gear, though her passports and miscellaneous paperwork are gone. The dog is with her or I would have stopped her. I thought Harvey would scoop her up. I'm sorry for not stopping her—that dog is vicious."

"Grace, take me off speaker phone." Tom needed a moment to decide what to do. *Father would terminate Beth. Tie up all the loose ends—or would he? Beth and Bob are years past their original termination date. The Line X double-agent role saved their lives. They were not supposed to live this long. They've no value if they can't control Betty and they're a liability if she turns them. What's Betty trying to accomplish?*

"Tom? Hello? Are you still there?" asked Grace.

Tom took the handset off speaker. "Grace, Beth is your half sister. You know her better than anyone. It is not usually your job to make a decision like this, but I don't know anyone better suited. Clean this up however you see fit, then let me know the details when you are finished." Tom ended the call and looked away from David. *Fuck! I can't delegate this. I don't want to kill Beth, so I tell her sister to decide? To think I call my father weak!*

"David, get Harvey on the line. Get a chopper in the air to back him up on the chase. Figure a way to track her without the GPS since she dumped her phone. Damn it!" Tom slammed his fist into the counter-top making the phone and keyboard jump.

"I'm already on it, Sir. Harvey lost them, but they headed toward the capital via George Washington. I'll start the search there. Harvey is in pursuit but can't be too aggressive; he has a state trooper in sight." David efficiently read the list of actions and reactions in progress. When he finished the list, he looked to his boss for direction.

"Call in a bank robbery to get the trooper out of there." Tom was thinking on his feet. *Do something! Anything is better than nothing!*

David put a call on hold and gave Tom a number two with his

fingers as he picked up another call. "Bud, I want a 911 call into the Virginia troopers for a possible bomb near Ronald Reagan Airport . . . No, two minutes ago."

✝

"Beth, what an interesting situation we have here. Makes you think, maybe you should have been nicer to me when we were kids, doesn't it?" cooed Grace with a wild look in her eyes.

"What do you mean? Grace . . . you wouldn't!" Beth did not like being in a corner. The binding was hurting her wrists; the swelling of her flesh had made the rope even tighter. She was shaking and beginning to cry.

"You were always the weaker one, Beth. I learned the hard way to be strong. I never told you about your boyfriend Ralph, did I? Remember when you wouldn't have sex with him?" Grace edged closer to her sister.

"You know what Mother put us through. I wasn't going to get pregnant and be left with a child to raise on my own!" Beth's objection seemed hollow.

"Remember when you were babysitting me and left him in charge?"

"I only left you with him for an hour. Mother called and needed more money for bingo. You didn't say anything happened. He and I made out afterward, he was a gentleman, and he didn't even try to grope me!"

"He raped me, Beth. I was only ten. Ten years old, Beth. I couldn't stop him. No. But I learned to be strong. Didn't you ever wonder why the police never found his body?" Grace started to laugh manically.

"Grace, I didn't know, I swear! You can't—how could you?" Beth pleaded, then let out a bloodcurdling scream as Grace came closer. "No!"

✝

"Grace, we lost her. Do you have any ideas?" queried Tom, avoiding the question he really wanted to ask.

"No, Tom. I told you everything I know." Grace's icy calmness eerily denied Tom the knowledge of what she may or may not have done.

"What did you need to clean up? Any complications?" asked Tom, not really wanting to know the answer just yet.

"Tom, I cleaned the apartment so it looks as it should. I didn't find any paperwork to indicate Betty's destination." Grace seemed to be avoiding something.

"What else, Grace? Any indications of tampering?" Tom pushed on.

"Her scrapbooks. They've been gone through recently—the dust is disturbed. It's hard to tell, but something is cut out of a hiding place from the one they had been looking at." Grace's tone was clinical, her pronunciation precise, almost mechanical.

"What about . . . Beth?" Tom's hesitation revealed a weakness his father would disapprove of.

"I've taken Beth to my place and have her sedated. She may be able to help me understand what's missing. She made the scrapbook."

Perhaps Grace is not the perfect cleaner after all; maybe she does have some humanity left, thought Tom. "What are your plans?"

"I think I need to clean her after I'm finished with her. I know you asked me to decide because you didn't want to, Tom," said Grace pointedly.

"Grace, do as you see fit. You're on the ground. however, I will make the decision if it helps." *She sees right through me,* thought Tom.

"I think she is salvageable, even if she deserves to die. I'm going to give her electroshock therapy. She won't be able to remember what happened. We'll have to keep a close eye on her for a while."

Grace is as cold as they come. "See, that's why I deferred to your expertise. Very well, keep it simple." Tom was relieved.

"Simple would mean cleaning her right now, but I know what you mean, Tom." Grace hung up the line.

FORTY-FOUR

MOST EXCELLENT

August 6, 2009 — Vail, Colorado

THE VIEW UP THE MOUNTAIN from the second-floor condominium unit was stunning. The Aspens were just beginning to change color around Vail. The lodgepole, blue spruce, and Colorado pinyon stayed green year round, but the pine-beetle epidemic had hit the ski slope hard, with most of the blighted trees thinned out. The yellowing of the remaining affected trees gave the slope the unnatural appearance of a fall color change. The green grass clinging to the side of the mountain was just visible past the mottled hue of the pristine younger timber intermixed with the older, skeletal lodgepole pines.

The second-floor condominium space was narrow, tunnel-like. The balcony wrapped around from the side facing the other units. This southern exposure gave a view of the ski runs. The construction was first rate: hardwood floors and alder cabinetry, accented with marble countertops, high-end stainless steel appliances, interior doors with drop-down seals that silence a room, and extra-thick walls. It was the Ritz way. The pool area sat on a concrete plateau six feet higher than the first floor giving the second-floor balcony an odd feel. The first-floor courtyard seemed more of a moat. The architect's choice to give the front bedroom access to the balcony and a view of the mountaintop aggravated the narrow layout of the living room. *I would rather have a nice living room view of the mountain,* thought Jil. *Then again, it will make the penthouse seem that much sweeter.*

"I suppose this will do." Jil waved her hand dismissively as she exited the condo of the Ritz-Carlton Residences in Vail, Colorado. Richard Stockpoint, the local agent trying to sell the unit to Jil, looked exhausted despite his permanent grin. "Now, show me the sixth-floor penthouse we talked about. I think we want both units."

"Ms. Harper, I'm so sorry, the penthouse suite sold yesterday. May I interest you in one of the other large units? The fourth-floor units are nearly identical. Just a little different layout is all." Stockpoint gave a wave of his arm and started in the direction of the elevators.

"Listen, Dick. May I call you Dick?" said Jil.

"Well, my name is Richard, but if it pleases you, madam." Stockpoint stopped advancing to the elevator, waiting to hear Jil's desires.

"Has the contract been signed yet for the penthouse suite I told you I was interested in?" asked Jil coolly.

"Well, the signing is not until tomorrow. The client's flying in from Europe as we speak to close the deal." Stockpoint threw up his hands to emphasize there was nothing he could do.

"My firm will add an additional million dollars to the price if we can sign today." Jil took out her checkbook. "You can use your extra hundred thousand in commission to smooth the feathers of your other client."

"Oh, I couldn't possibly do that."

"Of course you can." Jil smiled a million-dollar smile.

"It just is not done."

"I don't understand your resistance."

"On the fourth floor, we have a five-bedroom unit, practically the same."

"Same? There is nothing the same as the penthouse."

"In fact, it has an extra one hundred and five square feet of space for two hundred thousand less!" Stockpoint placed his right palm to his face and held his right elbow with his left hand.

"I don't think you understand my position," said Jil in her I'm-getting-peeved way.

"Unit 405 is extraordinary! It has a second level, which 615 does not."

"Why would I care about a second level that is still below the penthouse?"

Stockpoint turned the charm on and made his voice silky smooth. "Your client's guards will be able to stay out of sight when necessary. It really is a better unit for your needs."

"I wish to purchase this unit here and the six-bedroom penthouse suite. Your client coming from Europe can have the five-bedroom fourth-floor unit. You lose nothing and gain an extra ten percent. What's the problem here?" Jil always got what she wanted.

"I . . . uhm, Miss Harper, that just is not done, not by Sotheby's or Ritz-Carlton," stammered Stockpoint. A dew of sweat had begun to glisten on his forehead.

Jil took out her cellphone and dialed a number. "Casper, I am so sorry to bother you," she purred, more to make Stockpoint nervous than to placate Casper. "Yes, as you requested, I am here to purchase the units."

Stockpoint's assistant, Rachel, breezed in and out long enough for him to murmur in her ear, "Why would I piss off Günter? She can upgrade like the rest."

"Would you please tell Dick Stockpoint our position." Jil listened intently to Casper. "Yes, I have him right here." Jil handed Stockpoint the phone.

Stockpoint reluctantly took the phone as he mumbled under his breath, "Damn it, who do they think they are? This just is not done!" Smiling and straightening his posture, he spoke clearly into the phone. "Richard Stockpoint, managing partner of Ascent Sotheby's International Realty, how may I—" He stopped before he could finish the sentence. His face became pale, blood draining from his face, as the sweat beads grew larger. "You wouldn't . . . I see . . . no, that will not be necessary. Thank you, Casper. I am so—" Wincing, Stockpoint was not permitted to complete his sentence yet again. He handed the phone back to Jil, the connection cut, so she put the phone away.

"Now, Dick. I am going to be nice and let you have the bonus money. As you now understand, I could ask you for a discount and still get what I want. Are we clear?" Jil smirked at the now-deflated man.

"Crystal clear, Miss Harper." Stockpoint pursed his lips as he finished the words, biting off the thought You bitch.

"Most excellent. I know my organization will be most pleased with your work." Jil's smile exposed her pleasure in witnessing Stockpoint's pain. *No one denies Casper!* Jil tried to crush the image of her father's missing finger from her mind, but she found herself feeling her own left ring finger involuntarily.

"Please follow me; my staff will draw up the necessary paperwork immediately. I must make new arrangements for my *less* well-connected client before he arrives." Stockpoint knew when he was defeated. He mumbled to himself, "There is nothing more to gain from polishing this apple. Best to hand it off and move on. How could they pull the financing from my valley project? I am leveraged too far out to get a new loan. They wouldn't, would they? It would be a disaster. That bitch!"

"Dick, I'm sorry, I couldn't hear you." A wry smile crossed Jil's face as she imagined the curses passing the schmuck's lips.

Stockpoint turned his upper body back slightly and radiated his best smile. "Yes, this way, thank you. Rachel, get Miss Harper anything she likes."

Rachel radiated her best submissive smile and sweetly cooed, "Miss Harper, water, coffee, Coke, or perhaps a snack?"

"A mimosa would be just fine, thank you," Jil waved her hand dismissively at Rachel.

Stockpoint left the room, sank into his office chair, and dialed his associate's number. "Get Craig in here, now."

Five minutes later, an agitated, dapper middle-age man rushed into the managing partner's office.

"Craig, I need you to do an immediate closing for the Harper woman."

"Listen, Richard, I had to put the Martins on ice to come take care of this. Why can't you close the deal?"

"I have to go take care of Günter, and that *woman* is in a hurry." An exasperated Richard Stockton reached for the bottle of glacier water that Rachel had thoughtfully placed on his desk just moments before.

"Is she taking both 405 and 215?" asked Craig.

"No, 615 and 215." Richard Stockton looked away from him.

"Günter's unit?" asked Craig, his posture stiffening.

"Yes, I know. Günter is going to be pissed. Why do you think I'm having you finish the sale while I go salvage Günter?"

"You're going to lose him. We need his money and his connections! You're trading dollars here." Craig threw his hands up with a worried look on his face.

"No, I'm going to go meet him at Eagle Vail Airport in an hour when his Challenger arrives. Oh, and Craig, the price is ten point two million. The extra million is for our trouble, but I will have to knock at least five hundred thousand off of unit 405 to make Günter happy, so don't start counting your chickens just yet." Stockpoint was starting to grin outwardly. Even with the concession to Günter to smooth things over, he would still come out ahead, but the smile faded as he thought of the bone-chilling voice named Casper.

"Well, all right. You're the managing partner." Craig left the office.

Richard Stockton groused at the ceiling, "That man knew how to twist my very soul into a knot!"

As Craig approached the conference room, he looked admiringly at Stockpoint's assistant, noting her fawning over the harpy of a woman. Rachel had prepared the forms and was waiting to be the notary on the deal. "Miss Harper? Craig Dalton. It is a pleasure to meet you!"

FORTY-FIVE

HOW DO YOU SAY "CHEESE" IN DANISH?

August 6, 2009 — Denmark

"**B**UD WAS RIGHT. The tanker had a container hidden in spray foam under a gangway. The ventilation duct work is still exposed." Karl was describing the scene in front of him.

"Excellent work. Can you send the rest of the photos over? We need to document this," said David as he enlarged the initial image sent by Karl, Control's top agent in the Netherlands district. Karl's Northern European work continued even during the mothballing of Control after the Chinese freighter incident. During the intervening years, Karl kept busy with daily trips to the outskirts of major cities, digging into the underbelly of commerce; Karl had free license to go where he wanted as a photojournalist for InterContinental News.

"I'm not sure how you're going to find these hiding places going forward, but you might look for freshly sprayed foam. They aren't trying to hide it or blend it into the old foam," explained the tall, lean field agent. His chiseled face and high cheekbones gave him the look of a stern Boris Karloff. His half-Dutch, half-Belarusian ancestry allowed him to blend into most European communities. He could speak six languages and understand nine. His technical knowledge extended to structural engineering and architecture, but his specialty was black operations. Karl was in his early fifties now and getting ready to retire from fieldwork. It was a young man's world. Karl had managed to carve out a niche thanks to his skills and technical abilities to stay in the game, but he longed for a retirement in the mountains of Colorado where he had grown up. The skiing was fabulous in Europe, but he missed the hospitality and warmth he experienced in his youth.

"See if you can locate the nest. We need to either eliminate the threat or recover the asset. We need to know what they know," David reminded Karl.

"David, please don't tell me how to do my job. I know what to do. Are you the photographer, or am I? If the lighting is poor, I will wait to take the shot." Karl easily masked the true nature of his conversation as passing workers grinned and waved at him to take their picture. Snap . . . snap . . . snap. Karl stayed in character in case any of the men were polyglots.

"OK, OK, Karl! I get the hint. The director is making this a priority, just so you know." David exclaimed, "Damn prima donnas!" as he slammed the handset into its cradle.

Karl put his phone away and quickly snapped pictures of the swarthy crew as they passed by the exposed skeletal remains of the camouflage for Gil's former prison. By the dimension of the gap, Karl guessed a twenty-foot intermodal shipping container had been used. Ragged edges indicated fast work by a coterie of thugs with reciprocating saws chewing aggressively through the foam—with dust and crumbs still evident. *Snap . . . snap . . . snap.* Karl documented the remains with his camera and took mental notes to identify the next sarcophagus. Karl turned and looked out over the shipyard. Switching to his telephoto lens, Karl scanned the yard for possible evidence of Gil's former tomb. *Snap . . . snap . . . snap.* In the distance, sandwiched between two other containers was an orange metal rectangle with yellow foam remnants crusted on the edges. The workers had been sloppy and lazy, thinking no one was watching them. Karl swiveled as he took a series of photographs. *Snap . . . snap . . . snap.*

"Hvad fanden laver du?" yelled the yardmaster in a drab, heavy overcoat.

"What the hell am I doing?" replied Karl in Danish. "I'm the guy who is going to make you famous!" *Snap . . . snap . . . snap.* "Move just to the left and the sunset will frame you perfectly with that windmill blade." Karl was improvising. The yardmaster was supposed to be drinking with his cronies right now.

"You don't belong here. I don't want to be famous. I want you out of my yard, now!" Two goons came around the corner to back him up.

"Keep your shirt on! Hans Krofton gave me permission to be here.

He wants new shots for the website." Karl flashed a pass for the ill-tempered man to see.

The yardmaster planted his hands on his hips, exposing an ill-fitting suit. The aroma of his lunch and the bad wine he washed it down with wafted up to Karl. "OK, OK, you can stay, but be careful—this is a dangerous place. I wouldn't want anything to happen to you if you got in the way." The squat, burly man turned and left, but the two goons stayed behind to keep an eye on Karl.

"What the hell, the light's fading anyway! Tell Hans I will send him the photos in a week after I clean them up." Karl turned to go but kept an eye on the goons as they slowly followed him down the gangplank. Karl had an itch to shove them over the side, but that would be giving in to his feeling old and cranky. Even though he liked the surge of adrenaline, he recognized the sign that this really was the time for him to hang it up and retire.

The men edged a little too close for Karl as they came off the gangplank together. They kept closing as Karl turned the corner near some shipping containers waiting to be loaded. Swinging the camera behind his back, Karl quickly spun around. With a swipe of his left foot, he broke the kneecap of the larger man, then swung his right elbow hard into the other goon's right temple. The second man slowly turned as he fell, and landed on his face. "Don't crowd me! See, I have a pass." Karl flashed the pass at the goon lying on the ground holding his now-ruined knee. "That's going to leave a bruise!"

Karl was feeling better now. He would pay for this collateral damage later, but then again, this was his last job.

While driving back to his hotel, Karl called in. "David, remember I told you I wanted a stateside posting soon? It's time. I'll finish this shoot for you, but that's it."

"Karl, are you sure? Do you just need some time off? Maybe go skydiving or base jumping?" asked David, not sure how to take the news from one of Control's most reliable field agents.

"I'm sure, David. I just know that if I don't get out now, I'll do something really stupid—go for that perfect shot just 'cause I can. I know it's time." Karl paused, then reflected, "I'm not getting any younger, you know."

"OK, I will pass it on." David tried to make his voice sound sympathetic, but it came out snarky instead: "You looking to get out or do you want to go to a nice quiet post somewhere?"

That made Karl nervous. No one ever really got out of Control. He made a mental list of the retired agents he knew. They all left on their backs. "Yeah, that's what I want. I want to be somewhere I can keep an eye on things for you." He would soon miss the action, but he hoped to replace it with outdoor activities. In the meantime, somewhere he would not have to stick his neck out seemed appealing.

"I will let you know," David answered noncommittally.

FORTY-SIX

WHICH WAY DID SHE GO?

August 6, 2009 — Washington, D.C.

"**H**AMID, THIS DEBIT CARD has a thousand dollars on it. You can take out two hundred per day. I want your cellphone in exchange." Betty was starting to think on her feet. *Time to use Control's tools against itself—send them on a wild goose chase.* Her credit and debit cards were useless in the normal sense because Control monitored their use. *I need a phone, a place to stay, and transportation. How can I even go to Margaret's house without drawing attention to her?*

"Lady, you're kidding, right?" Hamid was trying to look back at his fare and keep one eye on the road at the same time. Traffic was not bad since it was after the dinner hour, but it still was important to pay attention.

"I've never been more serious. Give me your cellphone and I will give you the debit card—or I can put a bullet in your head. Your choice." *Guess since I'm going rogue, I might as well go all the way!* "I really don't want to harm you. I have other options, but you are the easiest if you cooperate. It's worth your while. Make sure you use the card in the swipes, not at ATMs that can eat your card. Do not use the same one twice. The pin is 4444. Now give me your phone!" Betty's tone was insistent.

"Fuck. Shit! I knew you were trouble!" Hamid tossed his cellphone back to Betty through the open Plexiglas portal.

She dropped the ATM card onto the front seat by reaching between the gap in the Plexiglas sliding door. "Remember: 4444, two hundred per day, and never the same machine twice. Walk to the machine, do not drive up, and wear a hat, for God's sake. Here's the other half of the hundreds. Pull off here onto Pennsylvania. There is a Starbucks just down the road. Drop me off there. Don't look back. Forget what I look like." Betty readied Surry and her bag for a quick exit. She had no reason to trust Hamid, but she did not need to. *They'll cancel the card by midnight unless they decide to follow the transactions. I need him to be greedy. Go for it all, Hamid!*

Hamid screeched to a stop outside the coffee shop. He could not get rid of this fare fast enough. After Betty exited the cab and as he pulled away, Hamid exclaimed, "Al-hamdu lilah! If I survive, this is the best tip ever!" Hamid grabbed his prayer beads and began muttering.

†

"Any signs, David?" asked Tom as he hung up on the call with Grace.

"Bud called in a burglary, but Harvey hasn't caught up to the cab. We have a call in to the company, but they have no idea where their cab is—they say the GPS suddenly stopped working." David's expression, one eyebrow raised and a smirk starting at the corner of his mouth, raised the questions how and why.

"When did they say they lost the GPS?" quizzed Tom.

"Funny thing, that. It happened right near Betty's apartment, not even a quarter-mile down the road. We have the state troopers looking for the cab on the pretense of an escaped felon, but unfortunately, we also have them checking on the robbery," David noted wryly.

"Surrounding states?"

"Spreading the search to Maryland and D.C. Don't want to call in the Capitol police yet, but ready to do so if you think it's necessary," responded David, having already thought out all the permutations.

"No, I don't want those guys involved. Keep it as a stolen cab with a felon report," answered Tom. "Start watching the airports. It's her only quick way to Europe."

"You thinking she's headed for Gil?" asked David.

"Who else?" Tom sighed as he rubbed his forehead.

†

"Shhhh, Surry, it will be all right," Betty calmed her dog as a customer approached the coffee shop from the attached parking lot. "Excuse me, my phone battery died." Betty waved the cabbie's phone at the woman for show. "Can I borrow your phone to make a local call?"

"I don't know." The woman shied away from the excited Surry.

"I'm so sorry, my friend was supposed to meet me here to pick up my dog. It will only take a minute, she probably already called, but my phone's dead."

"OK, I suppose, but make it quick, please. My blind date is waiting for me." The nervous woman handed over her phone. Betty handed her Surry's leash and began getting everything tangled up together. The woman dropped her purse and keys, but could not bend down to get them because of her tight skirt, high heels, and the dog leash wrapped around her knees.

"Oh, I'm so sorry!" Betty smiled inside as she helped the woman get untangled. She pretended to trade back phones with the woman while simultaneously palming the disheveled woman's car keys. "Oh, I'm so sorry for bothering you. Go on to your date—I'll find someone else to help out." Betty nudged the now-free woman into the store with her purse and the cabbie's phone. The startled and confused woman went in and attempted to put herself back together before presenting herself to her blind date.

Thirty seconds later, Betty rolled out of the parking lot in her new ride, a late-model coupe with a day's worth of shopping bags in back. "Perfect!" Betty smiled. The woman had been about Betty's size. "Can't wait to see what I bought today," she mused as she drove the short distance to her legal assistant's house.

The bureaucrats who lived in District Heights, Maryland—a name nicer than its 1950s vintage brick bungalows—kept things plain: no fancy garages or extravagant embellishments. *Why does Margaret stay? She's paid twice what she needs to move up.* Betty pulled into the driveway on the six thousand block of Merritt Street and left the motor running.

She waited impatiently for Margaret to come to the door. Instead, Margaret's domineering husband—with a day's growth of beard, a receding hairline, and a beer gut the size of the Jefferson Memorial—loped slowly to the door. "What the hell do you want?"

"I'm looking for Margaret. Tell her Betty is here." *Fuck, I need this guy to be scared of me.* "Listen." Betty stepped in closer and screwed up her face into a menacing glare. "Burt, right? I'm Margaret's boss." She poked him in his booze-hardened belly covered by a hole-pocked, grease-stained T-shirt and raised her voice loud enough for anyone inside to hear her. "Get your fat ass in there and roust Margaret for me if you want to keep living off of her salary, you lazy piece of shit!"

Burt took a step back and looked over his shoulder. The worried look on his face indicated he did not like the idea of Margaret being unemployed.

Grabbing the initiative, and with Surry in tow, Betty used her elbow to push her way into the house and past the chastised brute.

His voice went up an octave and sounded worried. "Lady, you can't bring that dog in here!" Surry started growling at Burt, who fell backward into his well-worn recliner, holding his hands up to protect his face from the pissed-off dog in front of him. "Who the hell do you think you are?" he asked.

"I'm the one keeping you in lottery tickets and cheap beer. Stay the hell out of my way." Then she called out, "Margaret, be a dear and come out, I need to talk to you!"

Margaret slowly emerged from the kitchen, carrying a bowl of freshly made popcorn. "Betty, you look like hell! You miscarried, didn't you?" she asked.

"Good to see you too, Margaret." *She never misses a thing, does she?*

"Margie, I don't care if she's your boss, she can't have that dog in here!" yelled the scared little man cowering in his throne of faux leather.

"Shut up, Burt!" Betty and Margaret shouted simultaneously as Surry growled at him.

"Betty, what's going on?" asked Margaret.

"Listen carefully, Margaret. I'm going to disappear for a couple of weeks. I need you to take care of Surry for me. If I take longer, you can put her into a nice kennel," said Betty.

"A couple of weeks!" shouted a disbelieving Burt.

Surry charged and clamped onto Burt's crotch with a low growl. "Ahhh! Get . . . 'em . . . off! Get . . . 'em . . . off!" screamed Burt.

"Surry, stay!" Betty commanded sharply. "Margaret, I need you to do this for me. An old boyfriend has made some threats. He will kill Surry and try to hurt me if he finds us." Betty was not really lying, *except Tom probably will kill me if he finds me.*

"Oh, Betty, please make Surry be gentle," said Margaret, giggling.

"Stop it! Let go!" demanded Burt.

"Burt, shut up!" yelled Betty and Margaret simultaneously as Surry stayed clamped on Burt's crotch.

"Here is two hundred dollars now to cover your expenses. More later if you need it . . . don't tell anyone about me. Just say you're fostering a dog." Betty handed two crisp one-hundred-dollar bills to Margaret, who looked at the money as if she did not understand. "Do as I'm asking and my ex will not find out you're helping me. He might try to hurt you if he thinks you know anything."

"Listen, lady! We don't like dogs . . . ahhh . . . tell it to let go!" pleaded Burt.

Margaret pushed the money back into Betty's hand. "Keep it. Sounds like you need cash more than I do right now. You can pay me later."

Betty turned to Burt, pondering whether the tears in his eyes were from Surry clamping down or Margaret refusing the money. "If you give her any trouble, you'll have to worry about me *and* my dog, not my ex!" Betty glared at the Neolithic boar in the clutches of her prized pooch, then turned back to her legal assistant. "Margaret, you're a doll!" Betty gave her a hurried hug before heading out the door.

Burt tried to muffle the sound of his anguish, but his moans of pain and fear continued, albeit through clenched teeth.

"Do you need anything?" asked a worried Margaret from the stoop.

"I've got it handled from here. Thanks, I knew I could count on you." Betty ducked into the stolen car and drove out of the suburban nightmare that was Margaret's home.

Margaret came back into her tiny living room and looked at her husband with a strange look in her eye. "Burt, I don't think you should move—just in case," Margaret said with a newfound confidence as she took control of the remote and changed the channel from the football game to *Dancing with the Stars*.

Forty-Seven

Follow the Money

"SIR, DOMESTIC ESPIONAGE IS JUST not our specialty. I'm doing the best I can!" David's frustration with his task and his boss's pressure was starting to show.

"David, this may be the most important tail we ever have. You don't know Betty as well as I do. She's just pissed enough that nothing is going to stop her. She's just rational enough that she'll figure out how to get where she wants to go." Tom rubbed his eyes with the heels of his palms. It was two a.m. and no sign of her. *I always feared this day would come. Me hunting Betty and Betty able to hide because I trained her.* "It's like a graduation ceremony," muttered Tom.

"What?" David did not take his eyes off his monitor but turned his head slightly.

"Betty. This is sort of a graduation ceremony. She'll either survive and prove she's the best agent there ever was or we will hunt her down and terminate," said Tom as he sighed.

"Kind of hard to not cheer for her, if you put it that way," stated David wryly.

"Get Bud in here. We need an update and a face-to-face. I need to know if she's been using her credit cards, any signs of her driver's license, has she checked into any hotels or motels, has she used an alternate ID? Did we interview the cabbie yet? Did she have contact with any other civilians? Everything!" Tom was ready to take charge. *I have to be in control of this mess.*

†

"Hamid is an alcoholic; he misses work from time to time when he goes on a bender. He's been attacked by a maniac; I bet he's already three sheets to the wind." The manager of the Mercury Cab Company, Louie, spoke with an Indian accent.

"Did you find Hamid's cab?" Bud asked, cradling the phone with his shoulder while he threw a stress ball into the air and caught it with his opposite hand.

"Sure, sure," Louie snidely remarked. "We found the cab."

"Where?" Bud sat up, missing the stress ball, and began typing on one of his keyboards.

Bud could hear Louie leaning back in a squeaky office chair. "Parked right outside the gate."

"Did you get this on tape?" Bud had access to several different security camera streams, which he currently had on multiple monitors set to fast-forward while he watched for a sign of Hamid's cab.

"The security tape shows Hamid dropping off the cab around . . . seven thirty p.m."

"I'll send a unit by to pick up the tape." Bud typed in a command that instantly fast-forwarded the security footage to 7:25 p.m. "Any damage to the vehicle?"

"The GPS cable was cut by a knife." The manager sounded impatient. "Someone *must* pay for the damage," he growled.

"Was anyone else on the tape?" Bud spotted the cab going through an intersection two blocks from the cab company. Only Hamid was visible in the grainy black-and-white footage.

"No, just Hamid." The manager cleared his throat.

"We need to impound the car. An agent—hold on." Bud caught himself misspeaking. He meant to say "an officer."

"What was your name again—and badge number?"

"I will get back to you when we know more." Bud hung up on the manager, realizing he was not going to get anything more worthwhile. Betty would not have left anything useful behind. "I will never get that kiss—or even a date now. Fuck! I was so close!"

"Close to what, Bud?" asked David as he rolled into the geek den of Bud Stux. Computer monitors filled a wall: some scrolling green text, others flashing images from security cameras, hacked police computers, spy satellite imagery, a satirical news show, and network news stations. "I can understand the news services, but Comedy Central? You're kidding, right?"

"No, no . . . some of the best reporting comes from these guys. The good jokes are from real material. These guys get it!" Bud was trying to pick up his accumulated trash of high-octane soda cans, candy wrappers, microwave popcorn, and potato chip cans. Holding up one of the chip cans, Bud smiled and shared a secret. "These are the best for making quick Wi-Fi snooping antennas. You want one? A chip, I mean."

"No, Bud. Get your information together."

Bud frowned. "What's up?"

"We have a meeting in fifteen minutes with Director Howell . . . and Bud, make it good."

"I'm always good." He reset his baseball cap on his head.

"Make me believe you're worth your own hype." David looked tired. He was not amped up on caffeine and sugar like Bud. The physical toll of his injuries made it difficult to do these all night adventures. He could take uppers like an agent in the field, but sitting in his chair he would just get all edgy and wired. He needed to stay focused and cool on this job.

†

"Oh putain de merde! She wasn't lying!" The receipt from the ATM machine showed Hamid's withdrawal of two hundred dollars, leaving a balance of eight hundred dollars in the account. It was ten thirty p.m. and he had taken the Metro to the capital area from the cab company headquarters in Alexandria. After midnight, he could take another two hundred out. It was time to go somewhere else. Hamid headed back to the Metro station and took the train to Georgetown. He pulled his hat down low and turned his quilted Redskins jacket inside out before going to the next ATM machine. "Crazy lady! If I survive the week, I'm going back to Morocco! It's much safer there!"

†

Betty needed to ditch her hot ride. *The last thing I need is a conversation with the police!* A lit-up cruiser, siren blaring, barreled past. *Best to stay three moves ahead of everyone.* A block ahead, the lights went out and the din waned. *How the hell am I going to get to Europe?* Control agents would watch the airports. No other transportation would be fast enough. *I need to talk to Bud!* A dark and silent state trooper briskly passed going the opposite direction. *I need a mud puddle!*

Betty pulled into a manual car wash and stuffed a handful of quarters from the car's ash tray into the machine to activate the wand. She sprayed the car down with just water and put the wand back before the timer expired. Across the street, the construction site of a future strip mall offered some camouflage. She began doing donuts in the barren lot, kicking up a cloud of dirt. She stopped long enough to get out and throw a handful of dust from the ground onto the license plate. Smiling to herself, she thought, *Nice work!*

Pulling into a parking garage two blocks down, Betty parked the stolen coupe with a group of other long-term parked cars. Her handiwork was no match for the dust on the neighboring vehicles, but a busy rogue spy could only do so much. She took out a few essentials from her duffel and transferred them to the department store bags, placing the purchased goods on top. She double-checked the tags to see the sizes. *That will work, a little loose—but better than skintight! Wow, definitely not my shade of makeup, though.*

Betty left the parking garage and found an all-night diner around the corner. She gave a fake smile to the sixtysomething man folding napkins near the front door—"Table for one, please. I'll be right back"— and headed straight to the bathroom. She took some paper towels and wet them down. *Thank God, the handicapped stall is open.* She proceeded to clean up after a mad day of espionage.

Just before leaving the privacy of the stall, Betty let herself have a moment of pity and a good cry for her baby. Wiping her face, she shook it off. *OK. Time to suck it up. Gil has it worse than me. Lord knows what they're doing to him!* That was enough to get her mind straight. A short cry for her loss and another future shattered. *I'm getting a little too good at handling life's little disappointments.*

Taking a booth to herself with a view of the kitchen and the front door made her feel a little more comfortable. *They won't find that car for at least a week. Now, time to get some food ordered and find out what Bud knows.* The cellphone lifted from the woman at the coffee shop was still functioning. *Her blind date must be working out!* Betty thought with mild jealousy. The smartphone already had a Twitter app installed. Betty signed on and created a new handle, @bettygirl. She had toyed with the social network tools, but was not much into them. *Who am I going to connect with, anyway? People like Bud?*

Within seconds of sending her message—"Hello?"—the phone app notified her that a direct message from @stuxboy had arrived: "Stay low! Line X is the least of your worries. Make your tweets private, and for God's sake only direct message me!"

Betty was not sure what that meant but dug into the site to figure it out. Sure enough, hidden in the preferences was an option to make all tweets private and a tutorial on how to direct-message. She tapped the keys with her thumbs, getting used to the new toy. "Watch my back. Where is Gil? How do I get to him?"

Seconds later, a direct message came back from @stuxboy: "Frederikshavn Denmark. Go to FedEx at Reagan. Talk to Strivner. Take catheter, oxygen, food, water, blanket. Get technical gear on arrival. Don't wish I was you."

"Damn, he types fast!" Betty muttered.

"My grandkids love that texting thing," said the man as he walked up. "What can I get you?"

Betty smiled her first real smile of the day. "Full stack of pancakes and two, no three eggs over easy, wheat toast."

"A little thing like you must be eating for two." The manager started to put his hand on her shoulder but stopped when he saw the dark circles and sad expression on Betty's face. "Is everything OK?"

Betty tried to manage her best imitation of Jil's pageant smile, but it just made her look like an insane person about to crack.

He started to back away, opened and closed his mouth without saying anything, and just shook his head as he wrote the order while walking back to the kitchen. He shoved the order ticket into the track and mumbled to the short-order cook, "Let's get her back on the road, shall we, Leroy?"

"Everything was OK," muttered Betty. "I *was* in a good mood."

Forty-Eight

Whack-a-Mole

August 6, 2009 — Control

"**D**AMN YOU, BETTY!" muttered Howell as he tried to gather his thoughts before his staff came through the door. *Other operations need my focus. We have agents sitting idle waiting for nothing more than you to pop up. We don't have much time left to get to the Cabal leadership this go-around.* One of several TV monitors played C-SPAN's coverage of the ongoing debate in Congress over raising the government debt ceiling: if Congress did not act by midnight, the government would technically default on its obligations. On another screen, a news program aired the Treasury secretary giving the administration's case for why borrowing another trillion dollars was a good idea.

"What the hell! It's our government and our money. If President Wilson hadn't given those bastards from Jekyll Island control of the currency, we wouldn't be in this mess!" yelled Howell to no one in particular. "Damn Federal Reserve is going to ruin the country if I don't stop the Cabal soon." Howell's mind returned to the meeting about to happen in his office. *Damn it, Betty! I do not need this shit right now!*

Howell could hear David and Bud talking as they came toward his office. David knocked on the door that was already open to get his attention. Howell did not turn around before saying, "Come in. Close the door. Bud, take a seat." Howell spun around in his chair to face his key operations aides. "David, anything to add before Bud gives us an update?" It was important to maintain the pecking order, make sure everyone knew the chain of command.

"There is one new development that's coming in from the police. A woman reported her car and cellphone stolen in a parking lot near Pennsylvania and I-95. Seems a tall, thin, black-haired woman conned her into holding a dog's leash while she swapped phones and stole the keys to her car," stated David for the record. "The police were not notified immediately. She didn't notice the theft until two hours later when she was leaving with her date. She ended up with the Mercury Cab driver's cellphone."

"Any calls on her phone?" Howell doodled his felt-tip pen on a pad of paper; the resulting marks resembled a Rorschach inkblot.

"No." Bud did not look up from his data stream.

"What about the driver's cell?"

"Not by Betty—or anyone else, for that matter, other than the woman's 911 call."

"Any word on her car?"

"Nope." Bud tried to look Howell in the eye but strayed back to his scrolling alerts.

"OK." Howell cleared his throat. "Well, then. Anything that resembles a lead?"

"I'm working on getting surveillance tapes of the area to see where she went." Bud did not like having so little positive news.

"Bud, care to enlighten me with what you've found out?" prodded Howell.

"The cab driver's name is Hamid Bouchtat; he's a Moroccan here on a green card."

"Family?"

"No family in the U.S., other than a cousin in New York."

"Where is Hamid?"

"Last seen on surveillance camera outside the Mercury lot when he dropped off his cab."

"Anything left in the cab?"

"Unfortunately, no, there was nothing left behind in the cab except the GPS cord that was cut with a knife."

"Where is he now?" pressed Howell.

"He's a known alcoholic and possibly on a bender after tangling with Betty."

"Any communication from him?"

"Obviously, he no longer has a cellphone, so no activity there. Harvey checked out his residence. Nothing there. Now we have it bugged in case he returns." Bud was checking his phone as he went through the uncomfortably short list of line items in his report.

"Any communications picked up from Betty?" asked Howell. His posture was weakening, like their chances of finding her.

Bud put his phone down after locking the screen. Lying by omission seemed to be the safest path at the moment. "Nothing picked up on our scanners as of yet. She is not using any known cellphone traffic. We've patched into the NSA's voice analyzer and are watching for any voice recognition matches."

"Credit cards?" Howell, waved his hand in a rolling fashion to prompt Bud to keep things moving. If there wasn't going to be any new information, there wasn't much point in stretching the meeting out.

"One of her debit cards is still active—"

Howell's eyes lit up and he sat up straighter. "Now we're getting somewhere! Why didn't you bring this up sooner?"

"We're still waiting on the surveillance tape. It's a local bank, so we can't access the live feed."

"Any vector on that location?"

"Nothing correlates yet."

David jumped back in to establish he was being proactive. "We're watching the airports around D.C. and the region. We have a flight restriction entered into the TSA's system. They'll pull her for an additional search and keep her sequestered until we come and get her."

"You've—"

"They have been notified that she's dangerous."

"OK, we need to monitor this until she makes her next move."

"Whack-a-Mole." Bud was fidgeting in his seat.

"What?" David interjected.

"She's popping up like a prairie dog, using tunnels to move around without being seen," elaborated Bud.

The roller coaster of Betty's situation was getting to Howell. He slammed his fist on the table and yelled, "Well, find the tunnels, damn it!"

The room went quiet for a minute.

Howell tried to shake off his morose thoughts of having to terminate Betty like his father wanted. He decided to refocus himself and his team on their primary missions. "OK, we have operations that need to move ahead in Europe and Asia. Come on, guys, Betty will show up. We need to stay focused on the Cabal. We only have a short window of time to bring them down this time around. If—and this is a big if—Betty pops up and slips through, tail her. Do not stop her. She may be our ticket to tracking down the core Cabal membership. She's pissed off and wants some scalps. I would not put it past her to slip out of the country. We need to start watching European destinations as well. Put calls out to whoever owes you a favor." Howell swiveled his chair away from the two men. "I want her to live long enough to find our real target—the Cabal." Tom Howell paused for a moment before turning away from the useless chatter on the screens. "I will be in D.C. tomorrow. Keep me posted on anything important. Go get a few hours of rest. We'll pick up in the morning; let the night gang keep an eye on things for now."

David and Bud quietly left the office and closed the door behind them. They did not see Howell remove his SIG Sauer P226 pistol and silencer from a drawer and place them in the holster under his jacket.

†

"Margaret, call this dog off of me!" Burt yelled to his wife, who had just gone to bed.

"Here, Surry!" Margaret called her charge to the bedroom. "Good girl!"

She heard Burt moan—he was probably checking the condition of his genitals. "Margaret!" he yelled, half as a reproach and half to demand her attention.

"Up." Obediently, Surry jumped onto the comforter. "Lie down." Margaret and Surry snuggled together in bed. Burt appeared at the bedroom door.

"What the hell! Get that dog off my bed!" Burt yelled as he gingerly massaged his crotch with his right hand and leaned against the door frame.

Surry began to growl and edge toward the foot of the bed.

"Burt, why don't you sleep in your recliner tonight? I'd hate for Surry to feel lonely with Betty away," said Margaret as she fluffed her pillow and rolled onto her side.

†

The prepaid cellphone was not fancy, but was all Betty needed in order to text and communicate with Bud via Twitter. By registering a phone with the system, he would see her tweets and vice versa, with no calls or Wi-Fi hot spots to trace. They were tweeting back and forth regularly now. No one would know about this backdoor into Control as long as he fed his group the minimum information needed to avoid suspicion. A magician's audience expects to be deceived, and Howell was a paying customer. Bud kept her at least one step ahead of being caught while prepping her for an all-expense-paid trip in a can to Europe. If they got lucky, she would be free to pursue rescuing Gil—and Bud would be the knight gallant.

The thought of trapping herself in a FedEx container for the trip did not appeal to Betty, but her options were limited. The twenty-four-hour pharmacy had the catheter she needed, with the bonus of cereal bars and bottled water. *I cannot believe I'm doing this on Bud's suggestion. They'll be watching for my passports, though . . . no other viable options come to mind.*

Betty stuffed the supplies in a new black duffel bag and jumped a Metro train to Ronald Reagan Airport. Getting to FedEx and finding Strivner was her next priority. Her only open path was to go down the rabbit hole and see where it came up. *Maybe I'll find some information while I'm in the warren,* thought Betty.

Forty-Nine

Something Left Undone

August 4, 2009 — Observatory Circle, Washington, D.C.

"YOU COULD END IT FOR ME, Tom. I will even let you choose the means."

"Such as?"

"An overdose, suffocation, a shot to the forehead. Take that knife and twist it into my heart. Just end this suffering." Tom Sr. coughed to remind his son of the pain.

"Why don't you let the doctor euthanize you?"

"He won't do it."

"So, you want me to do it? You want me to slide down into the abyss, the one you looked over and could not go into yourself? The one you stared into when you needed to eliminate—no, kill—Uncle Jack?"

"Jack has nothing to do with this."

"You don't have the guts to go there, but you have no problem ordering me, your son, to go those extra lonely steps into hell."

"I just want you to finish what I started."

"You couldn't do it, your successors couldn't do it—by God, your handpicked man, General Getner, certainly couldn't do the job!"

"Well, if you put it that way."

"You expect me to hand my soul to the devil, to be the uncaring, emotionless leader of Control, for what? Power, money, and prestige?"

His father glowered at him. The pain was too much to put up a proper intellectual fight.

"None of these can be used or I divulge the essence of Control! You're asking me to damn my own soul—for what?" asked Tom Jr.

"Damn your soul? No, I am only asking you to take charge."

"Same difference."

"Someone has to accept the authority and take responsibility."

"It is always about you. It isn't about Control. Like killing you to ease your pain. Keeping Control running as a legacy of your life."

Tom Sr. did not take the bait and stayed on message. "Only you can save the world from those soulless monsters at the foreign spy agencies and the World Order Cabal. Those bastards are out to end our way of life. We are the first country to stick our heads up out of the bunker long enough to see that there is a better way."

"So, I do the dirty work so some asshole in Washington can claim all the credit?"

"Someone has to do the dirty work so the politicians can keep on claiming they are the saints leading the sinners to paradise."

"Why not let them do this? They have the CIA, NSA, DOD—"

Tom Sr. could not let his son continue. "If you shirk the dirty work, then you can just kiss our nation goodbye."

"What, someone in the Cabal is going to take it over?"

"It will be up for sale to the highest bidder the week after next, and you can watch the spiral into hell from the war that will follow . . . and it will take us all down . . . except me." He wheezed desperately to regain his keel. "You might not end it for me out of mercy or necessity, but thank God, I" —Senior's voice became so weak for lack of breath, his voice faded as he spoke—"only here for . . . very short . . . time."

"You might die right now if you keep talking like that."

After sucking on his oxygen mask, Senior continued more fluidly, "You will be rid of me soon enough—today, tomorrow, or surely by next week. When I am gone, no one will tell you what to do."

"Do?"

"You are inheriting the power to control our nation and all the other nations of the world." Tom Sr. began to yell, blood and spittle spraying from his mouth as he pointed his finger at Tom Jr. for emphasis. "Hell, you will have the World Order running in under a year if you suck it up right now and put a fucking bullet through my brain!" His eyes were bloodshot and angry, the long hairs of the ancient man's eyebrows curved up as if they were horns of the devil, his once-proud mane a bramble of anger, pain, and vengeance.

Tom Jr. slowly reached into his jacket. He had entered the house without a weapons search. Barnes would excuse himself from the building each time he entered, leaving him alone with his father. It had been obvious for the past few months that Tom Sr. wanted his son to end his pain and suffering. At first, Tom Jr. thought his father wanted a mercy killing. Now, he could see it for what it was: the old man trying to take his son over that precipice of morality he had jumped himself. To take to that throne next to the devil himself; to become a fallen angel whose mission it was to keep the other princes of darkness from controlling the world; a manager of devils. *Is that what I want?* Tom asked himself.

He slowly pulled the SIG Sauer P226 from its holster and screwed in the silencer with care and patience, like a hangman carefully checking the knot of the noose and placing it over the condemned man's head. A hangman had responsibilities: a clean death, no lingering, no thrashing corpse slowly suffocating. It was the hangman's job to do it quick and clean. Tom Sr. had tossed Tom Jr. a gold coin, a tip to ensure a clean job. The gold coin was Control. With his father dead, Tom could do as he wished. He could allow Betty to live or even leave Control for a new life. He could use Control or even destroy the monster itself.

After moving his plate aside, Tom Jr. placed his pistol on the table. Lunch had gone uneaten today. The filet mignon was most likely the finest he would have ever eaten. Power has its privileges.

"If I kill you, you won't be able to harm Betty."

"I could have had her killed, you know that?"

"Why didn't you?"

"She is your responsibility, your dog to put down, not mine."

Tom paused and reflected on his situation. "No one will be in a position to stop me from my simplest whim. You know this, yet you want me to end it for you."

"I just want the pain to stop."

"I don't think you want me to end your suffering. I think you just want me to be a cold-blooded killer."

"You have killed for us before. Why is this so different?"

"Yes, I've done my share of wet work. You know that—like José in the church, for example. I kept to protocol even though he was about to give me valuable information. If that wasn't cold-blooded, I don't know what is." Tom Jr. paused for a moment. Tom Sr. sat in his chair, still and silent. His eyes began to glaze and his breathing became labored. He appeared to be giving up, slumping without really moving.

"I . . ." Tom Sr.'s shoulders slumped slightly as he exhaled for the last time.

Tom Jr. sat in his chair unmoving. Waiting to see what the old man would do next. He was not sure if his father could actually die. The old man had been such a fixture in his life, a sturdy post, even if the insides were rotten. He sat in his chair for ten minutes simply watching. Making sure it really was the end. Finally, Tom unscrewed the silencer from the pistol and replaced the weapon in its hidden holster. From inside that same jacket, Tom retrieved his secure cellphone and dialed the number for Barnes, the butler. "It is time," he said. There would be no funeral to worry about, no wake, or open casket. No one left to attend except Tom Jr. and Barnes.

Barnes arrived within five minutes. He could not have been far. "Master Howell, will you be staying tonight or will you be moving your things tomorrow? If you give me the particulars, I will have everything here by the morning."

"Oh, there is not much more than a toothbrush and a change of clothes. Nothing I need, really, but I suppose it should be cleaned."

"Shall I inform Ms. Grace."

"Yes. Wait. You better tell Miller to leave first. Grace and Harold tend to be thorough," joked Tom as a slight smirk crept into the corner of his mouth. "I suppose I'm the end of the line now." The smirk faded as he envisioned his future and the weight he would have to bear.

"You are the line, Master Howell. There is still time to resolve that issue," said Barnes with a twinkle in his eye.

"I'm afraid that will have to wait. I think I need to focus on pulling the organization back to a safe position—too many loose ends right now. What shall we do about Father?"

"His instructions were explicit. Cremation this afternoon. The arrangements are already in place."

"Anything else?"

"The cleaners will be here shortly," said Barnes as he reached into the old man's jacket to retrieve his wallet. Without looking at its contents, he handed the wallet to Tom. "Inside is the code to the safe and a key to his lockbox. In the safe, you will find the instructions and information he wished you to have. There is a signed quitclaim deed transferring this and several other properties to you. Your name is on all the accounts. Your father has already transferred all his wealth into your name, so there will be no probate. You are in control. You are Control," stated Barnes.

"Thank you, Barnes. I suppose you will be staying on. And the rest of the staff as well?" asked Tom.

"If that is what you wish, Master Howell. We are here to serve. Your father took very good care of us, and we would serve you without further compensation, if it were required of us. The cleaners will be here in a—" Before Barnes could finish his sentence, the doorbell rang. "Well, here they are."

Tom followed Barnes to the door. Barnes checked the peephole just to be certain, but he knew who was outside. "Grace, Harold, even on this sad day it is a pleasure to see you," remarked Barnes.

"Mr. Howell," said Grace as she nodded at Tom. Tom nodded back. The change had occurred. He was no longer Tom Howell Jr. He was *the* Mr. Howell.

FIFTY

WALL OF DARKNESS

August 7, 2009 — Washington, D.C.

I T WAS DECEPTIVELY QUIET at four a.m. in the D.C. Metro
area. Betty found herself sitting on a bench across from the Vietnam
Memorial in the dark. The low lighting of the monument cast an
eerie glow on the etched granite. Just visible in the gloom, the names
of the fallen linked together as one unbroken-chain of destiny. Heroes
and average Joes blended as one, those who gave their lives trying to
save others and the unfortunates in the wrong place at the wrong time.
Volunteers and conscripts—some were probably laughing the moment
before they died, while others were grim with determination, throwing
caution to the wind in the name of honor.

Betty was at her crossroad. She was in the sights of three enemies:
the Cabal, Control, and time. She could only control time—or rather,
control what she did with her time. The Cabal wanted her dead. Once
she got past the hurdle of surviving the first forty-eight hours, Control
would be a nonissue. She knew their methods and their resources; easy
enough to evade them. Destroying the Cabal was her true mission, her
true calling. She had been raised for this, whether she liked it or not.

Sitting at this memorial to the dead, Betty allowed herself a
moment to mourn the loss of her child to miscarriage; to mourn her
parents' death just after she was born. Betty unwound the pain that had
been part of her psyche, hidden deep below the surface, and measured
the length of her sorrow. The rawness of the hurt startled her. The fresh
wound of her lost child, perhaps her only chance for motherhood, the
one she would never hold, tore off the scab covering the hole in her soul.
The child she had decided to change her life for, defying all the wishes
of those around her.

Betty reached out to the raw nerves of her childhood and strummed the pain in the dark morning of D.C. No one was there to disturb her; no one to comfort her; there never had been and never would be anyone so close to her. She was completely alone in the middle of a vast metropolis. The single strand of purposefulness was all she had left: the purpose of bringing down those in power who sought to subjugate the people of the world—the bastards of the Cabal. This strand, was it strong enough to hold her weight as she clung to it? *Will I have the strength to pull myself up this silken thread?* Her bleeding heart and shredded soul would have to wait a little longer. For a time to heal when the world was not spinning around the sun, a day when she was six feet under the ground or buried facedown in the sand of some long-forgotten corner of a desert.

This was her time to rise above the pain of her childhood, to rise above the hurt inflicted upon her by Tom, Jil, José, Bob and Beth Thursten, and even her real parents, who had chosen a life ill suited for raising a child. Now was the time for Betty to take complete control and responsibility for her life. She made no pretense of wiping away the brine rivulets on her cheeks. This was her moment to let go of everything. Surry was her last responsibility, and Margaret was a good woman for the job. Surry would only live a few more years. *What I choose to do— what I choose to sacrifice—will affect everyone's quality of life, not just my dog. Damn it! This sucks!*

Betty forced herself to rise from the bench, to gather her meager belongings and head for Reagan International Airport. She had a ticket out and a private carriage to do all the crying she wanted on her way to Europe. *Strivner better have his shit together!*

At exactly 6:55 a.m., Betty entered the parking lot of the FedEx facility at Reagan. She walked up to the idling black SUV with tinted windows. Before she could rap on the glass, the window rolled down.

"Yes?" asked a clean-shaven man wearing sunglasses, a white shirt, and a black suit.

"Strivner?" replied Betty. *I was expecting a FedEx worker, not an agent type!*

"And you must be the package?"

"In living color." Betty was not feeling perky but tried to fake cordiality.

"I've heard about you people, but I've never met one."

"Aren't you the lucky one?" Betty bit her lip. *What did Bud tell him?*

"Bud said you pissed off your boss and needed to get back for the politburo meeting."

"Really?" Betty's face screwed up, incredulous.

"I thought you guys had given up and thrown in the towel."

"We don't like to talk about it anymore." *Bud is going to pay for this!*

"Hop in. I'll take you to your 'quarters.'" The locks on the SUV popped as the window rolled up. Betty threw her duffel bag of supplies into the back seat. As she climbed in, Strivner turned to her and said, "I mean . . . I don't exist. I'm the mythological secret agent people talk about. Your people are the myths we talk about to our junior agents."

"You should hear about the mythological people we talk about!" Betty thought of the Cabal and their invisible hand in the world.

Strivner chuckled as he put the SUV in gear and headed to the gate. The guard did not even wait to see who was driving, opening the gate as the SUV drove in slowly, unchallenged. "I've arranged a special berth for your travels. We use it to transport people in and out of hot spots. Not particularly comfortable, but I've personally had worse and can only imagine the rides you've suffered," smirked the rugged-looking secret agent.

"I can't complain, really." Betty was not in a very talkative mood. She would gain nothing from chatting up this man and he was trying to get information.

"I guess I can't blame you for keeping a lid on things. I'm like the biologist who just discovered a species we thought was extinct. I want to know everything about you." They pulled into a low building next to the hanger and the door closed behind the SUV.

"I guess you'll just have to get use to it."

"Get use to what?" Strivner frowned as he looked at her and put the SUV in park.

"Disappointment."

Strivner chuckled slightly, and then became serious. "Stay put until I clear the building. Be ready to go in two minutes. You'll board in fifteen."

"How long is the flight?"

"You will be in the air for eight hours total with a stop in Paris."

"Anything happening in Paris?"

"Your crate is going to be moved to a different plane. You'll take off and land approximately one hour and fifteen minutes later in Copenhagen."

"What is my exit strategy?"

"After landing, it won't be gentle."

"I've survived rough landings."

"I bet." Strivner took another look at this unknown woman with poise and confidence. "Just the same, make sure you're buckled up."

"How will I know it's safe to exit?"

"Your container will be specially routed to a building similar to this one. The ground crew will slap the side of the container twice. Wait another ten minutes for everyone to clear."

"Will I have a handler at that end?"

"You'll be alone. Coveralls with a security tag will be sitting on a desk about twenty-five feet away."

"So, I just walk out?"

"Not my problem."

"Hmm. So, I guess I should say thank you now?" Betty smirked.

"Well, I'd like that, but you should really thank Bud. I owed him big time or you wouldn't be here."

Getting out of the vehicle, Betty looked catawampus for a moment. "How well do you know Bud?"

"I don't . . . other than his online handle. He takes care of some freelance hacking for me; saved my butt in Turkey last year."

"Has he ever asked for your help before?"

"Never."

"So . . . I guess I better get loaded up."

"I'll probably never hear from you again, will I?"

Betty could not decide if Strivner was asking for a date or treating her as a hostile foreign agent with a get-out-of-jail-free card. "Not unless I need to get back to the politburo on the fly again."

"Then I will spend the rest of my life trying to find you. I wish you the best." Strivner made a quick move for the door of the building to intercept the workers coming to move Betty's container onto the plane, so she would have enough time to settle in.

Her new quarters were sufficient but plain. There was a built-in cot with blankets. A five-point harness attached to the bulkhead turned the cot into a seat for a secure takeoff and landing. Nets to store miscellaneous items hung on the walls. The contoured box was designed to fit into the cargo area of a Boeing 727 jet. The space was roomy enough, ten feet long and seven feet wide, but only five feet three inches tall. *I won't be standing up in here!*

Betty pushed on the battery-operated touch light stuck to the wall and began to seal herself in. The door latched from the inside to prevent workers from snooping or accidentally exposing the secret cargo. She stowed her gear, ran the oxygen mask tubing to dangle above the cot for in-flight breathing, and strapped herself into the five-point harness. The next phase had begun. *I will let myself cry once the plane is airborne. I can hold it together just a little longer. Gil, I'm coming for you!*

FIFTY-ONE

TO SLEEP, PERCHANCE TO DREAM

August 7, 2009 — Somewhere over the Atlantic Ocean

THE GLOW OF BETTY'S ROLEX was the only source of illumination her cramped quarters currently provided; she did not know how long the battery on the touch light would last and wanted to save that for the landing. Rubbing the crystal with her thumb, she thought back to happier times: her engagement to José at Ceiba restaurant, the adrenaline-filled sex with Gil to consummate their partnership, even her time with Tom before he became the bastard Howell. *Interesting,* she thought, *each man wore a Rolex. A common thread between my men. Each had also been about the same build and size. Come to think of it, they keep getting a half-inch shorter. At this rate, I'll be dating a dwarf by the time I'm a dowager!*

So far, the flight had been all right. A little turbulence over the Atlantic before the aircraft could climb above the storm system. Most of the cargo did not care how rough the ride was, but the freight company wanted to balance fuel efficiency with safety, so the pilots had to fly around bad weather if it was not more than forty nautical miles out of the way. Better to spend a little more in fuel than to have to fix electronics or patch holes from lightning strikes. Most storm systems rose too high for cargo planes to fly over. With flight ceilings of 43,000 feet, the pilots had to deviate or just ride out the weather. Today, the pilots were able to fly around the worst of the storm. *Finally, I can get out of this harness! I really need to get some sleep.* Betty had not slept in two days. Between running from Control and avoiding entanglements with the law, there had been no time to rest. Bud had sent her a large file with information on the operations of the port area and the officials in charge. She would grab a short nap, then get busy memorizing the details. *I need to plug my cellphone into the portable charger and set the alarm. I can't afford to land lying down on the cot!*

This storage area of the 727 was pressurized and heated to protect the cargo. If the pressurization failed, a "passenger" in the cargo area would suffer from decompression sickness, barotrauma, altitude sickness, and hypoxia. The lower cargo areas of the plane included an area for transporting pets, but Betty was in the main cargo area that allowed for a container twice the size of the lower deck. She would have enough room to stretch out and sleep. *Bud really is looking out for me. The oxygen tank in here will make me recover faster and will protect me in case the main system fails. Sleeping with this oxygen mask is going to be like having a CPAP machine on, though.* Bud's list was mainly functional items to ensure she would be at her maximum capability upon landing, but he also included some for her comfort: hydration, catheter, earplugs, sleeping pill, blanket, pillow, food, and oxygen. All things Betty expected on a Control operation, but not included on this cut-rate government fare package.

Bud did not put a phone charger on the list, but being an excellent planner, she brought a lighter-size battery pack that plugged into her phone's standard micro 'B' USB port. *I'll have to get a new phone when I land. Need to keep changing things up or they'll spot me on the grid.* The blinding glow of the phone as its screen lit up signaled the charger was working. Her eyes had become accustomed to the near total blackout of her temporary home. *This place wouldn't be half bad with a fireplace and a microwave, in a Ted Kaczynski sort of way. Like Ted, I'm plotting to blow up, maim, and kill my targets too! Jesus, when is my life ever going to be normal: a cat, a dog, and two kids in the suburbs? With my biggest problem being juggling meetings with the PTA and the soccer club.* Betty's thoughts had come full circle and she knew it was time to let things go, to finally allow herself to cry, to sleep, perchance to dream . . . This would be her last opportunity before hitting the ground running to let herself feel the emotions buried deep inside her heart. *Just until I fall asleep—then I will take back control, I promise!*

The searing pain of the flooding emotions ripped open her tear ducts as she saw images of her past: lovers; the imagined, mangled bodies of her parents' car crash; José's broken body; the terrorists she had killed. On and on, the images flashed across her brain as she gave herself just a moment to cry for each wrong done to her and by her. The images melded into one long blur as her mind drifted to much needed sleep, until one image emerged stark and alone, taunting—Ernesto Montoya, the man at the center of everything. The man who would know who killed José, where Gil was, and who in the Cabal held the ultimate power. Montoya held the key to Betty moving onto a "normal" life beyond the world of espionage.

We'll be landing in seven hours. I'll study Bud's info for that last hour of the flight. Normal, I want normal . . . whatever normal means, thought Betty as she finally began drifting off to sleep for the six-hour nap she was going to allow herself. *No sleeping pill, though! I don't want to oversleep.*

Just as she had dozed off, her bad dreams began. The nightmares reared their ugly heads and snarled in Betty's mind. Images of Howell, Ernesto, terrorists alive and assassinated pulled her from her sleep. Scenes of Howell screaming at Betty, "Take the shot!" while the terrorist screamed, "No!" Ernesto taunted Betty with knowledge of who had killed José, showing her sealed envelopes with the name that burned instantly into floating carbon sheets that disintegrated as she tried to catch them. Explosions and death tore at Betty's sleep. Each time she surfaced from a nightmare, she would regret not taking the sleeping pill, but it was too late to change course. Surfacing was quick; the exhaustion accumulated over the past week just as quickly pulled her back down to REM sleep. The dual forces of fatigue and memories were whipsawing her—each winning for just a moment, each losing its grip on the rope of Betty's mind as they played tug-of-war with her conscience until finally, mercifully, fatigue won over. The nightmares still reigned, but she stopped waking from the awful terrors raging in her mind. Even the pressure of the poorly fitted plastic oxygen mask could not arouse her from the deep sleep, which she finally succumbed to until the sudden impact of a rough landing knocked her out of her cot and onto the floor of the container. Wind shear and further bouncing on the tarmac jostled her hard against the padding of the aluminum sarcophagus.

Taking raging breathes of air, she pulled at the mask clinging to her face. At first, she had no idea where she was, but Betty was shocked back to the stark reality of the inky darkness in her cave. As the plane righted itself and rolled down the Charles De Gaulle runway, the hum of the aircraft engines and the careless bumping of the cot forced upon her mind the true nature of the darkness. *Fuck! What the hell!* She had slept through the alarm. *Oh.* Betty shook her head to clear the mist remaining from her sleep. *Only two hours to get ready.* Packages for France would be unloaded and new packages added for Denmark. One more hop before she would be discharged from the plane. *At least I'm awake!* Betty felt her body, checking for blood, bumps, and sore points. Using the phone as a light, she found the water bottle in the net above her head. Sitting upright now to keep from falling back asleep, Betty splashed the cool water on her face and rubbed the back of her neck. Inside her kit was an assortment of medicines in small plastic envelopes. Acetaminophen, aspirin, ephedrine, antibiotics, cold medicines, finally the one she was looking for—ibuprofen. "If it hadn't been for the rough landing," she muttered, "I'd be taking the ephedrine." Ephedrine would have calmed her hunger and made her alert—something that would not matter until her adrenaline from the landing wore off.

The downloaded information included maps, diagrams, employee lists, bank numbers, and general information. Bud had given Betty more than she could have hoped for, considering she was now a rogue agent of Control. *Oh, hell! I can't even think about how I'm going to pay that little geek back. I have to survive first!* Betty stowed the remaining gear and strapped herself into the five-point harness to prepare for the transfer to the second plane and the next takeoff. She sent her only friend a message via Twitter:

@stuxboy CDG. Barely. #roughlanding

Fifty-Two

Perfect Timing

"**W**HAT THE HELL ARE YOU talking about?" asked Karl. "I have it right here. She's on the termination list."

"Karl, you know I have the most recent data right in front of me." Bud hoped he sounded more boastful than nervous.

"Well, if anyone had the most current shit, it would be you."

"Listen, Karl, speaking of current information—" Bud was using his authoritative voice.

"I only talked to David five minutes ago," stammered Karl out quickly.

"Exactly my point . . . I'm surprised, though, to see that you requested the Kyrgyzstan posting."

"You little shit!" growled Karl. "There's no way David put that in there."

"Seems there is an opening in a folk music group." Bud attempted to suppress a smile. "You know how to play the komuz, don't you?"

Karl was confused. "What the hell is a komuz?"

"A three-stringed lute, of course." Bud loved to flaunt his knowledge of the obscure. "Your Russian will work . . . and since you're Belarusian, you should fit right in."

Karl was quick to correct. "Half Belarusian . . . wait, I asked to be at a desk in America!"

"Listen, Karl, I don't know what you did to piss David off—I mean, he is pretty new here, compared to you."

"I haven't done anything!" Karl was becoming befuddled by the course of the conversation. He felt a need to reassert his bonafides. "You know my missions are always top notch."

"Which is exactly why you are still alive at your advanced age and you shouldn't be stuck monitoring terrorists in a remote and desolate location."

"Get to the damn point, nerdman." Karl's face was flush. The weaselly little geek was getting to him.

Bud tried to sound hurt. "No need to start calling me names. I'm here to help you."

"OK, OK, you want something from me and you're willing to help me in return. How far am I sticking my neck out?" Karl's spine tensed visibly, his knuckles turning white as he clutched the secure phone in his hand.

"Not at all. I'm just telling you about opportunities."

Taking a deep breath, Karl calmed himself. The idea of being stuck in Kyrgyzstan touring with a folk band was enough to make him do almost anything. "Bud, how may I help?"

"Betty needs our help to sort out the who, what, and where of a captured agent. Director Howell has given me clearance to assist her anyway I can."

"She's not on the terminate list?"

"No."

"I'm to help her?"

"Yes."

"You're going to help me stay out of Kyrgyzstan?"

"I'm going to get you your dream job as a concierge at the Ritz in Vail."

Karl's shoulders relaxed visibly. "Vail?" He sounded incredulous.

"Yes, a remote and not-so-desolate location that has tremendous opportunities for monitoring the rich and powerful at play in nature without worrying about a bullet in the back of your skull."

"You'd do that for me?"

"Karl, I wish I could do more."

"Is there anything else I can do for you?"

"Don't get in Betty's way. Help her however she wants and back her up."

"I can do that."

"I knew you would. Wait, hold on . . . check that out!"

"What?" Karl's curiosity got the better of him.

"Your record now indicates a perfect match for Vail! Can you say concierge? I better keep my eye on that to make sure David doesn't change it back."

"You're a good man, Bud. I've always said that."

"Right. Go pick her up at the hanger next to FedEx cargo in Copenhagen."

"I'm on it."

"Have transportation to Frederikshavn and a disguise for her. Get her to the safe house there and show her what you know about Gil's container prison."

"OK."

"And Karl?"

"Yes?"

"She's pissed! I wouldn't tell her about the terminate order."

"Anything else?"

"She *will* kill you *if* you get in her way." Bud clicked the save button to change Karl's future status and ensure his retirement in Vail. "Good luck." Bud terminated the connection, smiled to himself, put his hands behind his head, and leaned back in his chair, admiring his empire of screens.

David rolled by his office door and knocked before coming in.

"Did you get Karl set up for Vail like I asked you?"

†

August 7, 2009 — Copenhagen, Denmark

Betty waited impatiently for the specified ten minutes to pass before opening the door to her mini hotel. The remaining flight time had been uneventful, which gave her enough time to study the materials Bud had provided her. There remained the question of how she was going to travel unnoticed and locate Gil once she arrived in Frederikshavn. *I'm resourceful. I'll figure something out.* During her wait, she bundled her equipment into her backpack and wiped the crate down for any prints. *Grace would be proud,* she noted wryly. Silently counting down from ten, to prepare herself in case the cargo area was not clear or if she was getting out earlier than she should, Betty drew her Sig Sauer P226 and attached the silencer. She quietly counted down, ". . . 3 . . . 2 . . . 1 . . ."

Bursting out of the container and sweeping her weapon over the top while using it as a shield, she stopped cold with her muzzle pointed at a very tall man's head. He was sitting on the desk where her coveralls where supposed to be, his left leg half on the desk and the other planted on the floor. His hands were raised, with his pistol in his right hand.

"I'm here to help." Betty's scowl gave Karl a feeling he needed to clarify further. "Bud sent me."

"Drop the weapon!" Betty growled and waved her piece at him.

Slowly and delicately, Karl placed his weapon on the gray concrete floor of the hanger. "Really, I'm here to help you. Bud said to give you whatever you need."

"I need to figure out why Bud sent you. I wasn't expecting anyone here."

"I'll wait."

Betty calculated in her head where Bud would be: her phone said it was 12:03 a.m. local time, and Bud was now six hours behind; therefore, he would be eating dinner at his desk. Betty checked her Twitter account and found a message from @stuxboy:

> @bettygirl Karl offered to help. Trust him.
> Let him know what you need. Don't kill him
> . . . unless you have to.

"I guess I need to check in more often." Betty stowed the phone and her gun. "Bud says you're OK."

Karl chuckled. "Let's get you dressed." He held up a headscarf and a stylish cloak.

"Seriously?"

"We don't want to be noticed, do we? You don't speak Romanian by any chance, do you?"

FIFTY-THREE

MESSAGE IN A FLOWER

August 7, 2009 — Frederikshavn, Denmark

"T OMORROW," DR. ERIC SALIZAR SAID.

"Tomorrow? Finally!" said Michel.

"Prepare yourself. This isn't your first time, of course."

"And I have been careful to follow your directions by the letter."

"You mean 'to the letter.' You've followed my instructions to the letter, haven't you, Michel?" The doctor looked out his hotel window at the late summer landscape of Frederikshavn Harbor.

"Yes, yes! I now realize the error of my ways . . . last time with Yuri."

"You don't want to have a rejected kidney, right?"

"Of course not. That is why we have waited for my son to get healthy, is it not?"

"Yuri's kidney failed because of your hypertension," Dr. Salizar reminded Michel. "We have to keep that under control. You haven't smoked recently?"

"No, of course not. And I won't start again!" Michel was beginning to feel defensive.

"Good." Dr. Salizar smiled to soothe his patient. "We had to wait because of Gil's smoking and the dysentery."

"Will these affect the transplant?"

"I am sure it will be just fine."

"Will we be using the horse serum again?"

"Prophylactically, of course. I don't think you should concern yourself with the details of the surgery. Just stay focused on your long-term health. Stay focused on your diet and exercise."

"How long must he rest before he returns to his life?" asked Michel.

"Well, just like you, three to six weeks, depending on how he recovers and what he chooses to do."

"He will be able to do everything like Yuri, right?"

"He won't have any restrictions as far as I'm concerned, though he should not lift more than nine kilograms and he should avoid contact sports until he is fully recovered."

"I see. Thank you, Dr. Salizar. Your bedside manner is an improvement over your father's, may he rest in peace." Michel looked up at him with a plaintive face.

"May God forgive your brother for what he did." Dr. Salizar placed a hand on Michel's shoulder and gave him a reassuring smile. "I have forgiven him."

✝

"Keep down!"

"Why? I'm wearing a disguise, right?"

"I'm not the only one looking for you."

"So," Betty began as she tried to settle down in the trunk behind the removable rear seat covering her. The trunk's false wall created an area just barely large enough for a passenger or packages her size. The rest of the trunk contained hard cases storing lenses, cameras, tripods, miscellaneous equipment, and the spare tire.

"Listen, there are people expecting you to show up. They have your general description and are going to ask too many questions."

"Like who? And why aren't they looking for you?"

"No one suspects I'm anything more than a photojournalist. I'm a loner, so I never have anyone in the car with me."

"OK."

"So, if I'm suddenly seen running around with a woman like you . . ." Karl shrugged his shoulders slightly.

"Well, just imagine if I was seen running around with a man like you? I'd probably get shot!" Betty could not resist a snarky retort.

"Now, shut up! We're coming to the gate. Don't breathe."

Just to be ornery, Betty grunted at Karl, timing it so she would not actually blow their ruse.

Karl showed his credentials to the guard, who seemed nonplussed to see this particular photojournalist leaving the cargo area of the Copenhagen airport one more time. He waved Karl through without closely inspecting the car.

Ghosts were receding into the distant crevices of Betty's mind, their arms outstretched toward her with fingers contorted and pointed at her, begging for one last moment of attention before they faded into the darkness. Sleep.

Fifty-Four

Overlords

August 6, 2009 — An island in the Indian Ocean

"YOU ARE CERTAIN HE'S DEAD?" The woman had a hint of a Bavarian accent. Perhaps Oxford had worn the edges off her familiar tongue. "I was not sure he could die."

"Most certainly, our American cousin has passed into the void." Gustav's accent remained strongly Teutonic despite the best efforts of many tutors. Perhaps his lisp foiled them. "He's gone." Gustav sighed, sounding as if he were describing a favorite four-legged companion.

"For all the grief he has caused you . . . you are still fond of him!" Charles spoke in perfect English without a hint he had spent his youth in a Spanish boarding school.

"I believe Pierre and Marie can attest that even in pain one can find pleasure," Gustav retorted drolly while eyeing his half brother and stepsister.

"Yes, he is gone but not forgotten," Marie quickly chimed in. "Can we count on the son?"

"That is to be determined." Charles stretched his left arm out and used the tip of his second finger to remove a speck of dust from the desk. "We are giving him enough, just like the woman, to guide him to the next level. Failures happen; we are all human. Hence, we have contingency plans."

Pierre raised an eyebrow at Gustav, sending the signal with his smirk that he could deliver pain without pleasure.

"Will he continue his father's work or will he turn on us?" Gustav queried.

"We have gotten our investment back many times over, so he *is* the bonus round." Pierre slid the stack of paper with today's agenda, facts, figures, and trivia off the table and placed it into an incinerator by his side.

"One last item." Charles looked directly at Pierre to remind him who was in charge. "The woman."

"She arrived?" Pierre asked in a hushed tone.

"Is everything in place?" Gustav inquired as he lifted his espresso to his lips.

"As planned." Charles concurred, nodding as he looked over at Pierre.

"What contingencies do you anticipate?" Gustav placed the thin bone china cup gently on its saucer. The gold border rim on the setting gleamed brightly.

Charles took a large drink of his obsidian-colored beverage. "Besides the usual? My greatest concern is the information she is receiving. Is it reliable enough to guide her were we want her to go?"

Marie shuffled her pages until she came to a pink-colored sheet. "The information is solid enough, yet vague enough to hide its source. Clear enough to guide her in."

"We are the only ones who know about her." Charles clasped his hands behind his head and leaned back in his chair. "Casper is doing his job well. If we stick to our plan she will tilt the balance of power our way."

"Your OCD and micromanaging will be our downfall," Pierre scolded.

Gustav jumped to Charles's defense. "Your lack of follow-through and slacker tendencies are more likely to expose us, I should think."

"Well, I for one am glad we are finally done with this minutia; why not focus on the big picture? We have people taking care of the little things, right?" Charles unclasped his hands, sat up, and pushed slightly away from the densely carved African blackwood table.

Pierre rolled his eyes.

"I have decided to have our next meeting at the chalet outside Bern," Marie stated with obvious restrained excitement. "Any objections?"

"What of that hideous view?" Gustav asked derisively.

"Give it a rest, will you?" countered Charles.

A hurt but prideful Marie spilled her words out, unable to hold back any thought. "Oh, yes, the village. He had it removed but I am rebuilding it around the corner. I'll miss it, you know."

"For years you've complained that it spoiled the view!" retorted Pierre.

"Village? I thought they were your outbuildings." Gustav slid his cup and saucer to his left.

"Well, sometimes we just like to complain, we don't necessarily want the problem solved. Can't you see that?" Marie huffed, holding on to her cup a moment longer to take one more sip. Her unique color of lipstick stained the rim of the cup, a color no other woman in the world could obtain. Its pigment was derived from the riverine rabbit, a species on the brink of extinction with only two hundred adults remaining in Sutherland, a town in the Northern Cape of South Africa.

"Well, an avalanche was due to happen eventually! They never should have built—"

Charles waved the conversation away. "Enough! Berne in two weeks. Progress reports as needed. Your staff shall prepare for a month's stay."

"But . . . but . . . Monaco?" stammered Pierre.

"It will have to wait." Charles glared at Pierre. "We need to sort out our longer-range plans. The fifty-year plan needs updating, let alone the hundred-year. Hell, the twenty-year plan barely held up, what with the inconsistent implementation of the field staff." Charles looked away from Pierre and out the thirty-by-ten-foot window overlooking the Indian Ocean. Charles turned his gaze squarely on Gustav. "Don't you agree?"

"Yes, of course. We should be focused on long-range planning." Gustav fiddled with his shirt button as he considered how to express his sympathy for the death of Slim. "Charles, I'm sorry for the loss of your son."

"Slim should have known better. He strayed from the plan." Charles somehow sat straighter in his chair.

"Still, it's a tragic loss." Pierre restrained himself from making a cutting remark.

Marie looked like she was about to speak but held her words when Charles pushed back his chair and stood up. "Please feel free to do as you wish. The helicopters will leave in twelve hours. Anything you desire, as you know, is at your disposal. Marie, Pierre . . . you will be quite pleased with the trollop I've arranged for you in your guest bedroom." Charles smirked and chuckled slightly. "From one of the finest families of Europe, I've been told. Can you believe it? She's a virgin at twenty-one."

Charles left the others in the observation room and walked out onto the parapet to gaze into the ocean. He would stay there for several hours to watch the sunset. None of the others would join him.

"Pierre," Gustav called, "Charles did not issue new codes. Should we bring him back?"

"Please! For once, let us leave the minutia behind. I only just memorized the code for Frederikshavn . . . 5xx723bq . . . right?"

"That's correct, Pierre. I suppose we should leave him to his grief."

FIFTY-FIVE

MEA CULPA-BILITY

WITH A NOT-SO-GENTLE THUD, Betty hit the compartment wall and woke up. "Why are we stopping?" Betty hissed sharply. The sound of the garage door closing and the settling of the car signaled this stage of the journey had ended much quicker than she had expected.

"We're at the Copenhagen safe house." Karl gave her a hand to help her out of the hidden compartment of the trunk.

"Why didn't you tell me we were headed here?" grunted Betty as she slithered into the back seat.

Karl held the door for her as she clambered out and stretched her tired muscles. "I wasn't going to bring you here, but I need some answers before I take you any farther." He ambled over to the refrigerator in the garage and threw her a cold water bottle before grabbing another.

The safe house was unusual for the neighborhood. Most homes had carports or short drives for parking. This property had an extended driveway; the house was set behind another home where the yard was not visible from the street. Control owned all the homes surrounding the safe house compound. Behind the main building, a long permanent dock jutted out from the Dragør coastline with direct access to the ocean. This afforded Control the ability to transport people and equipment in and out of Denmark—as well as other coastal towns similarly situated—without going through customs. Cover documentation protected those who left the compound if there was a chance they would interact on an official basis.

"What do you want to know?" Betty gulped half of the liter container of springwater before pointing the sloshing bottle at the man she was not completely sure she could trust. "I probably should be asking *you* questions." Keeping her distance from the lithe agent, she followed him across the garage to the house entrance.

The secure door opened by a retinal scan and a palm-print machine hidden behind a panel disguised as the electrical box. Karl opened the door and escorted Betty through a hallway lined with shelves and wire-cage cabinets filled with weapons, bombs, chemicals, costumes, and the nick-knacks of the espionage trade. Betty whistled low as she ran her fingers across some of the gowns, but stopped short in front of the less lethal cabinet containing tranquilizer equipment.

"Mind if I borrow some of this?"

"Later. Bud has told me some things about you—things I want confirmed." Karl walked into the house after unlocking the matching secure door leading to the kitchen.

Following him in, Betty checked the refrigerator for anything without a beard of mold that looked edible. "Like what?"

"Why are you going solo?" Karl began pacing the floor.

Betty balanced her sense of hunger with a lack of trust for the Black Ops specialist at her back while she explored the unusually large refrigerator. "You're helping me, and Bud's got my back." She began throwing rotten food on the counter. "This is anything but a safe house with food like this in the fridge."

"That isn't what I mean."

"What do you mean, then?" Betty shook a bottle of dressing and put it back.

"Shit. I'm not supposed to ask you this." Karl stopped pacing and stared at the ceiling as if it could give him the answer or the courage he was looking for.

"Spill the beans or I'll spill your guts." Betty looked annoyed as she threw a rotten bag of vegetables into the trash.

"Listen . . . I don't know what is going on. You raised some hackles back at Control. Your number came up on the termination list . . . shoot on sight."

Betty looked at the pile of food determined to be unfit for human consumption. "I suppose I brought that on myself."

Karl took a step toward her with his hands plaintively asking for answers.

Betty pulled her P226 out of her waistband behind her back. "Then why didn't you kill me when I came out of the container?" She waved for Karl to turn around and put his hands behind his head. "Spread your feet." The gun barrel poked deep into the small of Karl's back as she searched for weapons. "Has McFluffy tested these spy suits for close range?"

"I trust McFluffy and his spider goat silk, but I don't wish to be your test subject."

Betty stepped back to look over the several guns, knives, and a garrote she had removed from Karl and placed on the kitchen island. "Have you taken a round?"

"Both . . . with a suit and without. I prefer the suit."

"Me too."

"You've taken rounds?"

"One in the calf. The others bounced off me like Superman. My glider was shredded with bullet holes."

"Your suit didn't stop the bullet?"

"The shot was from below; it went through my boot, along my ankle, and under the suit . . . lodged in the meat of my calf." Betty cringed inside, thinking about her rehabilitation. "I guess I was lucky it didn't shatter my ankle."

"Damn. He had a lucky shot. May I put my arms down now?"

"I suppose. I had lots of bruising from his not-so-lucky shots."

"So, that's when Gil was captured?"

"He drove the truck off the mountain so I would get enough lift with the glider. Bastard risked his life for me twice that night."

"Is that why you're risking termination to find him?"

"I wouldn't be alive without him. He deserves my best effort."

"What next? After you . . . I mean *we* save Gil."

"What do you mean?"

"Are you going to return to Control?"

"Yes . . . I suppose I will. I have some questions of my own Howell needs to answer."

"OK. Let's pull up the latest from Bud on the computer. Maybe come up with a plan instead of just going in shooting. What do you say?" Karl moved over to the computer and made a secure connection to Control.

"Can we order some food first?" Betty asked with a famished look.

✝

An hour later, with full bellies, Karl and Betty had assembled an outline for a basic plan to breach the perimeter of Gil's presumed prison based on the information fed to them by Bud via a secure live chat over the Internet. Frederikshavn Harbor figured prominently throughout the naval history of the Baltic Sea. Inside the modern commercial harbor was a marina building that most likely, according to Bud, contained a temporary surgical unit and a squad of guards protecting Michel Vasilyev and his prize, Gil.

"How do you know Vasilyev is dying of kidney failure?" Betty was looking over the different manifests of deliveries to the shack.

Even through the distortion of encryption, Bud's nasal twang came through, "I've traced a dialysis machine delivered to this building." A bull's-eye blinked red over a map to the right of Bud's image on the screen.

"Why couldn't it be someone else?" Betty retorted.

"There is no other reason for it being there. If he wasn't trying to hide, he could just go into the local hospital for treatment," Bud confidently stated.

"But what does Gil have to do with Michel?"

"The only connection I can find is that Gil was born in a Salizar hospital in Belarus while his dad was stationed at the embassy. Michel's sister-in-law died during childbirth the same day."

"Weird in a small-world way, but how is that a connection?" interjected Karl.

"I thought that was a little too coincidental myself. I checked into Gil's parents' medical files. They aren't his parents."

"How the hell did you figure that out?"

"Gil is B positive, right?" Bud stated cryptically.

"So? How could that matter?" Betty squinted at the two-inch-square video image of Bud back in Control.

"Both of Gil's parents were A negative. They couldn't genetically produce a B positive child. It's impossible."

"Whose kid is he, then?" Betty shook her head incredulously.

"Either Yuri's or Michel's. My money is on Michel, making Gil a perfect match for a kidney donation."

"Holy shit," stated Betty flatly, half in disbelief. Her own heritage only just revealed in the past week, and now Gil's.

"Betty?"

"Hmmm . . . What?"

"Try not to kill Michel, OK? We kind of need him for intelligence purposes."

"If he doesn't get in the way, sure."

"There is more you should know."

"Like what?"

"Getner was the source for the mole."

"Wow. Didn't see that coming."

"The source of the mole originated with José."

"José? Are you sure? That doesn't make any sense!"

"Quite sure, I traced the communications."

"What happened?"

"He was terminated."

"Getner? Who did the job?"

"Howell. He did both Getner and José."

"That son of a bitch!" Betty yelled at the floating image of the nerd on the computer. "Bud, warn him, no, tell him I'm coming to kill him. It will not be a slow death, either."

"Betty, calm down. What's the big deal about Tom terminating a traitor like José?" questioned Bud as he turned down the volume on his earpiece.

"Traitor? Why the only traitor is the arrogant bastard you call the 'director.' He said he would help me find the killer of José! If I worked for him I would get my revenge! Ha! He was the killer all along, and he did it to get me to join Control! Tell Strivner that I'm on my way . . . as soon as I get Gil."

"Wait, you don't understand!"

"Tell Howell he better gear up, 'cause this is war!" Betty killed the connection and then killed the computer with a round from her P226.

"Uhm. Betty. We kind of needed that computer."

"Don't piss me off, Karl!" She aimed her pistol squarely at Karl's forehead and pierced through him with her cold stare. "Now grab the shit we need or make a run for it. You're either with me or you're dead."

"I'll grab the gear," gulped Karl.

FIFTY-SIX

THE CONS OF PROS

"**T**HAT SHOULD ABOUT DO IT." Karl gently pressed the trunk of the Audi closed. If it were not for the load-leveling suspension, the tailpipe would have touched the concrete from the mass of the weapons: assault rifles, pistols, rockets, mines, tear gas, tranquilizers, communications gear, and—of course—the assorted odds and ends. For lack of room in the rear, he put his camera gear in the back seat next to Betty's train case.

Betty gracefully made an entrance into the safe-house garage in an ensemble of clothing that could have come straight from the latest fashion magazine: the straw hat with a giant green bow completed the ankle-length, split-front dress with matching bow on the backside. Karl stood at the rear of the car and made a low whistle.

"Thank God I went to all those pageants with Jil!" mumbled Betty.

"All those what?"

"I was talking to myself. Pageants. My best friend growing up competed in beauty pageants and I was her assistant. Based on my usual choice of clothing, you'd never know."

"You look great, like you're about to go to a polo match or bocce tournament." Karl walked to the driver's door but hesitated before opening it. "What now?"

Betty cleared her throat as she stood by the passenger door and waited.

A bewildered Karl held onto the handle of the driver's door trying to think of what he might have forgotten.

Betty darted her eyes to the door handle while keeping both hands on the brown leather strap of her canvas Chanel purse.

"You're kidding, right?" questioned Karl.

"A gentleman always opens the door for a lady," replied Betty.

Karl shook his head as he slunk around the front of the sedan. "I suppose I need to learn how to serve the snooty wealthy with a smile if I'm going to be a concierge in Vail," he mumbled. He opened the door for Betty with a wave of his left hand, bowing to his lady.

"Much better!" declared Betty as she carefully guided her dress onto the seat and protected her bow from being crushed.

Karl clambered in, started the engine, and opened the garage door.

"So, you and I are just going to waltz around the harbor as I pose and you take photos?"

"It's what I do all day while I wait for an assignment."

"Have you been in Frederikshavn before for either an assignment or a photo shoot?"

"Wow. I suppose so. It's the way to Sweden and points north. I've been up and down most of Europe for the past twenty-five years . . . so, yeah, I'm sure I've done a couple of shoots. It's a strategic port." The A6 began rolling backward, angling into the parking spot teed off the driveway to turn around.

"You don't remember?"

"There are a lot of things I try to forget. Don't you?" Karl put the car in drive and looked squarely at Betty.

"I suppose so. Yes." Betty looked at her hands, examining them for signs of blood. Of course there were not any, but she could see the blood just the same.

"Are you ready for this?"

"Absolutely."

Karl pushed the accelerator and gently guided their quasi-assault vehicle into the street, heading for their photo shoot at Frederikshavn Harbor.

"Oh, you may need these." Karl handed Betty her new passport indicating her cover name. "Fresh off the printer while you were dressing."

"Irena Basta?"

"Ask Bud. You look amazing in that dress. Better than some of the models I've shot professionally."

She gave him a knowing look.

Karl realized the unintended pun and added, "Photographically."

Betty began to laugh out loud and seemed to be releasing all the tension and anxiety that had built up over the past several months. Karl wondered if he needed to pull over for her to calm down. He turned right onto Stationsvej instead of left to the planned route via Kirkevej. Nordre Dragørvej had a more rural setting with many places to stop without notice in case Betty could not regain her composure or if he had a problem on his hands.

Betty recognized the change of direction quickly. "Karl, what are you doing?"

"You scared me there a little. I'm taking an alternate route."

"Why?"

"Does it really matter?"

"Yes!"

"I thought you were losing it. Having a psychotic break with reality."

"And you were going to do what?"

"That all depended on you." Karl looked over at Betty briefly and noted she had recomposed herself. "You seem fine now. This will only add a few minutes to our journey. Besides, I kind of like this route better."

"Who do you think I am, Karl?"

"I'm not following you."

"I've spent my life thinking I was the daughter of my parents and only recently I've learned that I was adopted."

"OK."

"Not just adopted, Karl, I was the daughter of spies handling my adopted father who is a double agent for Control."

"Go on."

"I was trained from birth to work for Control."

"What's your point?"

"I could kill you in under three seconds with what is sitting in this front cabin; faster than you could kill me with your holstered pistol."

"If we are getting down to brass tacks—"

Betty got to the point, "I think we have."

"This is my last assignment before 'retiring' to a cushy job in Vail."

"So, you'll be sitting on your ass. What's your point?"

"I don't have anything to lose."

"Neither do I, Karl." Betty looked around and considered the ordinary lives of the people they passed. People who were not trained to do the dirty work of a world-class secret spy agency. In a nearly inaudible whisper she repeated, "Neither do I."

"OK."

"OK." Betty turned down the visor and opened the vanity mirror to check her makeup. "Why did you join Control?"

"Seriously?" Karl slowed the sedan for a sharp hairpin left turn as Nordre Dragørvej ended and became Hovedgaden at the perimeter of Copenhagen Airport.

"Seriously."

"I was recruited by a man who pandered to my pride and self-confidence. I see that now. I don't regret it, but I see it for what it was."

"What was it?"

"Just like when we're in the field. You use a contact's weaknesses against themselves. I didn't know where I wanted to go in life, I just knew I wanted to go everywhere and see everything."

"You were OK with walking away from your family?"

"Usual story. My dad, the Belarusian, was an alcoholic—hell, he died in a gutter outside a bar after he threw up on himself. Aspirated the vomit. Choked to death." Karl was quiet for a while and Betty let him have his moment of reflection. "My mom died of breast cancer just before I was recruited."

The sun was shining. The air was clear. A stark contrast to the dark picture Karl painted of his childhood.

Betty waited a long time for the kilometers to pile up before she pushed him again. "Then what?"

"I'm passionate about photography. Being an assassin wasn't part of the vision, just a necessary evil to pay the ticket."

"Have you ever worked up close?"

"Only when I've had to. Usually, I'm at a distance. Rifle with a scope. You?"

"Both. All of the above." Betty got quiet and Karl took the hint.

Betty looked over at Karl after they turned onto the highway from a small village area. "Why do you keep looking in your rearview mirror?"

"The car behind us is hanging back. They are following us but at a distance."

"How is that possible?"

"It probably isn't anything. I'm just way too paranoid these days. It's why I'm getting out of fieldwork."

"How long have you been in?"

"Too long." Karl took a deep breath and sighed. "About thirty years."

Betty gave a low whistle. "That's a long time. You really know your stuff by now."

"I'm tired and getting sloppy. If I don't get out now, I'm going to start making mistakes. The unrecoverable kind."

"Why—" Betty stopped her deposition voice and tried to keep it casual instead. "What were you running from when you joined?"

"I had a bad breakup. I didn't want to be anywhere near my high school sweetheart. My hitch in the army was up. With my Mom buried and the house sold, it was either reenlist or leave town. Europe sounded really cool."

"You chose to leave. Was it salvageable?" Betty pried.

"Maybe. Probably. Damn. It was my fault anyway. I had a fling and she punished me by fucking my best friend." Karl shook his head and went back to the rearview mirror to see if the car had gained ground. It was still one hundred yards back, but easier to spot now that they were cruising on E20, Vestmotorvejen Highway.

"Kind of hard to overcome that."

"Yes. Ummm, Betty, we are still being followed."

"I can't see it." Betty tried to look casually in her passenger-door mirror, but the angle was not good. "What make and color is the car?"

"Red. A small VW, I think. Odd, it's too obvious for a tail."

"Right. Someone wants us to know they are following us but not be threatened."

"If it was me, I would have a car in front guessing where the subject was going. Trade off if you miss a turn."

"OK." Betty's surveillance training was extensive, but not for this type of situation.

"If I had to guess, it's the blue Volvo up ahead." Karl began slowly edging up to the blue sedan. At first, the mop of hair framed by the headrest only casually noticed his subject closing in. Then it became a torrent of motion as the driver attempted to figure out what was going on.

"I think you have his attention now," Betty cracked dryly.

"Put this headscarf on." Karl tossed Betty a silk wrap from his coat pocket.

"I don't need a scarf, I have a hat. What's going on Karl?"

"You need to change your look for what comes next."

Betty placed her hat on the back seat, covered her head, and placed her large-size sunglasses squarely on her nose. "So, what comes next?"

"Either I've been compromised or you're the target. Take your pick. Either one won't end well if we don't take control."

"What are we going to do?"

"There is a petrol station at the rest stop ahead. We'll pull in and see if one or both cars follow." Karl slowed down and turned his blinker on a kilometer too soon for the rest stop. The blue Volvo got the message and pulled off at the rest stop ahead of Karl. The red VW followed Karl in. The Statoil station had four sets of pumps. The last space was open and Karl slid the Audi in. The first chase vehicle had pulled into the first available slot. The red VW guy headed to the rest room in the service station and took up a watch post inside.

"Betty, I don't like this."

"What do you propose?"

"I really don't like following the rules anymore."

"What rules?"

"Not making a scene, don't get noticed, abort if report. I mean everything they have trained us for needs to be thrown out."

"OK." Betty casually shrugged her shoulders and smirked at the thought of Howell having a conniption over the rule breaking.

"I'm going to place a plastic explosive with phosphor on the gas tanker there, on the second half of that tandem." An island wedge separated the station from the rest stop road. The Statoil truck driver tamped his freshly purchased cigarettes as he walked back to his waiting load.

"That will get someone's attention. Why phosphor? What about cameras?"

"The phosphor will make the gas burn better—think napalm. Ever seen one of these?" Karl pulled out of his camera bag a cylinder two feet long by eight inches in circumference. It looked like a telephoto lens case.

"I'm not following you."

"EMP."

"What?"

"Electromagnetic pulse. If you lob this up on the roof within twenty seconds of pressing the button that looks like the hasp release, the entire electronics system of the station, including the video recorder, will fry. But we have to pull past that intersection before it goes or our car will lose its electronics too."

"What's the point of blowing the tanker?"

"In case their chase cars still work, the tanker will take out the road and maybe them."

"Collateral damage?"

"Lots. I can live with it. Can you?"

Betty glared at Karl.

"You're in the revenge business, right?"

Betty rubbed her temples. "OK, OK. Fuck!"

"Wait for my signal. I have to place the plastic explosives and make sure the driver is ready to leave. Then you toss the EMP on the roof after pressing the button. Walk as fast as you can or run back to the car."

Karl headed to the trunk and rummaged in a black tactical bag for the device he needed. He placed the explosive in a black sack and casually walked over to the truck with his camera in hand, yelling to the driver that he wanted to take his picture, if he was not in a hurry. While Betty waited, she kept an eye on the guys from the chase car.

Karl explained that he wanted a photo taken from the front of the truck looking back. The driver shrugged, turned, and headed for the cab of the truck while Karl placed the black sack on the metal grate under the tank at the very rear and waved to Betty. Karl unhitched the rear half of the load as the driver got into his cab. He walked to the front of truck and began taking pictures while directing the driver to stick his torso out of the window and wave. The guys from the chase car became agitated and Blue Volvo prodded Red VW to get closer to see what Karl was up to.

Betty walked quickly, as if she suddenly wanted to use the restroom before resuming their trip. Just as she reached the door, she initiated the countdown and heaved the cylinder onto the roof. Changing her mind about the bathroom, she trotted back to the car as Karl climbed in. The Audi began moving before Betty could sit down in the car. "Jesus, Karl!"

The tanker began rolling, leaving the tandem behind. Betty slid down in the seat and tried to click her seat belt. Karl moved from the outer drive to the inner drive of the rest stop with a hard left, cutting off the fuel truck. They barely got past him, causing the driver to slam on his brakes. The driver of the tanker truck threw up his hands in utter frustration. Karl counted down "3 . . . 2 . . . 1 . . ." and pressed the remote trigger. The tanker ruptured gas and began to burn.

"Why wasn't there a fireball?" Betty asked as she righted herself in her seat.

"That's just in the movies. Only vaporized gas burns. The phosphor keeps burning for ten minutes and thus the vapor remains ignited." The fire spread as the gas spread. The tanker driver scrambled out of the cab and scurried away from the disaster. A second trucker, who abandoned his fueling, began backing his transport up as quickly as he could, leaving a fuel hose dangling and spilling diesel. He jackknifed at the entrance to the station when he tried to make the turn backing up. Trapped on one end by a massive wall of fire and the other end blocked by the jackknifed semi gave the pursuing drivers a moment to panic before jumping back into their vehicles. The red VW driver gave up in frustration when his engine would not turn over. The EMP had done its job. While rejoining the chase, the blue Volvo made a five-point turn and then slammed over several curbs, damaging the vehicle's suspension. He drove through the burning gasoline and a fire briefly broke out on the underbody of the car, but extinguished itself from lack of fuel. The car became erratic due to the damaged suspension and the roughed-up tires, unbalanced by the curbs and softened by the fire.

On the fringe of acceptable driving for Denmark, Karl accelerated out of the rest area. The blue Volvo observed no such niceties, clipping a Porsche and causing several drivers to slam on their brakes and blast their horns. The rest area looked more like a demolition derby than an island of tranquility.

Fifty-Seven

Shaken, Not Stirred

"**T**AKE THE WHEEL!"

"What?" Betty kept looking back at the devastation of the fire and the scattering people.

"I got shots of the guys following us. I want to check the pictures, but I need to put on my reading glasses." Karl let go of the wheel but kept his foot on the accelerator. He grasped his camera with both hands and quickly reviewed the shots he had taken while walking back from the tanker. "Son of a bitch!"

"What?" Betty checked over her shoulder to make sure their merge onto the highway was clear.

"The guy in the blue Volvo was at the pier two days ago."

"What pier?"

"The one where I found the sarcophagus remains of Gil's transport from Venezuela to Copenhagen."

"So they're after you, not me! What did you do?"

"They got a little too nosy; I told you I am only one mistake away from retirement. Those guys pushed my buttons . . . I sort of broke one guy's knee."

"I thought—holy shit!" A motorcycle veered away from the Audi and narrowly missed the back end of a truck as he got out of their way. "I totally didn't see that guy coming."

"He's OK. Don't worry about it." Karl took back the steering wheel from Betty and handed her the camera so she could memorize the goon's face. "Watch for the Volvo. He was just far enough out he might have survived the EMP."

"Yeah . . ." Betty spied the blue Volvo closing in quickly on their position. Smoke poured out of the wheel wells. "I think he survived it . . ." Sparks flared from underneath the carriage of the automobile. "Here he comes now . . ." Something was loose underneath, either the muffle or part of the suspension. ". . . but I don't think he'll be with us long."

"Why do you say that?" Karl took a longer look in the rearview mirror. "I see. Shit! He'll catch up to us before the bridge."

"He won't catch us." Betty stated in a calculated way.

"How do you figure?" Karl quizzed.

"Basic math. Since leaving the rest stop, we have driven an average of ninety-five kilometers per hour, two minutes ahead of him. We are eight kilometers from the fire. He has to be driving around a hundred fifty to a hundred sixty kilometers per hour to catch up. From the look of his car he won't catch us before one of his tires blow."

"Get the fuck out of here! Math genius."

"Speed up just a little and we'll have a better cushion."

"I'm impress—" A bullet struck the rear window. "—ed."

"I think he might be a math whiz too."

Karl looked over his shoulder and frowned. "Damn it!"

"What?"

"He's marked us."

"It's OK. Look, his tire blew." Betty grinned for being right. The Volvo came within twenty meters of them before markedly slowing down due to the ruined tire. The car lurched back and forth briefly before veering under the trailer of a semi. The rear tires of the heavy truck crushed the hood of the smaller vehicle but continued on its way, as if a small speed bump popped out of hiding. The Volvo began rolling unmercifully, unpredictably bouncing three meters into the air like a swimmer catching a breath between butterfly strokes. All traffic behind them came to a halt as the car slowly turned for another revolution; the metal creaking as the heap rumbled to a stop blocking both lanes of traffic. Additional accidents to the rear would complicate the mess.

"Holy shit! It must have rolled twenty times!"

"Five complete turns." Betty confidently corrected him. "Basic physics, actually."

"What? Oh, never mind." He drew in a deep breath. "I think the police will find their bomber conveniently waiting for them in the Volvo," he finished dryly.

"What now?" Betty took the scarf off and replaced her hat.

"The tollbooth for the Storebæltsforbindelsen Bridge is next. Look bored."

"Why? What's the big deal here?"

"Nothing really . . . just a checkpoint where they will see us clearly."

"Who?"

"Anybody watching: cameras, eyes, toll agents, other travelers. Our rear window makes us stand out. No time to fix it right now. I'll put some packing tap over the damage before we stop for the toll. Wish I had a popular bumper sticker to cover it."

"Whatever." Betty sounded bored as she waved her hand dismissively.

"Good. That's exactly what I meant."

Karl exited the Vestmotorvegen at the Tårnborgvej exit. He drove south from the roundabout and crossed under the highway. At the next roundabout, he spied a 7-Eleven and pulled into the parking lot. "I'll be right back."

"Whatever." Betty pulled out a fashion magazine from Karl's bag and pretended to be only slightly interested.

The hole was low in the glass, just off center. The bullet had lodged in the dash just in front of Betty. Karl placed a sticker over the fractured glass, covering the worst of the damage, and reentered the car. "That should do it."

"Whatever."

"You aren't the least bit curious?"

"If I had to guess you picked the European Union flag."

"Not a bad guess." Karl was impressed.

No reason to tell him I caught the yellow stars on a blue field as he walked up.

"Ready?"

"Whatever."

Karl smirked. "You have the whole bored routine down."

The tollbooth split into different payment methods: green for the prepaid BroBizz pass, blue for automated credit cards, and yellow for cash or manual credit card transactions. Karl pulled into the sole yellow lane and waited his turn.

"Why are we paying cash? Why not a credit card so we don't have contact?"

"If they're following me, they'll be watching any expense account they tracked down. Cash is king." Nodding and smiling through the entire transaction, Karl paid the 230 Danish kroner and took his change.

"How much was that . . . in dollars?" queried Betty as they rolled away from the booth.

"The exchange rate is about six to one."

"What a rip off! Thirty-seven dollars?"

"What do you expect for the privilege of crossing the world's third-longest suspension bridge?"

Betty yawned, threw the glossy magazine back into Karl's bag, and rubbed her eyes.

"Nap time?"

"I forgot how tired I am." Betty attempted to settle into her seat, adjusting the leather back to a comfortable angle. She was asleep as the road changed from the smooth highway to the rougher bridge decking.

Karl settled in for the remaining 350-kilometer drive. They would arrive at their destination in under three and a half hours. He looked over at the sleeping, nonlethal looking woman. He planned on waking her a half hour before arriving. Karl admonished himself for getting softhearted. She was an agent, not an objective; a partner, not a potential conquest. He took several deep breaths and returned his focus to driving.

✝

August 7, 2009 — Control

"Bud, you have some explaining to do." Howell glowered at his intelligence director.

"What? You told me to watch out for her." He fidgeted with his baseball cap and licked his lips.

"Twitter? Seriously?" Howell slid the printout of Bud's communications with Betty across the glass-covered wood desk Tom Howell Sr. and a few lesser men had occupied. Tom momentarily felt unworthy for missing Bud's deception. "Seriously?"

"You never asked about social media. I gave you truthful answers and took care of her just like you asked me to. Like you said, I told you what you needed to know."

Bud pulled out a single sheet of paper with a digital copy of the codes Howell had found on the Belarus security officer. "I figured out the codes. Just so you know, I do my job." Bud summoned the courage to make direct eye contact with his boss, something he rarely could do. "All of it."

"What are they for?"

"Access codes."

"For what?"

"They are the password for entry."

"For whom?"

"Initially, I thought it was just wireless networks set up for communication. These people are lazy. It's also their secure door codes."

"Whose?"

"The Cabal, of course."

"What about Minsk? Gil isn't in Minsk, is he?"

"He's in Frederikshavn, Denmark."

Howell slammed his fist on the desk. "Did this slip your mind earlier?" he demanded.

"You said you wanted Betty to have a long leash, to see where she took us. If I told everybody what was going on, then maybe that info gets out to the Cabal. Asset reallocations are telltale signs just as much as intercepted messages," Bud studiously explained.

"Seriously? This is how you defend your actions?"

"I did what you asked me to do."

"Get the hell out of my office." Howell turned away to hide a slight smile; however, he turned back with a frown and declared, "Tell me everything. I want a full report on her status in twenty minutes." Howell looked Bud squarely in the eyes, making sure he had his undivided attention. "Everything."

Bud slinked away, sulking for the chastisement for doing his job, even if it was pretty far into the gray area of not obeying protocol. "He wants it all?" sneered Bud. "By God, he'll get the whole fucking haystack!" A crooked smile crossed his lips. "Time for a document dump!"

Fifty-Eight

Needling Things

TWENTY MINUTES LATER, Bud dropped a thumb drive onto Howell's desk and plopped down into the leather chair, waiting for a reaction.

Howell slowly turned around, picked up the drive, and dropped it back onto his father's mahogany desk. "So?"

"You asked for all the documents. What, did you want me to print them out?"

"Why don't you summarize them for me." He leaned forward and placed his chin in his left hand. "I'm all ears."

Bud cleared his throat and took a swig from his water bottle before beginning. "Betty became suspicious of Grace when she found a note about cleaning José stuck between her refrigerator and the counter. This spiraled out of control when she discovered that Grace was her aunt and the mother of Timmy, your half brother."

"My what?"

"You didn't know that Grace had an affair with your dad?"

"There is a lot I don't know. I'm not particularly surprised in a general sense, but . . ." Howell waved his hand for Bud to continue, but he leaned in a little closer.

"As you know, Timmy died a year ago while cleaning the early fallout from Getner's leaks to Susan Miranda, a.k.a. Babs McGillicutty."

"Yes."

"Grace maintained a shrine to Timmy. Betty saw it, along with pictures of Grace with Beth, let alone with your father and Timmy while she was doing surveillance. This led to her drugging and questioning Grace."

"Really . . . and how did she manage that? This is Grace we are talking about."

"She slipped STP-17 into Grace's drink when she got her to leave the room."

"And why didn't Grace remember this?"

"Betty had included a dose of flunitrazepam with the STP-17." Howell did not have a look of recognition. "Rohypnol? Roofie?" Still no recognition. "Date-rape drug?"

"Oh, memory loss. Go on." He waved his hand again.

"Right. So, she interrogated Grace, learning that Grace is Beth's half sister and the aunt she never met. Betty also began learning about her adopted family's history with Control. That is when she contacted me about Line X."

"Right, Bob's transfer of rigged technology back to the Soviets—"

"—through Belarus; hence, the Yuri and Michel connection . . . Salizar . . . Gil . . ."

"Do we have a map connecting everyone or do I need to start diagramming this?"

"It's on the thumb drive." Bud pointed at the electronic storage between them with a quick smile of pride.

"Do you really think I'm going to plug that thing into my computer knowing you were primarily responsible for Stuxnet?" Howell looked quizzically at his director of intelligence.

Bud ignored the compliment cum accusation. "So, Gil is really the son of Michel and Yuri's wife, who died during childbirth and provided the tissue for your mother's eye transplant."

"You aren't making this up, are you?"

"Salizar the elder also had transplanted a kidney from Yuri to his twin, Michel, fifteen years ago. Now, with Yuri dead, Gil became the ideal match, which is why Michel rescued him from Montoya's compound before he was tortured enough to divulge anything. I don't think Michel gives a rat's ass about Control and probably hasn't gotten anything out of Gil."

"Rather convenient."

"Per your request, I arranged for Betty to make a clean break from D.C. via a CIA contact who flew her in a cargo container to Copenhagen, where I had Karl pick her up for additional assistance."

"Now, Bud, this is the crux of the matter. What gave you the idea I wanted you to take this kind of initiative?" Howell leaned back in his chair and played with the center drawer of the desk, repeatedly sliding it in and out half an inch as he contemplated Bud's story.

Bud looked up at the ceiling and tapped the side of his head. "'If—and this is a big if—Betty pops up and slips through, tail her. Do not stop her. She may be our ticket to tracking down the core Cabal membership. She's pissed off and wants some scalps. I wouldn't put it past her to slip out of the country. We need to start watching European destinations as well. Put calls out to whoever owes you a favor.'"

"Nice parlor trick." Howell slid the drawer out a full inch and stopped. "Recording my office, are we?"

"I guess you forgot I have a phonographic memory."

"Phonographic?"

"If I want to remember something, I tap my temple, otherwise I'd go insane from some stupid song playing over and over in my head." Bud held his index finger at his temple, ready to store information.

Howell cleared his throat and slid the drawer back in. "Continue."

"I took the liberty of having David arrange transportation for you and an extra jet standing by for extraction. You need to leave in"—Bud looked at his watch—"five minutes."

"Where am I going?"

"Ålborg. Just down the road from Frederikshavn and where all the action is tonight. I'm sure Betty's looking forward to talking with you."

"I should make you come with, but I suppose you'd whine the whole way about not having your gear."

"You're correct, Director."

"Bud." Howell pulled his drawer all the way out, removed his SIG Sauer P226 and silencer, and put them in his jacket as he stood up. He then grabbed a velvet box before closing the drawer firmly. "I want you to have this medal. For taking initiative and risk beyond reason and . . . for being right."

"Thank you. What if I'd been wrong?"

"Let's focus on the positive, shall we? I have a plane to catch." Howell swiped the thumb drive off the desk and strode out into the hall.

August 8, 2009 — Near Frederikshavn, Denmark

"Wakey, wakey." Karl nudged Betty lightly in the shoulder. Betty grabbed his hand and began to twist his wrist before she realized who was poking her. Karl yelped, "Hey . . . yow! Let go . . . you'll make us crash!"

She let go and sat up in her seat, rubbed her eyes, looked around at what appeared to be the same scenery as before, and gathered her thoughts. *Oh. Denmark. Gil. Karl is helping me. I need to check in with Bud. I need to check my makeup!* Betty opened the vanity mirror in the visor and looked at the damage done to her face: the damage of time, martial arts, and hand-to-hand combat with terrorists, but most of all the mileage. *What the hell am I doing here? How did I let this go on for so long? How the fuck am I going to stop this carousel?* She freshened her makeup and smiled at herself. "I never did mind the little things."

"What?" Karl drove their urban assault vehicle, née Audi A6, with his left knee as he rubbed his right wrist.

"Oh. Did I say that out loud?" Betty put her things back in order and squared her posture with her hands in her lap. "So where are we and what's the plan?"

"We will be arriving in twenty minutes. First stop is the Bangsbo Fort."

"The what fort?"

"It was originally a German World War Two installation. The Danes expanded it and now most of it's a museum."

"Why are we going there?"

"It has a commanding view of the town. We'll be able to do surveillance and planning from there. Besides, you will look incredible next to those fifteen-centimeter guns."

"Whatever." Betty rolled her eyes. "I'm not sure we have time to mess around. Remember why we are here?"

"I know why we're here—Gil. We have to make sure we know what's down there."

"Can't Bud get us some satellite views?" Betty looked at Karl with a dismissive frown.

"We need horizontal views, not just vertical. We're the closest assets available. It'll only take a half hour—hour tops."

The Bangsbo Fort covered a hillside with a strategic view overlooking the North Sea Bay of Kattegat and the island Læsø. To the north lay the shipyards of Frederikshavn, the location of Gil and his captors. Karl paid their hundred-kroner entry fee. After he selected his camera gear, the two traipsed off to the concrete bunkers for their photo shoot.

"This really is a nice location for a shoot," Karl said. I love the contrast of the old concrete and the overgrown vegetation." The subtle noise of the camera shutter flicking open and capturing Betty's image stood out over the peaceful surroundings. There were no other visitors nearby, so Karl gave up the pretense of photographing Betty and began to focus on their objective.

"Can you see it?" Betty asked casually.

Karl had a single pole to balance the thirty pounds of camera and telephoto lens. Stability was needed to take in the five-kilometer view of the docks. "Yes, nothing yet. Hang on." His digital SLR camera lacked the sound of film advancing, but the shutter clearly indicated he was taking shots. "Here, take a look."

Betty leaned in and looked at the grainy image of a gray metal building with a black roof surrounded by a chain-link fence. Standing outside a steel door was a stout man smoking a cigarette. Another man was stowing his pistol as he stepped through the door for his own smoke break. "I think we have a winner."

Karl returned to taking surveillance photos, not wanting to miss any opportunity of capturing their target's identity before they attempted to breach Gil's jail. "Go stand over by that bunker and pose, just in case someone comes our way." He pointed toward the raised 15 cm gun turret from the sunken World War Two Danish Niels Juel artillery ship. "Go look pretty."

Betty glared at him. *Why do all men need to be such assholes?* "Just for you, Karl," she sneered. *We know where Gil is. There can't be more than five guys in there . . . why are we . . . shit. I have to work on my patience. I need more sleep.*

Karl continued taking photographs for an hour until a young couple appeared with a picnic basket for a private lunch. They slowed and stopped talking when they noticed Karl and Betty.

Karl called down from on top of the bunker, "I think we have enough here. Let's head into town for some industrial shots."

The pair worked their way around to avoid any interaction with the young couple. Thirty minutes later, they were back at their original destination—a block away, just out of sight of the door where the guards would take their smoke breaks.

Fifty-Nine

A Nick in Time

"I FIGURE THE NEXT GUYS WILL be out in ten minutes. We'll position ourselves over there." Karl was pointing at a pile of material on the pier waiting to be loaded. "Take this rolling luggage with you."

"We're coming back to prep before going in, right?" Betty felt vulnerable in her outfit. *Damn disadvantage. Always the case when you're eye candy. How do you hide a gun?*

"What if an opportunity presented itself? Would you want to pass it by to come back for gear?"

"You have full body armor and a complement of weapons. I have my spider-goat-silk camisole top and panties, backed up with a pistol in my handbag. What more could a girl want?" She gave a false smile and grabbed the rolling bag. "Shall we?"

They walked down the pier to a jumble of castoff material before Karl stopped to take her photo. He had changed the lens to a smaller telephoto, light enough to skip the monopod. The camera hung by its strap on his side when not in use. "Don't turn around. A Mercedes just pulled up." Snap . . . snap . . . snap. "Two men are getting out." Karl aimed just over Betty's shoulder, with the camera focused beyond her. "We have Yuri's twin brother and a rather well-dressed, midforties, swarthy, European-looking guy. He has a bag." Snap . . . snap . . . snap. "Looks like a doctor's satchel."

"What are they doing?"

"The tango." Snap . . . snap . . . snap.

"Har, har, har." Betty pretended to be laughing as part of her pose. Inside, her nerves were on fire as she thought about all the possible ways this could go down. *I just have to remember that Gil has to still be alive. Why else would a doctor be checking in on him?* "You're too funny."

"Punching in a code to unlock the door." Snap . . . snap . . . snap.

"Are you getting it?" Betty asked with an unintentionally snarky bent. Calm down. He's doing his job. I need to do mine. Betty struck a new pose for the camera.

"What do you think?" Karl moved slightly to his left. "Fuck!" Michel shifted to Karl's left as he punched the code before grabbing the handle to open the door. "He blocked the view for the last digit." Snap . . . snap . . . snap.

"This is good." Betty tried a different pose. She began channeling her inner Catwoman.

"Why?" Snap . . . snap . . . snap.

"They must be shorthanded or a guard would be letting them in."

Karl stopped taking pictures and looked directly at Betty. "Good point. Let's move over there—I want to work around the building in a big circle."

They strolled down the pier with Karl occasionally snapping a shot or telling Betty to take a pose to keep up appearances. A ten-foot chain-link fence separated the compound from the pier. Two German shepherds patrolled the perimeter. Karl reviewed the pictures of the keypad and announced, "I've never seen a keypad like this, fully alphanumeric."

"What code did he type?"

"Lower-case letters . . . 5xx723b . . . I missed the last character. Too many possibilities to guess."

"I've sent it to Bud. He'll have the answer," Betty stated confidently.

"How the hell could he know the—"

"It's 'q,'" Betty interrupted.

"What?" Karl was astonished by both the rapidity of the answer and the confidence Betty had in Bud's ability to know the unknowable.

"Lower case 'q.' Bud says the first part matches an intercepted code list. This is a Cabal safe house."

"Get the fuck out of here!" Karl's phone buzzed. "Hello? . . . Bud?" Karl nodded his head a few times and turned to Betty with a shocked look on his face. He covered the mouthpiece and whispered, "He's monitoring the scene from a satellite." Karl took his hand off again. "Right . . . OK . . . now?"

"Karl, tell me what's going on before I kick your shin!" Betty moved closer with purpose.

Karl put his phone away. "That was Dr. Eric Salizar with Michel at the security door. Bud thinks they're going to start surgery any moment for a kidney transplant. He says we need to get in there now."

"Of course, and I don't have a thing to wear!" Betty said sarcastically, looking quite annoyed.

"Open the bag. Grab some concussion grenades and extra magazines. I'll take the charges and what's left."

Betty grabbed the tranquilizer magazine and stuffed the live magazines in her bra. "Not quite the fashion-model look, is it?"

"If looks could kill," Karl drolly remarked.

They moved in closer, Betty pulling the bag with their remaining arsenal and Karl continuing to check the building for movement with the camera. "As soon as we breach the fence, their security is going to activate. You don't have that kind of a touch pad if you don't also have surveillance and trip wires."

"Bud said now."

"I know. I don't like it. This is the kind of shit old man Howell never would have allowed."

"You know the director's name?"

"You don't spend thirty years working for someone without figuring a few things out. If you only knew how deep you're really in." Karl looked her directly in the eye. "But that will have to wait till another day, won't it?"

"Tease." Betty approached the fence, prepared to knock the dogs out when the steel door opened again. Dr. Eric Salizar stepped out and said some parting words to Michel, who lingered for a moment, looking out into the darkening sky as if he could smell something in the air. "Back." The two operatives moved behind a trailer covered with a dark, weather stained tarp. It stank of salt, fish, oil, and years of humidity.

Dr. Salizar made direct eye contact with the shepherds as he approached his car. This only incited the dogs to come closer and act menacingly. "Can't you control them!" he shouted nervously at Michel, who was standing in the doorway. Eric opened the car and backed into his seat while keeping the door between himself and the dogs. Michel closed the secure building door as the Mercedes headed for the open gate.

"Now!" Betty pushed Karl toward the opening and rushed the dogs that were growling and barking with bared teeth and closing in on the duo. Nervously, she waited a moment to be sure she would hit her target, but not so long as to have a still-conscious canine on her throat before pulling the trigger. Double taps of tranquilizer for each dog, and because of her excellent marksmanship, all four shots hit their mark. The dogs stumbled and whimpered before they staggered and dropped at her feet. Karl pushed past and with ten quick steps he arrived at the keypad. He began punching in the code when Michel burst out the door to investigate the disturbance.

"Fuck!" Betty had not changed her ammunition, but she took the shot anyway, hitting Michel with three successive tranquilizer darts in the upper chest and neck. Surprised by the impact, he stumbled out the door and made it five feet before collapsing on the asphalt.

With a smile of appreciation, Karl looked back at the approaching vixen who had just saved his life.

Reaching into her cleavage, Betty switched the tranquilizer magazine for live ammunition.

"That is a dangerous place; remind me not to go there." Karl leered.

"Don't go there," Betty quipped. "Grab his ankles."

"In we go." Betty fired over Karl's shoulder, the ejecting shells bouncing off his head.

Karl grabbed his ear and swore, "Fuck me!" He opened his mouth wide, trying to clear his ear canal to no avail.

"You wish. I just saved your life. Again!" The guard lay bleeding on the floor, gasping for air. He had dropped his Glock pistol and was attempting to find it. Karl popped a round from his silenced P226 into the guard's forehead. He returned to help Betty pull Michel into the building.

Both Betty and Karl turned sharply, standing with their backs against the wall and Michel at their feet. The sound of guards approaching was ringing out. There were two distinct sounds of footfalls: one, the standard sound of hard-soled, military-issue combat boots; the other muffled as if wrapped in a cloth layer. As they came around the corner, it became obvious. One man was dressed in typical military uniform while the second man was wearing green operating scrubs with an AK-47 firmly grasped in his latex-gloved hands. Karl silently shot the military-clothed man while Betty once again fired too close to Karl's head as she neutralized the surgically dressed guard.

"Son of a bitch! Stop doing that!"

"I saved your life again."

"I hear bells ringing in my left ear!"

"Come on!" Betty moved past Karl and walked swiftly down the hallway. *If anyone sees me, they'll be too shocked by my outfit to shoot, mused Betty.*

Karl followed behind, turning backward from time to time, checking for a rear-guard approach.

Betty dropped her magazine from her pistol and grabbed another from her cleavage. As she slid it in, she realized her mistake. *Fuck, the tranq magazine.*

Two more guards began firing from behind a door frame ten feet ahead of them. The shots were too random to hit their target. Karl hit one of the guards, who fell into the hallway wearing surgical gear. "What is with these guys?"

They pressed up against the wall as bullets sprayed through the plaster, narrowly missing Betty, but several rounds harmlessly bounced off Karl's protective body armor. Betty held her ground next to Karl.

I need to change my ammo. She began to pull out a live magazine when a sound from behind got her attention. Michel approached them, dragging his feet and clinging to the wall for support, his eyes half open from the effects of the tranquilizer. She aimed and squeezed off a round into his neck, dropping him to the ground.

"The operating room is in there!" Karl hissed after ducking his head around the corner for a split second. "Gil is on a gurney. One more bad guy to go." He counted down from three with his fingers raised in the air. On zero, he and Betty ducked around the corner. No one was present and no threat was evident. "He has to be here somewhere!"

A large knife split the difference between the two Control agents and stuck a solid inch into the wood door frame. The surgically clad guard was inserting a fresh magazine and aiming for Betty.

Karl lunged in front of her and drew his Sig Sauer P226 sight on the sole remaining guard. A younger man would have gotten the shot off in time. Karl did not. The first bullets caused only bruising thanks to McFluffy's spider-goat-silk body armor. The third shot arrived after Karl returned fire, the bullets passing in flight; the guard's shot grazed Karl's neck, nicking his jugular vein and striking Betty in the chest. The guard instantly dropped; the old pro's shot had pierced the bridge of the guard's nose and blown out the back of his skull. Betty paused long enough to realize she would have a large bruise on her right breast and that Karl would bleed out quickly if she did not act immediately.

"Fuck! Gil!" She yelled for the one man who could save Karl. The same man they had come to save. *Think . . . quick! I need a compression bandage.* "Gil! I need you!" Using the knife embedded in the door frame, Betty cut her dress at the hem. "He's bleeding out!"

Gil slowly raised himself off the gurney, rolling onto the floor. He dragged himself to his feet by pulling on the frame of the surgical bed. The general anesthetic still held him in its grip. With complete lack of clarity but a strident purpose, he pushed himself toward the medical supplies while using the gurney as a crutch. He collapsed.

"Gil!" cried Betty as she heard the crash in the makeshift surgical unit. The binding from her dress combined with the pressure of Karl's palm slowed the flow of blood. This gave them more time, for now. "Gil! Are you OK? Karl . . . his neck . . . lots of blood . . . *I need you*!" she screamed. Again, Michel began to rouse from his tranquilizer-induced sleep. Betty found her pistol and shot another dart into his thigh near the femoral artery. *I hope I shot him in his . . .* Karl attempted to sit up. "Karl, gently, gently." Betty pushed him back down. "Stay down. Gil isn't out of the anesthetic yet. Stay calm and we'll get through this."

The outer door opened and Dr. Eric Salizar entered, wearing surgical scrubs. "Michel . . . Holy shit!" For the first time, Salizar and Betty looked at the complete destruction of the room: Michel laying unconscious, his chief guard laying in his own pool of blood with his skull blown open, the nurse and guards in the surgical unit bleeding to death, and Gil flailing about as he tried to overcome the effects of the drugs injected for removing his kidney. Dr. Salizar dropped his clipboard and medical charts.

Betty dropped her gun and grabbed Karl's. "You have thirty seconds to put your medical degree on the fast track! Karl's neck needs to be repaired."

Dr. Salizar hesitated as he calculated the proper triage order of the victims.

Betty impatiently asked, "Which leg do you want me to shoot first, your left or your right?"

Dr. Salizar moved to the surgical unit, snapped on gloves, grabbed the surgical tray intended for Gil, and returned to Karl.

"What the fuck has been going on here?" He peeked under the dressing and immediately had Karl put pressure on the wound as he prepared for surgery. He handed Betty a pair of gloves. "Put these on, you're assisting."

Betty put her gun on the floor before chiding the doctor for looking around at the dead and tranquilized. "Don't you think Karl deserves your undivided attention at the moment?"

Dr. Salizar took a deep breath and removed Karl's hand. "This is going to be a little sloppy, but you'll survive to tell your grandkids about how lucky you were." After clamping both ends of the vein, he helped Karl move, albeit gently, to the gurney in the surgical unit. Betty brought the surgical tray back into the operating room.

Gil sat with his back against a wall. "What the hell is going on?"

Dr. Salizar did not look up from his work. "You're coming out of the anesthetic. You will be groggy for a while. Stay here until you're ready" He handed Betty a bottle of saline solution and instructed her, "When I ask you, wash the wound and wipe with gauze. Gently."

Karl grimaced from the pain but maintained his composure.

"You're going to need some antibiotics when this is over," the doctor said as he finished stitching. The wound closed and the danger cleared, Karl gingerly regained his feet. "Take it easy . . . don't overdo it or you'll tear my sutures!"

"Thank you, Doctor." Karl touched the bandage covering his neck and relaxed, closing his eyes briefly and exhaling deeply. Mortality remained.

Michel began rousing again, but Betty had placed cable ties around his wrists. A gag kept him from talking on his own. Gil had recovered somewhat during the repair of Karl's neck. With a low whistle he commented, "Nice work, Doctor! Just like Clint Malarchuk!"

Karl looked over and queried, "Clint who? Some surgeon you worked under?"

Gil chuckled, "No, dummy. The goalie for the Sabres . . . he got his throat slashed by a teammate's skate. Just like him, you're lucky to be alive."

Betty looked closer at Gil. "You're one to talk. Go get some clothes on!" she tsked.

Karl removed his blood-soaked shirt and examined the two bullet holes. "God, I love McFluffy!"

Dr. Salizar looked at the shirt and then at Karl's chest. "Do I have more work to do here?" He inspected the body armor and found no corresponding holes. "Impressive. Let me check you out."

Karl unzipped the front and exposed two swollen and bruised sites forming where the bullets impacted.

"No broken ribs." Dr. Salizar gingerly pressed the surrounding tissue and examined his skin. "An x-ray is in order to check for fractures. You'll be sore for a while. Ibuprofen as needed." He nodded appreciatively of McFluffy's handiwork. "That is an impressive fabric!"

Betty touched the bullet hole in her dress just below her breast. *I think I'll wait until later to get checked out. I don't think I want to strip to my waist in front of all these guys.* She adjusted her clothing to make sure the damage was not obvious. Her camisole body armor had done its job—barely.

Dr. Salizar walked over to the prone mastermind of the surgical unit. "Well, Michel, it looks like you are going to need a kidney from the secondary market after all."

Michel gave a muffled invective and glared at his surgeon.

Gil sauntered back into the room with his clothes on and a large grin on his face.

"What are you smiling for?" asked Betty with her own wry smile.

"It all worked out. Just like I told you." Gil thumped his chest and pointed his index finger at her.

"Whatever."

With no other living members of the hostage/surgical team alive to tend to, Dr. Salizar sat down to rest. With his elbows on his knees and hands clasped between his legs, he contemplated his situation. "Well, what now? I'm supposed to be in Århus in the morning for a lung transplant."

Betty asserted control over the situation. "You'll be coming with us. You'll need to be debriefed before you go anywhere. Karl, we need to get this wrapped up. Are you and Gil up to keeping tabs on the good doctor and our friend Michel?"

"I don't think they'll give us any trouble." Gil approached Michel and searched him for weapons and communications devices; he confiscated a cellphone and car keys. "Dad, can I borrow the car?" Gil jangled the keys at Michel, then looked at Betty and Karl, who did not get the joke. "I crack me up!"

Karl took up the first-guard position, with his pistol back in his hand and his feet propped up on a second chair. "Go ahead, give old what's-his-name a call in the other room. This should be interesting."

Betty headed out of the anteroom and into the corridor. Her first call went to Bud. "Well, Stuxboy, it looks like we got our man."

"You are incredible, Betty! Hey, uhm, speaking about that . . ."

"Sorry, you never gave me the information on Line X. So, I don't owe you a date."

"But, wait a minute—"

"Bud, I don't owe you a date, but I certainly owe you dinner at a very nice restaurant to thank you."

Bud gulped. "It's a start."

"You can pick the place." Little bastard. He'll probably want to go to that lame burger joint instead of a proper restaurant. "Now, on to our main situation. We stopped the operation before they cut into Gil. We killed the guards and captured Michel Vasilyev. We also have Dr. Salizar in custody."

"Holy shit. That's awesome!"

"How do we get them transferred to Control?"

"I've initiated several flights. You need to get to the airport in Ålborg, really Nørresundby. It's about forty-five minutes southwest of your current position. Is that a problem?"

"I think we can handle it. We'll need a doctor on board."

"Why? You stopped the operation before Gil got cut open."

"Karl was shot, his jugular cut. Dr. Salizar closed the wound, but Karl will need immediate help if it reopens."

"I see. Gil's a medic, but I see your point. I'll make the arrangements."

"How long?"

"Two hours. Oh, and expect Director Howell."

"What the hell, Bud!"

"He's in the loop, Betty."

"What the hell, Bud!"

"I was wrong about José."

"What do you mean?"

"Director Howell killed a different guy. A José from Colombia, not your José."

"Are you pulling one over on me?"

"Seriously. This guy was cleaned in a church. Honest."

"I should've known by your pronunciation."

"But they're both spelled the same."

"My José is zho-ZE, his is ho-ZAY."

"OK. Don't kill him."

"The thought crossed my mind, once or twice."

"Seriously, Betty. He's on your side. He did what was necessary. He gave me authorization to help you and put assets at your disposal. Just don't kill him."

"I might beat the crap out of him."

"Not my problem if he can't defend himself."

"Two hours."

"I'm sending directions to Karl's phone. Call him."

"Karl?"

"You know who I mean."

"I guess I have to wear my big-girl panties now."

"Whatever. Just call him. He has something for you."

Betty could not think of anything Howell could offer. "What could that SOB possibly have?"

"Information—Jil." Bud hung up the line.

"My, how the world turns."

Betty collected her thoughts and began searching the adjoining rooms before dialing Howell's number. "That son of a bitch owes me. I do all the dirty work and he gives me nothing."

She came upon Michel's private room and ransacked his belongings. The usual clothing, personal items, and artifacts of life provided nothing extraordinary. She lifted the mattress and exposed a vest. "Ooh, what do we have here?" Inside the plain canvas were pockets containing gold coins. "I'll be damned." She counted roughly forty Krugerrand coins and two hundred Credit Swisse one-ounce gold bars. The vest weighed close to twenty pounds. Betty finished checking the room. A suitcase looked suspicious, so she cut it open. A money belt fell out of the lining as she shook the medium-size luggage. The currencies inside the pocket included Swiss francs, euros, pound notes, and American dollars. Combined with the gold, she had discovered a small fortune.

"Well, I suppose I should call the boss." She dialed Howell's direct number and waited tensely for the coming exchange.

"Betty! Bud has filled me in. Are you ready to come in?"

He has some fucking nerve! "First, you have some explaining to do!"

"Yes, I do. I owe you an apology."

"Well?" Betty's anger began to boil. An apology? Just an apology?

"I'm sorry I couldn't tell you more before. We were still piecing things together when you went rogue."

"What the fuck, Howell?" She was on full-roiling boil now. "My parents are agents, you were recruiting me, and my *Aunt* Grace is a cleaner for Control. You forgot to mention some things? Pretty big fucking things."

"Well, yes, I suppose I learned to lie through omission from my father."

"How is the old bastard?" Betty spit the words out sarcastically.

"Dead."

"Oh. I'm sorry." Betty cringed at her faux pas.

There was dead air on the line for several seconds. Howell felt defensive and Betty just had the wind sucked out of her sails.

Betty licked her lips and thought of her own parents. "Is Beth OK? I kind of left in a hurry."

"Beth and Grace are having a long chat. I'm sure she'll be . . . fine."

"About what?"

"Family business. Old scores and such."

"Like what?"

"I wouldn't bring it up, myself."

"Let sleeping dogs lie, eh?"

"Exactly." Howell cleared his throat. "Betty, Jil's mother is waiting for Dr. Salizar. She's to have a lung transplant from Ruth."

"What? I didn't know. Jesus. I mean, she was always nice to me, kind of like a second . . . mom." Betty had a weird look on her face as she tried to process the idea of a second, let alone third mother figure in her life.

"I want you to take good care of Dr. Salizar. He'll be able to get some interesting information for us from the Harpers. I think they're deep into the Cabal.

"Small world."

"Yes. I also have some information for you on who killed José. I don't think you'll like it."

"You know I'm going to kick your ass when I see you, right?"

"I would expect nothing less, but I would hope we could sit down and talk things out."

"Betty? Betty?" Karl was calling from the other room.

"See you in two hours, Howell." Betty disconnected the call and gathered her thoughts. When she returned to the operating room, she discovered Gil and Karl were ready to leave.

"Time to get a move on, Betty." Karl, focusing on the vest and money belt, gave her a quizzical look.

"Thank you for saving my life. I have a retirement gift for you." She handed him the vest. Michel began gurgling behind his gag and Dr. Salizar chuckled. "Gil, here is a small token of thanks for saving my life as well. You get the smaller one because I just saved your ass for once." Betty winked at her partner and then whispered into his ear, "You ever get left behind again and I will kick your ass from here to eternity." She gave him a kiss on the mouth while holding his cheeks as he reached for her ass. Betty slapped him hard across the left cheek. "You don't have that privilege at the moment. Keep your hands off my ass!"

He grabbed his cheek, looked at Karl, and shrugged his shoulders. "Women! It doesn't pay to save them."

Betty gave Gil a matronly look and said in her best lecturing-mother voice, "You and I need to talk. Later." Betty wagged her finger. "Time to blow this Popsicle stand!"

"Bud sent me the coordinates. We'll need a bigger car."

"Dr. Salizar, you drove here, correct?" Betty cocked her head slightly.

"Of course."

"I think you and I should go to Ålborg, don't you?" She checked her magazine and examined the chamber of her P226. "Ready?"

"But of course."

"Gil, you drive while Karl keeps an eye on Michel. Don't let him exert himself too much."

"I'm the medic, remember?"

"Oh, yeah." Betty turned and took Dr. Salizar by the arm and pressed the pistol into his ribs. "A beautiful night for a drive, don't you think, doctor?"

SIXTY

INTO THE POOL

August 8, 2009 — Ålborg Airport

BETTY STRAINED TO HEAR Howell while the loud thrust of the first G6 pushed Karl, Gil, Michel, and Dr. Salizar down the runway. "What?" Betty pushed her hair behind her left ear and turned in closer to the director of Control, her one-time lover and promised husband, and now her boss and all-around bastard.

"This photo was taken by a woman across the street from José's apartment." Howell shoved the still image toward Betty. "We found out about her by canvassing the neighborhood again." The picture showed two men perched on either side of the open sliding-glass door of José's balcony. One man of average height, but thin; the other muscular and extraordinarily tall. "She uses a telephoto lens to keep track of the neighborhood."

"No!" *It can't be.*

Howell shuffled through a series of a dozen photos, which indicated the men clambered down the balconies below until they found another open door on the ninth floor. "She's wheelchair bound and rarely leaves her apartment. Her only hobby is spying on her neighbors with her telephoto lens on her digital camera."

"You staged this or Photoshopped them in!"

"You wanted to know without a doubt who killed José. There's no doubt . . ." He sorted through the photos until he found the best frontal view of the men. "Slim and Michel."

Betty threw an uppercut into Howell's solar plexus. The photos scattered to the ground, blowing and hopping down the tarmac, just out of reach of his outstretched left hand as he grasped his gasping chest with his right. She kicked his ribs viciously, hoping one would break. Howell crumbled to the concrete and tried to protect his vital organs from future blows. Before her cocked leg could release another damning blow, Betty turned away and began crying, herself collapsing to the concrete as the emotional pain inside her began to rise up, tar loosened from a pit deep inside gurgling into her lungs. She coughed out the single word, "Why?"

Howell recovered enough to gamely hobble about, picking up the photos, saving the evidence from dispersing further around the Århus airport. He came back to her but kept his distance. "Slim was Cabal, the son of a leader. I'm still figuring out what happened. Michel's an errand boy. He'll spill his guts for us—that I guarantee."

"Your word means shit to me." Betty spat out the poisonous hate. "Fuck off!" She composed herself and rose to her full height; with her jaw tight with rage she reminded him of his broken promise. "You said I would get my revenge and you wait until Michel is in custody to tell me? What . . . am I supposed to be pleased?"

"I don't expect you to be happy."

"You put me on the kill list!"

"You were acting bizarre until I understood your motives. I would have rescinded the order earlier if you had only come in!"

"You dangled me in the wind!"

"I gave you Bud and Karl to keep you safe."

"Then why are you here?"

"I need to know if you still want to continue."

"With what? Slim is dead, Michel is off to your gulag, and Gil is saved. What the hell do you need me for?"

"I want to get the guys who gave the orders. I don't care if Michel lives or dies. I want the Cabal leaders, not their lackeys."

"You can do that without me."

"No, I can't. I need you."

"You don't need me, you just want to use me. Again and again and again. I'm only a tool to you."

"Betty, I still—"

"Mr. Howell!" Miller came running up with a secure phone in his outstretched hand. "David."

"What?" Betty gave Howell a sharp look. "You still what?"

Howell turned as he waved her off, listening to David on the phone.

Betty walked in front of Howell and glowered. "Damn it! You still what?" Her fists were balled with rage. Betty adopted her signature look, meant to pierce the inner thoughts of a client or a witness—her look that asked: I know what you were about to say, but did you really mean it or were you just saying it to get an advantage?

Howell held the phone away from his mouth, but still at his ear. "Miller, take Betty inside. Our flight leaves in fifteen minutes and we need to gather our things."

Miller reached out to comfort Betty and guide her to the waiting room while the jet pulled up.

"Touch me and I swear to God, I'll break your wrist!" snapped Betty.

Howell spoke quietly to David with his back turned until the agents were about to enter the building. Betty paused to look back at him as Miller held the door for her. *He did love me once. That I know. It wasn't an act then. The loft. That was real. Is it possible? Could it even work? Do I even want that anymore? Or am I just a beaten lover going back for the apology and the moment of loving affection before the abuse starts all over again?*

Howell turned sharply and with a smile on his face said, "That will do, David. That will do." He gave a thumbs-up and headed to join them as the second G6 pulled up for loading. Howell tried to say something, but the muted scream of the jet smothered his words.

"Come on, Betty, let's get our gear." Miller let the door close just a little to prompt her.

"Yeah, yeah, yeah." She grabbed her tactical bag and headed back out to the tarmac and her flight home. *I'm exhausted. Sleep. I need sleep.*

As the luxury G6 gained altitude, Howell began debriefing Betty. "So far we've figured out that Slim was a plant into Control facilitated by Getner."

Betty yawned. "Why would the general do that?"

"I sincerely believe he was duped. I don't think he understood how compromised he was."

"Why was Getner even in charge if he was an easy mark?" Betty rubbed her eyes.

"He was a distant relation to President Merryweather."

"So, he was trusted more than he deserved," Betty taunted.

"Blood is thicker than water, usually." Tom rubbed his face with the warm towel handed to him by a flight-crew member.

Betty took a towel but turned down the pillow and blanket. "I'm sorry about your dad."

"He stuck around just long enough to lock me in. He should have died years ago."

"Still, he's your dad. Now you have no one left."

"Not exactly. The Salizars."

"Dr. Eric Salizar?"

"Yes. He's my cousin."

"What the hell?"

"I know. I knew his father only as Guali."

"Did you know we were spying on your uncle when we were in Panama?"

"No. My father didn't give me all the details. His favorite method of lying to me."

"Did you ever meet him?" Betty asked inquisitively.

"A couple of times, I was away at school or a camp, usually, when he came through. But, I never met Eric before."

"How are you related?"

"My mother and Eric's mother are sisters. Dad and Guali were the outlaws."

"How did they meet? Your dad and mom."

"Dad was recruiting Nazi scientists in Argentina after World War Two. One of the recruits was my grandfather. Guali was Grandfather Fritz's pupil."

"Oh my God!" Betty took the still warm towel and wiped her face and hands. *Hmm. Lemon. God, I'm tired, but I want to know more.* "What did he specialize in? What was his place in the Nazi Party?"

"Token membership. Grandfather Fritz specialized in organ and tissue replacement. He created amazing techniques in the pursuit of replacing my mother's eyes."

"Her eyes?"

"Yes, she lost her sight from measles."

"Did he succeed?"

"Grandfather didn't live to see it accomplished, but Uncle Guali was able to perform the surgery successfully. Yuri was one of his first trials."

"No way!"

Howell rubbed his cheek, thinking about all he knew. "Yes, the scar on his face was caused by an infection when he couldn't take the anti-rejection medicine."

"Who else has he worked on? You?"

Howell laughed and rapped his prosthetic leg, "No, I lost my limb honestly." His face drew serious. "There's more you should know. Michel is Gil's—"

"Father. I know."

"What you might not know is that his mother, Yuri's wife, became an organ donor for my mother and others. Gil was adopted, like you but not by spies."

"Let me get this straight. Yuri killed uncle Guali, Michel and Slim killed my José, you killed José the traitor from Colombia, Michel is Gil's genetic father, his genetic mother donated her eyes to your mother . . . is there anything else I should know about this fucked-up family we call Control?"

"Eric is on his way to transplant lung tissue from Ruth to Linda."

"Is that why he got on the plane with Karl, Gil, and Michel?"

"Larry, Jil, Ruth, and Linda are waiting for him to come. By rights, I could keep him from them, but I want to see where they lead us. Jil knows things she shouldn't. Larry owes someone big, plus he has a death sentence hanging over him. I want you to figure all this out."

"Me? Why?"

"Karl is going to Vail for his quasi-retirement. We're placing him as the concierge at the Ritz-Carlton. Jil's company just purchased two units there. You can rest up and keep an eye on things with Karl. He'll watch your back and you watch his. Make sure he settles in and has someone to talk to. You . . . you just need to stay there and relax until something comes up."

"What could be easier, right? Your shit always stinks, Howell. There are never easy things when it comes to you." Betty rubbed her temples. "Fuck. OK. I'll do it, but not for you. I'll do it to find out what Jil has gotten herself into. And you're paying all the bills."

"Whatever it takes. I don't expect the Ritz to come cheap, but we can afford it and you're worth it . . . but keep the receipts."

"Of course." Betty yawned. "I need to sleep. Bug off while I sleep on . . ." Betty was instantly asleep. Howell left his seat and came back with a pillow and blanket for her. He tucked her in, kissed her forehead, and whispered, "I love you."

Betty stirred just a little and snuggled into her pillow. *I know, Tom, I know.*

SIXTY-ONE

POWER ABSOLUTE

August 9, 2009 — Valdés Peninsula, Argentina

THE ASHES FLOATED without sound to the rocks one hundred meters below the cliff. The waves crashed onto the beach as sea elephants belched out sounds reminiscent of a poorly tuned vintage sports car. In the distance, a southern right whale crashed into the ocean, giving a final crescendo to the orchestra of nature as it saluted the final resting place of Tom Howell Sr. The man had done so much to manipulate the actions of others; yet now he was dispersed amongst the forces of nature, which did not care one whit about his future. The ashes were consumed by the ocean and the terrain so quickly that Tom could not discern their passing the moment they landed.

Seeing the raw nature that his father had favored during his time in Argentina brought a peace to Tom he did not expect. The fractious unraveling of the secrets of Control during their many lunches together seemed more planned than Tom had originally given his father credit. *The bastard foresaw every reaction. He planned and orchestrated every moment.* The sighs, the tears, the upset stomach, and the fits of coughing suddenly crystallized in Tom's mind as pure symbols created to get specific reactions. His father knew not only how Tom would react, but also what it would take for Tom to understand the nature of the beast his father had created. The nature that Tom would have to understand if he was to control the power he now held.

He took a deep breath and let it out slowly, pausing for just a moment before turning away from the vast ocean. Twelve years before, Tom Sr. had cast his mother's ashes in the same location. Now the two were together again, in the same ocean that had played no small part in bringing the lives of two mere mortals together. *No*, thought Tom. *He was no mere mortal. God, no. Demigod . . . perhaps.* Tom Howell Sr. had been a force to reckon with. The evil forces of the world had paid a dear price for their lack of knowledge concerning this powerful man. *He controlled the destiny of millions—no, billions of people by what he chose to do and not do. A kingmaker and destroyer. With a wave of his hand, people lived or died.*

Tom now understood the awesome power his father had wielded. The awful toll it had cost him, especially the burden of Jack's inability to stay sober. Tom thought back to his school days reading the Odyssey and for the first time in his life understood what Homer had meant.

> Nothing feebler than a man does the earth raise up, of all the things which breathe and move on the earth, for he believes that he will never suffer evil in the future, as long as the gods give him success and he flourishes in his strength; but when the blessed gods bring sorrows too to pass, even these he bears, against his will, with steadfast spirit, for the thoughts of earthly men are like the day which the father of gods and men brings upon them.

"Master Howell, you will catch your death in this cold," said Barnes as he handed Tom his coat. "It is time for you to read your father's final words. I have started the fire for you to burn them after you have committed them to memory." Barnes handed Tom the sealed envelope with a red wax seal and silk ribbon. Tom was ready—perhaps for the first time in his life—to hear the words his father had damned him to breathe into his own psyche. The outside of the envelope had a quote emblazoned in gilt letters:

> Power tends to corrupt, and absolute power corrupts absolutely. Great men are almost always bad men.
>
> —John Emerich Edward Dalberg Acton, first Baron Acton (1834–1902) to Bishop Mandell Creighton in 1887

Acknowledgments

I owe a debt of gratitude to my sources and contributors. Some I can name.

Dan from Lookout Mountain Hang Gliding is responsible for the accurate portrayal of Betty's escape. I am responsible for the inaccurate parts.

The kind folks at the Ritz-Carlton, Vail, for showing me around, especially Karl Middelburg.

Specialist L. M. and Chris Ameling, for your continuous moral support.

An extra-special thank-you to Meghan Dee, a damn fine editor and an excellent person.

Please read on for an excerpt from A. J. Mahler's next thriller

CONTROL

THE BETTY CHRONICLES

Volume III

Available from White Bradford Publishing

ONE

THE LAWN GOODBYE

Observatory Circle, Washington, D.C.

"**G**IDEON, DRIVE AROUND the bend and park—Master Howell, something is amiss." Barnes gave a pensive look over his shoulder at the Howell mansion receding from view Tom Howell Jr., newly elevated head of Control, scanned the same scene as Barnes while he continued his phone call with David, the second in command at the bunker deep in the Virginia wilderness.

Betty was fidgeting with her smartphone. David's call had interrupted their conversation about her new assignment in Vail, let alone her continued employment with Control. The previous forty-eight hours had been a roller coaster of emotions. She and Karl had rescued Gil from his biological father and stopped the kidney transplant. Betty's feelings for Gil were a jumbled mess, now that he was safe. They were only together for a few minutes before he jetted off with Dr. Eric Salizar to catch up with the Harpers for Laura's lung transplant using tissue from Jil's sister Ruth. Michel, the contract killer of Betty's fiancé José, was in Control custody and out of Betty's reach—for now. *I need a vacation! If only Tom were here to run off with me. Instead I have Mr. Hyde/Howell trying to corral me into another stint as a tool for Control.* She ruminated on the recent past and considered her options.

Howell raised his finger to signal to her that it would be just a moment longer. "No, David, I'm sure we are just being overly cautious since the Cabal's probe into our territory."

Yep. Tom is absent as always these days, thought Betty. Her choices were limited to unrequited love while working for Howell full time in the revenge business, or a return to law full time, and hoping for the best with Tom and seeking satisfaction part time. *If I don't work for him, how will I get my revenge? If I do work for him, how do I get my revenge when he keeps putting the people responsible out of my reach? I love Tom, but I hate Howell. Will the two ever split up? That would be nice. Maybe McFluffy has something that would do the job?*

Gideon slowly pulled up to the curb around the bend in the road, but left the car in drive with his left foot firmly on the brake, his right poised over the gas, and his shooting hand on the grip of his SIG Sauer P226. The Audi A8 sedan had been retrofitted with the latest in armored protection: laminated bulletproof glass with a transparent spider-goat-silk middle layer, courtesy of McFluffy; a beefed-up suspension, transmission, and engine to handle the extra two tons of protection; and a wet bar to calm the nerves of any ruffled occupants.

The sight of the wet bar and the ice bucket reminded Betty of her Aunt Grace's freezer with the severed hand. *Do I want to know whose hand that is? I'm sure I could find out now. Though, curiosity did kill the cat.* Betty was tired from catching up only slightly on her sleep after being debriefed by Howell on the flight back to the United States from Denmark aboard Control's G650 jet. *A nap in the sun in a hammock would be a thing of beauty right now. Tom promised that I could get some sleep at the house. My God, what all did he inherit from his father? I'd be set if I were a gold digger!* Betty gave Howell a squinty-eyed glare and tapped her Rolex GMT-Master to remind him of the time and his promises.

Howell smiled and nodded his head.

That didn't seem to have much effect on him. Betty looked away from her former love and stared out at the expanse of expensive homes and Third World–country embassies. *Maybe if I flashed my breasts like Gil suggested in Caracas.*

Something caught her eye on the other side of the road from the Howell mansion. A rickety old 1985 Ford F250 with "Hombre Landscaping" hand painted on the ratty plywood siding sputtered to life. The workers tossed their equipment onto the bed loaded with lawn debris as they scrambled up the sides. Something about that beat-up old truck and the men screamed at her for attention. *Is it the men? Their tools? The debris in back?* Whatever it was, something nagged at her to give it her full attention, and it was not Howell.

"Betty." Howell tapped her on the shoulder. "We're going to the

Capital Grille for lunch, OK?" Just as quickly, he was back to his phone conversation with David while flicking through paperwork on his touch-screen laptop. "Aha." Howell either nodded approvingly or scrunched up his face as he responded to David. "Yes, that will work." Betty had become an afterthought once more. "Send it anyway."

Jesus! I just can't win with this guy! Betty was about to make a scene by closing the laptop and killing the link to David when Barnes caught her attention as he checked his M1911 pistol for a round in the chamber and a full clip.

Barnes opened his door and stepped halfway out of the heavily armored sedan before stating, "Wait here, Master Howell, while I check things out. Mandala is either dead or incapacitated." With his free hand on Gideon's shoulder, he gave a final missive to his understudy: "Remember your mission. Always protect him—no matter what the cost."

Betty looked back at the truck and then at the enigma. "Barnes—"

Gideon spun in the driver's seat to ask how Barnes knew Mandala was so indisposed, but the bulletproof door sealed with a sound similar to a vault closing.

Howell tried to peer past his neighbor's house to his own newly inherited kingdom while maintaining his conversation with David. "I don't know, David, what do the security cameras show?" No alarms had been tripped at the house, and Mandala was the only occupant of record for the previous two days. The motion detectors indicated he had not left his room since his morning rounds just an hour before.

Betty screamed at the top of her lungs, "Barnes!" as she reached for the handle, but because the car was in drive, the doors were locked.

Howell looked at Betty and then back at his valet, who was about to enter the front door. The live feed of the house interior showed nothing out of the ordinary. "David—

David had been reviewing the security status of the mansion and relayed the summary to Howell. "Everything looks OK. Nothing out of the ordinary. Wait—"

An enormous explosion rocked the car despite its massive weight. Car alarms in the neighborhood began blaring all around them. Gideon quickly surveyed the area and then accelerated hard, swerving from the curb to the middle of the road, continuing around Observatory Hill and as far from the explosion as he could get in the following thirty seconds.

The security partition that separated him from his passengers swiftly rose up and hermetically sealed Betty and Howell into the safest rolling seventy cubic feet on the planet.

Debris began raining down from the sky as the house returned to earth in pieces varying from the size of a fist to a section of roof, chimney still attached. Just when everything seemed to settle down, a large chunk of sod landed on the hood of the car, grass side up.

Howell yelled, "Gideon!"

Gideon rolled the partition down and asked, "Mr. Howell? Everything OK back there?"

Betty screamed, "Barnes!"

About the Author

A. J. Mahler lives in the Athens of the Midwest, also known as Iowa City. On nice days you might find him writing or editing on the Ped Mall or perhaps in a local coffee shop. Give him three nouns and he will tell you a story.